"ROMANTIC SUSPENSE IS HER TRUE FORTE."
Minneapolis Star-Tribune

"VINTAGE ELIZABETH LOWELL . . .
SNAPPY DIALOGUE . . .
LIKABLE, INTELLIGENT, AND INTRIGUING CHARACTERS . . .
A FUN READ."
Columbia State (SC)

"LOWELL'S KEEN EAR FOR DIALOGUE AND INTUITIVE
CHARACTERIZATIONS CONSISTENTLY PLACE HER A CUT
ABOVE MOST WRITERS IN THIS GENRE."
Charlotte News & Observer

"I'LL BUY ANY BOOK WITH
ELIZABETH LOWELL'S NAME ON IT."
Jayne Ann Krentz

Also by Elizabeth Lowell

Contemporary

BEAUTIFUL DREAMER • MIDNIGHT IN RUBY BAYOU
AMBER BEACH • JADE ISLAND • PEARL COVE
REMEMBER SUMMER • TO THE ENDS OF THE EARTH
WHERE THE HEART IS • DESERT RAIN
A WOMAN WITHOUT LIES • LOVER IN THE ROUGH
FORGET ME NOT

Historical

ONLY HIS • ONLY MINE • ONLY YOU
ONLY LOVE • AUTUMN LOVER • WINTER FIRE

UNTAMED • FORBIDDEN • ENCHANTED

And in Hardcover

EDEN BURNING

Coming Soon

RUNNING SCARED

ELIZABETH LOWELL

MOVING TARGET

AVON BOOKS

An Imprint of HarperCollinsPublishers

AVON BOOKS
An Imprint of HarperCollins*Publishers*
10 East 53rd Street
New York, New York 10022-5299

For Cissy Hartley
web goddess extraordinaire
and
all the great global habitués of
http://www.elizabethlowell.com/wwwboard

murfle

Prologue

The sky was a seamless blue, empty as a murderer's heart.

The woman who had three names smiled grimly into the rearview mirror of her old pickup truck. The man following her in the white Toyota sedan had blended right into the freeway, but he ran out of luck as the roads grew narrower and lonelier on the dirt track that led to her isolated home.

It was hard to hide in a desert. Even hanging way back, trying to be invisible, he stuck out like a neon tongue.

The dry, wild land looked unchanging, but wasn't. It was full of hidden life, of surprises that ranged from sweet to deadly. Some of those surprises were sand traps that had nothing to do with golf courses. Other surprises were rocks and potholes.

She hoped the little white car broke an axle and the driver's neck. It would save her the trouble of shooting whoever was following her—assuming she could still see well enough to get the job done before it was done to her.

You're getting old, she told herself roughly.

For more than fifty years she had outfoxed the fox; now

she finally had been run to ground. But she wouldn't be easy prey. Nor would she surrender the ancient, priceless Book of the Learned. She would die first.

The pickup truck lurched upward as it took the final steep quarter mile to her cabin. NO TRESPASSING signs rushed by in jolts of red. Stones spun and spat beneath the wheels as balding tires struggled for traction. Time went so fast these days; there was never enough to get everything done.

Or perhaps it was simply her certainty that death was closing in on her that made time hammer like a waterfall on the stubborn boulder of her life.

Was that how the female descendants of the first Serena felt when their death time came? Did they look at the old, worn loom that had passed through generations of Weavers? Did they lift frail hands to the shuttle to add their own final lines to the ancient pattern?

She didn't know. She never would. So much had been lost to the devouring cataract of time. So much, but not all. Words whispered through generations of women told her that in the beginning the Book of the Learned had been more than six hundred pages long. Time and desperate circumstances had reduced the number to five hundred and seven. Those pages held the accumulated history and wisdom of the Learned, pages illuminated in gold and crushed lapis lazuli, bright with the green of life and the scarlet of blood.

No Weaver in seven generations had been able to decipher the lean, elegant words that graced the Book of the Learned, but no one doubted the value of the object itself: the binding was studded with vivid gems that were the heart of the intricate, mysterious designs etched into the solid gold cover.

And now, again, the ancient pages were at risk.

As the last in a long, long line of Weavers, she had had a lifetime to prepare for just this situation. The torch was waiting to be passed. If her own race was over, so be it. The Book of the Learned was safe from man's greed.

Shielded from sight by a low ridge, her cabin lay in a small hollow. The wooden planks in the wellhead and in the walls of the cabin had been cooked to iron by the Mojave's relentless sun. Though cool now, the piles of granite that poked up like bones through the dry land would be burning hot in a few months. Then she would bake bread and beans in the little oven she had made outside the cabin and feel midnight's cool benediction whisper over her face.

If she was still alive.

She braked in a cloud of grit and dirt, shut off the engine, and grabbed for the package on the seat beside her. It was the precious pages inside that had lured her out of hiding, forced her to reach back into the dangerous past she had spent her life running from. Just as she must run now.

With the determination that had gotten her through almost eight decades of life, she forced her thin legs to run the short steps to the cabin. Sand ground under her worn sneakers. A Joshua tree's twisted arms stood black against the burnished sky. Overhead a hawk keened into the emptiness.

She heard only her own ragged breath and saw only the beckoning door of her weathered cabin. Panting, she wrenched open the door and stumbled inside just as a white car shot over the crest and into the hidden hollow. She slammed the cabin door and levered a yard-long iron bar into place across it. Then she closed the interior shutters on the two windows and bolted them into place.

The darkness inside was nearly absolute, but she didn't need a light to find her way. As a young "widow" she had built the stone and wood cabin with her own hands. As an old woman she knew every inch of the place: its strengths, its weaknesses, its secrets, everything.

She limped to the pegs over the door where the shotgun waited. She knew it was loaded. It always was.

A fist pounded on the front door. "Mrs. Weaver? I'd like to talk with you about—"

"You're trespassing and I've got a shotgun!" she shouted over his words.

* * *

The man on the other side of the door looked around quickly. No sign of cameras or spy holes. He hadn't expected any, but he was careful; that was why he was alive and free when others were neither. There was no sign of telephone or electrical wires, or even a radio or TV antenna. He knew from personal experience that cell phones didn't reach into this particular corner of the Mojave Desert. The old woman was truly alone.

He smiled.

With a smooth efficiency that told its own tale, he reached under his lightweight wind jacket. A gun appeared in his fist.

"There's no need to be frightened," he said reassuringly. "I don't want to hurt you. I want to make you rich. I'll give you two million dollars for the Book of the Learned. Won't you let me in so we can talk?"

"I'll give you sixty seconds to get off my property."

"Be reasonable, Mrs. Weaver. Two million dollars is a lot of money. It's better than anyone else will pay for what's left of that damned Druid book."

"Thirty seconds."

"At least take my business card."

The only answer he heard was the unmistakable slide of metal over metal as she readied the shotgun. He gauged the thickness of the stone and walls, the sun-hardened thick wood of the door, and the surprising strength of the prey. He would need armor-piercing bullets for the cabin. For her, too. That was one tough old bitch.

With a vicious curse he turned, got in his car, and drove away from the very thing he wanted enough to kill for.

The wind came up after sunset. The invisible rush of air was dry, cool to the point of chill, and smelled of time rather than life. The kerosene lamp inside the cabin threw odd, living shadows over the windows and walls. An old loom waited in one corner with an unfinished weaving partially filling the frame. Bobbins wound with colorful yarn dangled from the loom's warp strands, waiting for the moment when they would be woven into a seamless design.

A young fire burned companionably in the hearth, chasing the desert's nightly chill. The woman wore around her neck a long scarf that was as old as the loom itself. Normally the scarf felt rough to her, and she left it with its companion, the Book of the Learned. But tonight her own spirit was chilled, and the scarf soothed.

Numbly she sat in front of the fire, staring at the sinuous flames without really seeing them. All she saw were the pieces of thin, blank cardboard that she fed one by one into the fire.

He had promised to send her the stolen pages of the Book of the Learned. He had betrayed her again, promises made and broken. He had sent modern paper, not ancient vellum. There were no pages of lean, somehow dangerous writing, an old language speaking in silence of people and places long vanished. It didn't matter that she couldn't read the words themselves. It was enough that she kept the book safe and passed it on to the next Serena.

Family tradition held that the Book of the Learned was the soul of a man written on vellum with ink made of oak gall and iron. A powerful man. A proud man. A mysterious man. A deadly man. Erik the Learned. Erik, who had learned too late. But what he had learned and what he had lost were themselves forgotten when the keepers of the Book of the Learned no longer could read the ancient language.

Yet even without knowing the words, she knew the book itself was a treasure beyond price. Beyond the value of the ancient strip of cloth that she now wore as a scarf, beyond the value of the hammered gold and brilliantly polished gemstones on the cover, knowledge called from the Book of the Learned with its ancient, double-edged lure. Elegant, intricate capital letters teased the mind with designs whose meaning went deeper than words. The *feel* of previous generations, her own ancestry, people who were wise and foolish, saints and criminals, warriors and witches, advisers and hermits, peasants and aristocrats: the whole experience of humanity called forth in rich colors—sapphire, ruby, emerald, and gold. Above all, gold, illuminating darkness with a light like no other, shimmering with timeless endurance.

And she was but flesh, worn-out with enduring.

A sound from outside jerked her from her bitter reverie. She turned in time to see one window burst inward. A bottle hit the stone floor and exploded, showering the small room with burning gasoline. Another bottle followed, then another and another and another in a merciless rain that burned even the air.

At the end she saw the pattern that had eluded her for her entire life. Laughing, she reached to embrace it. Her only regret was that she wouldn't be alive to see his face when he discovered that she had outwitted him again.

She had already passed the Book of the Learned to its next keeper.

One

Like much of the town, the law offices of Morton Hingham were left over from a more leisurely, luxuriant time. Second-story arched windows framed a view of low-roofed buildings, tall palm trees, and stony mountains that dwarfed everything human. Inside the reception area, creamy walls and rich green plants soothed the eye. Solid wood furniture gleamed with polish. The carpet was worn, but tastefully so, like a dowager princess.

The secretary-receptionist was the same. Her voice was crepe, irregular without being rough. "Ms. Charters? Mr. Hingham will see you now."

For a moment Serena stared blankly at the receptionist. In this cool, gracious room with its stately aura of law and civilization, it was hard for her to remember that her grandmother had died from a random act of violence of the kind more often associated with inner cities than with the desert's ageless wilderness.

Very few animals killed simply because they could. Homo sapiens was first among them.

"Thank you," Serena said in a husky voice.

The older woman nodded, ushered the client into Morton Hingham's office, and shut the door behind her.

A quick glance told Serena that the lawyer's office had shuttered windows and no visible wallpaper. Every vertical surface was concealed by books whose covers were as dull and dry as their titles. Various legal documents lay stacked haphazardly on Hingham's heavy desk. An array of computers along the far wall looked out of place amid all the leather-bound monuments to past decisions, writs, and opinions.

Hingham's swivel chair creaked and jerked when he stood to greet his client. Long past the age when other men retired, the lawyer kept his shrewd mind engaged with the trials and tangles of people generations younger than he was.

"Sorry to keep you waiting, Ms. Charters," Hingham said, clearing his throat. "There is a particularly difficult custody case that . . ." He cleared his throat again.

"I understand," Serena said, a polite lie. "It doesn't matter." The truth. She had been quite willing to look out the windows at the mountains that had ringed her childhood and formed her adult dreams. "I take it that the State of California is ready to close the books on my grandmother's murder?"

"The books will never be closed until her killer is found. But, yes. I'm empowered as her executor to turn over to you all that remains of Lisbeth Charters's—er, your grandmother's—worldly goods."

His use of her grandmother's real name—Lisbeth Charters—told Serena that her grandmother had trusted this man as she had trusted only one other person on earth: her granddaughter.

Then the rest of the sentence penetrated Serena's mind. She compressed her lips against bitter laughter. *Worldly goods.* Her grandmother had lived a simple, spartan life. Her reward had been a cruel, savage death.

"I see," Serena said neutrally. "Does the fact that I'm finally receiving my so-called inheritance mean that I'm no longer a suspect in G'mom's murder?"

The controlled anger beneath his client's voice made Hingham examine her more carefully. Middle height, casually dressed in blue jeans and an unusual woven jacket, a slender yet female body that once would have aroused him and even now interested him, red-gold hair in a long French braid down her back, triangular face with eyes as cool and measuring as a cat's. The papers in his hand told him that she was in her early thirties. Her face looked younger, though her oddly colored eyes held an unflinching power that belonged to an empress twice her age.

Lisbeth Serena Charters had had eyes like that. Violet blue. Wide-set. Fascinating.

Unnerving.

Hingham cleared his throat again. "You were never under serious suspicion, Ms. Charters. As the detective explained, it was simply routine to ascertain your whereabouts the night your grandmother died, especially as you were her sole surviving heir."

"The detective explained. It didn't change how I felt."

"Yes, well, it must have been very difficult for you."

"It still is. Even though G'mom and I weren't close, she was the only family I had."

And every day, Serena asked herself if she and her grandmother had been closer, would her grandmother still be alive?

There was no answer. There never would be.

Abruptly her hand moved in an impatient gesture. "Let's get this over with. I have work to do."

"Work?" Hingham glanced at the papers in his hand. "I understood that you were self-employed."

"Exactly. No time off for good behavior. My employer is a bitch."

A ghostly smile rearranged the wrinkles on the lawyer's face. "Would she mind if you took time for coffee?"

Serena smiled despite her unhappiness with the law, the legal profession, and the bureaucracy of the State of California. "Thanks, but I really should get back to Leucadia before the freeways turn into parking lots."

"Then if you'll be seated . . . ?"

Despite the restlessness crackling along her nerves, Serena went to the wing chair that waited beside Hingham's desk. Outwardly calm, she forced herself to sit quietly. She had spent a lot of her life masking the energy and intelligence that poured through her with such force, they made other people nervous. Deliberately she leaned back into the chair, crossed her legs, and waited for the old lawyer to tell her what she already knew: her grandmother had no *worldly goods* worth mentioning.

Hingham's chair creaked sharply as he sat. "I take it you don't need all the ruffles and flourishes."

"Correct."

He nodded and shifted papers. "Your inheritance is what remains of the house and five acres it sits on. There are no liens nor outstanding debts." He handed a plat map and deed across the desk to Serena. "The taxes have been paid through last year. I filed for a reappraisal due to the fire." He handed over more papers. "There are no utility bills because there are no utilities. Lisbeth—Mrs. Charters—was self-sufficient to the last."

If Hingham thought it strange that his client was Ellis Weaver on the publicly filed deed and Lisbeth Charters in her very private life, he said nothing. So long as a person didn't take a second name in order to conceal illegal actions, multiple names were quite legal.

As Serena took the papers, she gritted her teeth against emotions that owed as much to anger as to sorrow: Lisbeth Charters hadn't deserved a violent death.

"I recommend that you request another appraisal on the land itself," Hingham added. "The assessor is greedy."

Serena tried to care. She couldn't. Not now. Not when she was holding the sum total of her grandmother's life: a handful of official papers that added up to less than Serena received for weaving the kind of textile that gallery owners called "important." But the papers, like the galleries, left out so much, everything that mattered; the laughter and the silences, the tears and the warmth when cold winds blew, and the memory of lanterns shedding golden light over the safe little world of her childhood.

She had never felt poor in her grandmother's house, though she knew now that they had been impoverished.

Hingham cleared his throat. He was accustomed to reading people, yet the composed young woman across the desk from him was a closed book. As Lisbeth Charters/Ellis Weaver had been. He cleared his throat again, rearranged papers, chose one, and handed it across the desk.

"She has one bank account," he said. "In Bern."

As the words registered, Serena focused on the lawyer rather than on the memory-haunted past. "Where?"

"Bern, Switzerland. A numbered account. That's why there isn't any paper. Just the account number written in Lisbeth's hand. Even as her executor, I had a devil of a time getting any information about the account out of the Swiss."

"Are you certain it was G'mom's account?"

"Quite." Hingham smiled, pleased to have ruffled his composed client. "From the number, I would guess that the account is rather old." He waited for Serena to ask how much money there was in the account. He was still waiting when he cleared his throat and told her. "There is enough in the account to cover any final expenses associated with her death. As you know, she wanted to be cremated and her ashes scattered over her land."

Rage and tears fought for control of Serena's voice. Rage won. "How clever of her murderer to carry out her last wishes."

Hingham winced at the slicing edge in her voice. At that moment he decided to spare his client the whole truth: he had given Lisbeth's charred remains a formal cremation as soon as the sheriff's office permitted it. Then he had driven out into the desert wilderness Lisbeth had called home and had given her ashes to the wind.

Serena crossed her legs again. It was the only sign of the near-wildness that swept through her whenever she thought of someone killing her grandmother on a brutal whim. But thinking about it did no good. So she forced herself to think about something else. "Why would my grandmother have a numbered Swiss bank account?"

"The usual reasons, I assume."

"But she wasn't involved in anything criminal."

Hingham smiled. "There are many legitimate reasons for having anonymous bank accounts. Your grandmother was an extremely, um, private woman. And the account is quite old. Well before your time, I would guess. It has nothing to do with you, except if you choose to close the account. I could do that for you."

Serena looked at the piece of paper in her hand. There was $12,749.81 U.S. in the foreign bank. "I'll take care of it myself."

The lawyer's mouth flattened. He couldn't count the times Lisbeth had said the same thing to him. *I'll take care of it myself.* No matter how hard he had tried, she had refused all but the most neutral legal necessities from him. It hadn't been anything personal. She had disliked and distrusted all men equally.

"As you wish." The impersonal words stuck in Hingham's throat now as they had in the past. He cleared his throat roughly and handed over a small envelope with the logo of his office as a return address. "This is a key to her safe-deposit box."

"In Switzerland?"

He smiled. "No. Palm Springs. In my position as executor, I—"

"—opened it." Serena's voice was cool. She didn't like the thought of anyone pawing through her grandmother's life. There had been too much of that at her death, the lonely cabin and its burned-out pickup truck festooned with bright crime-scene tape, and gray ashes lifting with every bit of breeze.

"She requested it when she amended her will. I am an officer of the court, Ms. Charters. I ascertained that there was nothing of interest to the state in the safe-deposit box."

"Why would the state care if G'mom left me a few mementos?"

"If the, um, mementos were sufficiently valuable, there would be the matter of death taxes to pay."

"Of course. How could I forget." There was no inflection in her voice, simply the flat line of her mouth to reveal her disgust. G'mom had never taken a thing from any government in her life—city, county, state, or federal. But that didn't stop the various governments from wanting a share of her spoils, however meager they might be.

Hingham unlocked the belly drawer of his desk and gently removed a worn leather portfolio that all but filled the wide drawer. "There were several items in the safe-deposit box." He put a fresh, magazine-size envelope next to the portfolio. "And this was found in the ruins, near your grandmother's loom."

"What is it?"

"Cloth. She was lying on it, apparently."

In fact, the investigators speculated that she had started out curled around the cloth as though it was a child; then the pain had come. But Hingham didn't think Serena needed to know the clinical details or see the gruesome photos in the police files. Some things were simply better left unknown.

"Apparently?" Serena asked. "I don't understand."

Hingham sighed and rubbed the bridge of his nose. "There was little left but stone walls and the stone chimney. It's a miracle that this survived the fire at all."

Frowning, Serena took the envelope, opened it, and drew out the cloth. Perhaps a foot wide, more than a yard long, the fabric smelled of smoke yet wasn't burned. The threads were supple, gleaming, every color and no color, opaque and transparent, whispering to her in an ancient tongue, luring her deeper and deeper as the unfinished pattern teased her with a feeling of absolute rightness.

This is mine.

I wove it.

Yet she had never seen the cloth before in her life.

Two

"Ms. Charters, are you all right?" Hingham asked.

Serena forced herself to look at the lawyer rather than the pattern hidden like a puzzle within an ancient textile. She had always had an excellent imagination and a vivid feeling of being connected to a long, long history of weavers; that was what made her textile patterns so unusual that galleries were beginning to show a real interest in her art. But this certainty of direct connection was too real, too unnerving. Too . . .

Dangerous.

"Ms. Charters?"

"Sorry," she said. "The memories are difficult." That, she realized wryly, was truer than she wanted him to know. In this case, impossible was a more accurate description; there was no way she could have woven it. "This cloth is very, very special to a weaver like me. The pattern is fascinating and the cloth itself feels like the softest kind of satin. Or maybe velvet. The feel changes in the most extraordinary way. What an incredibly skilled weaver she must have been."

"Your grandmother?"

"No. The woman who wove this cloth. It was a long time ago. Very long."

A feeling of agreement echoed through her, softer than a whisper, as definite as thunder: *Almost a thousand years.*

Hingham looked at the scarf Serena was holding. It had a nice enough mix of colors, he guessed, but he didn't see any particular pattern. As for the feel of the stuff, well, it had made his flesh creep. He had hardly been able to hang on to it long enough to stuff it in an envelope. Yet here she was stroking it like a pet cat. Amazing.

Shaking his head, he turned away from the cloth. At least there was nothing ugly about Lisbeth's other bequests. In fact, they were among the most beautiful objects he had ever seen. With great care he opened the portfolio.

Serena's breath wedged in her throat. Against the scarred, faded leather, colors gleamed richly in deep tones of ruby and lapis, emerald and gold, incredible color soaring like a song in the quiet room. Elegant black calligraphy described a time and a place long gone, using an ancestral language that few alive today could understand.

Her heart stopped, squeezed, then beat quickly. When she spoke, her voice was barely a breath. "My God."

Gold gleamed and shimmered as the lawyer turned a page over. More colors sang in a design a thousand years old. Awe prickled over Serena's skin like electricity. *It was her design, the one that had haunted her dreams her entire life.*

"You didn't know she had these, did you?" Hingham asked.

"I—I thought I dreamed them." Serena's eyes shut, then opened. The dream was still there. Reverently she ran a fingertip down the supple edge of one vellum page. "It's real!"

"Oh, yes. Quite real. Four loose sheets written on both sides. Eight pages total."

"Real." She was having trouble accepting it. "But you said there was nothing of value in the safe-deposit box."

"For all I know, these aren't."

Reluctantly she looked away from the unbound remains of what had once been a beautifully illuminated whole manuscript: and that, too, was a memory she shouldn't, couldn't have. "I'm afraid they are very valuable."

"If so, then they are far older than any government that would hope to tax them." Hingham's smile was gentle and indefinably sad. "Your grandmother wanted you to have these pages. I saw no reason to get them appraised, and thus probably force you to sell your inheritance in order to pay death taxes to a state which did nothing for Lisbeth, least of all keep her alive."

"You . . ." Serena hesitated. "You cared about her, didn't you?"

"I would have loved her. She wouldn't permit it."

"I'm sorry."

"So am I." He sighed, pulled off his glasses, and rubbed the high bridge of his nose. His eyes were as black as his hair once had been. "A more stubborn woman I've never known. It was her biggest vice. And her biggest virtue." He sighed and replaced his glasses. When he spoke again, his voice was neutral. "The final item is this."

For the space of a breath, Serena simply stared at the small sealed envelope the lawyer was holding out to her. Then she took it, slit the bottom of the envelope with a letter opener he handed her, and read what Lisbeth Serena Charters had considered important enough to pass to her granddaughter from beyond the grave.

Serena,

When you read this, I'll be dead. No sorrow there. I lived longer than most, and all the useful parts are worn out.

If this note comes to you with only four leaves from the Book of the Learned, then I've failed in my duty. For a thousand years this book has been passed down from mother to firstborn daughter. We've lost some pages through the centuries, but damned few.

Until my generation. I'm taking steps to get them

back. I'm old enough now that death is more a lure than a fear. If I fail and you decide to go after your heritage, remember me when I was in my twenties. Think like the woman I was. Then think like the child you once were, when the desert was new to you. The Book of the Learned will follow.

Be very careful. Forgery is a dangerous art.

A wise woman wouldn't pursue this. But since when have the firstborn women of my clan been wise? Certainly not for a thousand years. If you follow where these pages lead, don't make the mistake I did—be a moving target, not a sitting duck.

Trust no man with your heritage.

Your life depends on it.

Serena read the letter again. Not for the first time, she wished her grandmother hadn't been so suspicious of everyone. She had trusted Hingham enough to leave the letter with him, but obviously she hadn't trusted him not to read it. She had given no more information than she thought absolutely necessary for her granddaughter to have.

That wasn't very much to work with. Just enough to tell her that there was a more or less whole manuscript somewhere out there, and it was her heritage, and to be careful. The warning was clear enough—*moving target*—but the way to reclaiming her heritage wasn't.

Frowning, she refolded the letter and put it back in the envelope. Though Hingham was obviously curious, he didn't appear to notice when she put the letter in her purse. Nor did he ask any questions about what the letter contained.

"I need to know more about these," she said, gesturing toward the vivid pages. Maybe they were too vivid. Maybe they were forged. "Do you know anyone who could give me a discreet appraisal?"

Hingham had expected some such request. He pushed a piece of paper toward her. Beneath the lawyer's logo were two addresses with telephone numbers and E-mail addresses. One was in New York. The other was local.

"The Palm Springs number belongs to Erik North," he said. "For a young man, he has an excellent reputation for knowing the nuances of old English manuscripts. I understand he travels a lot, though, so he might not be in town right now."

"The second number?" was all Serena said.

"The House of Warrick."

Serena recognized the name. Anyone would. The auction world had three giants: Sotheby's, Christie's, and the House of Warrick.

"Warrick has long specialized in old manuscripts," Hingham continued, "so I would recommend them. Due to the nature of this community, they have a small branch here, but New York handles major appraisals. I would be happy to ship the pages for you."

Trust no man with your heritage. Your life depends on it.

Silently Serena wondered just how stable her grandmother had been when she wrote the letter. Yet caution and distrust were almost as deeply ingrained in the granddaughter as in the grandmother.

"Thank you," Serena said, "but I'll take care of it myself."

"As you wish. I took the liberty of making color copies of these sheets myself." He emphasized the last word slightly, assuring her that the matter had been conducted with great discretion. "While the pages don't appear to be fragile . . ." He shrugged. "Surely being hauled around in a suitcase can't help them. A competent appraiser should be able to tell from a few color copies whether it is worth the trouble and expense of having the entire block of eight originals appraised."

"Again, thank you. You've gone to a great deal of effort for someone you don't even know."

He smiled faintly. "It was worth it to see Lisbeth's eyes again."

Serena didn't know what to say, or if she could say anything at all past the sudden tears in her throat. Without thinking, she picked up the ancient scarf and wrapped it around her throat. It soothed her like a caress. She touched the cloth in return, gently.

Then she collected her surprising inheritance and left Morton Hingham to his memories. She needed to go somewhere and think, hard, about what she wanted to do.

Or not do.

Trust no man. Your life depends on it.

Be a moving target.

Three

Erik North sat in a lounge chair in his walled backyard. Sun brought out every bit of blond in his thick, golden-brown hair. Barefoot, naked to the waist of his worn hiking shorts, he waited for his morning visitor and thought about the manuscript page he was translating.

Not since Eve has a woman been so deceitful. I was trapped in the cloth woven by her own hand, spellbound cloth, unclean, wrapped in her plans like an insect in a web; and I thought all the while that she loved me. She did not. She loved only her own clan, needed nothing of me but my seed.

Cursed sorceress. I dream of her still.

I yearn.

I need.

I see her bright hair in every hearth fire. I see her eyes in every violet. I smell her scent in every summer garden.

God spare me from the torment of the Devil.

The modern Erik almost smiled but didn't disturb his stillness. No doubt about it, Erik the Learned had been one unhappy camper when he wrote those lines. The elegance of the script couldn't disguise the savagery of his emotion. At a distance it was hard to tell whether hate, love, or some unholy combination of the two drove the Learned scribe. One thing Erik North knew for certain. Internal evidence in the design of the illuminated capital letters indicated that the page belonged toward the front of the Book of the Learned. The design, like the gather marks along the margin, became increasingly complex through the years of the book's creation.

Despite the comfortable surroundings and sun-warmed January day, Erik didn't slouch carelessly beside the swimming pool. Instead, there was an uncanny stillness to his body, the stillness of a predator. Beneath a tawny thatch of hair, his chest barely moved with each slow breath he took.

Most people shift position or fiddle with a button or pick at their clothes or scratch their nose or drum their fingers. He didn't do any of those things. Even his eyes were narrowed so that he could blink with almost no movement of his eyelids. It was a hunter's trick.

A roadrunner appeared on top of the castle wall as though teleported there. Round, glass-bright eyes examined every bit of the large yard with its vine-covered arches and rosebushes whose lineage traced back to the Middle Ages. The bird's black crest flared and settled like a nervous heartbeat. In the desert, water and sex were the only things an animal risked its life for. The pool's turquoise allure was irresistible.

No matter how long and hard the roadrunner peered, it saw nothing but a breeze moving among the bougainvillea vines, jacaranda and citrus trees, and medieval herb garden. Satisfied that it was safe, the brownish hawk-size bird dropped seven feet to the interior flagstones and zipped over to the curving edge of the spa that was attached to the pool. In the center of the curve, water only a quarter-inch deep sparkled and murmured over a small ledge leading from spa to pool. Daintily the roadrunner waded to the precise center of the ledge and began dipping water from the pool with quick, oddly graceful jerks of its head.

The bird was within reach of Erik's hand. If he wanted a feathered snack, the roadrunner was lunch.

Motionless he watched the bird, storing up each nuance of its movements, the subtle pattern of light across the mottled brown and cream feathers, the elegant balancing act of wings and neck, feet and long tail. The chaparral cock was uneasy, but not nearly so nervous as it had been four days ago when Erik had first sat in the yard and waited for the thirsty bird to gather its courage to drink. During this winter's unusual drought, the pool had become a daily stop on the roadrunner's rounds.

In another week, two at most, Erik would have the bird eating from his hand. Animals of all kinds accepted him. They always had. Maybe it was his stillness. Maybe it was simply that he respected them for what they were: independent, blissfully self-centered, and completely alive in the moment.

The roadrunner's throat fluttered rapidly as it drank one last time. Then its narrow tail jerked like a conductor's baton. An instant later the bird turned, ran lightly across the flagstones, and half leaped, half flew up to the top of the high wall. There was a rustle, a flirt of black tail, and the chaparral cock vanished into a cascade of deep-pink bougainvillea.

"So much for my coffee break," Erik said to the empty yard.

Nothing answered him, not even a stirring of shadows.

He stood, stretched, and headed back for his workshop, which was in the tallest of the estate's fanciful turrets. He had inherited the land and the Scottish stones that had been collected at an ancient ruin, shipped, and reassembled in the desert. It had been an expensive indulgence, but in those days there had been money—new money—from Erik's great-grandfather, who had swashbuckled with Errol Flynn across a lot of movie screens. Like many other Hollywood denizens, Great-grandfather Perry had made enough to indulge himself in a Palm Springs fantasy getaway.

A love of the medieval had always been part of the family. Erik's paternal grandfather and his wife were both well-known medievalists when they met. His father had been a medieval scholar and children's book writer. His mother's drawings had been as enchanting as the stories they illustrated.

Stretching one last time, Erik sat down on a tall, beautifully made cherry-wood stool that had once been his mother's. He leaned over a steeply tilted drafting table of ancient design which had, like "North's Castle," undergone a few modern renovations.

Even though it was ten o'clock and there were windows all across the north side of the big turret room—Perry had drawn the line at gloomy authenticity—there was barely enough daylight to meet the demands of Erik's work.

"I really am going to have to cut back that old bougainvillea," he muttered.

He needed good light, but he hated to curb the vine's cataract of blazing pink blooms. Sooner or later a rare freeze would come to the desert and take care of the exuberant bougainvillea. Until then, he would enjoy the flowers.

And squint.

He tilted the table slightly to catch the north light better, then tilted a little more. There were two sheets of paper on the table. One was vellum, blank except for the carefully ruled lines waiting to be written upon. The other sheet was a photograph taken in ultraviolet light of a very faded old Celtic manuscript that dated back to twelfth-century Britain. In ultraviolet light, the original manuscript showed through, despite having been erased so that more spectacular—and far more modern—illumination could cover ancient vellum. It was a monk's way of reusing expensive vellum, by replacing a secular text with the sacred word of God.

It was also a forger's trick to cover plain, pious text with something more flashy to catch a rich collector's eye. A carpet page of bright colors and figures was a lot more saleable than sixteen or twenty lines of text in a language the buyer couldn't read.

As always, the voice of the man known as Erik the Learned seemed to vibrate in his modern namesake's mind as he read the faded lines of the glossy photograph:

> *I stood at the boundary today, the year-day of my "marriage." Through the cursed mist I heard the bells of Silverfells ringing out the birth of a clan daughter, the first such birth in memory.*
>
> *And the mist held me back like chain mail.*
>
> *My horse refused the trail. My peregrine was blinded by sorcery's light. My staghound's nose was like unto stone. I was the most helpless of all. There was no means for me to pick a way through the mist, thus to get my hands on the source of my undoing.*
>
> *Cursed be all of Silverfells!*
>
> *I could taste the dark clan's joy even as I raged against the foul sorceress who had charmed me into being her willing slave.*

Erik winced as he had the first time he translated the passage. His namesake had been well and truly pissed off, so enraged that it radiated up through time from the faded letters, so furious that he never even wrote the name of the sorceress; at least, he hadn't in any of the seven pages Erik had managed to find over the years.

"Poor son of a bitch," Erik muttered. "She really stuck it to you, didn't she. Or maybe you stuck it to her. A birthing bell, hmmm? Well, unless they conceived babies differently in twelfth-century Britain, I suspect you were willing enough in the saddle. Wonder what went wrong . . ." His mouth turned down. "The usual, I suppose. She wanted more than you could give her and still call yourself a man."

It had happened that way to Erik North. His fiancée had wanted his undivided attention. She hadn't wanted to be "stepmother" to two teenage girls who happened to be his younger sisters. There were plenty of second or third cousins, weren't there? Let them raise the girls.

End of engagement.

Beginning of single parenting.

Carefully Erik put away the tools he had used to mark lines on the vellum. Because this particular client was exceptionally fussy—to put it politely—he had used a bone stylus with an embedded metal tip for marking on the vellum, just as had been done for more than a thousand years. Now the lines were waiting to be filled with calligraphy. All he had to do was see the ancient text well enough to copy from it.

It would have helped if he could have worked with the original vellum longer, but the owner was understandably possessive of his treasure. Works by the Spanish Forger were in high demand in the twenty-first century. Erik had been lucky to get permission to put the leaf under UV and photograph it, thus reclaiming the original text.

Slowly he tilted the wooden drafting table until what had been merely a hint of thin shadows just beneath the surface of the original vellum condensed into a photograph of elegant yet spare calligraphic lines. He made a deep, rough sound of approval that was rather like a growl. The sound went quite well with his tawny blond hair and predatory golden eyes.

"Gotcha!"

Humming a chant passed down from medieval times through generations of men, he fixed the table at the proper angle. Only then did he select a quill from a rack bolted to the edge of the drafting table. As he was left-handed, the quills he preferred using came from the right wing of the bird—usually a turkey, sometimes a goose when he was copying a page down to the last finicky historical detail.

Today he was using goose quills. His client was himself; when it came to the Book of the Learned, he was the fussiest client on earth. If a total re-creation of the original meant finding goose quills in Palm Springs, then by God he found goose quills.

The ancient monks and scribes had no problem getting good feathers. Old World medieval monasteries had never heard of New World turkeys, but the monks had kept flocks of geese to supply their pantry and their calligraphers.

Erik hadn't been driven to that extreme yet. He had chatted up some organic turkey farmers and a woman who raised European graylag geese for restaurants specializing in unusual foods. Once he had worked past the farmers' disbelief, they were glad to give him the pick of the feathers.

As expected, Thanksgiving was best for getting bushels of turkey feathers. Christmas was best for geese. Just a few weeks ago he had prepared hundreds upon hundreds of goose quills, plunging each shaft into hot sand to "cure" the quill, then peeling away the frail, slippery skin, and finally scraping out the soft core. After that a few practiced strokes of his penknife transformed a feather into a writing instrument.

It had taken incense to chase the smell of processed feathers from the old castle he had inherited from his grandfather. In fact, Erik suspected that monks had used incense for the same reason. Wet, scorched feathers had a smell that ranked right down there with skunk.

Automatically he held the quill up against the daylight and inspected the tip. Perfect. It wouldn't last long, but that was why he had a sharp penknife always at hand. Literally. He had picked it up in his right hand even as he reached for the quill with his left. In the twelfth century, all church-taught scribes were right-handed. The fact that this calligrapher was left-handed explained his choice of text as well: a secular history of the Learned clan as seen through the eyes of their greatest scholar rather than ruminations on the nature of God.

Erik settled in to begin work. Calligraphy in the medieval style required two hands, one to hold the quill, one to hold the penknife. The quill did the writing. The penknife did everything else: keeping the sleek vellum in place on the slanted table, sharpening quills at the bottom of every page, and erasing any errors by scraping off the ink before it could dry.

Holding the pen in a way which seemed odd to a modern man—so that the quill was at a right angle to the vellum, and the whole arm rather than the hand provided the motion—he reached out to dip the point into a pot of ink which he had made following a recipe that was older than the chant he hummed. Though he preferred lampblack as a personal matter when he was replicating ancient manuscripts, the stubborn client had insisted on the ancient combination of iron sulfate and ashes of oak gall. The resulting ink was pleasing enough to work with but faded to brown as years piled up like autumn leaves.

That wouldn't be Erik's problem. When the ink began to fade, he would be long dead. At least now that he was no longer working for the Security side of Rarities Unlimited, he had a better chance of living long enough to collect most of the Book of the Learned.

Before he could touch virgin quill to ink, the phone rang.

Four

Erik was tempted to ignore the ringing demon, but didn't. It might be a paying client. It might be a medieval scholar wanting to discuss some arcane aspect of calligraphy or mixing paints for illumination.

It might be Rarities Unlimited.

He set aside the quill and picked up the portable hand unit that was fixed to the side of his drafting board. As soon as the unit left its charging cradle, the ringing stopped.

"North," Erik said curtly.

"Niall."

Adrenaline kicked. S. K. Niall—*rhymes with kneel, boyo, I'm not a bleeding river*—was the cofounder of Rarities Unlimited, which wasn't so much a business as a collaboration of international talents held together by a shared reverence for the best that human culture had to offer. Some of Erik's most interesting assignments had begun with that low-voiced growl or Dana Gaynor's soothing, feminine tenor. Niall's specialty was Security, which covered a multitude of operations, some of them quite private.

"How's life in Smog City?" Erik asked.

"Up yours."

"That bad, huh?"

"You're just jealous. L.A. is all clean from the last rain and you're stuck in Palm Springs with dusty sidewalks and bars full of bad Elvis imitators."

Erik waited. The other man hadn't called to talk about the weather and they both knew it. The dark, highly trained head of Security had more work than he had time to handle. On the other hand, Niall and Erik were rock-climbing buddies as well as professional allies. Friends, in a word.

"I have a question for you from Factoid," Niall said.

Erik blinked. Factoid, aka Joseph Robert (Joe-Bob) Mc-Coy, was the Rarities computer expert and the completely wired twenty-first-century man. Due to the peculiarity of his mind, with or without benefit of computer, Joe-Bob McCoy had command of a staggering number of unconnected facts.

"You still there?" Niall asked.

"I'm speechless. What do I know that Factoid can't find in his databases or his terrifying brain?"

"The mind of a woman."

"Sorry, you must have called the wrong number."

Niall laughed. "He figures that anyone with shoulders like yours must have the secret of the feminine psyche."

"Better he should ask you," Erik said dryly. "You're the original tall, dark, and handsome. Hell, I've never even been married."

Niall gave a crack of laughter. "That's just it. He figures you've got it wired. Women chasing you and none catching."

"The boy has a great fantasy life," Erik said. "Tell him to keep on dreaming. It beats the hell out of my reality. Anything else on your tiny little mind?"

"Gently, boyo. This is your boss you're insulting."

"I work for Dana."

"The Fuzzy side," Niall said in disgust, referring to the Fine Arts side of Rarities, as opposed to the Security side, which he ran. "When are you going to come back to the real side? I could use you."

"I'm a born-again Fuzzy."

"Balls."

"You've assured me that Fuzzies don't have any."

Niall snickered and gave up for the moment. "McCoy wants a birthday present for Gretchen. I told him to get a vat of oil and a—"

"Way too much information!" Erik cut in swiftly.

"Then what's your suggestion?"

Erik opened his mouth. Nothing came out. Factoid's seething ambition to get his boss Gretchen into bed was the running joke of Rarities Unlimited. Gretchen was ten years older than her would-be lover and built like a Wagnerian diva. McCoy had a turbocharged metabolism; no matter how much junk food he ate, he had to stand beside himself to cast a shadow.

"Prayer," Erik said finally. "If that fails, virtual reality has my vote. There are websites out there that are guaranteed to rot your dick right off. Anything else?"

"One of our sources at Sotheby's heard rumors of some unknown, very high-quality manuscript pages surfacing."

"Twelfth-century Celtic?" Erik asked instantly, knowing that this was the real reason Niall was on the phone.

"I called you, didn't I?"

"Insular script?"

"I don't know."

"Latin or vulgate?"

"Hell, boyo. I'm no Fuzzy."

"Did the pages come to Sotheby's?" Erik asked.

"No. House of Warrick. New York office."

"Shit. If the pages are really good, the old man will buy them for his auction house, or even himself. Just because he prefers fifteenth-century manuscripts doesn't mean he doesn't buy others. Did Warrick contact you?"

"No. Our mole did. The stuff is in for preliminary appraisal only. Color copies, not the real thing. Nothing was said about selling."

"Any kind of appraisal is the first step to selling," Erik said impatiently. "I want to see those pages. If that fails, at least get me the copies. Find out the owner's name."

"Factoid's working on it, but nothing has been entered into Warrick's computer yet, or if it has, it's on a secure computer. Or maybe the boy's holding out for a really spiffy gift suggestion from you."

"Chocolate syrup."

"What?"

"Tell him to pour it into her—"

"Talk about too much information!" Niall cut in hastily. "I'm too young to hear this stuff."

"Bull." Before Niall could argue, Erik said, "Get me the information about those pages."

"Since when did you start giving orders to your bosses?"

"I'm an independent consultant, remember?"

"On retainer."

"Want it back?"

"Not today, boyo. I'll wait until you piss me off."

The sound changed, telling Erik that his employer/friend had hung up with his usual lack of ceremony.

"Good-bye to you, too," Erik said.

He punched the END button and put the unit back in its cradle. His left hand picked up the quill. His right hand reached for the penknife.

The front-gate buzzer went off.

Erik cursed. He turned, looked through the south window, and saw the white, purple, and orange van of FedEx delivery service. For a moment he was tempted to ignore the interruption. He wasn't expecting any shipments. On the other hand, the unexpected was often the most interesting thing that happened on any given day.

He went to the intercom on the other side of the room, punched a button, and said, "Need a signature?"

The crackling "Yes" was just barely audible.

He really had to do something about that intercom. Antiques were fine in their place, but that place wasn't in a security system. Although the rest of the system was beyond cutting edge, one of Rarities's security consultants had a brilliant, if bent, mind. Erik admired Joella's work, even if he didn't understand her genial paranoia.

"I'm on my way," he said into the intercom.

Setting aside the virgin quill, he went quickly down the stairs and out the large remodeled kitchen to the side gate where all deliveries came. The driver was new, female, and didn't look old enough to vote. But then, since Erik had turned thirty-four, more and more people had started looking young to him.

"Thank you," she said with a quick smile.

He took the package from her and smiled back automatically, but his attention was all for the package. She left while he held the parcel with fingers that were sensitive despite the scrapes and calluses left by his rock-climbing hobby. The package was too thin to hold much of interest, unless some cultural moron had shipped him naked manuscript pages.

Curious, he pulled a big pocketknife out of his jeans. The black plastic handle was deliberately rough, which allowed a good grip despite mud, rain, ice, or blood. The wicked, serrated edge of the knife could go through nylon webbing like lightning through night. The blade made short work of the package. He closed the knife with a distinct click and pulled some papers out of the parcel. The cover sheet was written in a modern hand that had no patience for beautifully executed letters.

Dear Sir,

Enclosed please find color copies of two manuscript leaves. If you feel they are worth a formal appraisal, please contact me at the number on top of this page.

Thank you.
Serena Charters

He raised tawny eyebrows at the energy that fairly crackled through the words. He wondered if Serena knew that her name, like his, dated back at least to the twelfth century. If she knew, she probably wouldn't care. Twenty-first-century people were obsessed with the future, not the past. At least, most of them were.

Erik wasn't. It was the past that haunted and intrigued him, the past that was his passion.

He flipped the cover page over to show the copy that lay beneath. He wasn't expecting much, because color copies were difficult to judge even when they were made carefully. This one was barely adequate. The colors were faded and uneven, as though the printer had been out of ink or out of adjustment. The writing was so light as to be indecipherable.

Yet his breath came in and stayed: what little he could see of the text was written in an elegant calligraphic hand that was as familiar to him as his own.

The language of the text was Latin. The marginal commentary was in the vulgate that was Anglo-Saxon and Norman combined. The few words that were dark enough to make out sent adrenaline spiking into his blood.

The Book of the Learned.

The thought echoed in Erik's mind, the pattern as clear to him as if it had been printed in letters an inch high. He had been enthralled by the Book of the Learned since he was nine and had seen his first leaf in a collection of old books and family papers his great-aunt had showed him. He had seen many other manuscript leaves since then, pages from books older and newer, more richly illuminated, more perfectly written script . . . but he had never seen a manuscript that moved him the way the Book of the Learned did.

Perhaps it was simply that the name of the Learned calligrapher and illuminator of the book was also Erik. Whatever the reason, his fascination with the book had driven him to learn Latin, Old English, and the fine arts of illumination and calligraphy.

Heart beating rapidly, he looked at the next color sheet and the next. The copies were so bad he wondered if it was deliberate. The pages weren't sequential, but they were definitely part of the Book of the Learned. The calligraphy was unmistakable, as was the style of the decorated capitals, a combination of pagan and Christian sensibilities that was unique to the manuscripts he described as Insular Celtic.

There were four pages, both sides of two unbound sheets that looked like they had been removed from a bound manuscript. The last page had no writing. Its colors had been so badly reproduced that the painting was almost impossible to make out. Erik stared and kept on staring until he finally saw the images.

A man and a woman in medieval dress.

The man had sun-bright hair cut so that it would fit beneath a war helmet. His cloak floated on a breeze, revealing the chain-mail hauberk beneath. A peregrine falcon rode his left arm. At his feet lay a staghound the size of a pony. He was watching a woman weave on a loom that was taller than a man. Her unbound hair tumbled in a fiery torrent down her back to her knees. She was looking over her shoulder at him with eyes the color of woodland violets. Instead of castle walls, the two people were surrounded by a rain-drenched forest, as though nothing on earth existed but a man and a woman caught in the mists of time.

More than anything else, the lifelike rendering of the people told Erik this was a secular rather than a religious manuscript. In the early twelfth century, the church was still so concerned about the possibility of idolatry that it insisted all representations of human figures be two-dimensional to the point of woodenness.

Slowly Erik let out a breath he hadn't even been aware of holding. Nor did he remember walking back up to his turret studio and studying the wretched color copies. Yet he must have done just that, because when he looked up he was in his studio and the copies were spread across the floor in a patch of sunlight.

The woman's hair, which he remembered as fiery, looked

more like a wan taffy color. The man's hair was equally faded. His clothes weren't distinct. The proud peregrine was only a shapeless bundle on his left arm and the staghound could have been a mound of earth at his feet. Her incredible violet eyes had no color.

Yet Erik had seen it so vividly. All of it, the sun-bright and the fiery, the violet and the gleaming links of chain mail, the peregrine and the sleeping staghound. He was as certain of it as he was of his own heartbeat.

After a few moments Erik shook himself and came to his feet with the coordination of a man used to climbing rock faces. Without looking away from the copies, he picked up his phone and punched in the number at the top of the cover letter.

No one answered. Not even a machine.

He punched in Niall's private number. Not his really private one, much less his most private one; but still, not the usual number.

"What?" Niall snarled, his accustomed telephone greeting.

"Tell Factoid that the woman who sent the color copies to the House of Warrick is called Serena Charters. She lives in Leucadia. She wants to know if the pages are worth a formal appraisal."

"Are they?"

"Yes." Sighing, Erik mentally kissed his next few Rarities Unlimited consulting fees good-bye. He should have done this years ago, but had been too stubborn. Too cheap, too, with the girls finishing off advanced degrees. "Also, I want a complete provenance search on some illuminated pages I own. I'll forward the specifics to Gretchen. And yes, I'll pay for a rush job."

"Bugger." Niall sighed. "I'll tell Dana that her favorite Fuzzy is off on a private quest."

"It shouldn't take long."

"Neither does dying, boyo."

Five

Local tradition held that Serena's house had been built by a man who had made his first million smuggling hashish during the Hippie Sixties. He had paid that million, plus a lot more in hashish, to his lawyer to keep him out of jail. As a result, house plans that had begun in grandeur and excess ended in a drastically trimmed-down version that required a "special" buyer to appreciate.

The house had three thousand square feet unevenly divided into one bedroom, one palatial bathroom, one kitchen, and one huge, vaulted room overlooking Leucadia's flower farms, Interstate 5, and the Pacific Ocean. There was no office. No media room. No spa or sauna or exercise room. There wasn't even a walk-in closet. None of the essential luxuries for the telecommuter of the late twentieth or early twenty-first century. As a result, the house had stood empty as often as not.

By the time Serena bought it, the house was approaching its half-century mark. The vaulted "great room" became her weaving studio. Five looms cast long shadows in the afternoon sun. Two of the looms were tall, one was medium height, one was small, and one was tiny enough to use sewing thread for the actual weaving. A tall loom stood empty but for the warp threads, ready for a new weaving to begin. The other big loom held a wall hanging that was almost finished. The pattern was a heraldic device that had been carried into the Second Crusade. Tear-shaped white Norman shields with simple red Christian crosses on them formed a huge patterned cross against a black background.

Critically Serena looked at the hanging. It was a commission piece from a wealthy high-tech entrepreneur who was trying to feel some connection to his past—or at least the past he would like to have had. As with most commissions when the design was simply handed to her, she didn't find the result particularly satisfying, but she wasn't in a position to refuse a guaranteed paycheck. Especially one of this size.

Though a few of her weavings were now on display in galleries in Manhattan, Milan, Los Angeles, and Hong Kong, it might take years for any single piece to sell. In the meantime she still had to eat, make house and car payments, buy quantities of fine yarn, pay taxes, and find cat food that Mr. Picky wouldn't turn up his black nose at.

The only things Picky really liked were fresh Pacific lobster, tiger prawns, smoked salmon, and chicken pâté from the French deli at the beach. Since Serena didn't have enough money to eat such things on a regular basis, she and Picky had to make do with tuna, cheese, and peanut butter. And rodents, of course.

For the cat, not for Serena. She had never been tempted by any of the mice, voles, shrews, or moles Picky proudly laid out for her inspection every morning—particularly as the cat had already eaten the choice bits. It was his way of telling her what he thought of commercial cat food, canned tuna, cheese, and peanut butter.

The cat in question yeowed loudly and stropped against the back of Serena's knees with enough force to make her grab the heavy wooden pillar of the loom for balance. Picky was almost as big as a bobcat. He had wonderful orange eyes, sleek black fur, a bobbed tail, and a tuft of hair on the tip of each ear. Knee-high, muscular, predatory, he ruled the house with velvet paws and sheathed claws. Other than attacking salesmen, he had no faults worth mentioning, and certainly none worth the trouble of breaking.

"If you're hungry, go hunting." Serena reached down and gave the cat a thorough rubbing. "If you're thirsty, go terrorize the koi in the garden pond. If you want to go out, you know where the cat door is."

Picky rubbed his chin against the ancient woven cloth she wore around her neck.

"You like it, too, don't you?" Serena said, laughing. She hadn't been able to let go of the scarf since the lawyer Morton Hingham had given it to her. She had even slept with it under her pillow.

And her dreams had been both vivid and troubling: violet eyes like her own beseeching . . . something. The wild cry of a peregrine frustrated in its kill. The hell-deep baying of a staghound circling at the edge of a mist that kept retreating. *Soon. Soon. He will see me and I will see him and there will be no more barriers, no safety, nothing but the fate I wrought on my loom.*

Picky purred hard enough to make her hands vibrate. The dream-memories evaporated, leaving Serena feeling unsettled. Both the scarf and the purring cat were welcome distractions from the uncanny memories. No, dreams. She couldn't possibly have remembered them, no matter how real they seemed at the moment.

"Too bad somebody fixed you," she said to Picky. "I'd like to have a couple more like you."

The look he gave her said: *Eat your heart out. There aren't any more like me on earth.*

"Scoot. I have to work."

As soon as she picked up the shuttle, Picky stalked off. He had learned that the fastest way to get locked out of the house was to be underfoot while Serena was weaving. He could watch. He could pace. He could lust after the rapidly moving shuttle. But if he made a pass at it or at even one of the dangling yarn-wrapped bobbins or lovely heaps of yarn piled around the room, he was out in the cold.

Absently Serena snapped her fingers. A remote switch kicked over and music poured out of speakers all through the house. Normally she preferred chamber music, Renaissance motets, or twentieth-century blues, but the austere Crusader design seemed to call for martial music and laments. At the moment, American Civil War ballads wept in all their sad beauty. Not exactly the same war as the Crusades, but not all that different, either. Hell on earth in the name of a higher morality.

The phone rang.

She made no move to answer it.

She had ignored the phone twice already. It was a bad habit of hers, one she had promised various galleries that she would break, or at least get an answering machine that was reliable. But Picky adored any blinking light, and batted with his paws until answering machine, computer, telephone, whatever, was well and truly fouled up. She had tried to explain this to people who insisted that she find a better way to receive their messages. She no longer bothered. People always found a way to get to her. If it wasn't easy, that just gave her more time to weave.

The phone rang. And rang.

And rang.

Serena finished the row and reached for the phone, hoping no one would be there. "Hello."

"Good afternoon. Is this Ms. Charters?"

"If you're selling something, I don't buy over the phone. I don't do surveys, either."

"This is the House of Warrick," a woman's voice said crisply. "Janeen Scribner speaking. May I please speak to Ms. Serena Charters?"

"Oh. Sorry." Serena put a lock of silky, wavy red hair behind her ear with a motion that was half exasperation, half embarrassment. "I'm Serena."

"You sent us four color copies taken from an illuminated manuscript, correct?"

"Yes. I wondered if it was worth the trouble of getting a full, formal appraisal."

"The person who could best answer your question is Mr. Norman Warrick himself. His specialty is illuminated manuscripts."

"I'm reluctant to send the original pages to New York," Serena said, "and I don't have time to bring them myself right now."

"That won't be necessary. Mr. Warrick divides his year between New York and Palm Desert. He and his family are presently in Palm Desert. They will expect you this evening, if at all possible."

"Tonight?"

"Yes. Mr. Warrick is almost one hundred. He never wastes time."

"Oh." Serena looked at the nearly finished wall hanging. Then she thought of the luminous pages lying inside their leather envelope in her locked van, where Picky's curiosity couldn't get to them. "Fine. What time and where?"

Janeen gave her directions and added, "Naturally, Mr. Warrick will want to inspect the originals."

It wasn't exactly an order. Nor was it a question. Serena's full mouth firmed even as she told herself that she was being ridiculous. If she couldn't trust the head of the House of Warrick, she couldn't trust anyone.

Even so, each time she looked at the pages, her sense of possessiveness toward them increased. In some indefinable way, they were *hers*. The thought of sharing them with anyone made her uneasy. Or maybe it was just that she couldn't forget her grandmother's warning.

Even at nearly one hundred, Norman Warrick was still a man.

"Seven o'clock?" Serena asked.

"Mr. Warrick will be expecting you and the sheets."

Click.

Serena looked at the dead phone, shrugged, and picked up the shuttle again. She didn't have to leave for half an hour. Forty-five minutes if she pushed it.

She would push it. She always did.

Six

PALM SPRINGS
WEDNESDAY AFTERNOON

Erik looked at his twenty-six-inch flat-screen monitor as intently as he would a manuscript for appraisal. He wouldn't buy pages over the Internet, but he sure didn't mind previewing them that way. It saved a lot on airline tickets or special-delivery services.

For more detailed research and comparison, he preferred using his extensive CD-ROM library of entire manuscripts or collections. Viewing by CD-ROM wasn't as good as thumbing through a manuscript in person, but it was a hell of a lot more convenient. In any case, most of the manuscripts that interested him were locked away and simply not brought out for viewing by anyone, for any reason. As a way of protecting the precious manuscripts, it was very effective. It was real good at frustrating scholars, too.

Fortunately, the pages he was looking over right now were being put before the public quite cheerfully. They were for sale to the highest bidder. His favorite auction site to search was the Bodleian Market, named after England's world-famous Bodleian Library, with its breathtaking collection of illuminated manuscripts. He keyed in his usual request: palimpsests; fourteenth- or fifteenth-century-style illumination; sheets or whole manuscripts; new listings for this month only.

Because of the short time frame for the listings, and the narrowness of the request, he didn't expect much. He checked often enough that there were usually only a handful of new entries.

This time there were six, but the only one that interested him was posted by Reginald Smythe, a small-scale trader who had once been a curator of manuscripts at a minor museum and then an estate chaser with his own agenda. Erik had never met Reggie personally but knew him by reputation.

The man was perfect for Erik's purposes. Erik wanted the pages that slipped beneath other people's radar, the pages that said they were one thing on the surface but really were something else underneath. Palimpsests, in a word, vellum sheets on which the original text had been scraped off and a new one painted or penned on top.

He clicked on the photo button. Instantly a picture appeared on his screen. One of the side benefits of consulting for Rarities Unlimited was the uplink to Rarities's satellite-supported computer system. Light speed beat the hell out of even the most recent commercial Internet offerings.

When he saw the picture, adrenaline kicked in in a tingling rush. Then he frowned. The miniature wasn't up to the standards he had come to expect of the Spanish Forger, a man whose illicit work had become quite valuable in its own right. Instead of the near lyric style of a late-nineteenth- or early-twentieth-century forger imitating the Romanesque style of the early fifteenth century, the drawing appeared almost clumsy. Almost, but not quite. It was certainly close enough to fool most people. It could possibly be genuine; even the best artists had bad periods.

Thoughtfully Erik checked the leaf's availability. No bids

yet. The leaf could be inspected at Reggie's shop in Los Angeles or at the International Antiquarian Book Celebration.

With a grimace that said he really didn't want to attend the world's biggest antiquarian rummage sale, Erik moved on to the category called "Provenance." The first of the leaf's three most recent owners all that were required to be listed—was Christie's (brokered on behalf of a very private client); it was later sold to a private collector by the name of Sarah Wiggant, who died last year, and was then owned by Reggie himself, the ultimate death chaser. He had purchased it from her estate less than a year ago.

Erik didn't have to look at his hand-size portable computer/ cell phone to key up the Research department at Rarities Unlimited. He could find the code in the dark—and often had, when he got up in the middle of the night with an inspiration.

Since his own code automatically registered as he "dialed," his call was routed directly to the person who was handling his previous research request.

"Shelby here. Whadya think I am, God? I haven't had your stuff long enough to—"

Erik cut in quickly. "Just wanted to add to the search list. I copied my screen to your computer, so all you have to do is—"

"Yeah yeah, got it. Anything else?"

"No."

The cell phone went dead.

"Say hello to the wife and kids for me, Shel," Erik said into the useless phone. "And good-bye to me, too."

But Erik was smiling as he dumped the handset back into its charging cradle. Shelby Knudsen was a black former pro football player who had broken his back during scrimmage and discovered while in traction for a long, scary recuperation that he had a gift for tickling facts out of computer files.

Researchers could be trained. Born researchers had to be found. Next to Factoid, Shel was the most brilliant researcher Rarities had. Erik knew it was a sign of Dana Gaynor's high regard that he had been given Shel on such short notice.

Or else she knew something about those pages she wasn't telling Erik. It wouldn't be the first time.

It wouldn't be the last.

Seven

By the time Serena followed the directions to Warrick's Palm Desert estate, it was dark. Even at night, the place was impressive. The Mediterranean-style house was set dramatically against the stark black rise of the mountains, pinned by static swords of security lights, and surrounded by stucco walls, wrought-iron gates, palm trees, ocotillo, and barrel cactus. Exterior security lights set off vast colorful plantings of snapdragons and petunias. Sprawling bougainvillea vines shed bright petals that piled up in windrows at the base of the high walls.

The twelve-foot-high front gate had cameras as well as the usual number pad. Because she hadn't been told the gate code, she punched the button marked VISITOR and spoke her name into the microphone grille.

"Welcome, Ms. Charters. The Warricks are expecting you." The voice was clear, pleasant, and male. "Please follow the main drive to the house."

The gate retracted just enough to allow her through. The instant her van cleared a hidden detector, the gate closed so quickly that it all but banged into her bumper. Soon she was surrounded by tightly mowed lawns, fountains, and trees that owed more to Italy than to the New World. The drive was at least a quarter mile long. The house itself was big enough to be called baronial: pale stone facade, three stories, with vertical windows set at regular intervals on all levels. Olive trees and cypress pruned into unlikely shapes lined the long walkway to the entrance.

Though Serena knew this tract of land had been nothing but rocky desert when she was a girl, the house and grounds looked as if they had been in place for five hundred years.

Wonder if they need any hangings for their castle walls? Serena thought wryly.

The Warricks certainly could afford her weaving. One of her continuing sources of bittersweet amusement was that she didn't have enough money to buy her own work. She could barely afford to keep a favorite piece off the market and in her own home.

As soon as Serena turned off the engine, the massive front door opened. She half expected to see a leggy young thing in a French maid's outfit, but the person waiting for her was very tall and masculine in outline. She got out of the van and stood, waiting for him to come to her. As she waited, her fingers strayed to the ancient cloth she wore beneath the neck of her blouse. Soothing, almost silky, yet somehow even softer than silk, the texture calmed her.

The man walked down the stairs with an ease that suggested youth, fitness, or both. His hair looked dark, except where it was woven through with silver that glistened in the artificial light. Erect and clean-shaven, he didn't appear particularly casual despite the slacks, golf shirt, loafers, and light wind jacket he wore.

Without being obvious about it, he looked through the van's windshield to see if she was alone. He scanned her with equal discretion. There was nothing to raise warning alarms in her black jeans, black cotton pullover, and black sandals. The black leather purse she carried was big enough to double as an overnight case, but many women had such purses and carried nothing more lethal inside than makeup, water, and comfortable shoes.

"Welcome to the Warrick estate, Ms. Charters."

"At the moment, I feel more like Alice in Wonderland."

White teeth flashed. "I reacted the same way the first time I saw it. I'm Paul Carson. The Warricks are eagerly awaiting you inside. May I help you carry anything?"

"Like the pages?" she asked.

He had the grace to look chagrined. "Sorry. We're all excited. The color copies were intriguing, but not particularly useful." He shrugged. "You understand, I'm sure."

"You want to see if the pages have more to offer than the copies, is that it?"

"Of course."

"That's why I brought them. I'd like to know, too."

Intent, pale eyes that could have been blue or gray or green watched while she pulled a large leather portfolio from the rear of her van. She noticed his scrutiny and raised her left eyebrow in silent question.

"I'm sorry if I seem rude," he said quickly. "Some habits are impossible to break. I spent twenty years in the Secret Service and ten more as Mr. Warrick's chief of security. We have so few strangers to the estate that, frankly, I'm nervous."

"I'm getting that way myself," she said. Then she smiled. It was hard not to. The idea of someone who looked like Carson being nervous around an unarmed woman was amusing.

"Again, I apologize," he said. "It's just that so many young women carry concealed weapons today."

"I'm not one of them."

"Good, because I would have to ask you to leave any weapon in your van. House rules." He smiled again. This time he let his approval of her feminine form and elfin face show in his voice. "Have you eaten?"

Serena blinked. The man was damned handsome, even if he was twenty years older than she was. The twinkle in his eyes hadn't aged one bit. "Eaten? I think so."

"You don't know?"

"I was weaving. When I'm weaving . . ." She shrugged. "My stomach isn't growling, so I must have eaten something somewhere along the way."

"As soon as I introduce you to the Warricks, I'll see what we have in the kitchen."

"That's not necessary, Mr. Carson."

"Paul." He gestured for her to precede him up the wide marble stairs. "And it's very necessary. I have a niece your age. I'd feel terrible if she fainted at my feet because I hadn't thought to feed her."

"That must be how Picky feels."

"Picky?" He opened the massive front door and turned to her.

"My cat. He's always leaving, er, delicacies around for me to eat."

"Delicacies?" He closed the door behind them. "Such as?"

"Obviously you don't have cats."

"No."

"Picky catches all manner of small things, but he only eats the juicy bits. He leaves the crunchy stuff for me."

"Ugh. No wonder you don't eat. This way, Ms. Charters."

"Serena."

"Serena. Unusual name. Quite lovely."

"I'm told it's a very old name." As she spoke, her eyes took in the extraordinary etchings, paintings, armor, and framed pages from illuminated manuscripts that lined the hallway. They were more striking than even the Louis XV rug whose plush length softened the stone floor. "According to family legend, the first girl born in every generation is given Serena as part of her name. It's been that way since the twelfth century, one Serena per generation."

"Dammit, Paul, where is she?" demanded a rusty, irritated voice. "I could die before I—"

"We're in the hall," Carson cut in quickly. Then he said softly to Serena, "I'll apologize in advance for Mr. Warrick. He is rude, arrogant, and brilliant."

"I'll try to concentrate on the last part."

"We all do," he said ironically. "Some days it's easier than others. This way."

Serena didn't know if the space she entered was officially called a "great room," but it should have been. French and Italian antiques lined the walls and made graceful conversational groupings that any museum would have been proud to own. The Warricks seemed to have a special fondness for the ornate. Ormolu decorated or held everything that could support its gilded splendor. She was certain that the porcelain thus displayed was the best of Sèvres, the crystal was hand carved, and the furniture was signed by the master craftsmen of their times.

Though it wasn't Serena's style, she smiled at the luxurious result and admired the painstaking artistry that went into each piece.

Then she saw the medieval French tapestry hanging on the far wall and all thought of furnishings vanished. The complexity of the hanging could only be fully understood by another weaver: the delicate weft, the intricacy of the pattern, the hachure technique of blending colors so that there appeared to be many more than the medieval palette of two hundred, the gold and silver threads among the fine wool, the thousands of hours of work, and the keen eye that first imagined and then taught others the design. Unicorn and aristocratically dressed maiden, knights arrayed for battle, colorful tents where favored members of the court rested after a picnic of wine and cheese and meats; the tableau was a slice of time that had survived to cross the years into the twenty-first century.

The tapestry's humanity cried out to Serena. Aristocrat or peasant, knight or knave, all people hungered for food and rest and beauty. The weaving both described and understood the imperfections of human nature and the fleeting perfection of a certain moment in time.

Motionless, she simply absorbed the faded yet extraordinary tapestry that had been woven and embroidered by nameless workers so many centuries ago. Silently she saluted the long-dead men and women who had created such beauty from nothing but a handful of threads.

"—stand there like a sheep caught in headlights. Bring that portfolio to me!"

Belatedly Serena realized that there were people in the room. They were all but hidden by the magnificent furnishings.

"Father," a woman's voice said wearily, warily, "there's no need to be that rude. Not everyone is used to living with antiques that once graced the castles of French and Italian kings."

"And queens," Serena said, looking back to the far wall. "That's a woman's tapestry. Extraordinary. Except in the Louvre, I've never seen anything to touch it." Reluctantly she turned her attention from the enthralling woven portrait of a time long lost. "I'm Serena Charters."

"Of course you are," the old man retorted. He was thin, quick, had wispy white hair and hands that looked delicate despite their enlarged knuckles. He seemed more like a vigorous seventy than nearly one hundred. "Anyone else wouldn't have been allowed past the front gate."

"This is my father, Mr. Warrick." The woman was like her voice: of medium coloring except for her skillfully bleached hair, of medium height, and educated yet still casual, with a strong flavor of New York. "I'm Cleary Warrick Montclair. The young man with the good manners is my son, Garrison Montclair."

Serena nodded at Garrison, who looked perhaps eighteen at first glance. When he moved to greet her, she noticed the Safavid rug beneath his feet for the first time. Only the French tapestry could have kept her from noticing such a glorious example of textile art. The rug's colors were still vibrant after five centuries, the designs both crisp and flowing.

"Delighted to meet you," Garrison said.

Serena realized that she was staring at the rug rather than paying attention to her hosts. Talk about rude. Guiltily she forced herself to look away from the gorgeous rug to the hand Garrison was holding out to her. As she shook it firmly, she realized that up close he looked at least ten years older than she had thought. He had the assurance that came from wealth and exclusive education. If he also had the arrogance, he hid it well.

Probably one arrogant man in the house was enough, she decided with faint humor.

Having been raised essentially without men, Serena found them amusing and impossible by turns. Fascinating, too. Rather like large cats. Really large. But, as G'mom had assured her granddaughter many times, *Men aren't worth the trouble of housebreaking.*

Serena had always taken her grandmother's words at face value. Only when she grew older did she wonder why—if men were that much trouble—women went to such unlikely extremes of dress and cosmetics to get one of their own.

Garrison's friendly hazel eyes smiled at her. Two warm hands surrounded her own. Softly curling chestnut hair caught and held light as he gave her a slight bow.

"My pleasure, Ms. Charters. Or may I call you Serena?" Garrison asked.

She wondered if a woman had ever refused him. "Serena is fine, Mr. Warrick."

"Oh, please," he said, laughing. "There's only one Mr. Warrick here, and that's Granddad. I'm Garrison, chief flunky for the House of Warrick."

Cleary gave her son a sidelong glance that he ignored.

Serena hid a smile. Perhaps a possessive mother was the reason that the charming young scion didn't have a wife at his side.

"Enough nonsense," Warrick said curtly. "Bring me the bloody sheets now."

Garrison rolled his eyes but made no other objection. "If I may . . . ?" he asked, holding out his hand for the portfolio.

For an instant Serena's fingers tightened on the leather. A peculiar sense of possessiveness gripped her. She had to force her hands to loosen. It was ridiculous to be so wary. The man who owned the baronial splendor surrounding her certainly wouldn't simply grab four leaves from a manuscript nobody had ever heard of.

"Of course," she said.

She handed over the leather portfolio and told herself she was an idiot for the silent cry of objection that rose within her when the pages left her hand. She was acting like a mother cat with only one kitten.

It was an effort, but she forced herself not to follow Garrison as he crossed the costly rug and laid the portfolio on an antique table in front of his grandfather. The surface of the table gleamed with a mosaic of semiprecious gems—lapis and malachite, ivory and ebony, carnelian and mother-of-pearl. For all the attention Warrick paid to the table, it could have been made of clay.

With surprisingly nimble fingers, he undid the buckle on the portfolio and opened the leather wide with the impatience of a conquering knight spreading a woman's thighs. Silence filled the huge room while he turned the first sheet, then the second, the third, the fourth.

He looked up, pinning her with dark eyes. "Where did you get these?"

"I inherited them from my grandmother."

He said something that she couldn't hear, something that sounded very much like *bullshit*.

"Excuse me?" Serena said.

"Where are the rest of the sheets?"

Serena was sure that hadn't been what the old man said, but she answered anyway. "This is all I have."

He snorted. "Likely story. Want to try again? Where are the rest of the sheets?"

"Yes, let's try again," Serena said tightly. "I don't have any other pages."

Warrick gave her a look out of eyes that had faded from their original brilliant blue but had lost none of their searching clarity. "When did she die?"

"A year ago."

"Why did it take you so long to get these appraised?"

Irritation flared. Serena subdued it and tried to remember that Warrick had the reputation of being as brilliant an appraiser as he was rude. Even so, she had no intention of going over the whole sad, sordid tale of her grandmother's death.

"I'm a busy woman," Serena said through her teeth.

"And I'm an old man. I don't have time to waste with a clever young baggage who thinks to take up where her purported relatives left off."

She stared at him, wondering suddenly if he wasn't more than a little bit senile. "I'm afraid I don't understand."

He snorted.

"I'm sorry to have bothered you," she said evenly. "I'll take the pages somewhere else to be appraised."

"Waste of time. We both know exactly what they are. How much do you want for the lot? A hundred thousand?"

"There has been a misunderstanding." She spoke with great care, because she hated to add to the stereotype of redheads and quick tempers. "I'm not here to sell these pages."

"*That* I believe," Warrick retorted. "Two hundred thousand."

Serena looked at the other people in the room. They met her glance with barely subdued curiosity.

"Three hundred thousand. Each," Warrick said. "But for that I want the rest of the book. All of it, mind you. I won't be fooled."

With a feeling of unreality, Serena turned back to the old man sitting in the high-backed carved ebony chair. "No."

A flush of anger tinted his pale, wrinkled cheeks. "If you think you can fuck with—"

"You're tired," Carson cut in. His cool words overrode his employer's rusty voice. "It's been a long day for you. We'll discuss this again when you're rested."

For several moments the two men traded stares. Then Warrick hissed something under his breath, stood, and stalked from the room.

Garrison sighed in relief. "I'm sorry, Serena. Grandfather is a man of strong opinions."

"His home. His privilege." Serena went to the table and began buckling up the portfolio.

"You have every right to be angry," Carson said, "but there's no need for you to have made this long trip for nothing. We have a guest room for you and a safe for the portfolio, if you like. In the morning we can talk again. He'll be more reasonable. I promise you."

"Thank you, but no." Serena gave Carson a tight smile. "I have work to do tomorrow."

Actually, she planned on staying in Palm Springs, sleeping late, and then driving out to her grandmother's house—her own house now—to see what was left after the triple disaster of fire, crime-scene investigation, and a year of neglect.

"Obviously Mr. Warrick thinks the sheets are valuable," Carson said. "I'm uneasy about letting a young woman alone go driving off into the night with more than a million dollars' worth of art. Let us keep it for you until you decide to sell."

She tucked the portfolio under her arm and looked straight into Carson's light-blue eyes. "Will the gate open automatically or do I have to call the house again?"

"I'll show you out," Garrison said.

"Nonsense," Cleary cut in. "Let Paul do it." She gave the portfolio a glance that was as cold as her voice. "When you change your mind about selling those sheets, call us. But don't wait too long. The offer won't be open indefinitely."

In silence Cleary and Garrison watched Serena walk out of the room. The line of the younger woman's back suggested all the things that she had wanted to say, *Go to hell* being foremost among them.

"Too bad Granddad was in such a pissy mood," Garrison said. "She's quite pretty in a fey sort of way. Nice ass, too."

"Get your mind out of your crotch."

"Not until I'm at least as old as Granddad."

"You'll never see the day," Warrick said from the interior doorway. "Call Rarities Unlimited. It's time for them to start earning their retainer. That blackmailing little bitch will regret trying out her teeth on me."

Eight

Head thrown back, muscular neck bulging, the bighorn sheep stood on a dry, rocky ridge and sniffed the wind for danger. There was man smell on the air, but it was a familiar odor to the ram. That particular scent had never meant danger to the small herd. On the contrary, sometimes the smell might mean that a salt lick would appear nearby. In the desert, salt was a treasure, almost as necessary for life as water or food or ewes.

The ram blew out air, rubbed his head on one front leg as though to rearrange the massive, curving weight of his horns, and began grazing again. Four ewes foraged nearby. Their woolly bellies protected and warmed the next generation.

Sixty feet away, Erik sketched rapidly to catch both the wariness and the acceptance of the wild sheep. The land around him was steep, desolate, rocky, and dry. It was also much more accessible than the sheep's summer range. The bighorns had been driven to lower elevations by the coming of winter storms. A recent snowfall had made their normal haunts icy and covered over everything edible, but the only other sign of water was a wisp of cloud curling down from the highest peaks.

Today there was rain on the other side of the mountains, the wet side where clouds piled up and darkened until they shed life-giving silver tears. But there wouldn't be any water at lower elevations on the Palm Springs side of the peaks, Erik's side. It took a bigger storm to push rain over mountains more than two miles high.

The wind blew hard enough to make Erik glad for the Pendleton shirt he was wearing. The sheep came equipped with their own wool, but he had to import his. The thought made him smile while he added a final stroke to the sketch, turned over a new page, and began drawing quickly again.

He had spent much of the night poring over the maddening copies of pages from the Book of the Learned. No matter how much, how little, or what kind of light he had used, he could only make out occasional phrases written by a man long dead.

The thought that this time I will see her drives me like a starving wolf . . .

May Christ forgive . . .

I cannot . . .

. . . cursed mist, let me by!

On another page he had fretted and worried over a note concerning the marriage of a young woman, Caoilfhionn of the Mist, to the son of Simon and Arianne, called Ranulf of the Rowan. The birth of a shared grandson to Dominick le Sabre and Duncan of Maxwell was noted. A full harvest received prayerful thanks. The arrival of three books from a Norman duke was celebrated. A place or a people called Silverfells was either cursed or mourned, perhaps both.

The fragments were maddening. He had worked until he was cross-eyed and bad tempered. Then he had checked for anything new from Rarities on tracing the provenance of his pages—Shel's response was succinct and obscene—before he had finally fallen asleep.

Three hours later he had awakened restless and filled with

adrenaline. He had dreamed of flying like a peregrine, coursing like a staghound, holding on to a violet-eyed sorceress who burst into flame that heated without burning. The colors had been vivid, the language that of his specialty, twelfth-century British, which was a mix of Norman French, Anglo-Saxon, and the exuberant patois that ultimately became known as English.

Too restless to sleep any more, he had pulled on hiking clothes and headed up into the San Jacinto Mountains. Illuminated manuscripts were his passion and his profession; sketching the vanishing bighorn sheep was his relaxation and his hobby. Before dawn, he had needed both.

He looked up, then resumed sketching. He doubted that the sheep would be around when his children were old enough to hike the steep sides of the desert mountains. That was assuming he ever had any; at thirty-six, he was no closer to fatherhood than he had been at sixteen. He had never expected it to turn out that way. If he had thought about the matter at all when he was young, he had assumed that he would have descendants stretching out into the unknown future just as he had ancestors stretching back into the unknown past.

Then the years had gone by and nothing had changed but his age. Realistically, he had to wonder if anything ever would. With each passing year he was getting harder to please, not easier. Females who would have interested him twenty years ago looked like children now. The twenty-somethings he met were married or caught up in their careers. The thirty-somethings were often harried and bitter after a divorce, wholly committed to their careers, or interested only in an undemanding affair.

Erik wasn't an undemanding kind of man. He wanted a woman who was intelligent, passionate, honorable, strong enough to be a true partner, and interested in working with him to build a shared life. He had found many women with one or two of those qualities. Once he had found one with four out of five, but she was interested only in his mind.

A golden eagle plummeted down out of the sky, distracting Erik from his unhappy reverie. Instants later a rabbit broke from cover and raced in unpredictable zigzags through the rocks. Either too eager or too late, the eagle missed its kill. The bird screamed its irritation to the sky.

Erik whistled in exact imitation of the eagle's angry cry. The raptor wheeled in a swift circle overhead, peering down as though to discover who his rival was. Erik whistled again. The sound was less fierce this time, more questing than threatening. The eagle answered in kind, made another circle over Erik, then beat its broad, powerful wings and flew up into the sky. The whistle that tumbled back down to earth sounded almost like a good-bye.

The vibration of Erik's pager against his body was definitely a hello.

He would have been tempted to ignore it, but his bosses at Rarities were two of the few people who had his pager number. If they wanted to talk—especially about the pages from the Book of the Learned—he was more than ready to listen. The copies had haunted him all night long. He had dreamed of their letters whispering to him, telling him the secrets of the past. And then he had dreamed of mists and forests, a staghound and a falcon who was his eyes.

Smiling at his fanciful, medieval mind, he punched a button on the pager. One of Dana Gaynor's numbers at Rarities Unlimited blinked in the pager's small window. Moving slowly but not furtively, for he didn't want to alarm the sheep, Erik reached into the rucksack beside him and pulled out his combination cell phone and computer. A flick of his thumb activated the first number in the speed-dial file.

Dana picked up her phone before the second ring. "Morning, Erik. Can you talk?"

"The sheep haven't sold me out yet."

"Lord, are you doing your mountain-goat bit again?"

"Sheep, Dana. We don't have mountain goats in southern California."

"Sheep, goats, whatever. Hooves and a bad smell."

He laughed softly. Dana was a stickler for some kinds of details, but wildlife wasn't one of them. "I hope this is about the pages Serena Charters sent to my home."

"It is. Your private quest just went public."

His heart kicked up the pace. "How so?"

Dana ignored the question in favor of her own agenda. "Is your request to Research for provenance searches on your manuscript pages part of your private quest?"

"Yes."

"Then it's on the house," she said dryly. "The House of Warrick, that is."

Erik thought quickly. Serena hadn't hired him; she had merely made inquiries. If she decided to have him do the appraisals, there still wouldn't be a conflict. Whatever he learned during his Rarities research became part of his expertise, which was exactly what she and Warrick paid for. "Is the old man having trouble deciding if the pages are worth appraising?"

"I'll let Paul Carson explain. Garrison and Cleary Warrick Montclair will probably be here, too."

"By here I assume you mean Rarities headquarters in Los Angeles?"

"Yes. Ten o'clock this morning."

"Today?"

"The old man is nearly a hundred, what do you think?"

"I think I can't make it before two o'clock even if the freeways are clear, and they won't be."

"The chopper will pick you up at nine."

Erik let out his breath in a very soft whistle. The last time he had been chauffeured by the Rarities helicopter, he had been riding with the president-for-life of a small African country. The president's passion, and eventual downfall, had been illuminated manuscripts. He had spent money on them that should have gone to military salaries, ammunition, and outright bribes.

"Factoid is now head researcher," Dana continued. "Shel is swamped with chasing some damned Old Master through four wars."

"Factoid? Should I be flattered or worried?"

"Be whatever you want except late."

Nine

The helicopter wheeled like a falcon beneath the pilot's steady hands. Idly Erik wondered if rides like this were the source of his recurring dream. Then he decided it must be his own imagination. He had dreamed of flying like a falcon and running like a staghound long before he had ridden in his first helicopter. In any case, Los Angeles was the opposite of mist-shrouded oak forests and wild meadows swept by wind-driven rain. The hills of L.A. were carpeted by houses and eucalyptus trees. Coyotes rather than wolves sang, and they sang to each other about garbage cans set out at the curb for trash collection rather than a blood-humming chase through ancient oak forests after elk.

The headquarters of Rarities Unlimited was cut into a hillside high above the concrete sprawl of the city. On the border of commercial and residential zones, Rarities had the best of both worlds. More compound than office or house, Rarities was laid out like a small, very exclusive college campus, with walkways connecting five buildings. No building was more than three stories high. All except one of the buildings were set in a landscape design that owed much to Japan: serenity and evergreens, the sculptural presence of boulders, the soft murmur of water trickling over dark stones.

The exception to all the clean lines was Niall's house. It was surrounded by an English cottage garden. No matter what the season, flowers climbed, towered, sprawled, bunched, and ran in careless riot around the wood-and-glass residence. Among the flowers grew herbs that were the source of a running argument between Niall and Dana. He insisted they were useless. She insisted that they were the only part of his garden that *was* useful.

The pilot lowered the helicopter down to the pad as gently as a butterfly settling onto a flower. Larry Lawrence was a former marine, former National Forestry Service firefighter, and former traffic reporter for KCLA. If it could be done in a helicopter, he could do it.

"They're waiting in Dana's conference room," Larry said.

"Anyone else?"

"I brought in Garrison and Cleary Warrick Montclair. The Eiffel Tower, too."

Larry was five feet seven and one-quarter inches. He disliked really tall men on principle. At just under six feet two inches, Erik was right at the edge of Larry's tolerance. Paul Carson, aka the Eiffel Tower, exceeded Larry's personal limit by several inches. Paul had been chosen for the Secret Service because there had been a series of presidents who topped six feet two. As Charles de Gaulle had figured out generations ago, tall guards made excellent bullet catchers for tall presidents. Larry had wanted to be a presidential guard in the Secret Service, but wisely had opted for the marines instead.

"You've never forgiven Carson for taking the job you wanted, have you?" Erik asked.

"The taller they are, the shorter their business," Larry retorted.

"You just keep telling yourself that."

Erik ripped off his headset, grabbed the envelope with the

copies from pages of the Book of the Learned, and jumped out before he could hear Larry's undoubtedly raw reply. Marines swore like the sailors they were supposed to be, even when they were helicopter pilots.

Larry got even by taking off with enough force to rock Erik on his big feet.

Niall waited until the dust settled before he walked up. He was dressed the way Erik was, comfortable jeans, comfortable shoes, and a clean long-sleeved dress shirt rolled up to the elbows. If he had worn a jacket this morning, it was hanging over the back of a chair somewhere.

"How many times do I have to tell you, boyo?" Niall asked, shaking Erik's hand. "Never piss off a short pilot."

"Or a tall one, for that matter. What are you doing here? Have you joined the Fuzzy side?"

"Somebody has to keep the dainty little darlings alive."

Erik cocked his head and looked in Niall's blue-green eyes. "Something up?"

"I wish. Things get any quieter here and I'll fall into a coma."

"What about that Old Master you were guarding in one of the clean rooms?" Erik asked, referring to the special rooms where potential buyers, sellers, and other interested parties met to discuss business. It was one of Rarities Unlimited's most popular services—a safe, neutral place to view priceless pieces of art.

"The Van Dyck?" Niall shrugged. "It went back to its original owners."

"Too bad."

Niall grinned. "Not really. Patrick said the paint on the bastard was barely dry."

Patrick was Patrick Marquette, who vetted a lot of paintings for Rarities Unlimited.

"There's one born every minute," Erik said ironically.

"Optimist. I'm thinking it's more like a sucker born every second."

"Lots of business for you."

"Idiots. They never figure out that if it sounds too good to be true, it damn well is a lie."

Niall opened a glass door. It was bulletproof, like every other piece of exterior glass—and most interior glass—on the premises of Rarities Unlimited. Dana had fought the whole idea until some crackpot with a grudge and a pistol went hunting a former girlfriend who was working part-time for Rarities. Niall had been cut up by flying glass before he disarmed the man. The bulletproof glass was installed a week later. Niall had never mentioned it. Neither had Dana.

"What about those color copies the Charters woman sent you?" Niall asked. He glanced at the large envelope. "Do you have them with you?"

Erik nodded.

"Still fancy them?" Niall asked.

"Yes."

"Interesting."

"Why?"

"I'll let Dana tell you."

Erik lifted his eyebrows but didn't say anything more.

Dana was waiting in her office, which had a garden view on one side and a city view on the other. When the two men walked in, she glanced at her elegant gold watch.

"Don't blame me," Erik said. "Air traffic in L.A. is almost as fouled up as the freeways."

"You were the one off chasing goats."

"Sheep," Erik corrected patiently.

"Whatever," Dana said, dismissing the subject. "They all have fur."

"Wool, actually," Erik said, deadpan.

Niall snickered.

She glanced over at Niall with soft, dark eyes. "Kill him."

"Before or after he talks to our clients?" Niall asked.

"Bloody hell," she muttered.

"I love you, too," Erik said.

She grimaced. "What do you know about Norman Warrick?"

Erik was accustomed to Dana's lightning shifts of conversation. "More than you have time to hear."

"Is he as good as his reputation?" she asked.

"Are we talking about his ability as an appraiser?"

"I'm not vetting his sexual skills or putting him up for sainthood," she said impatiently. "Is he any good or is he coasting along on an old reputation?"

"Last I heard his eyesight was good and his mind was intact. That puts him right up there with the world's top appraisers of illuminated manuscripts in general, and fifteenth-century French manuscripts in particular."

"But not of twelfth-century Insular Celtic manuscripts?"

"He's as good as anyone else that comes to mind."

"What about you?"

Erik looked hard at the petite brunette who appeared much too delicate to be as fierce as he knew she was. And as bright. "His reputation is international and long-standing. Mine is just getting to the point that my name is on the must-consult list for Insular Celtic manuscripts, if that's what you want to know."

"What I want to know is will you be right or will he?" she asked bluntly.

"Should be interesting to find out."

Niall laughed out loud. "You don't belong with the Fuzzies, boyo."

"Stuff it," Dana said quickly. "You're not getting him."

"If I screw up," Erik said to Niall, "I'm yours."

Dana shot Niall a lethal glance, pulled her maroon silk jacket into place over a pearl-gray sweater, smoothed her matching slacks into a clean line, and said, "Don't screw up. You're the only manuscript expert we have who speaks English."

With that, she walked out. The men followed her into a hallway lined with photos of some of their more spectacular finds. Erik's personal favorite was a wall hanging that dated to twelfth-century Britain; the design was intricate to the point of dizziness, yet fascinating. Everyone saw something different in it. The priceless textile had been discovered in a flea market. Rarities had certified that the textile was genuine.

Dana's high heels clicked rhythmically on the tile floor. Though her stride was shorter than that of her companions, she didn't hold them back. She moved the way she thought: quickly, confidently. Despite the fact that she was his boss, a decade older, and not interested in him sexually, Erik couldn't help admiring the rhythmic, essentially female motion of her hips beneath the fitted silk jacket. She had a walk that would melt steel plate.

"Watch where you're going, boyo," Niall said under his breath, "not where she's been."

"Her view's better."

"Shut it, children," Dana said crisply. "It's showtime."

Ten

Cleary, Garrison, and Paul were seated around a steel conference table that was big enough to comfortably seat eight. Steaming cups of coffee and plates of dainty pastries and biscotti told Dana that her assistant had been on the job.

Dana introduced Erik to the clients. A glance told him that Cleary was expensively if unexceptionally dressed, her son likewise, and Paul less so. If Paul could afford a four-thousand-dollar suit and thousand-dollar loafers, he wasn't wearing them today. His slightly graying hair was well cut. Garrison's cut was better, just short of Hollywood flashy. Cleary's hair was frosted, shoulder-length, and frothy, a style suited to someone her son's age. But then, a lot of women in southern California's body-conscious society dressed a generation or two younger than they were. Some of them even believed it.

At a discreet signal from Dana, Niall sat where he usually did, in a chair with its back to the wall and its front facing the door.

"Thank you for seeing us so promptly," Paul said.

Cleary gave Warrick's head of security a look that said they were paying enough for the privilege of Dana's company that they didn't need to be polite about it. The yearly retainer the House of Warrick gave Rarities Unlimited only ensured a place on Rarities' busy schedule; after that, expenses on specific assignments sometimes piled up rapidly. But then, so did the results.

"Our pleasure," Dana said briskly. "You said it was urgent."

Garrison examined the toes of his expensive shoes. The expression on his handsome face said that he had lost an argument on the subject of just how urgent this business was.

"Mr. Warrick," Cleary said, "insisted the matter be concluded as soon as possible."

Dana wasn't surprised. A man leaning hard on his century mark didn't have time to be patient. In any case, it wasn't in Warrick's nature to wait. The man should have been born an emperor, a god, or a czar. Tyranny came naturally to him.

"A young woman sent copies of four pages from a purported illuminated manuscript for Mr. Warrick's appraisal," Cleary said stiffly.

"Purported?" Erik asked.

Cleary gave him an impatient glance. "You heard correctly. Purported. May I continue?"

"Of course," he murmured. Apparently the old man wasn't the only one who had a wide streak of impatience.

Cleary took in a jerky breath. For a moment she ducked her head. Then she turned to Erik. "I'm sorry. This has been very upsetting. My father is, frankly, in the kind of fury that a man his age can't afford. For the sake of his health, this must be settled immediately."

"Exactly what is the problem?" Erik asked.

"That woman tried to sell him fake pages."

Erik waited. When Cleary didn't say any more, he said carefully, "Surely that has happened before."

"Yes. Of course." Cleary looked at her manicure as though seeing it for the first time. Her expression said she didn't like what she saw. "Mr. Warrick—my father—has been a target for such people from time to time."

"It adds to my collection," Garrison said, smiling.

Cleary sighed. "My son collects fakes. He insists they're art in their own right."

"When you think of it," he said, leaning forward, "there's no difference between well executed—"

"Not now," his mother interrupted. "This is no time for one of your lectures on reality, expectation, and post-postmodernism."

He smiled in amusement at himself. "Sorry. I do get carried away. I'd love to have Serena's pages for my collection. Not at the price she's asking, of course. The thing about fakes is that they're cheaper, once they're uncovered."

"You want us to prove the pages are fraudulent so that you can buy them at a good price?" Erik asked neutrally.

"No proof required," Garrison said. "Granddad had a fit when he saw them. He hates frauds the way some people hate snakes. A phobia, you know."

"One you don't share," Erik said.

"Nope." Garrison grinned. "I think the Spanish Forger is one of the great artists of the late nineteenth, early twentieth century."

Erik's bronze eyebrows lifted. He had a fondness for the Spanish Forger, too, but only because the miniatures were painted on "erased" vellum. Some of those pages had come from the Book of the Learned. But all he said aloud was, "Must make for some loud discussions at home."

Garrison laughed. "Are you kidding? He'd blow something vital. I don't talk about my hobby at home."

"Since you're certain the pages are fraudulent, why do you need Rarities?" Erik asked.

"Granddad," Garrison said simply. "He said he wanted them off the street. We can't talk him out of it."

"Our services don't run to confiscation," Niall said.

Cleary started as though she had forgotten Niall was in the room. It would have been easy to do. For a big, well-built man, Niall could take up very little space when he wanted to.

"We don't want anything that drastic," Paul said with a smile. "We were trying to buy the pages when Ms. Charters became irritated at Mr. Warrick's abrupt manner and left. We called her house repeatedly, but there wasn't any answer. We decided to turn the whole thing over to you."

Niall glanced at Dana.

"Then you want Rarities to find Ms. Charters and negotiate on your behalf for the purchase of the pages Ms. Charters brought to you," Dana said. "Is that correct?"

"Correct," Cleary said. She glanced at Niall. "I believe that is within the company's purview."

" 'Buy, Sell, Appraise, Protect,' " Niall said, quoting the company motto.

"Precisely," Dana said. "What is the upper limit of Mr. Warrick's price range for the pages?"

"He didn't mention one," Paul said before Cleary could. "He was really quite furious."

"A million dollars' worth of mad?" Erik asked dryly.

"Two million. Three. Whatever it takes." Cleary's voice was clipped. "This isn't business. This is a matter of life and death. My father's."

Eleven

Dana waited until she heard the helicopter taking off to return Cleary Warrick Montclair and her escorts to Palm Desert. Only when she was certain that the chopper was airborne did she reach for the envelope Erik had brought with him.

"Does this mean I'm walking home?" he asked, watching the aircraft make a wide swing past a bank of windows.

"By the time Larry gets back, I might be finished with you," she said, laying out the color copies.

"Sounds ominous," Erik commented to Niall.

He grunted. "You still fancy those pages?"

"Who wouldn't?" Dana asked, looking at them. "The copies are execrable but it looks like the pages themselves might be quite beautiful."

"So was the Spanish Forger's work," Erik pointed out.

"Who was he?" Niall asked.

"Could have been a she. Nobody knows." Erik shrugged. "The Spanish Forger's specialty was erasing genuinely old vellum and then painting and selling miniatures that were supposedly taken from old illustrated manuscripts."

"Erasing? How?" Niall asked.

"Lots of ways. Sometimes he scraped the old words off

and painted a miniature on the 'erased' vellum. Sometimes he cut out a rectangular piece of the undecorated margin of an old choir book and painted a highly decorated capital letter on the scrap. The result looked like it had been cut from an old Book of Hours or Psalter."

"What good was just a capital letter?" Niall asked.

"There was a Victorian craze for alphabet books whose letters were made up entirely of elaborate capitals that had been cut out of old manuscripts."

Dana winced. "You mean they would take something as elegant as this and butcher it for the pretty letter?"

Erik looked at the page she had pointed to. It took a good eye and a better imagination to see the clean, balanced columns of calligraphy that filled the page. The only relief was in a palm-sized capital *T* made of intertwined dragons whose eyes, claws, and scales were probably picked out in gold foil; the copy showed the color more as a sickly bronze. As was customary in illustrated manuscripts, a heavily decorated and gilded capital letter signaled the beginning of an important passage: *The thought that I will see her drives me . . .*

The idea that Erik the Learned might have arranged a meeting with his mysterious sorceress/lover/enemy intrigued his modern namesake. The words vibrated with emotion, but there was no hint as to whether such a meeting was in the past, in the future, or only in the scribe's mind.

"That's exactly what the forgers did," Erik said to Dana. "They couldn't read the old Latin, much less the common language of the day. Few people could, and that included the folks buying the illustrated manuscripts. Even fewer people could read the vulgate commentary between the lines and in the margins."

"Vulgar comments?" Niall asked, looking interested for the first time.

Dana gave him a black glance that could have left holes in two-inch steel plate.

"Vulgate," Erik said. "Same root. Much the same meaning.

Common or coarse. Latin was the language of education and writing. English was considered a vulgar tongue."

"Still can be," Niall said.

"In your mouth, certainly," Dana said.

"Stop, now, you're hurting my Fuzzy feelings," Niall said.

"I'd have to find them, first."

"Anytime you want to go looking, luv. Any time at all."

Her lips fought a smile. She lost. One of the things she liked about Niall was that he wasn't a bit intimidated by her sharp tongue and even sharper mind. Just as she wasn't intimidated by his intelligence, strength, and lethal skills. From time to time they fought like hell on fire, but they respected each other just as fiercely.

"You were saying . . . ?" Niall invited Erik.

"Alphabet books," prompted Dana.

Erik didn't even blink. He was accustomed to the free-wheeling conversations that passed for business meetings at Rarities Unlimited. "At the end of the nineteenth century, when self-made men like J. Pierpont Morgan were buying art by the carload to shore up their claim to social legitimacy, illustrated manuscripts in whole or in tiny parts became all the rage. Morgan bought them by the pound. Quite a few of them were compliments of the Spanish Forger."

"You mean the old robber baron bought a lot of frauds?" Dana asked, smiling at the idea.

"He was buying what was available on the market at the time. The Spanish Forger was a big part of that market. Interesting thing is, today the work of the Spanish Forger is collectible in its own right. He or she was an artist. He couldn't read Latin—the miniatures didn't match the sense of whatever words survived on the page—but the images themselves were beautiful."

"Then it's hardly something to have a heart attack over, is it?" Niall muttered. "A rose by any other name still has thorns. If Warrick had been suckered by these," he said, waving at the pages, "then I could understand him popping a vessel over them. But he wasn't suckered. So what is he really after?"

"Irrelevant," Dana said immediately. "People lie to themselves, much less to other people. If we had to know all of our clients' motives before we acted, we would be lip-deep in stink. That's why I made certain we were hired for a specific job: attempt to buy the pages for the House of Warrick. Why the Warricks want the pages is their problem."

"Until it becomes *our* problem," Niall said.

"We'll burn that bridge when we get to it. *If* we get to it." She gave him the kind of look that had shriveled lesser men. "At the moment, I don't want your convoluted, paranoid military mind screwing up a simple, profitable assignment."

"Convoluted," Niall said, savoring each syllable. "Is that a Fuzzy word for brilliant?"

"What if the pages are real?" Erik asked quickly, heading off one of his bosses' famous, furious slanging matches. Niall and Dana might consider them invigorating, but everyone else headed for the nearest exit.

Dana swung toward Erik. "Are they?"

"I won't know until I see the originals, but if I had to put a bet down now, I'd say they're real. The calligraphy certainly is right for the time. If the images match the text . . ." He shrugged. "Get me the originals. Then I'll tell you if they're fake or real."

"Bloody hell," Dana said. "That might complicate things on our end. The House of Warrick thinks the pages are fake. They could go sideways on us if we insist the pages are real."

Then she was silent but for the movement of her fingertips on the conference table's burnished maple surface. It wasn't the random drumming of an impatient person but rather the intricate moves of someone who was accustomed to playing the flute.

Erik waited.

So did Niall. He might enjoy jerking Dana's chain at every opportunity, but he had a profound respect for her intelligence. She was a Fuzzy by choice, not because she lacked the unflinching pragmatism to see the world as it really was.

"If the pages are real, of course we protect them," she said. "Our allegiance is to the art, not to the client. The House of Warrick knows it as well as we do. It's in the contract they sign with Rarities Unlimited each year."

"Good," Erik said simply.

"Otherwise you were going to freelance this one, is that it?" Niall said.

Erik nodded. "Serena Charters approached me, remember?"

"Were you interested on general principles or personal ones?" Dana asked.

"Both."

"Do you have a conflict with the client's request?" she pressed.

"I'd rather buy the pages for myself, but I can't outbid the House of Warrick and I know it." He shrugged. "Given that, I have no conflict with carrying out the client's wishes."

"All right," she said. "You're on."

"I'll need a complete background on Serena Charters," Erik said. "And on the grandmother, too, since that's where Serena says she got the pages."

"Grandmother's name?" Niall asked.

"All I know about Serena is that she lives here"—Erik handed over the cover letter that had come with the copies—"and she doesn't answer that telephone number often enough to matter."

Niall's winged eyebrows twitched but he said only "How long do I have?"

"The usual," Erik said. "Yesterday."

"Somehow I'm not surprised." Niall stood and looked at his watch. "Is this one of Factoid's telecommute days?"

"He's been coming in more often." Dana smiled slyly. "He says that telecommuting isn't as good as being in the flesh, so to speak."

"I like that boy's ambition," Niall said, heading for the door. Then he stopped and winked at Dana. "Good job he's after Gretchen's flesh, not yours. I'd hate to break every bone in his Fuzzy body."

"You break him, you replace him," Dana said.

"Gretchen isn't my type. I prefer tiny little brunettes."

"I'm not tiny!"

"Who said anything about you?"

The door closed behind Niall.

"Some day I'm going to kill that man," Dana said thoughtfully.

"How?"

"In his bed."

"I doubt that he sleeps that soundly."

She smiled like a cat. "Did I mention sleeping?"

Her fingertips began moving again as she stared at the bad color copies spread across the table. The possibility of jewel tones and the suggestion of graceful, intricate Celtic designs made her wish she could see the originals.

"Fake or real, they're really quite extraordinary," she said finally. "When will you know?"

"If they're real?"

She nodded.

"Once I get my hands on them," Erik said, "I'm going to take a long time deciding if they're what they seem."

"Will it be that difficult?"

He grinned. "No, but it will be that much fun."

Twelve

The Rarities helicopter dropped Erik off at the clean, uncluttered, and mostly uncovered Palm Springs airport. He passed up the dubious delights of airport food and drove to a little roach coach a mile away that served the kind of tacos that had claws in them. The chilies were as real as the tears they drew from his eyes.

No sooner had he taken a bite than the pager vibrated against his waist.

"Now what?" he muttered.

He wiped his hands on a napkin that was smaller than the taco he was eating and almost as greasy, punched a button, and saw a number. He called it and waited. Six rings later, someone picked up.

"McCoy. What do you want." There was no question in the voice, simply a kind of irritable snarl.

"You tell me," Erik said. "You called my number."

"Minute."

Erik went back to eating. Factoid's idea of a "minute" was notorious around Rarities. It came from the fact that McCoy wore his computer clipped to his belt, used a palm communications unit called a widget as a keyboard when it would have been impolite to address the computer verbally, and viewed various screens through special windows placed in the glasses he didn't otherwise need. Factoid could be face-to-face with you and at the same time on the other side of the world having a conversation with one or more mainframes. To him, reality was a virtual construct.

"Okay," McCoy said. "What did you want?"

"To find out why you called me."

"Oh. Right. I loaded what I've found so far under your access code."

"Usual place?"

"Yeah. Rarities folder, today's date as the file title."

"I'm renaming that file Book of the Learned as soon as we stop talking. All future info on this case should go there."

"Minute."

Holding the cell phone between his ear and his shoulder, Erik took the last few bites of taco, wiped his hands, and wished that his cell phone/computer could compute and talk at the same time. He had tried it once. The results had been unspeakable, but that hadn't prevented Factoid from mentioning it endlessly.

"Cool book!" Factoid said.

"You've got the Book of the Learned on one of your databases?" Erik asked.

"Just a few rumors. Want 'em?"

Erik smiled. He had never been able to afford a full Rarities search. Dana or Niall would have given him one for free, but he hadn't wanted to ask. The Book of the Learned was, after all, only a hobby. He wouldn't admit that it had become an obsession, no matter how riveting and frankly medieval his dreams were. "Hell, yes, I want what you have."

"So where do I pour the chocolate syrup?"

Erik blinked and said without hesitation, "In her shoe."

"Her shoe."

"Um" was all Erik could say without laughing out loud.

"Jesus, it's a wonder you ever get laid. Her *shoe*. I'm checking my databases on that one."

"Let me know how it goes."

"Shoe. Mother. You're sick, North."

"It's all that chocolate syrup."

Grinning, Erik punched out and went to the computing/Internet access side of his hand unit's silicon brain.

A few moments later he knew that Serena's full name was Serena Lyn Charters, she was thirty-four, self-employed, owned a house in Leucadia, a five-year-old van, no outstanding or recent tickets, had registered a neutered male cat named Mr. Picky with a pet recovery service, never married, and used no computer that was plugged into anything McCoy could tap. Social Security number was still out of reach, but it shouldn't take long. More information would come when Factoid cracked Serena's bill-paying habits. The telephone bill was first. As soon as he found her mother's name—especially her maiden name—he would go after credit and debit cards. Then it would be a piece of cake.

Erik glanced at his watch. Quarter of one. He could read this in comfort at his home computer, or he could keep squinting at the unit's small display.

He kept squinting, haunted by the faded copies with their hints of a long-ago life written in a man's slashing hand and introduced by two dragons, intertwined yet hostile. And he had no doubt the beasts were hostile rather than loving; he had managed to decipher a few more words.

The thought that this time, this day . . . I will see her drives me . . . starving wolf to food.

Though I know . . .

God's teeth, I was foolish. Why didn't I see?

Erik could fairly feel the rage and acceptance of his long-dead namesake. Then he blinked and saw the tiny readout rather than fragments and phrases that were almost a thousand years old, words that were seared on his memory as though he had once written them, felt them, lived them.

With an impatient movement of his thumb, Erik scrolled

down the screen for information that was more modern. A few moments was all it took to see that Serena's grandmother had offered even less fertile ground for investigation than Serena herself. The grandmother's full name was Ellis Weaver.

Erik paused, frowning. Odd name for a woman. Must have been an old family name that they stuck on a girl when they ran out of boys.

Ellis Weaver had no Social Security number. No work. No income. No retirement benefits. No pets. Nothing but a piece of land and a house out in the high desert that only Joshua trees cared about, because only Joshua trees were tough enough to survive there. The truck that had burned with the house was registered to Morton Hingham, her lawyer, in Palm Springs. She had no driver's license. Birth date unknown. No savings account. One safe-deposit box. One dead daughter. One living granddaughter.

One unsolved murder.

Even for a preliminary search, that wasn't much information. Factoid must be doing laps looking for more. Obviously Serena's grandmother had led an unplugged, unwired life. Cash only, no credit cards, no checks, no use for any of the multitude of official programs designed to make life easier for the aged while various governments tracked everyone to the grave, giving benefits with one hand and collecting taxes with both.

A warm breeze curled through the open car windows, bringing with it the faint herbal scent of the desert. The air was silky with sun and warmth. The sky was a radiant blue. The thought of going back and confining himself indoors with the requirements of calligraphy or illumination didn't appeal to him right now. He needed something more physical to appease his restless mind and body.

He scrolled back over Ellis Weaver's records, noted her address, and decided to look around. Any place where someone had lived for nearly fifty years had to have some kind of information to offer about that person, some trace, some *thing* that would yield an insight into the woman who had apparently owned—and concealed—four incredibly intact pages from the Book of the Learned.

Unless the whole thing was a story and Serena was exactly what Warrick had said she was, a woman out to make good money on bad art.

As Erik turned on the engine and pulled out onto Bob Hope Drive, he realized he didn't want Serena to be a fraud, because that would mean the pages from the Book of the Learned were fraudulent, too.

He could live with the woman being a cheat, but he really wanted those pages to be real.

Thirteen

EAST OF PALM SPRINGS
THURSDAY NOON

Serena knew there was nothing more she could do but watch the erratic breeze stir ashes across her grandmother's abandoned hearth.

It was hard to be here, to match past memories of warmth and safety with present destruction. The shoulder-high native stone walls were scorched and ruined. The wooden beams and roof that had been high enough to house a big loom beneath were less than charcoal. What had once been a stout wood door was nothing but a gap in the rock walls. The chimney stood alone, a tall memorial to the fire that had consumed everything but stone and the single ancient strip of textile that had miraculously survived.

That fragment haunted and compelled Serena in a way she couldn't describe. She still wore the cloth draped around her neck and tucked inside her blouse. The textile was quite wonderful—cool when she was warm, warm when she was cool, always kitten-soft and appealing to her skin.

The pages haunted and compelled her in a different way, like her dreams. Each time she studied the leaves they felt deeply familiar. There was a sense of relationship, of belonging, that was both eerie and inescapable. She wondered if it had been like that for her grandmother, if she somehow had been enthralled by the past, unable to move, caught by lives she had never lived yet knew too well to deny.

If I fail and you decide to go after your heritage, remember me when I was your age. Think like the woman I was then.

Even though the temperature was almost eighty, Serena rubbed the gooseflesh that roughened her arms. She didn't know precisely what her grandmother had meant by that statement—how could she think like someone she had never known as a young woman?—but there was no mistaking the warning that followed.

She just wondered if the warning had to do with madness or sudden death.

Trust no man with your heritage. Your life depends on it.

Shivering, she couldn't help thinking that the sheriff was wrong, that Lisbeth's death had been premeditated murder rather than a random violent act. If so, sending out copies to two appraisers who happened to be men was rather like putting raw meat in front of hungry wolves.

Forgery is a dangerous art.

Maybe the pages locked in the storage compartment of her van were extraordinary, elaborate, dangerous lies, lies that had ultimately killed her grandmother. Was the granddaughter now the next in the line of fire? Was that her heritage?

Without realizing it, Serena put her palms against her neck and let the peace of the ancient cloth seep into her. Her rational mind knew she shouldn't wear the textile, knew that her skin was leaving its traces on the weaving, but she couldn't bring herself to take it off. She felt naked without it. Vulnerable.

I'm getting as nutty as people thought my grandmother was.

Serena shook herself and forced her thoughts away from danger, murder, madness, death, everything that had haunted her since she had read her grandmother's note, seen the pages, felt the weaving warm to her touch like something alive. Whatever her heritage might ultimately be, nothing of it survived here in the burned shell of her childhood home.

Abandonment lay like a sooty shadow over everything. Long after the police had left, target shooters had moved in. Someone had tied a piece of crime-scene tape to the charred frame of the pickup truck and used it for shooting practice. The tape had faded to pale yellow and was ragged with wind and bullet holes. Brass cartridges—some tarnished, some bright—dotted the gritty face of the desert. Spent shotgun shells in a rainbow of colors lay scattered like giant confetti around the perimeter of her grandmother's yard. Obviously the locals had decided that the abandoned cabin was more entertaining for target practice than the place they had been using, which was closer to the graded road.

A pale flash of movement caught the corner of Serena's eye. She turned toward the dirt track that led to the ruins. Barely a mile away, a light-colored SUV kicked grit and dust into the air.

Instantly she knew the vehicle was headed right for her. There was no other place it could be going. The twin ruts dead-ended at her grandmother's isolated house.

Trust no man. Your life depends on it.

Without stopping to consider, Serena yanked her keys from her pocket and hit the remote-lock button for her van. Then she turned and sprinted away on a faint trail that went up the steep slope just behind the cabin.

For all their height and bold name, the Joshua trees offered no hiding places for someone her size. Neither did anything else. The brittle shrubs that grew out of the unforgiving earth were little more than waist-high. Their stingy, stunted leaves offered no real chance of concealment.

She didn't even give the plants a second look. She knew exactly where she was going, just as she knew there were two ways to get there. The shorter way was more difficult, because it involved climbing down the steepest part of a broken cliff. She had learned the hard way that it was easier to climb *up* rather than down. She had much less control in a descent.

Serena took the long way to her hiding place. Boulders bigger than a man poked out of the loose, rocky soil. She dodged around them and cut back into a narrow ravine. The farther into the ravine she ran, the steeper the trail got. Finally it ended in a fractured, jumbled granite cliff. Three quarters of the way up the uneven wall there was a shallow cave. As a child, she often had gone up there to sit, look out over the empty land, and dream of patterns she would weave on her grandmother's loom.

Exposure had softened the rough edges of the ragged stone wall until the outer surface crumbled and came apart at a touch. Decomposed granite, or DG as the natives called it, was tricky in dry weather and treacherous in rain. If it had been wet, she wouldn't have tried the cliff at all. Even as dry as it was, she still slipped and nearly went down several times before she pulled herself close to the lip of the hidden cave.

The old broomstick she had left jammed among the rocks was still there, weathered silver and hard as stone. She grabbed the stick, poked it into the overhang, and waited. No furious rattling sound came from the gloom at the back of the cave. She poked again just to be sure; rattlesnakes loved the little cave as much as she did, which was why she had stashed a broomstick nearby after she discovered the cave as a girl.

When she was sure she was safe, she pulled herself over the lip of the hidden cave. Wedging herself out of sight was harder now than it had been when she was eight or even twelve. Despite her slender appearance, there was a lot of her to conceal. The cave had been a skinny child's hiding place, not one designed for a woman five feet seven inches tall in her bare feet.

Lying on her side, she brought her knees up to her chin and hugged her legs back against her body until only the scuffed toes of her shoes poked out. As for the rest, her dusty jeans and dark-blue denim shirt blended right into the shadows.

Breathing hard, she looked down at the cabin just in time to see a man get out of a dusty silver Mercedes SUV. He glanced around, then called something that could have been her name.

She didn't answer.

He called again.

This time Serena was sure it was her name. It didn't make her feel any more like answering. As she hadn't told anyone that she was coming here, she had to assume that she had been followed.

It wasn't a comforting thought.

Silent, motionless, she watched while the man walked slowly around the house, zigzagging as though he was looking for something in particular. She had time to notice that he was a rather tall man, certainly too big for comfort. He also moved too easily, casually vaulting a wall here and leaping down an embankment there, landing lightly, and searching, always searching, the ground.

Whatever he was looking for, it didn't take him long to find. He went back to his SUV, took out some rough country shoes, pulled them on, and started up the faint trail that led to the cave. Very quickly he vanished into a crease in the land.

Serena waited, almost afraid to breathe. If he was following her trail, in about a minute he would appear in the open spot before the ravine.

She saw him in much less than a minute. His long legs devoured the ground at a frightening pace. His eyes searched the granite wall as though he sensed she was hiding in one of the dark pockets scattered across the crumbling face of the cliff.

Instantly she began planning her escape route. If he attempted the tricky climb up to the cave, she would scramble up to the top of the wall and then over and into the next ravine, which led to the back of the cabin. It was the short way down. She would be in her car and gone before he was halfway up the wall.

"Serena? Are you all right?"

When she didn't answer, he started up the broken cliff as though it was a walk in the park. His speed and coordination scared the hell out of her.

The cave had become a trap.

She shot out of the darkness and lunged at the crumbling wall that stood between her and a safe route back to the cabin. She was only a few feet from the top of the wall when a piece of rotten granite crumbled under her foot. Suddenly she was skidding, falling, turning. She threw her arms out wide, trying to catch something that would stop her fall.

Powerful hands clamped around one flailing wrist. Then she slammed up against the wall with enough force to knock her breath out. Even so, she would have kept on sliding if it hadn't been for something at her back, wedging her against the rocks.

That something was a man. A big one.

"I hope the pages are in a safer place than you are," he said in a rough, deep, impatient tone.

Serena froze, wondering if she was hearing the voice of her grandmother's murderer.

And her own.

Fourteen

"Are you all right?" Erik asked the woman whose back was to him as he pressed her into the cliff.

Serena made a stifled sound that could have meant anything.

"When you didn't answer my call," he said, "I thought you might have wandered off and gotten hurt. DG can be a real bastard to climb."

With a wild shudder, air returned to Serena's lungs. She breathed hard and deep until she trusted herself to say, "Who are you?"

"Erik North."

"The manuscript appraiser?"

"Yes."

Thank God. He wasn't a stranger. Not exactly. Which meant that she was probably safe.

Probably.

Relief turned her bones to sand. She took a broken breath and sagged against the rock face without even noticing its rough surface.

Erik felt the difference in her, as though strings had snapped and she could barely hold herself upright. He tightened his grip and leaned into her, holding her upright with his own body.

She went rigid and would have fallen all over again if it hadn't been for the hard length of the man pinning her to the rocks.

"Easy, Serena. I've got you."

"That's supposed to make me feel better?" she asked through locked teeth.

He laughed. The puffs of air disturbed some of her soft, flyaway hair at the side of her face. He was so close that he could admire the burning shades of red and gold in her loose braid, sense her heat, feel each breath she took. He could all but taste her. If he wanted to do that, all he had to do was nose aside the unusual, quite beautiful, scarf she was wearing loosely around her neck.

The thought of doing just that appealed to him. He didn't know which would be softer, the scarf or the luminous skin. He did know that he was going to find out. Soon.

Wryly Erik was glad that Serena wasn't a mind reader; she would have been clawing away at the cliff again, trying to escape him. His climbing skills were up to the chase, but he wasn't sure hers were. As he had pointed out, DG was treacherous stuff to climb on, especially if you were in a hurry.

"Can you stand, or did you turn your ankle?" he asked.

Odd sensations had rippled over her when his laughter stirred against her skin. At some elemental level, that laugh was familiar to her. That voice was familiar to her. Like the pages. Like the fabric that had slipped up her neck as though to protect her face from the cliff.

She knew this man.

The certainty was as shocking as feeling her footing give way had been a few moments before.

"Are you sure you're Erik North?" she asked hoarsely.

"Positive."

She didn't know how to say that he didn't fit her idea of an appraiser of medieval illuminated manuscripts and she didn't want to say anything as stupid as *Don't I know you from somewhere?* So she asked the question that had been bothering her since she first saw him. "What are you doing here?"

"Trying to figure out if you can walk or if I'll have to carry you."

"You can't. I'm too big."

Laughter stirred against her neck again. The scarf lifted on a bit of breeze and floated back to brush over Erik's lips. Smiling, he nuzzled the soft, clingy cloth in return.

"Niall is a lot bigger than you," Erik said, "and I had to pack him out of the Santa Rosa Mountains once."

"Niall?"

"Later. Or do you really want to exchange life histories while we cling to this rock pile by my fingernails?"

Without warning the granite beneath Erik's left foot crumbled. His foot slid, searched, but didn't find solid ground. He jammed his hands into cracks and crevices, clenched his fingers into fists, pinned Serena hard with his hips, and waited.

Nothing else gave way.

He probed cautiously with his left foot until he found a crevice that supported his weight. When he was secure again, he silently congratulated himself on taking the time to change his shoes before he followed the faint trail he had picked up. On rocks like this, city loafers were about as useful as Rollerblades.

"Are you all right?" Serena asked, shaken.

"Yes."

She stared at the big fists that were wedged into rough cracks in the wall. "That looks uncomfortable."

"It is. But it beats the hell out of falling. Hold still while I change my grip."

He removed first one hand, then the other from the crevices, and flexed his fingers. Some of the skin smarted and burned. He had expected that. Blood welled from several cuts, but not enough to interfere with getting a secure grip.

Slowly, confidently, he shifted his weight so that he could hold her safely against the rock without crushing her.

For Serena, the intimacy of his body moving against her was unnerving. She kept her mind off it by watching while he selected two more handholds. There was nothing random in his choices, nor in the muscle and sinew that flexed to take the new load.

"You've done this before, haven't you?" she asked.

"Scared a woman so much that she nearly killed herself trying to get away from me? No, this is a first."

She smiled despite the residue of fear and adrenaline lighting up her blood. "I meant climbing rocks."

"It's my hobby. But usually I'm dressed for the occasion."

For the first time she noticed the soft maroon cloth that was rolled up to his elbows. Expensive fabric from the look of it, but not as fine-grained and supple as the golden masculine skin that was only inches from her face. Sun-bleached blond hair gleamed along his arm. Blood trickled down the back of his hand.

"You're hurt!"

"What?" He glanced at the trivial cut and wished he knew Serena well enough to ask her to kiss it better. From where he was, her mouth looked capable of healing, among other things. Much more interesting things. "That's not even big enough to call an 'oww-ee.' "

She laughed, surprising both of them.

Erik let out a silent breath. He liked the feeling of her moving against his hips. He liked it way too much. If he didn't start thinking about something else, he would be pole-vaulting down the damned cliff.

"Do you want to go up or down from here?" he asked almost roughly.

"Up is easier."

"I know. I just wasn't sure if you did. Ready?"

"Wait. Let me test my footing."

Silently he endured some more of her subtle wiggling while she put weight on first one foot, then the other.

She slipped.

Reflexively he pinned her against the wall again with his hips.

"Slow is better," he said.

"I'm trying."

"Very trying," he said through his teeth. She wasn't meaning to, but her little movements had made him hard.

"If you hadn't come up the wall like Spiderman with his feet on fire and scared me to—" she began.

"As my friend Dana would say," Erik cut in, " 'Shut it.' You can chew me out later."

"Is that a promise?" she retorted.

"Yeah. Right after you thank me. Guess which one I'm looking forward to?"

As Serena moved to find a better position, she felt the unmistakable hardness of an aroused male pressing into the cleft of her buttocks. Her breath came in a strangled gasp.

"Don't panic," he said neutrally. "It's a simple physiological reflex. It will go away as soon as your tight little butt stops rubbing against my crotch."

"Give me more room and it won't be a problem," she shot back.

He bit back some hot words and eased away from her. This time she managed to stay upright without slipping. His mind was grateful. His dick wasn't.

"All right?" he asked.

"Fabulous," she said sarcastically. "I can finally stop licking the cliff."

He couldn't think of anything to say that wouldn't get him in more trouble than he already was. He eased farther away from her, but not so far that he couldn't grab her if she slipped again.

Without a word she began climbing up the jumbled rock face. Now that she wasn't trying to flee, she could choose her route for safety rather than speed. She went up with only a few minor slips and one fast scramble.

He followed. Rock climbing with a major woody was something he had never tried before. He would be happy if he never did it again. He glanced into the small cave as he went past it. All he saw was an old, weathered broomstick. She hadn't left anything else behind—pages from the Book of the Learned, for instance.

As soon as Serena gained the top, she glanced toward the cabin. If she ran, she could beat him to her car. Then she remembered his speed coming up the ragged jumble of rocks and decided that he would likely catch her before she got halfway there.

In any case, she had to admit that if Erik North wanted her dead, he was going about it in an odd way.

All the same, she watched him with wary violet eyes as he topped the cliff in a coordinated rush. He could be Santa Claus and she still wouldn't be happy about being alone in the desert with a strange man, no matter how hauntingly familiar he was.

I know him, dammit. I'm sure of it.

Maybe she had seen him in one of those ads for extreme outdoor equipment, the kind only strong, fit, and completely crazed people used.

As he walked up to her, she saw that he was even bigger than she thought, well over six feet. He moved like an athlete. His hair was every color of blond from flax to bronze. His eyes were as clear and tawny as an eagle's. And as measuring.

She had seen those eyes before.

Erik noted the tension in Serena's body and wondered if it was just a woman's normal wariness at being alone with a stranger or if it was the nervousness of a crook who had a lot to hide. He didn't like the latter idea but he had to keep it in mind.

No matter how much he wanted the pages to be real, Warrick had seen the originals and pronounced them fakes. Erik would be a fool to dismiss that appraisal simply because he had an emotional attachment to the Book of the Learned.

"Okay," he said, looking into her wary eyes. "Where do we go from here?"

"That depends."

"On what?"

"Why you followed me."

Fifteen

Erik stared at Serena. "What makes you think I followed you?"

"Get real. This isn't exactly on the must-see list for sight-seers in southern California."

He smiled slightly. Even dusty, scuffed, and perspiring in the desert heat, she was unreasonably attractive to him. Maybe it was her unusual combination of red-gold hair and violet eyes. Maybe it was the intelligence and wariness in those eyes and her quick tongue. Maybe it was the curves he saw beneath her casual clothes. Maybe it was the combination of dirt smudges and pale freckles on her high cheekbones. Maybe it was the fey, almost silky scarf she wore around her neck.

Maybe it was the memory of her hips rubbing against him.

She seemed both intensely familiar to him and totally unknown. It was a disturbing combination.

He wondered if she felt it, too, or if her wariness came from the circumstances: two strangers in the middle of an empty desert, one of them male, one female. Maybe she would feel more relaxed if they were surrounded by people. His younger sisters kept telling him that he just didn't under-

stand how vulnerable a woman felt when she was alone with
a strange man.

And maybe Serena wouldn't be more relaxed in a crowd.
Someone running a scam had lots of reasons to be nervous
around the person whose job it was to see through scams.

"Cat got your tongue?" she asked coolly.

Mentally Erik shrugged. Whether her edginess came
from an attraction to him, an instinctive feminine caution
around strange males, or something less savory, he needed
answers from her. He might as well go for broke right now,
where he could run her to ground if she bolted at his first
words.

"I'm a consultant for Rarities Unlimited," he said.

And waited.

"Is that supposed to explain something?" she asked.

He almost smiled. She hadn't flinched, hadn't tightened,
the pulse in her neck hadn't quickened, and the pupils of her
fey violet eyes hadn't dilated or contracted. Either she was a
great actress or she really hadn't heard of Rarities. If it was
the latter, it spoke well of her innocence. If it was the former,
she was a crook or simply an extremely cautious person bent
on getting more information from him than she gave.

"Rarities is a collaboration of specialists," he said. "We
buy, sell, appraise, and protect rare artifacts and art."

"For anyone who hires you?"

"Up to a point."

"What's that point?"

"Known crooks."

"You only work for the good guys, is that it?" There was a
cynical edge to Serena's voice.

"What do you think?"

"I think you'd go bankrupt if you waited for saints to hire
you."

He smiled thinly. "I think you're right. But our allegiance
is always to the art, not to the client. It's in the contract all
our clients sign."

"Meaning?"

"If it comes to a choice between the art or the client, the client loses."

Her left eyebrow lifted in a golden-red arc. "Does that happen often?"

"You'll have to ask Dana."

"Who?"

"Dana Gaynor. Along with S. K. Niall, she owns Rarities."

Serena jammed her hands in the rear pockets of her jeans and looked away from Erik's searching bird-of-prey eyes. "Buy, sell, appraise, and protect. Well, I don't want to buy or sell anything, but I sure could use a neutral appraisal."

She could use protection, too, but she wasn't about to bring that up. The way she had run from Erik North, he probably thought she was a little bit fractured. If she said she was afraid that her grandmother's murderer might be after her, he would assume she was fractured, period. Lisbeth's murder had been random, not particular. It said so right in the police files.

In any case, she wasn't a piece of art to be protected. She was just an ordinary human being who was afraid she was caught in a situation that wasn't ordinary at all.

"A neutral appraisal," Erik repeated, watching her elegant back and partial profile. "An interesting way to put it."

"Why?"

"Most people just want to find out how much something is worth."

Her smile was a quick, hard curve. Making a living from her own weaving creations had taught her that no matter how much work she put into a piece, the price didn't change. Not really. "It's worth whatever someone will pay for it. No more. No less."

Erik looked at her curving hips. His hands itched to feel what he was seeing, to shape her rear and squeeze, filling his hands with her flesh. The depth of his hunger baffled him; she was attractive, yes, but hardly the type to bring a grown man to his knees with lust.

Yet his knees were weak.

"Then why don't you just put the pages up for bid?" he asked irritably, looking away. "The marketplace will tell you what they're worth."

"I don't want to sell them. I just want to know if they're real."

"For insurance?"

Her mouth turned down. *If you decide to go after your inheritance . . . be very careful. Forgery is a dangerous art.* "In a way."

"What way?"

"Does it matter?" she asked tightly.

No matter how unnervingly familiar he seemed at times, she wasn't about to share her grandmother's lifetime secret with him: the Book of the Learned. Yet she had to know more about those pages to go after the rest of her inheritance. Right now she was playing a game of blindman's buff, and the penalty for losing was very high.

Trust no man.

He looked at her narrowed eyes and full mouth. "It's hard to work with someone who doesn't trust you."

"Trust isn't a problem for me," she said distinctly. "I always work alone."

"So do I."

"Is that why you came out here today? To be alone?"

Reluctantly Erik decided that the lady was as intelligent as she was attractive. "You never answer your phone."

"And?"

"I wanted to see the pages. I couldn't, so I came here instead."

"How did you find out my grandmother's address?" Serena asked baldly.

"Rarities."

"How did Rarities find out?" she asked through her teeth.

"Ask—"

"Dana," she cut in ruthlessly.

He smiled. "Right."

She thought of a golden wolf. Not the kind that seduced

maidens. The kind that dined on them. "You're here. She isn't."

"We could fix that."

"You're not going to tell me, are you?"

"Think of it as a trade secret."

"Think of me as your fairy godmother," she retorted.

His smile changed. It was warmer, but it didn't make her feel less hunted.

"There *is* an elfin quality about you," he agreed.

She made a sound of disgust and brushed off her dusty jeans. "Try again. I'm five seven. Hardly an elf."

"Witch, then. No. Sorceress. Witches have black hair and bad breath. All those toad stews."

She tried not to smile, but the wicked light in his eyes told her she wasn't fooling him. Absently she ran her fingertips over the cloth that nestled around her throat and lifted on the least stirring of the air. "Do you know many witches?"

"The margins are full of them."

"You lost me."

He held out his hand. "You found me. Now lead me out of here."

Before she realized what she was doing, she had taken his hand. She made a sound and snatched her fingers back.

"I'm not contagious," he said.

"You're way too charming."

He laughed out loud. "That's another first."

"What margins?" Serena asked.

He blinked and hung on to the slippery conversational thread with both hands. "Margins?"

"The ones with witches in them," she said impatiently.

"Medieval manuscripts."

"Oh." She frowned and absently grabbed her scarf, which had developed a will of its own; it kept lifting up and sticking to Erik's shirt. "I didn't notice any witches in mine."

"Not classic witches, certainly. The pointy hats came later. Your pages would have had Learned witches. Or what the Learned called Glendruid."

Serena blew out her breath with enough force to lift the wisps of hair that had escaped from her braid. It also launched her scarf again. She grabbed the wandering end before it could dive into the opening of his shirt. "Smart witches? A bottle of scotch? You sound like you're speaking English, but . . ."

"Scotch?" Erik asked, confused.

"Yeah. You know. Glenmorangie, Glenfiddich, Glendruid, whatever. Brands of Scotch whiskey."

Wryly he wondered how the ancient Glendruids would have liked being compared to a bottle of scotch. "Now that you mention it, I'm having the same problem speaking English with you. Maybe what we need is to get better acquainted. Want to take a walk?"

"Where?" she asked warily.

"Back to the vehicles. You'll feel less edgy about being alone if you're closer to a place with locks."

"What makes you think that?"

"I raised two younger sisters. What about you?"

"I'm an only. I'm used to being alone with the world." With locks, she amended silently.

"That explains it."

"What?"

"Your lack of trust in your fellow man."

"Reading a newspaper is all the explanation that's required," she said flatly, but she was thinking of her grandmother, trapped and dying alone in her fire-bombed home. "The fellow man you meet in the headlines is enough to give Pollyanna stomach cramps."

With that, she turned and began leading him down the shortcut to the cabin.

He followed, enjoying the view. Sunlight turned her hair to an intriguing shade of fire that was echoed in the floaty, flirty scarf she wore. The strength and ease of her stride told him that she wasn't a stranger to hiking over something more interesting than cement sidewalks. As she had pointed out, definitely not an elf.

But then, he had never had more than a scholarly interest in the delicate little things. He liked women who could go toe-to-toe with life—and him, if it came to that.

His sisters assured him it would. According to them, he was too overbearing to be endured. He didn't argue the point. Wasn't that what an older brother was for, particularly one who had had to be both mother and father to two teenage girls?

Thank God neither of his sisters carried herself like Serena. He would have had to chain them in the cellar and hold off eager males with a double-barreled shotgun. Watching Serena move was enough to make a statue come to a point, and he was a long way from unfeeling stone.

The relentless sexual pressure of his own body annoyed Erik. He was long past the stage of permanent adolescent rut where he got a woody just thinking about a girl's breasts. Or he damn well should be long past that stage. Otherwise, what was the point of the gray hair that had begun showing up over his left temple?

If you don't get smarter, getting older is more trouble than it's worth.

Deliberately Erik looked away from Serena's gently swinging hips and concentrated on the desert that surrounded him. Their footsteps made gritty noises on the trail. Plants slid over cloth with scratchy, whispering sounds. A quail boomed a warning from somewhere ahead. A distant hawk made an elegant spiral down to a spiky perch in a Joshua tree. Sunlight felt like a caress, far different from the hammer blows of stark power that was the desert sun in July. The air was dry and faintly fragrant, tasting of light and distance and time. Except for the vapor trails of jets far overhead, there was no sign of man. He and Serena could have been the last people on earth, or the first.

As always, the space and solitude uncurled nerves in Erik that he hadn't known were coiled. He didn't understand how people lived in a city's concrete canyons without going mad; even sedate and senile Palm Springs got on his nerves after a while. Dana, and to some degree Niall, were different. They didn't understand how he lived in Hollywood's graveyard out at the edge of the desert without going stir-crazy.

Erik smiled to himself. The interesting thing about people was that they came in so many flavors.

Ahead, a chimney rose like a soot-stained tombstone from the ruined walls. Serena stood waiting for him by her car. She had the air of a woman who had just run out of what little patience she owned.

"If you didn't follow me here—" she began.

"I didn't," he cut in.

"Then why did you come all the way up a bad road to my grandmother's burned-out house?"

Sixteen

"I came here to find out what I could about Ellis Weaver," Erik said evenly.

Part of Serena noted that he indeed had more to discover about her grandmother, including the fact that Ellis Weaver wasn't her real name. "Why?"

"You don't answer your phone."

"What does that have to do with my grandmother's death?"

He looked at her intently. "What possible connection could there be between your irresponsible phone habits and Ellis Weaver's death?"

Serena set her teeth. "Just answer my question."

He noted the tight line of her jaw and smiled rather grimly. "There's no connection that I know of."

"Then why are you here?"

"You don't answer your—"

"We've already established that," she cut in savagely.

"—phone," he finished. "If you did, I could have arranged to see the originals or at least asked you questions about them. But I couldn't reach you, so I decided to come here and see if I could learn anything about what kind of woman would have four complete leaves from the Book of the Learned and never let them see the light of day."

"The Book of the Learned?" Serena said instantly, remembering her grandmother's enigmatic note. "She never told me more than the book's name. What do you know about it?"

"See, I learned something already. She didn't know what she had. Or probably had. I can't be certain until I've had a chance to examine the pages themselves." He waited for her to offer him that chance.

She watched him with clear, wary eyes.

"If you don't trust me," he said evenly, "why did you send me copies of the pages in the first place?"

She blew out a breath, looked away, and gave him half of the truth, the half that didn't matter. "I didn't expect to meet you over my grandmother's grave. It made me . . . jumpy."

"Something certainly did," he agreed under his breath. He wanted to ask her outright to show him the pages, but reined in his impatience. Controlling himself was a lot more difficult than he expected it to be. The violet-eyed not-elf got under his skin faster than cactus thorns. He didn't expect women to drop at his feet, but he didn't expect them to turn and flee, either—especially a woman who could push his sexual buttons without even trying. "Would you be less nervous somewhere else?"

The edge to his voice made her wince inwardly. She supposed she couldn't blame him for being impatient. After all, she *had* come to him first.

"No." That, at least, was completely true. Until she found out if the pages were forged, and if pursuing the rest of her family's heritage had led to Lisbeth's murder, Serena knew she wouldn't be particularly relaxed no matter where she was.

Her grandmother had been in her own home, and look how much good it had done her.

Serena blew out another breath. "Here is as good as anywhere else." She made a gesture with her hand, half warding off Erik, half apologizing to him. "What do you want to know about G'mom?"

He opened his mouth to ask about the rest of the pages to the Book of the Learned. Then he thought better of it. In addition to wariness, there was grief in her eyes each time she spoke about her grandmother. "What was she like?"

Serena's eyes burned with more than the dry wind. "Solitary."

"No friends?"

"No." Then she remembered the lawyer. "Morton Hingham, maybe. He was her lawyer."

"Was your mother Mrs. Weaver's daughter or her daughter-in-law?"

"Daughter."

"Didn't they get along?"

"They must not have. Marilyn Charters ran away from here when she was seventeen. Joined a hippie commune, smoked pot, got pregnant, had me, took a bad acid trip, ran out in front of a car, and died."

"How old were you?"

"Five. I don't remember much about her except long, blazing red hair. It looked beautiful in candlelight. She taught me to weave and sold my bracelets for money."

The image of a young woman with fiery hair down to her hips, wary violet eyes, and a loom in front of her went through Erik like icy lightning. *She had stood and watched him just that way, as though uncertain if he meant to kill her.*

A chill flowed over his spine in the instant before he shook off the odd memory. No, it couldn't be a memory. He had never seen a loom like that except in his imagination. He sure hadn't ever seen Serena with her hair drifting in a blazing curtain down to her hips.

Get a grip, he told himself harshly. *Serena has a bad effect on what passes for your brain.*

He looked at her closely. Obviously whatever feelings there had been between mother and daughter were long past the stage of grief or anger. When she spoke of her mother, there was nothing in her face or voice but a kind of detached interest.

"What about your father?" Erik asked.

"I was what is so coyly referred to as a 'love child.' " Her lip curled in a cynical line. "Love had nothing to do with it. That's why my parents weren't married. They weren't even engaged, except sexually, and it wasn't an exclusive engagement. I had lots of 'uncles.' And what does this have to do with the pages, anyway?"

"I think you might underestimate your parents' feelings."

The angle of her chin told him that she thought he was wrong.

"She took his name," Erik pointed out. "A lot of women don't do that, even when they marry."

"What are you talking about? She never took his name."

"Your mother didn't change her name?"

"That's right," Serena said curtly.

"Interesting."

"Why? Most single mothers keep their maiden names."

"Did your mother ever marry?"

"Never."

"Did your grandmother marry more than once?"

"No." Serena gave him an impatient glance from the dark end of the rainbow. "According to G'mom, Mother was legitimate. I wasn't. Any more questions?"

"Yes. Why didn't your grandmother and mother have the same last name?"

Too late, Serena realized where Erik's questions had led her. Silently she apologized to her grandmother for giving away a secret she had carried to her grave. On the other hand, did it really matter anymore? Her grandmother was dead. So was her mother.

"G'mom was very touchy about her privacy," Serena said. "She raised Marilyn, my mother, under the name Weaver, but after my mother ran away, she changed her name to

Charters. That was why my grandmother never so much as spoke to her again."

The woman who chose to call herself Weaver had also made it very clear to her stubborn granddaughter—who refused to call herself anything *but* Serena Charters—that no one had a right to ask any questions about where "Ellis Weaver" came from or if she had any other names. As far as the outside world was concerned, Serena's name was Charters because her father's name had been Charters. Or at least, that was the lie he had given the girl he had seduced and abandoned.

And that was the story they told the outside world.

It didn't matter to Serena, as long as she got to keep the only fragment of her mother that time and circumstance had allowed—her mother's name. Even now the ingrained secrecy of a lifetime was hard to break. Especially now, with her grandmother's warning ringing in her mind. *Trust no man.*

Erik was definitely a man.

With brooding eyes, Erik looked around, waiting for Serena to keep talking. When she didn't, he prodded, "So?"

"She bought this land under her own grandmother's maiden name, Weaver."

"So her husband's last name was Charters and she simply changed it to Weaver when she moved here?"

"I don't know. She never mentioned her husband. Not once." Serena shrugged and told herself she didn't know Erik well enough to trust him with the name Lisbeth Charters. "My guess is she was never married, despite the gold band she wore."

"Like mother, like daughter?" he suggested ironically.

"Maybe. Does it matter?"

Only to Factoid and his computer search, Eric thought. But that wasn't something he was going to say aloud. "Provenance is a big part of any appraisal. In order to trace the provenance of your inheritance, I have to know what name to look for on sales receipts."

A thought struck Serena: she hadn't mentioned in her note how she came to own the pages. "How do you know I inherited them?"

Norman Warrick had told him, but Erik didn't think this was the time to bring it up. He had already said too much. He had been so tangled up in Serena's eyes and bedroom voice and long legs that he had made the kind of mistake even an amateur could pounce on. "A logical assumption," he said evenly. "Is it wrong?"

"Why is it logical?"

"Nothing like those pages has been on the market since before you were born."

"How do you know?"

"It's my business to know that kind of thing. Did you inherit those pages from your grandmother? Yes or no, Serena. If you can't trust me that much, we're both wasting our time."

She met his eyes squarely. "Yes. I inherited them from my grandmother."

He let out a long breath. "Progress."

"You're making me sound as difficult as you are."

"Then I'm not doing a very good job. You're more difficult than I ever thought of being."

She showed him a double row of hard, bright teeth. "Some things don't require thought. For you, being difficult is one of them."

He took a grip on his fraying patience and got back to the point he was pursuing: names. "Your grandmother bought this house under an assumed name, is that correct?"

"She bought the land. Everything else you see is her work. She built this with her own hands."

Erik turned and examined the small house with new eyes. He went to one of the ragged, remaining walls and looked at it closely. Native rock, cement, and sweat had built the wall. But Serena's grandmother hadn't been a nutty ascetic who found bliss in self-made ugliness. She had searched out iron-rich rocks and incorporated them into the walls. The rusty red of those rocks made a pleasing pattern against the common pale granite. The result was rather like a very simple weaving.

"She must have been quite a woman," he said.

"Why do you say that?"

"Obviously she lived close to the bone, yet she spent a lot of extra time and effort making the walls of her home more than just a support for the roof."

Serena looked at the pattern he was tracing with long-fingered hands, the hands of a poet or a priest or a pianist. Yet she knew just how quick and strong those deceptively graceful hands were. He had grabbed her, stopped her fall, and braced her against hard stone until she could move safely on her own once more.

The stone hadn't been all that was hard. The memory of unexpected sexual intimacy made her skin hot. She wasn't a saint, but she wasn't a party girl, either. Her deep, female reaction to a strange male made her nervous and curious by turns.

"My grandmother loved patterns. That's why she loved weaving. She created beauty from a handful of threads." As Serena spoke, she stroked the cloth nestled around her throat, as though she found comfort in its presence. After a few moments she stepped over the threshold of the cabin for the first time since Lisbeth had been murdered. "She kept a loom here, in this corner, where there was light from the north window. She called it smart light, learned light."

Erik went still, but before he could say anything, she was talking again.

"When I asked how light could be educated," Serena said, "G'mom just kept on weaving."

Serena knelt in the grit and charred fragments that had once been her grandmother's loom. So many memories . . . kerosene lamps turning night to gold, the cool gush of water when she worked the long pump handle, the smell of bread baking, a dazzling torrent of stars at midnight, dawn in a land brimming with black velvet and silence, the white-hot weight of the summer sun at noon when even shadows burned.

"That's all she ever said about the Learned?" Erik asked finally.

Serena's hand hesitated in its slow stirring through the ashes of her childhood. Her fingers curled around one of the burned stone bobbins that had once held bright yarn for the loom. She shivered as though someone had walked on her grave. But it was her grandmother's grave, and she was the one disturbing it. Her fingers opened. She left the stone bobbin where she had found it, scattered among other bobbins in the ashes of what had once been life.

"Learned?" Serena asked in an aching voice.

"She said something to you about Learned light." Despite his impatience Erik spoke gently, for her eyes were like twilight, haunted by increasing darkness.

"Learned light," Serena murmured. Then she remembered. "The Book of the Learned." The book her beautiful pages were supposed to have come from—unless they were forged, or the whole book was forged, or a lot of other things were lies that she didn't even suspect. "You asked about it before."

"Yes."

"You believe my pages came from it."

"Possibly." Almost certainly, Erik amended silently. But that, too, was something he wasn't ready to talk about.

"G'mom believed that they did. She called the Book of the Learned her heritage. The heritage she told me she lost. The heritage she tried to get back before she died."

"How long before?" Erik's voice was sharper than it should have been, but he couldn't help it. An ugly pattern was emerging around Ellis Weaver's life and death.

Serena didn't answer his question. She was wondering if a handful of forged pages would be worth killing for. It wasn't the first time she had wondered since she had read her grandmother's note. It wouldn't be the last.

And it would always chill her.

The midafternoon wind blew down the slope, over the remains of the cabin and Lisbeth Charters, known as Ellis Weaver to the outside world.

Despite the warmth, cold deepened in Serena. Her fingers rubbed soot from the stone bobbin against her jeans, rubbing so hard that a false warmth was created. Somehow it was worse to believe that her grandmother's murder had been a deliberate act tied to the Book of the Learned rather than a random act of madness.

Because if it was true, then she would be next in line to be murdered.

Bitterly Serena wished that her grandmother had left behind something more useful than a warning and a false name.

Seventeen

"Serena?" Erik asked, kneeling down beside her on the cold stone floor. "Are you all right?"

She tried to answer. Her mouth was too dry. She swallowed once, twice, but it didn't help. If she opened her mouth to speak she felt like sand would fall out.

His palm touched her cheek. The chill of her skin shocked him. "What's wrong, honey?" His voice was calm, gentle, the way it had been when one of his sisters woke up crying in the night and he went to her room and held her until the nightmare passed.

Serena closed her eyes and let the heat of Erik's hand sink into her, freeing her from fear. "This is her grave. I don't want it to be mine."

He barely recognized her hoarse voice. "Why would it be yours?" he asked reasonably.

"Why wouldn't it?" Tension ripped through her. She took a harsh breath and touched the ancient fabric that was also her heritage. "Never mind. I'm just . . ."

Erik waited, wondering if she knew that she was leaning into his hand as though it was fire and she was freezing. "You're just what?" he asked when she stopped.

Just an idiot, she thought roughly. *The more I learn, the*

*more I believe that G'mom's death was deliberate. And here I
am, kneeling on her grave in a strange man's arms. A man who
knows about the missing Book of the Learned.*

I wonder if he knows how to make gasoline bombs, too.

Serena shot to her feet and away from Erik with a speed
that told him they were back to square one when it came to
trust. He came to his own feet with a surge of power that was
just short of anger.

"Was it something I said?" he asked sardonically.

"What are you talking about?"

"You. Me. Trust."

"I don't know you well enough to trust you."

"And vice versa," he pointed out.

She looked startled, then shrugged. "Of course. But
you're a lot bigger than I am and your grandmother wasn't
murdered."

Silently Erik absorbed the implication that Serena hadn't
put into words. "Why do you keep going back to that?"

She gave him a disbelieving look. "That you're bigger than
I am?"

He made an impatient gesture, sweeping aside what he
sensed was a red herring. "You're acting as though your
grandmother's murder a year ago directly threatens you
now. Why?"

"Like I said, I'm jumpy." She folded her arms across her
chest. What good was a warning if she ignored it? "I'm leaving. There's nothing for me here."

"All right. You look like you could use a cup of Irish coffee
and a long soak in a spa."

"The place I'm staying doesn't have a spa."

"Mine does."

"Lucky you."

"Do you have a cell phone?"

"No."

Hoping she wouldn't realize that they were beyond cell
range at the moment, he pulled his communication unit
from its leather case at the small of his back. "Here. Dial 911

and tell them my name and license number, and if you don't call back every fifteen minutes they can send in the SWAT team."

She couldn't help it. She laughed.

"I'm serious," he said flatly. "I want you to know that you're safe with me. The quickest way to do that is to spend time together."

His eyes were intense, tawny, and far too intelligent for her comfort. He was a man who was used to getting what he wanted. Like Norman Warrick.

Oddly, the comparison made Serena feel better. Erik might be every bit as determined as Warrick, but he wasn't a tyrant. And he had tried to comfort her with a gentleness that she was only now appreciating. Despite her ingrained wariness, she found herself wanting to know more about this particular, impossibly familiar man.

"Why?" she asked. "Do you think I won't let you look at the pages until I trust you?"

"That's part of it."

"What's the rest?"

"I want you—"

"To trust you," she cut in. "You already told me that."

He shook his head. "I want you. Period."

Her eyes widened.

"The look on your face . . ." He threw back his head and laughed. "Do you think I get a woody every time something female rubs against me? Let me assure you, I'm well beyond that stage."

Heat burned Serena's cheeks. Even as she cursed the complexion she couldn't control, she held her ground. "I can't believe we're having this conversation."

"*We* aren't. I am."

"I don't know you well enough for this."

"Whose fault is that?"

"Fate's," she retorted. "We've known each other for less than an hour."

"And in that time I've saved you from a nasty fall, gotten

so hard my gut ached, and found out you're afraid of being murdered the way your grandmother was. How much better do we need to know each other to talk about something as normal as sex?"

"You left out the part where you followed me up a cliff and scared me to death."

"Details."

Serena bit her lip. "You've got a quick mouth."

"Give me a reason to go slow."

She blew out a breath that was close to a laugh and even closer to surrender. The longer she was with Erik, the more she was certain that she had seen him before, met him before, known him before. Yet each time she pursued the feeling, trying to nail it down as to when and where and how, it vanished. It was like an idea for a weaving condensing in her mind—very real and absolutely irrational.

So she would do what she did when a half-formed pattern haunted her. She would let it happen at its own pace, in its own way, and wait for the result.

If she didn't like what developed, she could always walk away.

"How about a get-acquainted truce?" she suggested.

"Interesting. You see us as being at war."

She started to say no. The part of her that insisted she knew Erik wasn't so certain. That hesitation was as startling as the groundless feeling of familiarity he evoked in her.

"Ask me after we know each other better," Serena said finally.

He wanted to push for more. Then he thought about a relentlessly self-sufficient old woman raising a granddaughter alone in the middle of the beautiful, desolate desert. Suspicion was probably built into Serena as deeply as bone and blood.

"I'll do that," he said. "Can I trust you to follow me to my home, or should I follow you?"

"You're pushing me."

"Then start leading the way."

"What if I said I'm not interested?" she asked.

"I'd say you were out of touch with your body."

"You're arrogant."

"See, we're getting better acquainted all the time. Your house or mine?"

"What if I didn't have pages from the Book of the Learned?" she asked before she could think better of it.

"We wouldn't have met and that would be a damned shame. But you do and we did and the only thing left is to go forward."

"I followed that. Scary."

"We've already established that you're easily frightened." Erik smiled crookedly. "Tell you what. I'll show you my leaves if you'll show me yours."

"Leaves?"

"Pages. As in illuminated manuscripts."

"You have some?"

"A few," he paused, then added, "hundred."

Her eyes widened. "I keep forgetting."

"What?"

"That you're an expert on illuminated manuscripts. You really don't look like one."

"No gold foil on my forehead?" he asked dryly.

"No thin shoulders and scholarly stoop."

"Sorry to disappoint you."

She ignored him, which was better than saying she wasn't disappointed at all. "Your house," she said, deciding. "It's closer than mine."

"How do you know?"

"My grandmother's lawyer told me."

Erik almost asked if that was where she had left the pages—with the lawyer—but he decided not to push her.

Yet.

Eighteen

Manhattan wrapped around the House of Warrick's headquarters like a concrete anaconda. The cry of sirens and the impatient, illegal blaring of taxi horns announced that everything was normal outside the building. Things were pretty much normal inside, too. Garrison Warrick was sitting back in his gray leather chair and watching his oyster-colored telephone as though it was ticking rather than ringing.

One red light on the phone blinked as steadily as a healthy pulse. Another light blinked in triple time, as though to say, "Okay, fine, you're deaf. Are you blind, too?"

The intercom on his desk buzzed. Since his grandfather hadn't come to New York with the rest of the family, Garrison assumed it was safe to answer the intercom.

"Yes?" he said.

"Excuse me, sir." The supposedly British assistant's tone was unbelievably plummy, probably because Sheila hadn't been any closer to Jolly Old England than the map on her office wall. "You have a call on line—"

"Grandfather?" he cut in curtly.

"No. Mr. Warrick is still on line two. Rather, his assistant is."

The rapidly pulsing red light winked off. Garrison let out a sigh of relief; the old bastard's assistant had gotten the hint and hung up. The remaining light blinked lazily. "Who's left?"

"Ms. Risa Sheridan."

"Sheridan, Sheridan," Garrison muttered. Nothing came to mind, probably because he was still thinking of his obsessed and obsessive grandfather. "Do I know her?"

"Socially?"

Garrison looked at the ceiling. Sheila's voice and body were first-rate, but her brains were touch and go. Mostly go. "Professionally."

"House of Warrick has sold her some fine gold artifacts," Sheila said primly.

"Collector?"

"Collector's curator."

Garrison reached for the dregs of his lunchtime coffee, swallowed, and grimaced. Some day he figured he would learn that transcontinental flights doubled the hangover effect of alcohol. But if several years as an Army Ranger hadn't taught him the price of too much of a good thing, he doubted that comfortable civilian flights had a chance.

"Who's her boss?" he asked, swallowing again. He had a taste in his mouth that even bad coffee couldn't cut.

"Shane Tannahill."

"Oh, *that* Sheridan. Sure. Risa. Black hair and . . ." His voice trailed off.

Risa was built like a teenager's wet dream and had the kind of mouth a man wanted to sin in, but he didn't think his relentlessly proper assistant wanted to hear about that. Not during office hours, anyway. After hours, sweet Sheila could suck chrome off a bumper hitch. She was such a talented and energetic little lady that a man could forgive her for weighing in on the light end of the IQ scale. Risa was the opposite, at least when it came to IQ. He hadn't had an op-

portunity to test-drive her in the bedroom, so he couldn't
speak for her sexual abilities.

". . . a semi-southern accent, right?" he asked.

"Is that what it is, sir? I thought she might be eating cold
oatmeal."

When Garrison heard the edge in his assistant's voice, he
decided not to meet her for a midnight snack in a downtown
hotel. Sheila was getting possessive. He didn't need that kind
of greed in an occasional lover, no matter how talented she
was. He had enough of that sort of smothering, grasping
thing with his mother. It had driven him into the army at
eighteen until he realized that saying *Yes, SIR!* wasn't that different from saying *Yes, Mother.*

He smoothed his silk school tie against his crisp white
shirt, rearranged his French wool jacket, and said, "Thanks,
Sheila. I'll take the call."

He punched in the blinking button, activated the speaker-
phone, and leaned back. The microphone was sensitive
enough to pick up the sirens out in the streets, much less his
carefully enunciated words.

"Ms. Sheridan, this is an unexpected pleasure. What can I
do for you?"

"Actually it's more like what you can do for my boss,
Shane Tannahill."

"Ah, yes. The Golden Fleece. I believe I read something
about Las Vegas's newest casino in the *New York Times* last
week."

"Suitably snotty, I trust?"

"Definitely."

"Excellent. Nothing irritates the cultural mavens as much
as someone with a lot of money who collects the kind of art
they don't approve of."

Garrison laughed. "Fortunately, the House of Warrick
doesn't limit itself to Manhattan haute art."

On the other end of the line, Risa Sheridan gave a businesslike laugh of appreciation and looked at her boss.

Shane Tannahill was watching her with eyes the color—

and softness—of dark-green jade. The long-sleeved cotton shirt he wore exactly matched his eyes, just as his slacks were the same shade of dark brown as his hair. He could have spoken at any time and revealed his presence to Garrison but chose not to. He was here to judge just how close Risa was to the charming scion of the House of Warrick. Some closeness was a business asset. Too much coziness could cost him money.

A lot of it.

"Not haute art, perhaps, but certainly haute cost," Risa said dryly.

"Of course. The first thing I learned in the army was that there's no profit in poverty."

Her laugh was less businesslike this time. She wasn't sure if she liked Garrison Warrick, but she had to admit he could be amusing. His cheerful capitalism was a refreshing change from the sanctimony of some gallery owners who sold cultural status at inflated prices to the nouveau riche and eternally gullible.

"There might be profit for both of us in an interesting rumor that has come to my attention," Risa said. "If it wouldn't take too much of your valuable time . . ."

He took the opening graciously. "I always have time for rumor. It's the lifeblood of the art industry. What do you have?"

"It's more like what *you* have. You know the gold gallery that Mr. Tannahill is creating for his casino?"

"Doesn't everyone? I was hoping you would need something that Mr. Tannahill's, er, resources couldn't supply. If so, the House of Warrick stands ready to provide you with what you need. And, of course, you will have the full weight of our excellent reputation behind any acquisition we make on your behalf. Clean provenance is our specialty."

Shane's black eyebrows rose. Although Garrison hadn't said anything outright, his choice of words and tone of voice certainly implied that some of Shane's sources for art were dubious.

Which they were. They were also some of his most reliable providers of gold art and artifacts.

"I'm aware of the impeccable reputation of the House of Warrick," Risa said. "That's why I called you as soon as I heard the rumor of a twelfth-century Celtic manuscript page that was heavily decorated in gold. While my expertise is in ancient gold jewelry, I believe that gold illumination was rare in Insular Celtic manuscripts?"

"Very rare," Garrison agreed.

Risa waited.

Listening, watching, Shane "walked" a solid gold pen end over end between the fingers of one hand: back and forth, back and forth, like a golden shuttle weaving hypnotically between his fingers. His eyes never left his curator's lush, oddly aloof mouth. There was no telltale tightening of the voluptuous lips, no flattening at the corners, nothing to indicate that she was under unusual tension.

Idly he decided once again that although his curator wasn't beautiful in the usual sense of the word, her face rewarded study. Her body was like her mouth, lush and inviting even though she did nothing in particular to emphasize the curving difference between breasts and waist and hips.

Risa was uncomfortably aware of Shane's assessing glance and leashed impatience. "Have you heard of such a page?" she asked Garrison bluntly.

"Yes."

"And?"

"The House of Warrick is investigating the possibilities."

Garrison's bland voice didn't fool Risa. "Have you seen the page?" she asked.

"Yes. Briefly."

"Is it for sale?"

There was a long pause. Then Garrison sighed loudly enough to be caught by the microphone. "It's a very delicate situation."

"In what way?"

"We feel the pages should be investigated with great, shall

we say, *skepticism,* before they are accepted into the market-place. Certainly before the House of Warrick represents them."

"Does this skeptical 'we' include Norman Warrick?"

"Most definitely."

Risa looked at her boss.

Smoothly Shane flipped the pen into writing position and printed across her desk calendar: GET IT.

"Nonetheless, Mr. Tannahill would like to see the page," Risa said.

The only hint of her disapproval was in the slight cooling of her smoky voice. Dubious provenance was the kind of red flag that warned off a reputable curator, and Risa Sheridan was determined to be reputable. She hadn't been born with a solid gold spoon in her mouth as Shane Tannahill had. Although in his case, it was more like a platinum spoon with pavé diamonds.

She was sure there had to be drawbacks to being the off-spring of one of the richest computer entrepreneurs ever to walk the earth, but offhand she couldn't think of any. It beat the hell out of having cockroaches crawl out of your bath-room plumbing.

"Which page, precisely?" Garrison asked.

"It was described to us as a carpet page consisting almost entirely of a major initial or joined initials heavily foiled in gold."

Garrison made a sound that could have meant anything from agreement to skepticism. "Was the person describing it to you familiar with illuminated manuscripts?"

"We're satisfied with the person's credentials." Wryly Risa thought that Garrison would be, too, if she told him the name. Jane Major was an adviser to the House of Warrick. Her specialty was medieval iconography. "Do you have such a page?"

"At the moment, no."

"Can we expect that to change?"

"Life *is* change, Ms. Sheridan. That's how we know we're not dead."

Risa rolled her eyes. "Mr. Tannahill had hoped for a more specific change."

"What if the page isn't what it seems?"

Shane's eyelids half lowered almost lazily as he walked the pen back and forth over his hand; it was a trick used by magicians and cardsharps to keep their fingers flexible. Then, with no warning, the pen vanished, he stood up, and walked out of the room.

But before he left, he tapped the piece of paper that said GET IT.

Risa settled back in her chair, crossed her nylon-clad legs, and went to work finding out just how much Shane's obsession with owning the best and brightest of all kinds of gold artifacts was going to cost this time.

Nineteen

"Thank you for coming in on such short notice," Dana said as she led several Donovans down the hall toward one of Rarities's clean rooms.

"No problem," Kyle Donovan said. "We were meeting with some of our Pacific Rim partners in L.A. when your call was forwarded from Seattle."

"Speak for yourself," Archer Donovan cut in with the ease of an older brother. "Hannah's going to have my head if I'm not home in time to bathe our sweet little monster."

Lawe Donovan snorted. Like Kyle, he had sun-streaked blond hair. Unlike Kyle, his face had been weathered under too many foreign suns. "Monster? Little Attila? What are you talking about, bro? Your baby son is just like you, right down to the black hair and jugular instinct."

"Talk about the pot insulting the kettle," Archer said, raising his eyebrows. "You're just jealous because you don't have one of your own."

"A wife or a kid? Forget it. I've got enough trouble as it is." Lawe looked at the firm flex and sway of Dana's hips. She was worth the trip across town to see. He had heard about that walk of hers from other Donovan men, but he hadn't believed it. Nice. Really nice.

Smiling to herself, Dana led the way to the clean room. Some people would have been overwhelmed by being in the presence of three Donovan males, all of whom had lived in some rough places and topped six feet by a margin that would have made Rarities Unlimited's modestly built helicopter pilot see shades of red. Dana wasn't in the least intimidated by the Donovans. She liked big men. It was ever so much more satisfactory to put them in their place. The first time she did it, they always had such an endearing look of surprise on their face.

Not that she expected to be putting any Donovans down. The whole tribe was known to be smart, honest, and tough enough to get the job done. That was all Dana asked of anyone, and a hell of a lot more than she usually got.

Except with Niall.

He was the exception to too damn many of her rules. Someday she would have to do something about it.

"I checked the list of Susa's works with her gallery in Manhattan," Dana said. "Julian said he'd never heard of *Sidewalk Sunset*. The signature is a little off, too, but nothing that really rings bells. Artists often change their signature throughout a career. Artistic styles, too."

"What did Julian think of the painting itself?" Archer asked.

"He waffled. Said he would have to see it in person." Dana shrugged and opened the door. "Knowing Julian, he would waffle after he got here, too. He's really testy about any of the Donovan matriarch's—er, Susa's—work that doesn't come through him."

"Understandable," Archer said dryly. "He's had her exclusively for twenty years."

"But," Lawe said, staring at the painting on the easel in the center of the room, "she's been painting since she was six."

There was silence for a few minutes while everyone

looked at *Sidewalk Sunset.* Though the Donovans had been raised in the presence of their mother's talent and therefore took it for granted, the older they grew the more they realized how unique she really was.

One after another, the Donovan brothers nodded.

"Is that a yes-this-is-hers or a yes-this-is-a-fraud kind of nod?" Dana asked.

"It's hers," Lawe said. He stepped forward and stopped just short of touching the painting. There was an odd, remembering kind of smile on his lips. "She did this for Justin and me on our eighth birthday. We were whining about wanting to go to the mountains or the coast or some other wild, beautiful place they couldn't afford back then, and Mom—Susa—said there was beauty everywhere if we knew how to look. To prove it she painted the sunset reflected in puddles of rain on the sidewalk." He touched the frame of the painting with gentle fingertips. "Lord, that was a long time ago."

"Stop," Archer said. "I'm older than you are."

"I'm not," Kyle said smugly.

"Up yours," Archer and Lawe said as one.

Lawe looked at the painting for a moment longer, remembering a time when the world was much simpler, but he had been too innocent to appreciate it.

"Is the painting for sale?" he asked.

"Yes," Dana said dryly, "but you just raised the price considerably by attributing it to one of the foremost living artists on the North American continent."

He looked over his shoulder and gave her the kind of quick, uncalculated smile that had made more than one woman decide it would be worth the effort to round off a few of his rough edges. "I'm good for it."

"If he isn't," Archer said, looking at Lawe intently, "I am." It had been a long time since he had seen Lawe truly smile. If it took one of Susa's pictures to keep that smile within reach, then *Sidewalk Sunset* was about to have a new owner.

Smiling back, Dana shook her head at the unexpected

flash of Lawe's smile. The man could melt glaciers with it. "No wonder the Donovans get away with murder."

"Not literally," Archer said easily.

But the look they passed among themselves said *Not recently.*

"Is one of your clean rooms available within the next four days?" Archer asked.

Dana knew when a subject was being changed. She also knew when not to point it out. "For the Donovans, of course."

Archer's smile was like Lawe's, surprising in a man who otherwise looked like a hard piece of business. "Lawe has some emeralds and several dealers we've never heard of want to look at them."

"Would Tuesday be all right?"

"Fine. You can bill it to Donovan Gems and Minerals."

Dana waved her hand in dismissal and turned to Lawe. "We could work out an exchange. My West Coast emerald expert just went to work for the Smithsonian. His wife likes Washington, D.C. Go figure. Anyway, if you would be willing to be listed as a consultant on faceted gems for Rarities Unlimited, we'd be willing to let you use the clean rooms for your own business."

"Take it," Archer said. "It's a good deal."

Dana smiled like a cat. *Gotcha.*

Twenty

As the automatic gate to Erik North's property rolled shut behind Serena's car, she wondered if she had done the right thing. She couldn't hear the gate lock behind her. Not really. It was more like something she felt. When all was said and done, no matter how much she needed to know about her inheritance, and no matter how deeply Erik intrigued her, she really didn't know the man.

I didn't know Warrick, either, but I went to his house alone at night, she reminded herself. *And I got insulted for my trouble.*

At least she could be certain that Erik hadn't come out to the desert to kill her. If he had, she would be dead. Then she wondered if maybe he had held back because he was looking for more than just a few pages from the Book of the Learned. Maybe he thought she had more treasures.

The feeling of playing blindman's buff with her own life was frightening. She was accustomed to taking care of herself, to needing no one else, to living with the rest of humanity at arm's length. She didn't take it to her grandmother's extreme of becoming a desert hermit, but trust still came very hard to her, if at all.

She glanced at the sleek electronic unit on the seat beside her and sighed. It was hard to keep on being afraid of a man who left his personal communications unit with you just so that you could call the cops if you panicked.

Hold that good thought, she told herself.

Stroking her scarf for luck and comfort, she followed Erik's silver vehicle up the curving driveway. From the layout of the land, she guessed that the lot was about two acres, perhaps more. Like the Warrick estate, Erik's property was bounded by a high, solid wall. Unlike the Warrick estate, she guessed that the rocks in this wall had come from a very old building. Except for the reddish color, the stones reminded her of London Bridge, which had been imported piece by numbered piece from England and plunked down in the middle of the Arizona desert.

Indeed, there was a distinctly medieval feel to the layout and design of Erik's home. Unlike the Warrick estate, Erik's didn't have any Old World trees pruned into unusual shapes along the driveway. Instead, there were random plantings of jacaranda trees whose lacy, fernlike leaves made fragile shadow patterns over the cement. Beyond the jacarandas there were mature citrus trees heavy with fruit, various kinds of palm trees, and bougainvillea vines, along with lavender, honeysuckle, and other plants she couldn't identify.

Rather wistfully Serena looked back at the shadows beneath the jacaranda trees. Several times a year she tried to reproduce or at least suggest the grace of a jacaranda in her weaving. So far, none of her efforts had lived up to nature.

When Serena saw Erik's house up close, she forgot about her failed weaving designs. The roof was slate, like an old country house in England. The walls were blocks of reddish stone of a kind she hadn't seen outside of the red castles of Caerlaverock and Carlisle in the Scottish borderlands. Medallions and occasional panels of colorful glazed tiles balanced the unrelieved stone. Instead of the griffins, lions, stags, or other heraldic figures she expected, the tiles contained stylized Celtic designs that could have graced anything from illuminated manuscripts to ancient weavings. Blue, gold, violet, red, yellow; the colors were as brilliant as the designs were surprising.

Belatedly Serena realized that Erik was standing by her van door, waiting for her. She grabbed her big purse and got out, handing over his phone/computer as she did. With a swift glance, he checked the readout window. Nothing urgent. At least, nothing as urgent as his impatience to see Serena's pages.

Factoid still hadn't checked in. Neither had Erik. He didn't want to talk to Rarities about Ellis Weaver Charters in front of Serena. Mentally cursing the restrictions of distrust, he shoved the unit back in its case at the small of his back.

Automatically Serena locked the van before she turned to face her host. He had just finished stowing the expensive electronic unit in a holder behind his back. His quick, economical movements told her that it was a familiar action to him, rather like picking up a weaving shuttle was to her.

"The illuminated manuscript business must be good," she said, looking at the spacious yard and big house. Then she heard her own words and winced. "Sorry. Some people have to work at putting their foot in their mouth. It comes naturally to me."

He smiled. "No problem. I'm the fourth generation to own North Castle. Granddad knew my father well enough to tie up all the loose cash in a trust to maintain the family home, so I can't take credit for any of it."

"Smart man."

"Me or Granddad?"

"Yes. Where on earth did you get those fabulous Celtic tiles?"

"My mother made them."

Serena's left eyebrow rose in a graceful arc of surprise and reappraisal. "The designs are quite incredible, both ancient and somehow modern. All the spirals and intensity of the ancient Celts but none of the claustrophobic feeling." She stared past him at the tiles set into a walk leading to the front door. These weren't glazed in vibrant colors. The tantalizing design came from subtle shadings in each tile and careful placement of every tile. "Extraordinary. Some of the most elegant design work I've ever seen."

"I'm flattered."

"Why? Your mother did it."

"Didn't I mention that I created the designs?"

She threw up her hands. "Right. Be flattered."

"Is this where I compliment you on your fine eye? No one else has realized that the designs were a modern take on ancient themes."

She shot him a sideways look. "Why do I *not* believe you?"

"Beats me. I'm telling the truth. No one else has noticed. Oh, they like the designs and all, but they don't understand them. You do. Want to see my attack cuckoo?"

Serena's jaw dropped. "One of us is crazy."

"I'm looking forward to finding out which one." He held out his hand. "Come on. He should be on the back wall gathering courage for his afternoon drink. If we're real quiet, he won't see us."

"Who won't?"

"Cuckoo."

"One o'clock and none is well," she muttered. "At two do we get to meet cuckoo-cuckoo?"

Erik laughed, pulled her close for a one-armed hug, and said, "I suppose I shouldn't tease you, but, damn, it's fun to fence with someone as quick as you are."

She was in the middle of hugging him back when she realized what she was doing. She pulled away so fast that she stumbled.

"Easy, there," he said, steadying her with quick hands. "The walk is uneven. Tree roots keep growing and tiles don't."

"Then I'll have to watch where I'm going very carefully."

His eyes narrowed. "Don't worry. I'll catch you if you stumble."

"Thanks, but I've been on my own two feet for a long time."

Hoping his irritation didn't show, Erik turned away and opened the front door lock without even noticing his favorite design set into the door, a stylized tree of life. It seemed like every time he made a little forward progress with Serena, she jumped backward. At this rate he would still be trying to see those illuminated pages on the Fourth of July.

"I'll show you around in a few minutes," he said, pulling her almost gently into the house. "But if we don't hurry, he'll be gone."

"Who?"

"My attack cuckoo, remember?"

"Erik, you're worrying me."

He glanced down, saw that she was mostly teasing, and urged her quickly through the house into the kitchen. A glance at the spa told him that they were just in time.

"Stand next to me here," he said quietly. "Now, don't move. Without turning your head, look out at the spa. See him?"

Serena did as she was told and saw a large mottled brown-and-cream bird drinking with quick, nervous darts of its head.

"Cuckoo my rear," she said, barely moving her lips. "That's a roadrunner."

"Which is a member of the cuckoo family."

"You're teasing me again."

"Not this time."

"Cross your heart and hope to die?"

"Bloodthirsty, aren't you?"

"About promises and vows, yes."

He looked at her violet eyes for the space of one breath, two, and then said, "Cross my heart and hope to die."

Serena wanted to smile, but couldn't. Erik's tawny eyes were intent, almost predatory, and so familiar her heart squeezed. A shiver went over her skin, leaving her feeling as though someone was walking on her grave. Again.

"Good thing death won't be necessary," she managed. "I wouldn't want to be responsible for yours."

"Another compliment." He smiled and wished she wouldn't run if he kissed her the way he wanted to. "You'll turn my head."

"Not before you turn my stomach."

He laughed so hard that the roadrunner started and flew up to the top of the wall. "Just for that, I may leave the Irish out of your coffee."

"Good idea. I have a long drive home."

"Leucadia, isn't it?"

She nodded.

He glanced out at the angle of the sun. "There's plenty of time. Did you eat lunch or would you like a snack?"

She hesitated.

"That means you didn't eat lunch and would like a snack," Erik said. "How do you like smoked salmon?"

"Any way I can get it."

"You're about to get lucky."

He walked around the kitchen pulling a plate, cups, silverware, and a can from cupboards and drawers. He handed her the can.

She looked at the label: KING SALMON CAUGHT BY ERIK NORTH. "Really?" she asked.

"Really. I have friends up north."

She pried up the tab, pulled off the top of the can, and inhaled deeply. "Yum. Mr. Picky will never forgive me."

"Mr. Picky?" he asked, even though he knew that was the name of her pet. She wouldn't know that he knew, which was something he had better keep in mind instead of watching her lick her lips.

"My cat. He'll smell salmon on my breath and be really mad at me."

"I'll give you a mint."

"You could give me gasoline mouthwash and Picky would still know. He has a thing for smoked salmon."

"Want some bread or crackers to go with it?"

"Only if it will make you feel better."

Smiling, he handed her a fork. "Enjoy."

She took a bite of salmon and made a husky sound of pleasure. "You must have caught this one in heaven."

"Alaska."

She was too busy rounding up a stray crumb of fish with her tongue to answer.

Abruptly Erik turned away and began cutting pieces of cheese from a big chunk of Gouda. If he kept on watching her lick salmon off a fork, he was going to start thinking with his dick. Not smart.

So he washed off grapes, sliced up an apple, and put out a tube of sesame crackers. "Coffee? Tea? Soda? Water? Beer? Wine?" he asked, not looking at her.

"Coffee," she mumbled, then swallowed quickly. "Please."

"Black or doctored?"

"Sugar."

He started to pour out the morning's leftover coffee, only to have her grab his wrist.

"I'd rather drink it out of a cup than the sink, if you don't mind," she said.

"I was going to make a fresh pot."

She glanced around, saw a microwave, and said, "Don't bother. I'll just nuke it."

"No wonder you use sugar."

He poured the cold coffee into a mug, nuked it, and handed the steaming cup to her. He smiled when he saw that most of the salmon was already gone.

"Want another can?" he asked.

"My cat would execute a contract on me if I ate more than one can."

"Mr. Picky is a cat assassin?"

"If you can have an attack cuckoo, I can have a cat assassin."

He grinned. "I'll send some salmon home with you."

"I should refuse."

"But you won't."

"Are you kidding? Do you know how good this salmon is?" She licked the fork clean and sighed.

Erik decided it was a good time to call Rarities. Either that, or do something really stupid like feeding Serena smoked salmon tidbit by tidbit—with his tongue.

"I've got to check on something," he said, turning away. "I won't be long."

She made an indecipherable sound and began eating grapes, apple, cheese, and crackers with equal parts of pleasure and efficiency.

Erik went up the stairs three at a time, strode down the flagstone hall with its old Persian carpet, and went into his bedroom. Everything was neater than he had left it, which meant that the housekeeper provided for by his grandfather's trust had been at work while he was gone. Without a glance at the familiar furnishings, he sat at his desk near the big bed and passed all the information/speculation he had on to Dana and Factoid.

Though he was only gone a few minutes, Serena was down to the last grape and slice of cheese. The look on her face said that she had enjoyed every bite.

"Okay," he said. "Wash your hands and you can see my etchings."

She gave him a look from beneath her thick mahogany eyelashes. "Etchings, huh?" She turned on the sink faucet and began washing her hands. "They better be illuminated."

"Will you settle for illumina*ting*?"

"No."

"Once more, you're in luck." He handed her a small towel. "They're illuminated. But you'd be surprised at what some of those scholar-scribes thought worthy of illumination."

"If sultans can commission instructive rugs for their seraglios, then I suppose medieval kings were entitled to amuse themselves, too."

"Instructive rugs? Interesting."

"Only if you read Arabic," she said, drying her hands briskly. "Poems, not pictures."

"Art, then, not illustration. I'm afraid the medieval scholars of Europe were more, er, direct in their description."

"De*pict*ion," she corrected. Pornography, after all, wasn't noted for wasting time on words.

"That, too."

Serena snickered, then fell silent, wondering what medieval lust would look like. Probably pretty much the same-old same-old, once the clothes and hairstyles were discounted.

"That's an odd smile," Erik said as he led her down a hallway. "Share the joke?"

"No joke. Just that some things don't change."

"Like body parts?" he suggested dryly.

She shrugged. "And looking at sex as body parts. Part A goes into Part B, repeat as necessary."

"Put that way, it sounds pretty boring."

"Put that way, it *is* boring."

He gave her a sideways glance.

She didn't notice. She had just discovered the old photographs that lined the hall, Edward Curtis's sepia chronology of a time and a people now gone.

Erik wondered what Serena was thinking about as she studied the weathered faces of Chumash Indians whose difficult lives were written in each wrinkle and line. When he looked at the photos, he couldn't help thinking about what it had felt like to know that your ancestral line ended with you; no second chances, no hope, nothing but a blank stretching into the future. Extinction.

What might someone do when faced with that certainty? What would a man or a woman be capable of to ensure that there was a future other than emptiness?

He had been asking himself those questions ever since the first time he looked into the dark, intent eyes of the vanished Chumash and was old enough to realize just how final and inevitable death was. He still didn't have any answers.

Then he thought about a recently deceased Ellis Weaver,

four ancestral illuminated leaves, and a modern grand-daughter who didn't know how much trouble ancient history could cause.

"Grandmother had a photo like this," Serena said slowly. "The oasis and the stout palms, and a woman who looked as worn and gritty as the palms themselves. G'mom said the woman's eyes were like holes burned in eternity, letting time bleed through."

"Cheerful woman, your grandmother."

Serena smiled slightly. "Yes, I guess she was rather dour. But then, how does a mother feel who loses her only child?"

"Not happy," Erik agreed. "Did she blame herself for her daughter's death?"

"She never talked about it. But she didn't believe in God or the devil." Serena turned away from the photo and met Erik's uncanny bird-of-prey eyes. "That meant she had only herself to blame."

"Do you blame her?"

"No. I blame whatever it is that makes people so different. I love the desert. My mother loathed it. It was a prison she escaped from as soon as possible. The fact that she ran to a different kind of prison . . ." Serena shrugged. "Who knows? Maybe she loved communal poverty. I hope so. She certainly didn't have much life to enjoy. When she died, she was almost ten years younger than I am now."

Erik thought of his own parents, who had loved each other and their children, and would have loved their grand-children just as much. Even though his parents had died too soon, they had left a legacy of love that grew each time their daughters laughed with their own children, kissed their hurts, and ran to their husbands' waiting arms.

For the first time Erik wondered how he would have felt about life and trust if his parents had died when he was five and he had been raised by his mother's mother, who was as mean-spirited a woman as had ever lived to see the far side of ninety.

No wonder Serena was reluctant to trust him. She had no reason to trust life. Fourth of July might have been an optimistic date to see the pages. Halloween, perhaps.

He just wished he didn't have a feeling that time was a luxury he couldn't afford.

Twenty-one

" 'Tis useless to moan and rend garments at the graveside of past betrayal. I trusted where I should not. I doubted where I should not. I lost before I knew what I had found.

"A Learned man is no different from other men. When a pitiless truth stands before us, we hide our eyes. When a beguiling lie sighs to us, we race toward it.

"No, not we. I. I and I and I . . .

"Fool, to love the lie and flee from the loving truth.

"Mother of God, pity me as I stand naked by the graveside of what might have been, my clothes rent around me, my soul bare and shivering, moaning the name I loved too late.

"Does she stand naked by a different grave?

"Does she call my name in Hell?

"Or does she live, and in living, curse my very soul?"

Erik's low voice seemed to shiver like black flame in the room as he laid aside the page he had been reading aloud from.

An unreasonable sadness gripped Serena, sinking through her rational mind like talons. She turned away from him and forced herself to focus on the room, on the walls, on anything but the written words, echoes of an agony that was almost a thousand years old.

Except for an efficient ventilation system that removed candle smoke from the air, she could have been in a medieval library. The windows were high and shuttered. Carved wooden chests filled with leather-covered books stood open around the room. High wooden tables held other volumes. Some were open. Some were buckled or strapped tightly closed to prevent the thick vellum pages from curling. There was no light but that shed by candles whose flames quivered and dipped with every invisible current of air, as though the candles lived and breathed in slow rhythms. It was the same for the open books, light shimmering across them so that pages with golden letters and designs seemed to breathe.

Time was in the room, surrounding them, and it was alive.

"That's one of the pages from the Book of the Learned that I've resurrected," Erik said.

Blindly she nodded, unable to speak.

"The original page is in a private collection in Florida," he continued, looking at her back, wondering at her visible tension. "It's a palimpsest. They were kind enough to let me photograph the page under ultraviolet light so that I could read the text beneath."

Not really hearing anything but a dead man's living cry of despair, she nodded again. Her hair burned red-gold in the candlelight with each tight movement she made.

"Do you know what a palimpsest is?" he asked quietly.

She shook her head.

"Do you want to know?"

She nodded.

"It's taken from a Greek word that means twice-scraped or scraped again. That's how scribes erased mistakes or reused vellum; they scraped off the original lettering and wrote over the newly blank space. Vellum was very expensive."

Serena gave a sigh that sent the candle flames to swaying. "How did they do the erasing?"

"If you were working with papyrus, you just washed away the ink. Vellum was more difficult, but more durable. Scribes scraped off small errors with a penknife. You could do a whole page that way, but it was quicker and easier to use a rough stone. Pumice was a favorite. I use it myself."

Slowly she turned around, one arm crossed defensively across her chest, one hand open on her neck as though to hold her unusual scarf in place. He kept wanting to touch it. Or her. Then he saw the shadows in her rare violet eyes and he felt like there were bands around his own lungs, squeezing.

"Still worried that I'll hurt you?" he asked quietly.

"I . . ." She lowered her arms and let out another breath that made flames sway. "There's something about what you just read. His pain. *I could feel it.*" She rubbed her palms against her arms as though she was cold and looked past him at the page lying so innocently against polished oak. "It's crazy, but I felt it just the same. Poor man. What did he do to earn such pain?"

"I don't know. It's one of the reasons I've been seeking the Book of the Learned or whatever fragments I can find. I'm curious. I've always been that way."

"Where did that page come from?" she asked. "I mean, before the people in Florida?"

"A small Chicago dealer."

"And before that?"

"A large auction house."

"Warrick's?" she asked sharply.

"Christie's."

She let out a broken breath. "And before that?"

"A private individual, now dead."

"And before that? When did it first come on the market?"

"I don't know."

"Can you find out?"

"Rarities is searching now," he said.

"Why now? Why not whenever you first found the sheet?"

"Then it was a hobby, and I only asked for the recent provenance of the sheet. The Florida couple gave me the three owners listed on their bill of sale."

"Only three? Even if there were more?"

"Three is the accepted number to prove provenance," Erik said. "Many artifacts don't have even that. Lengthy, detailed provenance is a relatively modern concern growing out of Nazi thefts and, more recently, looted archaeological sites."

Serena bit the inside of her lower lip and wondered how much she could risk in pursuing her heritage . . . and, probably, her grandmother's murderer. She didn't want to trust anyone, but she had to start somewhere.

"Do you have other pages from the Book of the Learned?" she asked finally.

"A handful."

"Do you know anything more about where they ultimately came from?"

"Ultimate provenance." He smiled thinly. "No. Do you want to see them?"

"Are they all like that one?"

"Some are illuminated. Some have exquisitely rendered miniatures. Some have columns of treaty alliances in Latin and pithy summaries of allies in vulgate marginalia."

She smiled despite the ice prickling beneath her skin. "I meant are all the pages so bleak?"

"No. And even that page isn't completely despairing."

"You could have fooled me." The torment in the words still made her shiver.

Erik held out his hand. "Come over to the table. I'll show you another way to look at what I just read to you."

She took his hand and let him lead her to the page he had just put down. It looked so cool and elegant, all stylized black lines and colorful geometries hidden inside capital letters. Bits of gold foil flickered across the face of the page like a haunting wail.

"The lines I read out loud are here," he said, pointing.

Serena followed his fingertip as he traced lightly down one of the two columns on the page.

"This"—his fingertip shifted to the facing column—"talks about the uses of various fruits and vegetables to relieve imbalances in the 'humors.' Even as he laments whatever he did that brought such pain, he writes about eating less leeks and turnips and more barley soup."

"Why?"

"Leeks and turnips were believed to encourage sperm production and enhance sex. Barley soup was believed to cool hot temperaments."

"The medieval equivalent of a cold shower?"

He laughed. "Yes. The placement of the lament and the wry advice was Erik's way of telling himself to cool off."

"Erik?"

"Erik the Learned. He's the scribe who wrote the Book of the Learned."

"How do you know?"

He opened a shallow belly drawer. Inside was a ragged sheet of vellum that could have been cut—or hacked—from a larger page. No bigger than his hand, the partial page was quite beautiful in a spare, black-and-white way. The calligraphy was stylish, yet somehow more personal than the illuminated writing on the other page.

"It's a letter *E*," Erik said. "It's also a name, a prayer, and a brief description of the man who created it."

Serena stared at the intricate drawing. "I can see the *E*."

"The prayer is here," he said, pointing to a stylized mark at what would have been the margin of the original page. "Christ's symbol, the fish, superimposed against the sign that wards off the evil eye. The scribes blamed errors on a particular demon."

"Handy."

"I've been thinking about doing it myself. But essentially Erik was praying for Christ's protection of this manuscript against sorcery. As a sign of respect and importance, the stylized fish is painted in red against a solid gold foil backdrop.

As a sign of his own humility, Erik's initial is in black, unadorned in any way."

"How do you know the *E* stood for Erik?"

"The rest of the name is spelled out within the capital letter itself. See? The *r* runs along the upper bar, the *i* down the spine, and the *k* is part of all the letters."

Serena stared for a moment, then let her eyes unfocus slightly, just enough to lose the decorative details. "Erik."

"Yes?"

"No, I meant the name. Erik." Sadness twisted through her, echoes of a life she had never lived, never known. She brushed the scrap of vellum with her fingertips and then snatched back her hand. "Sorry. I wasn't thinking. I didn't mean to touch it."

"No problem. There's a school of thought that says all vellum should be handled regularly so that it can absorb the oil from your hands and stay flexible."

"But doesn't oil attract dirt?"

"Spoken like a true twenty-first-century American."

She shot him a cool look. "And who told me to wash my hands before I played with the leaves?"

"Guilty as charged. But I don't wear gloves to handle my vellum manuscripts. Neither did previous owners. Life isn't lived in a vacuum, and these pages were once alive."

"They still are," she said softly, watching gold slide over the pages as though they breathed. "Like my scarf," she added, touching the ancient fabric.

"Lovely." He looked at the scarf and the elegant feminine neck it embraced. Both seemed more beautiful each time he looked. "Very unusual. But I meant being literally alive once. Vellum is animal skin, initially calfskin, but later it referred to cattle, sheep, lambs, whatever." He picked up the small scrap and laid it on her palm. "The size and shape of the book was dictated by the size of the animal. The choir books, which had to be read by many people standing at a distance, were very big and almost always came from cattle. They used one hide folded in half to make just two facing pages. That's one cow for a few large lines of musical notation."

He gestured toward a nearby wall. There, framed in isolated splendor, was a page that was at least three feet by two feet. The gold capitals shimmered with each flickering of candlelight. The black squares of individual notes climbed up and down the four-line ladder of liturgical chants. The size of the manuscript page, and its clarity, meant that a single book could be read by the whole choir.

"There were books for each important mass to be sung," Erik said, "plus Bibles and breviaries, herbals and bestiaries, and simple account books filled with details of housekeeping. Thousands of pages for just a small library. It took a wealthy monastery to support enough animals to turn into vellum, and enough monks to prepare the hides and write on the pages."

Serena tried to imagine seeing cattle as paper on the hoof. "No wonder we went with plant fibers as soon as we had a printing press."

"Quantity over quality," he agreed. "Like machine weaving rather than the unique handmade cloth of your scarf. But even today, when we can make paper in any size or shape, we nearly always stick with the traditional rectangle, a shape that was dictated by the basically rectangular shape of an animal hide."

Tentatively she lifted her hand to touch the ancient scrap of life.

"Go ahead," he said, guiding her fingers to the vellum. "Feel. You won't hurt it. Stroke it again with your eyes closed. The outer side, the side that once had hair, is textured."

He rubbed her fingertips down the margin of the vellum. Then he turned it over. There was more writing on this side, but it was obviously incomplete. A column had been cut in half so that only phrases remained. Slowly he drew her fingertips down this side.

"Feel the difference?" he asked.

"Yes. Smoother, almost cool. Not soft, though. Resilient."

"You have very sensitive fingertips. This was the flesh side. The page that faced it in an open book would also have been written on the flesh side of the vellum, because the two sides take ink very differently. A well-made book allowed for that. And since manuscripts were every bit as valuable in their time as gems, spices, and gold, extraordinary care was taken when making a book."

She opened her eyes and found herself caught in Erik's clear, probing eyes. Her breath stopped on a half-gasp. The heat of his fingers over hers was as intense as fire. *She had felt his touch before, in candlelight, but he had been naked then and she had worn a dress made of the same uncanny cloth that had come unharmed from her grandmother's burned cabin and now lay around her neck.*

Serena jerked so suddenly that the vellum leaped off her palm. He caught the scrap with an easy motion.

"What did I do now?" he said half wryly, half impatiently.

"What do you mean?"

"You jumped back halfway across the room."

She didn't deny it. She couldn't. She was pressed against another library table as though trying to scramble backward over it. All she could think of to say was, "Your fingers are hot."

"And yours are cold. Did I jump like I'd been bitten?"

"Surely I can't be the first woman who has found you unnerving."

His head tilted. He studied her like a peregrine falcon studying a particularly plump pigeon. "Actually, I believe you are."

"They must have been blind."

Erik thought it was a case of Serena seeing much more clearly than the others had, but he didn't think she would be comforted to hear that. Most people—men or women—accepted his easygoing exterior, returned his smiles, and never wondered about the man beneath.

Serena didn't wonder. She knew. Somehow she sensed the intensity he took such care to disguise from the rest of the world.

And here he was trying so hard to put her at ease.

Twenty-two

"The initial tells you other things," Erik continued neutrally. "Though our scribe was a practicing Christian, the Christianity he practiced was rooted in the paganism of the Celts."

Serena wrenched her mind away from the unnerving sense of time and memory combined like a river in flood, pushing her into Erik's arms. Instead, she thought of the histories she had read on the subject of weaving.

"How old did you say the Book of the Learned is?" she asked.

"I didn't." He smiled slightly. "But from the evidence of the text, the style of the calligraphy, and the choice of colors, I would be comfortable with an early-twelfth-century date despite the insistently Insular style, which belonged to earlier centuries."

"In the twelfth century, I don't think a mixture of paganism and Christianity was unusual," she said. She tapped her finger slowly against her scarf as she narrowed her eyes, searching her memory. "In fact, I think there was an early papal bull on the subject. The Pope made it very clear that missionaries were supposed to fit Christianity over any existing local religion rather than insist on strict theological purity. Practice tolerance as well as preach it."

"The Pope was a smart man. People love their customs and holidays. Holy days. Conversion is easier when it gives room for traditions to breathe." He looked at the scrap of vellum that had passed down through the centuries. "That's why dragons and griffins and other imaginary beasts appear in so many illuminated manuscripts. The powers they embodied in pagan times were given Christian glosses."

"What do you mean?"

"Take the stag. In pagan times it was considered a symbol of regeneration."

"Because of the shedding and regrowth of antlers?"

"Exactly. The stag had other qualities, too. Like the lion and the eagle, the stag wouldn't tolerate a snake."

"Where were they in Eden?" Serena asked dryly. "We all could have used them."

Erik smiled and just managed not to wind a stray tendril of her hair around his finger. "In medieval times," he said, "the stag was also used as a symbol of a pure and solitary way of life."

"Pure and solitary, huh? Obviously the good monks had never seen a stag in rut."

He paused. "I never thought of it that way. But who said a symbol has to make complete sense?"

"Certainly not the godlike, logical male of the species."

"Ouch. Do I hear your grandmother speaking?"

"Probably. G'mom was a wise woman."

"There have been a lot of them through the years. In the Middle Ages, they were renowned for their healing abilities. I think that's another reason Erik sometimes symbolized himself by the stag—stags were supposed to be able to recognize useful plants for treating the sick. From the little I've seen of the Book of the Learned, Erik was obviously a skilled herbalist."

"A well-rounded stag," she said, deadpan. "Any other qualities?"

"Sometimes the stag is pictured with a crucifix between its horns."

"Fully Christianized, as it were."

"Certainly on his way there." Erik shifted the scrap of vellum so that it caught more of the restless candlelight. "In the ancient Erik's case, the stag's horns support a peregrine falcon that has a crucifix dangling from its beak."

"Meaning?"

"I don't know. Obviously it had some meaning to Erik, because he uses a highly stylized version of that sign as a gather mark or catchword. Watching it evolve through the manuscript is one way of deciding which page came first."

"A gather mark?"

He gave her a slanting, gold-gleaming look. "You're going to be sorry you asked."

"Why?"

"It's complex."

"So is weaving. I get by just fine. What's a gather mark?"

Erik would rather have asked to see the original of the page that showed a flame-haired weaver watching a man with a peregrine on his arm and a staghound at his feet.

But he didn't say a word.

His pattern sense was nagging at his mind, telling him that he knew the name of the Silverfells sorceress who had humbled the proud Learned man. There was no reason for Erik's certainty, but he was certain just the same. It had happened to him many times in the past: a hint here, a speculation there, the sense of a pattern forming, and then certainty crystallizing in a rush. His younger sisters had joked that he was clairvoyant because he always knew they were in trouble before they did. He said he was just smart.

Smart, clairvoyant, lucky, or some other word, Erik didn't care. He simply knew he saw patterns that a lot of people overlooked.

The name of the sorceress was Serena.

He opened his mouth to tell her about the odd coincidence. Then he shut it. Coincidences like this were entertaining as long as they happened to someone else. In full daylight.

In the flickering intimacy of a candlelit room, coincidence could be frightening.

If he told Serena the name of Erik's nemesis, she would probably bolt from the house and never look back. Better to stick to explaining gather marks and catchwords.

"You asked for it," he said, smiling. "Just remember: One leaf equals two pages because a leaf is written on each side."

"One leaf. Two pages."

"Picture a cured animal hide that has been trimmed to a roughly rectangular shape," he said.

"Got it."

"Now fold it in half."

"Which way?"

"Down the middle so that the hair side is out."

"Which middle? Median line or waistline?"

"They did it both ways, but not in the same book. So pick one way and stick with it."

She blinked. "Okay. It's folded in half."

"That's a bifolium. Plural is bifolio. Now fold it in half again."

"Done."

"We'll stop there, even though most manuscripts were folded again and yet again. How many leaves do you have now?"

"I have ... eight pages, which means four leaves, which adds up to one hide."

He smiled at the intent frown between her eyebrows and really wished he could kiss the lines away. "Now nest your folded hide inside another hide that has been folded in the same way."

Her eyes half closed. "Got it."

"Do it again."

"A third hide?"

"Yes."

Her eyes closed completely.

He looked at the long shadow of her eyelashes, at her skin glowing with candlelight, at her lips gleaming with the recent passage of her tongue; and he wanted to taste her with a violence that loosened his knees. Part of him wondered if it had been this powerful for his medieval namesake, if that was why the cry of pain resonated through the years.

And most of him was afraid that he would find out.

He really hated coincidences. They reminded him of just how much of his own life was beyond his control.

"Now spread them all out again," he said. "As you figured out, one hide should make four good-sized leaves, which is eight pages, because the printing is on both sides of the hide."

"I'm spreading them out."

The pager on Erik's belt vibrated. He ignored it. He wasn't going to let anything—not even Rarities Unlimited—interfere with gaining Serena's trust. The pattern that he sensed forming was both complex and frankly eerie, as though time was a book that could be folded and unfolded, bound and unbound, and nonsequential pages put facing each other, staring across a gap that the body couldn't bridge.

But the mind could.

"Now write a continuous text on your unfolded hides in such a way that flesh side always faces flesh; and hair side always faces hair," he continued, fighting to keep his voice even.

There was silence for the space of about a minute. Then, "You lost me," she admitted.

"Lots of monks got lost, too. That's why they marked the margins of each page to tell themselves how to gather the book in the correct manner. Some scribes used symbols. Some used words to indicate where the pages should be caught together and sewed."

"Gather marks and catchwords," she said triumphantly, opening her eyes.

The pager kept on vibrating. He kept on ignoring it.

"It's a concept we still use today," he said, "even though we're long past the time of folded vellum. Once the manuscript was bound, the gather marks or catchwords vanished into the central seam of the book, the gutter."

Serena opened her mouth to say something, then realized that Erik was studying her lips as though he had never seen anything quite as appealing. A curious, shivery sensation went through her, something like fear . . . but not quite. The difference was both subtle and stunning.

"I never realized making books was so complicated," she said huskily.

He closed his eyes. When he opened them, he was looking anywhere but at her tempting mouth. What had seemed like a good idea at the time—viewing the manuscripts in the same kind of light they had been created—now seemed like the height of stupidity. Culturally speaking, for modern people candlelight and sex went together like lightning and thunder. Inevitably.

The pager finally gave up and stopped vibrating.

"That's not the half of it," he said. "I've barely touched on the complexity of the subject."

She waited for him to continue. When he didn't, she made an encouraging noise.

"Not this time," he said.

"What do you mean?"

"Simple. I've shown you mine. Are you going to show me yours?"

Twenty-three

"Erik didn't answer," Dana said in disgust. She pushed back in her black leather chair and glared at the phone.

Niall's lean, muscular hip was resting on a corner of her neat—in his opinion, way too neat—desk. "Maybe he's in the shower."

"Maybe he's in the saddle," she retorted.

"Hell of an idea. Why don't you come over here and—"

The intercom in Dana's office buzzed, cutting him off. Her assistant's voice floated from a speaker. "Factoid is here."

"Tell him to—" began Niall.

"Come in," Dana finished. Then, quickly, to Niall, "Put a sock in it, boyo. Remember the Gretchen Incident."

"What incident? She never saw us under that conference table."

"If she had come in sooner, she would have found us on *top* of it."

"Later, too." Niall smiled, remembering.

"Rain check?" Dana asked.

"Do I get one, too?"

"As many as you want, whenever you want them. Except now!" she said, laughing and evading a lazy swipe of his big hand.

When McCoy came in, Dana was at her desk and Niall was looking out one of the windows. L.A. was the same, but the fit of his pants had undergone some interesting changes. He wasn't planning on turning around until everything was back in its accustomed place.

"Erik needs a new pager," McCoy said.

"Why?" Dana asked.

"The old one doesn't deliver electric shocks."

"Ignoring you, is he?"

"Yes."

"Don't feel bad. He's ignoring me, too."

"I admire his TQ," McCoy said under his breath.

From past exposure, Dana knew that TQ was shorthand for testosterone quotient. She ignored McCoy's comment. It was easier than trying to deal with his elliptical sense of humor. "If it's urgent, I have a fallback position."

Niall gave her a hooded look that said, *Would that be under the table, luv?*

She ignored him, too. There were times when she thought her life consisted of ignoring the men in it. "Is it urgent?"

McCoy started to say that it was, had a rare attack of common sense, and sighed. "No, but it's interesting."

"We're listening," Niall said.

McCoy straightened his stringbean body and began talking. "The grandmother—"

"Whose?" Niall and Dana said instantly. "We're not mind readers," she added gently, if a bit tartly.

"Yeah. I forgot. It's the pages thing."

Blank looks from both his bosses.

"You know, the *old* pages," he said.

"Which client, boyo?" Niall asked.

McCoy's eyes unfocused and his right hand began to twitch as he played his palm widget like a five-fingered master pianist.

"Bloody hell," Niall muttered, but he didn't say it loud enough to disturb Factoid. "He's gone again."

"Patience."

"I'd rather unplug him."

"Then he wouldn't be much good to anyone, would he? Least of all himself."

"Someday I'm going to find out."

"Give me a head start," Dana said, unwrapping a tiny mint from a dish on her desk. "Factoid unplugged won't be a pretty sight."

His hand kept twitching.

"Has anyone ever told the boy that he's a rude bastard?" Niall asked easily.

"You have. Many times."

"Not often enough or hard enough to— Wait, he's back."

"Sorry," McCoy said defensively. He knew Niall simply didn't understand the plugged-in, fully wired generation. "That was C. D. She needed to know if there's any proof that bugs have sex for fun rather than for making little bugs."

"Don't ask," Dana said swiftly to Niall.

"I can't help it. Is there?"

"Some Brazilian did a study of Amazonian riverboat cockroaches that—"

"*No.*" Dana's voice, like her face, said she meant it. "About the grandmother?"

"Grandmother . . . grandmother . . ." McCoy frowned and twitched, but his computer didn't have a record of the previous conversation. His brain, however, did. Sometimes there just wasn't any substitute for old-fashioned hardwiring. "Warrick."

"Ah, Serena Charters. The manuscript pages," Dana said. "Continue."

"According to every computer source I have access to, the old lady didn't exist before November 8, 1949. That's when she bought five acres of the government's biggest sandlot real cheap with the promise of improving it within a year. She did. November 8, 1950, she became the owner of said five acres free and clear."

"No sign of her before that?" Niall asked, frowning.

"Nothing. No birth certificate, no Social Security, no marriage, no death, no passport, no visa, no driver's license, no immigration papers, not one entry. Ellis Weaver appeared one day like she'd been beamed down from a passing spaceship. She hasn't been here much since then, either. Her lawyer pays her property taxes once a year. That's it. No credit cards, no checks, no utility bills, no Social Security, no Medicare, no MediCal, no health insurance, no life insurance, no driver's license, no vehicle registration in her own name. *Nada,* zip, zilch, zero. The woman was like a terminal-stage Yogi living on air and pure thoughts."

"Keep after it," Niall said.

Dana said, "I assume you searched under the name Charters as well."

McCoy gave her a wounded look. "No Ellis Charters listed at all. I'm tracing every other female of her generation with the name Charters, but it's slow going. Ancient history just ain't computerized."

"Ancient history is older than 1949, boyo."

"Really? I didn't think you were that old," Dana said.

Niall's smile was more like a promise of retribution. "The harder the information is to find, the more useful it's likely to be. People don't bury clean secrets, only dirty ones."

"Can't you put a print researcher on it?" McCoy asked in a tone that was real close to a whine. Then light dawned: Gretchen was a flash at brick-and-board research. "Never mind. Thanks. I'm gone."

And he was.

Niall blinked. "I don't believe I've ever seen the boy move that fast."

"He just remembered that Gretchen is keen on print research."

"And he's keen on Gretchen."

Dana smiled like an amused cat. "It's all your fault, my little cabbage. You put him on the trail."

"He was born on Gretchen's trail and I'm not your little cabbage."

"My big one, then."

"My ass."

"That, too."

Niall started to leap in with both big feet, but a single look at her told him that Dana's heart wasn't really yanking on his chain; her fingers were doing the flute thing again. He sat back and waited to receive whatever revelation her complex, brilliant, and pragmatic mind had to offer.

Twenty-four

Cleary Warrick Montclair paced the living room of her personal area of the West Coast Warrick house. The wing with its ten rooms had been set aside for her use when she divorced and moved back home with her very young son. Some days she didn't know whether her father had rewarded or cursed her with his generosity. She did know that he had a hold on her that no other man could equal; she just didn't know why.

Unlike Norman Warrick, Cleary preferred modern furnishings, or at least more modern than Louis XV. There was no massive "brown furniture" filling her rooms. Textured rugs and geometric furniture covered by fabrics in shades of beige and cream and white gave an airy spaciousness to the main room. The art on the walls and tables was generic avant, which was to say quite expensive to buyers willing to put themselves in the hands of a contemporary-art expert. As the House of Warrick overflowed with such experts to advise the ill-advised and newly rich, Cleary had made it her duty to showcase twenty-first-century art in her home as a balance to her father's decidedly antique tastes.

The true passion in her life wasn't art or antiques, it was business: the House of Warrick. How she decorated her home and office was irrelevant to her, except in as much as it contributed to the Warrick reputation as a cultural taste-maker, and thus to the House of Warrick's bottom line.

Despite her otherwise practical turn of mind, Cleary had spent most of her lifetime trying to please her father by re-placing the older brother who had tanked up on vodka and married his Maserati to a concrete wall. Even though she knew intellectually that both being the replacement and pleasing her father were impossible, she kept believing deep in her soul that if she just did the right thing, and did it often enough, Daddy would finally approve of his little girl.

No matter how much or how often the woman's mind wrestled with the child inside, the child Cleary was stubborn and the woman Cleary was compelled to keep on trying to do the impossible.

Even after Cleary had divorced the husband her father didn't approve of and brought her son home, she had been rewarded by the rough side of her father's tongue more often than not. Regardless, she had spent years trying to convince him that she was at least as capable of sharing the responsi-bility of running the House of Warrick as her older brother had been.

She hadn't succeeded. Every day, several times a day, her father let her know that he was going to live long enough to train his grandson to take up the reins, not her. Until then, Paul Carson had a shrewd head for business as well as for guarding people and information.

Cleary told herself that her father's lack of faith didn't matter; what was important was family continuity. On good days she even believed it.

Today wasn't one of those days.

"Why won't he let me take care of it?" Cleary said loudly. "God damn it, you'd think I was still sucking my thumb!"

Paul stretched out his long legs, admired the expensive,

dark gleam of his loafers against the white carpet, and let Cleary's words roll over him. He had heard it all before. He would hear it all again. It was just part of his job as Warrick's chief of security and right-hand man, and Cleary's discreet lover.

"When I asked if he had made any progress in finding the girl, he told me to mind my own business," Cleary said in a rising voice. "As if his business isn't mine! Who settles all the staff complaints? Who makes sure taxes are paid and people are hired? Who sucks up to all the crabby old widows with money? Who is on the road three hundred days a year pressing the flesh and reminding people of the House of Warrick? Who—"

Paul flicked a brief sideways glance at his watch. Thin, gold, expensive, it was a foolish luxury because it did nothing but keep track of seconds, minutes, and hours. It didn't receive faxes or voice mail or E-mail, it didn't send them, it didn't do sums or play games or remember addresses and birthdays. It did one thing superbly and well: it told time.

In that single-purpose reliability, the watch was rather like a gun. No nonsense. No confusion about function. No doubt as to what happened next. Just aim and fire.

Biting back a yawn, Paul eased his long body into a more comfortable position in the low chair whose creamy oval shape and yellow feet reminded him of a duck. He wished he could close his eyes and doze for a few minutes. He and Cleary had torn up the sheets like teenagers last night. Or rather, he had. Cleary wasn't a sensual woman. On the other hand, she was willing, eager to please, and had learned to go down on him with gratifying skill and every appearance of enthusiasm.

In all, he had nothing to complain about and a lot to be grateful for. So he would keep his mouth shut and listen to his lover's unvarying complaints about the prick who was her father.

Not that Paul disagreed with her. Norman Warrick was a

real prick. No doubt about it. But once that was said, nothing changed, certainly not blood relationship or the much more tenuous relationship of employer and employee.

Or of lovers, for that matter.

"—even makes sure each of his three houses is staffed, supplied, polished, and ready to have him at a moment's notice," Cleary continued. She compressed her lips, caught as always between fury at her father for his callousness and at herself for still giving a damn. Today biting her lips didn't work. Neither did tilting back her head. Tears gathered, hot as a little girl's anger. "Oh, *shit!*"

Paul almost sighed. Once again she had worked herself into a froth over something that wouldn't change. Couldn't change. He understood Warrick's problem; it was one he had himself. The ecstasies and agonies of human emotions simply passed him by. He knew they were real, just as he knew he would never feel them. Nor would Warrick. The only difference between the two men was that Warrick had been born to a family that was comfortable enough financially so that he didn't have to learn to mimic emotions to be accepted.

Paul hadn't been so lucky. His family had been hardworking, fertile, and barely able to claw its way from poverty into the lower class.

Being a bright boy, Paul had soon figured out that when it came to emotions, he was different from the people around him. The next thing he had learned was that people who were different were outcasts. The final revelation had been that outcasts didn't get ahead no matter how smart or ruthless they were.

Paul had decided he wouldn't be an outcast. He studied people until he learned how to read their needs. Then, if it was worth the effort, he gave them what they needed.

Leaning forward, he grabbed one of Cleary's hands and gathered her into his lap. "Come here, sweet thing. Come have a good cry on me. *I* understand how valuable you are."

She resisted for a moment before she gave in and relaxed into Paul's familiar embrace. A few tears came, then a few more, then a swift flood that was gone almost before it could dampen his shirt.

The speed of her emotional shifts fascinated him. It was like a peephole into a world he could never enter, a world that held the secret to success.

His quick, narrow hands smoothed over her tumbled hair and down her thin back and fashionably meager hips. He preferred women with meat on them but didn't bother telling Cleary that. She desperately wanted to look like a little girl, the better to win Daddy's approval, no doubt. If that meant eating one lettuce leaf and one carrot shred per meal, then that was what she would eat.

Besides, the parts of her that really interested him were still soft, still wet. If the wrapping lacked sex appeal, he could close his eyes and get past it.

"Let me talk to him," Paul said. "Sometimes I can get through to him."

She breathed out air that could have been born in a sigh or a sob. "What if he gets mad and dies?"

If that happened Paul would get up and dance a jig, because Cleary would inherit a buttload of money, but he knew she didn't want to hear about that. "He won't. Not today."

Which was probably, unfortunately, true.

"He can't die." Her voice was tense, desperate.

Not for the first time, Paul wondered how in hell an otherwise smart woman nearing her fiftieth birthday could be so dumb about an elemental fact of life: People died. All the time. For every reason. For no reason at all. Every day. All day. Night, too.

But the one time he had pointed that out, Cleary had exploded and called him a cold monster. It had taken him a week to coax her back into speaking to him, and it was another two weeks before she went down on him.

Paul learned from his mistakes.

He kissed Cleary's forehead and stroked her back and hips. "That tough old man will live to blow out a hundred birthday candles."

She sighed and snuggled closer. "I know. I just worry about him. I don't want him to die before . . ." Her voice faded. *Before he realizes what a good daughter I am.*

"Before what?" Paul asked.

Her shoulders jerked. She didn't like admitting her needs to herself. She did her best to hide them from everyone else, even the man she loved as much as she could love any man after her father.

"I don't know." Her voice was petulant, like a little girl.

But the tongue licking his neck was all woman. So were the hands reaching for his fly.

Paul smiled and shifted to make it easier for her. The nice thing about giving people what they wanted was that the smart ones gave it back to you.

Cleary was smart.

"Promise you'll get those pages?" she said. "We've got to keep a lid on this or we'll lose out on the merger with smaller Internet houses. Then we'll get swallowed up by Christie's or Sotheby's or even—Christ forbid—Auction Coalition."

He felt her mouth burrow into the opening of his fly and groaned.

"Promise me," she said, licking him.

His hips jerked. "I promise."

She smiled and felt better. She couldn't control her father, but she could certainly hold his right-hand man's attention.

It was as easy as sucking on candy.

Twenty-five

The call came after midnight. Only one person heard the cell phone ring.

He had been waiting.

"I'm listening," he said in a low voice.

"She went into her own house the same way she left North's—empty-handed."

Shit! Had she left the stuff in a safe-deposit box in Palm Springs?

"Stay with her."

"You want me to toss the house?"

He had already considered and rejected the idea. If Serena hadn't carried anything into the house, then the pages weren't there. "No. This is legal all the way."

A lie, but a useful one.

If it came to another murder, he didn't want anyone to know but Serena, because she wouldn't tell anyone. Ever.

That was the really nice thing about dead people. Their mouths were sewed shut.

Twenty-six

"Okay, Shel. Let me see if I have this right," Erik said into the phone. He scrolled through the list of pages Rarities was researching for him. For the sake of simplicity he had numbered them one through eleven. "So far, most of the provenance trails go back only as far as the seventies, no matter how many owners."

"Right." At the other end of the conversation, Shel didn't bother to conceal a jaw-cracking yawn. He was used to working long shifts, but this one had gone beyond caffeine's ability to speed him up. His only consolation was that Factoid was at this moment cursing up and down the hallway at the slow—*for God's sake it's fucking Stone Age microfilm*—pace of searching through some of the mustier archives of the U.S. government. "We're contacting the last-listed private individuals or dealers on the East Coast right now. Midwest next. Mountain time next. Should know more by noon. Evening, latest."

"What about the auction houses? Sooner or later, I'll bet that quite a few of the leaves go back to them."

"Dana's working on that now. Christie's was slow until she pointed out that it was to their benefit to demonstrate how thorough their research was. Sotheby's took some of our expert opinion on various stuff as quid pro quo for checking their databases."

Erik grunted, unimpressed. "What about Warrick?"

"They've had their people on it since the request went in yesterday. Or was it the day before? Or—" He yawned so hard he nearly broke his jaw. "Damn, I've got to get some sleep."

Erik knew how he felt. His own sleep had been restless and unsatisfying, filled with images of himself wrapped around Serena like hot around fire. Except it wasn't quite him. His hands were more scarred, marked by sword and crossbow and his peregrine's talons, which sometimes pierced even his leather gauntlet. Nor was the sorceress quite Serena. The eyes and hair were the same, but the mouth was different, thinner, and she smelled of cloves, tasted of dark wine, wore a medieval dress whose fabric caressed him as though alive.

"You still there?" Shel asked.

Impatiently Erik forced his mind back to tracing provenance rather than the feel of a woman's body beneath unearthly, loving cloth. "I'm here. If you reach a wall on the provenance on any single piece, let me know where. Immediately."

"Yeah." Yawn. "Sure. I've got Takeo and Suelynn on it. They're fresh. They'll wake me if they stall out."

"Thanks, Shel."

"I should thank you. Dana promised me three weeks off after this is wrapped up."

"Don't take your Rarities communications unit with you," Erik warned.

"Oh, I'll take it, just like my employment contract says. But it don't say nothin' about batteries."

Driven by the impatience that rode him with razor talons, Erik disconnected, printed out the list of what he had so far, cursed savagely, and headed for the shower. Enough was enough. He was going to have a look at Serena's inheritance, and to hell with her lack of trust.

He didn't know why time was closing in like an enemy. He just knew that it was.

Twenty-seven

Promptly at nine o'clock, Serena's front doorbell chimed.
Then it squawked long and loud. Something had happened a
few months ago to its melodious electronics. Something expensive. So she had been forced to choose between buying
yarn for weaving and new tires for the van or fixing the
doorbell. No choice, really. She couldn't weave with musical
notes, no matter how pretty they were. Nor could she deliver
her smaller textiles to southern California outlets without
tires on her van. So as soon as the next check came in, her
van would get new shoes.

And the doorbell would just get worse.

"What the hell was that?" Erik asked the instant the front
door opened.

Serena didn't say anything. She felt like slamming the
door in his clean-shaved, handsome face. Wearing jeans, hiking boots, hunter-green shirt, and a soft leather jacket the
color of night, he looked like he had just stepped out of an
advertisement for the outdoor life.

She looked like the before photo in a You Can Do It spa

ad. She was showing every one of the long hours she hadn't slept because she was too stubborn—and too uneasy—to stay in the guest room Erik had offered her, complete with a telephone and an inside dead bolt to ensure her privacy. Instead of being sensible and staying behind the bolted guest room door, she had driven all the way home.

It hadn't been her smartest moment. She had arrived after midnight, spent more than an hour trying to fall asleep, and then awakened to a nightmare of cold sweat and fiery death.

She told herself that her ragged emotions were understandable. The last few days had been exhausting: the lawyer, her grandmother's estate, the Warricks, the pages that might or might not be real, the note warning of danger, and most of all the unnerving sense of déjà vu that had increased the longer she stayed with Erik North. So she had driven back to her own familiar home as though pursued by a demon.

And here the demon was, standing at her front door.

"The doorbell electronics are skippy," she said.

"They're more than skippy. They're twisted."

His voice was almost curt. He had been in a bad mood since Serena had gotten in her old beater and driven off into the night, leaving him behind. His mood had gone from bad to dangerous a few minutes ago; that was when he spotted the guy parked down Serena's street wearing a tiny high-tech headphone and driving a drab Japanese car.

Without seeming to, Erik watched Serena closely. If she was aware of the watcher down the street, she didn't show it. She never once so much as glanced in that direction. Even so, she looked plenty nervous. He wondered if she had changed her mind during the night, if she would back out of showing him the pages in the clean light of day.

"I'm glad you made it home safely," he said, giving the van in her driveway a narrow look. "Your tires have about the same amount of tread on them as the average egg."

"They're not that bad."

"Have you checked them lately?"

"Yes."

"Then get your eyes examined and look again. You need new tires."

"They're at the top of my list, right after cat food."

"If I go out and get some, will you let me in?"

"Cat food?"

"Or tires. Take your pick."

Startled, she looked directly at his eyes for the first time. They were as clear as sunlight and almost as golden. They were also serious. He meant just what he said: cat food or tires, whichever she wanted, he would supply.

She stepped out of the doorway and motioned him in. "I don't require guests to bring hostess gifts."

The fact that he had invited himself—in fact, he had nearly shouted at her that he would see her tomorrow, *early*—was something she decided not to bring up. Despite his crisp appearance, he was looking determined around the eyes and mouth. She knew that he really hadn't wanted her to leave last night.

And she really hadn't wanted to stay. It had been too unnerving.

Every time she looked at him, it was as though there was another Erik there, too, shimmering just beyond reach, a presence that was both darkness and light, the air smelling of cloves and wine. When she looked down, she saw herself shimmering, too, wearing a dress of an unspeakably clever weave, a dress just like her scarf; and an ancient ruby ring she had never seen before was on her right hand.

She had panicked.

I'm not crazy, Serena told herself for the thousandth time. *Crazy people don't worry about being crazy. They just are.*

A black cat the size of a dog slid up and looked at Erik with unblinking fire-colored eyes.

"What about the cat?" Erik asked. "He looks like he demands tribute."

Briskly Serena cleared her mind of weird dreams and even more startling waking moments. "Mr. Picky? Nah. He's love with four feet and black fur."

"Don't forget the claws and teeth."

"I take it you don't like cats."

Erik gave her an amused look. Then he sat on his heels and began talking to Mr. Picky. The rumbling, purring noises and the soft yeowings Erik made sounded remarkably like they came from a cat's throat—a very large cat.

Mr. Picky thought so, too. He leaped up into what there was of Erik's lap and burrowed in as though he had been born there. Smiling, Erik sat cross-legged on the floor and settled in for some serious cat petting. He missed having cats around, but he was gone often enough that he didn't want anything less wild than a chaparral cock depending on him.

As Serena watched her cat quite literally drool over the strange man, she was divided between jealousy and fascination. Picky didn't dislike other people, but he usually ignored them, especially if they paid attention to him.

Not this time. The cat's glazed eyes were half closed. He was ecstatic.

Erik made feline sounds.

"What are you saying to him?" she demanded.

"Damned if I know. He seems to like it, though."

Picky butted his big head against Erik's chin and purred like a tiger. *Pay attention to me, not her.*

Holding the cat, Erik came to his feet in a lithe movement. Picky shifted, clung less than delicately with sharp claws, and generally made it known that he wasn't giving up his long-lost, very new friend.

"You'd think I never petted the ungrateful rat," Serena said.

"Cat."

"*Rat*. See if I share any more fresh shrimp with him."

Picky turned up the volume on his purring as though to drown out her complaints.

"You want a cat?" she asked.

"You offering this one?"

"I'm thinking about it."

The big cat shifted, sprang, and flowed into Serena's arms.

The purring never stopped. She sighed and rubbed her chin against his soft, sleek fur.

"I'll keep him," she said.

"I never doubted it."

"Neither did he, the rat."

Picky ignored the insults, butted her chin gently, and leaped down. A few moments later the flap on the cat door in the kitchen slapped softly.

"Was it something I said?" Erik asked, deadpan.

She snickered. "All that purring worked up an appetite. He's gone hunting."

"The coyotes better take cover."

"That's what I like about Picky. He's big enough to give a coyote second thoughts about feline sushi."

"That's one of the reasons I don't have a cat," Erik said. "I haven't found one that can outrun, outwit, or outfight a coyote. Palm Springs is full of them."

"So far, so good here. Want some coffee or food before you look at the sheets?"

Sheets. Bed. Serena in it with me.

Then reality hit Erik. She was talking about the leaves from the Book of the Learned. The fact that he hadn't thought of that immediately told him just how deeply she had gotten to him.

"Coffee would be good," he said.

An ice cube shower would be more to the point, but he wasn't going to say it aloud.

"Cream? Sugar?" she asked, turning and heading for the kitchen.

"Black."

As soon as she was out of sight, he turned and looked through the etched glass panel in the front door. The dull Japanese car hadn't moved. The man had. He was looking at Erik's license plate with discreet, high-tech binoculars.

Damn!

Automatically Erik's hand went to the communications unit at the back of his belt. All that kept him from using it was the certainty that his reluctant hostess wouldn't understand why he was chatting on a snoop-proof cell phone with Rarities about whether or not they had put a tail on Serena Charters and told the tail to keep a license plate log of visitors.

Usually Rarities would tell Erik if they had arranged for backup. Usually.

Niall was nothing if not unpredictable. It kept everyone on their toes, especially the folks trying to penetrate the security at Rarities Unlimited.

Erik settled for second best: E-mail. He had already memorized the license plate and make of the tail's car. As for the tail himself, he was the type of middle-aged generic white male that had given the FBI a look all its own. But the FBI was still stuck with American cars. This guy had the perfect West Coast undercover car: foreign.

Composing a brief message in his mind, Erik grabbed a stylus out of the communications unit, which was designed for just those embarrassing moments when even a soft voice would be too loud. He sent his message the old-fashioned way, writing quickly on the small electronic pad, "original" to Dana, copy to Factoid. Then he replaced the unit in its carrying case at the small of his back.

A lot of men carried guns in the same place. Erik hoped he never would have to again.

Despite the quick E-mail, he planned to call Rarities as soon as he knew Serena couldn't overhear the conversation. Shorthand was no substitute for real words, real impressions, real dialogue.

He followed Serena's steps past a series of fabric screens that walled off the great room from the front door, creating an entryway. Under normal circumstances he would have noticed and appreciated the quality of textile in the screens, but at the moment he was thinking about something more urgent than artistry.

He was wondering what would be the most tactful way to ask Serena if she had noticed anyone following her home the night before.

As soon as he reached the kitchen doorway, he froze. It might have been his divided attention. It might have been his lack of sleep. It might have been a lot of things. Whatever it was, the sense of déjà vu he got when he saw her pouring a steaming mug of coffee stopped him like a stone wall.

For a few staggering moments he was certain he had seen her do that for him before. Not coffee, but something that had steamed and promised warmth on a cold day. And it hadn't been a mug. It had been a bowl incised with ancient runic symbols.

He could see it.

He shook his head sharply, ending the overwhelming moment. Now was no time to let the medieval part of his soul get fanciful. There were more pressing things at hand than the impossible sense of familiarity that came every time he saw the curve of her cheek or candlelight reflected in her violet eyes and red-gold hair.

"Did you have much traffic last night?" he asked.

With disbelief in the arc of her left eyebrow, she looked over her shoulder at him. "It was after midnight. Even in southern California, sooner or later rush hour ends."

He shrugged. "I just wondered. Sometimes a woman driving alone late at night, some guy thinks it's cute to follow her. . . ." His voice trailed off invitingly.

She put down the coffeepot. "Like the coyotes, so far so good."

"No one followed you?"

"If they did, I didn't notice." She looked at him closely. "Do you worry about this a lot?"

"I have two younger sisters." It was lame, but it was something.

"Were they ever followed?"

"Once."

"What happened?"

"They called me."

Serena waited.

Erik kept his mouth shut. He didn't think she would feel

any better knowing that he had taken the guy's license number, traced it to his cheap apartment, and had a little talk with him. Then he had given the license number to the cops so that they could tell the jerk how much they loved him. He had heard later that one of the female deputies gave the guy some curbside therapy when she found him tailgating a frightened woman at 2 A.M.

"What happened?" Serena asked.

"They kept their heads and got home safe and sound. Is that coffee for me?"

She looked at the mug in her hand. "Er, yes. Sorry. Black, right?"

"Thanks." He took the cup, swallowed, and made a sound of surprised pleasure. "This is good."

She smiled crookedly. "I rarely poison guests on the first visit."

"Second?"

"I try to wait until the third."

He smiled, drained half the mug, and licked his lips. "After the way you nuked the coffee at my house, I thought yours would be terrible."

"Sorry to disappoint you."

"I'm not."

He finished the cup, washed his hands, dried them thoroughly on the towel she handed him, and looked at her expectantly.

Despite her possessive, protective reluctance to share the beautiful leaves with anyone, she couldn't help smiling back at him. "And here I thought you made that long drive just to see me."

He winced. "No matter how I answer that one, I lose."

Laughing, she washed her own hands, wiped them on her jeans, and headed for the second exit in the odd kitchen. "Follow me."

He looked at the smooth swing of her hips and said huskily, "My pleasure."

Her head swung around in surprise, but he had expected

that. His expression was innocent and his eyes were on her face.

"What?" he asked.

She started to say something, saw the trap, and jumped back. "Now I know how you felt. There's no answer I can make that doesn't put both feet in my mouth."

"At least yours look tasty."

She blinked, looked at her bare feet, and then back at him. "Before we go any further, maybe you should eat breakfast."

"Why?"

"If my feet look tasty, you'll devour the pages in one gulp."

Erik's slow smile was a mixture of humor and male sensuality that stopped Serena's breath.

"When it comes to the good stuff, I'm a slow and very thorough kind of man," he assured her.

"I'm not touching that one."

His lips quirked. "You sure?"

"My grandmother raised only one dumb child. It wasn't me."

Erik thought about the man with the nearly invisible headphones and a relief tube no doubt tucked away in a handy place. He hoped Serena was right about her intelligence, but he wasn't betting her life on it. All her grandmother's secrecy and shrewdness hadn't kept her from a violent death.

He wondered if Factoid or one of his minions had cracked the county sheriff's computer yet. It would be nice to know what the guys with badges really thought about Ellis Weaver's murder. Or was it Ellis Charters? Given the information that he had sent last night to the Rarities computer, Factoid should have discovered something useful by now.

For once, Erik was looking forward to having his pager vibrate against his belt.

And for once the damn thing was quiet.

Twenty-eight

LOS ANGELES
FRIDAY MORNING

Dana Gaynor was wearing the kind of sleek wool pantsuit that was perfect for a blustery January day in Los Angeles, when the wind blew cold off the ocean and the clouds were serious about unloading rain onshore. The cranberry color of her clothes set off her smooth dark hair and provided a warm focus to the room full of windows overlooking a rainy day, but at the moment she wasn't conscious of such unimportant details. There was a frown line between her eyes and an unhappy curve to her mouth.

Joe-Bob McCoy shifted uneasily. He wasn't used to coming up empty on a Rarities assignment, particularly one that had Dana's full attention. He wished the job had involved Old Master paintings rather than medieval manuscripts; Dana's interest in Old Masters was barely room temperature in a meat locker.

The phone rang, giving McCoy a reprieve.

Dana gave the instrument a lethal look. She had told her assistant Ralph Kung not to bother her unless it had to do with Serena Charters and the manuscript pages.

"This better be good," she muttered as she grabbed the phone and snarled. "Who?"

"Cleary Warrick Montclair."

"Not good enough. Hold her hand."

"She declined. Rather shrilly, if you must know."

"Where's Niall?"

"He took the day off. It's bare-root time."

"What?"

"Time to plant bare-root roses."

"Flowers? I'm working my butt off and he's out planting ruddy *flowers?*"

"It's raining," Kung offered as a kind of consolation. "You can see him from your window."

She didn't bother to look. "Do bare-root roses have thorns?" she demanded.

"I believe so."

"I hope he sits on one. Give me thirty seconds and put Cleary on." She pinned Factoid with a glittering dark glance. "Spit it out."

"Nothing new on the grandmother except for death-scene stuff," he said in a rush. "She completely invented herself."

"Bloody hell, I knew that. Now I want to know who she was before that and why she reinvented herself. So quit sniffing after Gretchen and *get to work.*"

"I haven't been sniff—" he began, turning to leave.

"No." Dana cut in. "Work here. In my office. Where I can watch you."

"But—"

Dana was talking again, and not to McCoy. Even if he couldn't have heard the words, he would have known she was talking to a client. Her tone was calm, cultured, confident, and above all, reasonable.

"Hello, Cleary. How is your father?"

"Livid."

Dana wished she could feel sorry about it. She couldn't. Warrick was a very rich, very unpleasant, very old man, and his daughter had been on the phone to Rarities every half hour since 6 A.M.

"Have you tried adjusting his medications?" Dana asked pleasantly.

Cleary was too surprised to speak.

Dana took advantage of it. "Ms. Montclair, I will be blunt. It is difficult for us to accomplish anything when the House of Warrick is on the phone demanding minute-by-minute updates. We appreciate your concern, we share your sense of urgency, and we will work much more efficiently if we are interrupted less often. We have your phone number, your fax, your E-mail, your cell phone, your pager, and your instant Internet connection. We have a man with Ms. Charters right now. If anything opens up in regard to purchasing the leaves, we will notify you immediately."

The client was unimpressed. "Look, the House of Warrick pays a lot of money to Rarities for—"

"Exactly," Dana cut in smoothly. "You expect a return on your investment. You will get it. You will get it much faster if you let us work unhindered."

Silence, then, "But he's so angry," Cleary said, her voice ragged. "His heart . . ."

Privately Dana doubted that the old bastard had one. "Have you called his doctor?"

"Of course!"

Every half hour, no doubt. Dana sighed. The passions that art or business created in people were difficult enough to deal with. The more personal traumas and dramas of family life were impossible.

"We are doing everything we can," Dana said soothingly. "Would you like me to reassure your father personally?"

"No. When I suggested it, he said your time would be better spent working rather than baby-sitting."

Dana's eyebrows lifted. Maybe the old man wasn't so bad after all. He certainly seemed to have a better grip on the realities of the situation than his daughter.

"In that case, Cleary, we'll be in touch. Soon."

"At least have your assistant send in hourly updates."

"During business hours, of course."

"But—"

"Thank you for calling, Cleary. We appreciate your concern."

Dana hung up and looked at McCoy. She expected him to be in some kind of computer trance, but he was looking at her.

"What's wrong?" she asked.

"Erik was trying to reach you a minute ago but he settled for E-mail, copy to me."

"Urgent?"

"There's a guy augered in down the street from the Charters house. Erik sent the license plate and description. He wants to know if the guy is ours."

"I didn't request anyone." She reached for one of the two-way radio units that Niall insisted she keep within reach at all times. He had the matching one. By tacit agreement, it was used only for emergencies. "Niall, you there?"

"What's up, luv?"

"Did you assign anyone to watch Serena?"

"No."

"Backup for Erik?"

"No."

"Bloody hell. We've got a bogey."

Twenty-nine

Erik looked at the old leather portfolio tucked beneath Serena's arm. "I still can't believe you kept that in your van in a locked plastic toolbox that was bolted to the floor."

"Don't sound so horrified. The box is waterproof, clean, and the alarm system and lock are good on the van. The locks on my house are as wonky as the doorbell. As for an alarm system . . ." She shrugged. "My smoke sensors have batteries, does that count?"

He opened his mouth, thought better of it, and shut it again. The sooner they were in the house with the pages, the better. Not that there was any real hope that the guy down the street hadn't seen her open the van and casually pull out the big portfolio. Their tail was probably calling in right now, which meant things could get lively at any time.

Unless the man belonged to Rarities.

Silently Erik wondered if the tail was friend or felon. If the latter, it would be really nice to know if Serena's grandmother had died randomly or because she had something somebody nasty wanted. Pages from the Book of the Learned, for instance. Or even the whole bloody book.

Damn it, Factoid! Where are you when I need you?

Nothing answered, particularly not the pager on Erik's belt. He had an uneasy feeling that a gun would do him more good than the silent pager. It was the kind of feeling he hated, because he didn't like guns. He liked the pattern that was forming even less.

Burning was an ugly way to die.

"Do you have a flat table that has good light?" he asked, heading for the door to the house.

Serena looked sideways at him. Though nothing in his voice or expression had changed, she sensed he was wary or angry or both. It was something about the clarity of his eyes and the predatory way he carried himself.

"How about the one in the kitchen?" she suggested.

He thought of the little knee-knocking café table that she used for solitary meals. It would hold a plate, silverware, and a cup. Salt and pepper were pushing it.

"Anything bigger?" he asked.

"I can clear off my design table."

"Perfect," he said. Anything used for designing would have good light.

Serena wondered how he would react to her studio. Other than various delivery people, no one had seen it. She had been raised to be self-sufficient, a loner. Nothing had happened to change that, including men.

When she graduated from her twenties, she had decided to join that curious modern phenomenon of "born-again virgins," single women who had quietly decided that living without sex was better than living with it. She didn't need a man to support her; she supported herself. She didn't need a man to get her pregnant; a sperm bank could take care of that. She didn't need a man to keep her car going; there were a gazillion eager mechanics in the telephone book—ditto for landscapers, house painters, plumbers, and electricians.

As for company, she had never met a man who didn't limit her possibilities more than he expanded them. Given that, Mr. Picky was the perfect male companion: he could take care of himself and only demanded occasional petting.

A trilling whistle cut through Serena's thoughts, a sound like a wild falcon. She spun toward Erik.

He didn't notice. He was studying the looms with something close to reverence. "Jesus, Joseph, and Mary."

She blinked. "Actually that's Big Betty, Middle Betty, K. L. Betty, Little Betty, and Betina."

"You name your looms?"

"I spend most of my life with them. Should I call them one, two, three, four, and five?"

"You've got a point. Five of them, actually. What does *K. L.* stand for?"

"Kinda little."

He looked at the nearly six-foot-tall loom and laughed. "Kind of is right."

"You should have seen G'mom's. It was the reason her cabin had a twelve-foot ceiling. The loom had been passed down through more generations than anyone could remember."

Erik didn't have to ask what had happened to the loom. Wood burned. Old wood burned even better.

Serena went to Middle Betty. The loom's warp threads were fully strung but had no weft threads to give substance and pattern. Eight harnesses held heddles that were waiting for her to have time to start the design that had haunted her since she was six. She had dreamed it, drawn it, redrawn it, chosen yarns and colors, strung the warp, checked the drawing one last time, and promised herself that she would begin as soon as she tied off the Norman cross weaving she had finished during the long, restless night.

Despite her lack of sleep, eagerness fizzed through her blood at the thought of beginning a new weaving. Especially this one. She had been building her skill as a weaver for a lifetime with this design in mind. Finally she was ready. She was certain of it.

She had dreamed it last night, only . . . not quite. It was a loom holding cloth that looked like her scarf, and she was weaving, dreaming, humming.

Lure to one, deterrent to all others.

Erik watched Serena's face while she stroked the warp threads as lightly and lovingly as a harpist stroked her favorite harp . . .

Ariane with her midnight hair and amethyst eyes and slender white fingers which could draw forth such sadness from a harp as to make his peregrine weep. Ariane, with her vibrant Learned dress, the cloth a guardian stronger than armor and a lure to just one man. Uncanny cloth woven by the sorceress Serena of Silverfells.

Cassandra had meddled brilliantly in Ariane and Simon's match. Would that his own match had been so charmed.

With a lurch of adrenaline, Erik yanked his mind away from the haunting not-quite memories. It was one thing to have a medieval profession—calligraphy and illumination. It was quite another to have medieval memories that he had never written, never illuminated, never even read. That was called imagination, and his was entirely too vivid.

He was obsessed with the Book of the Learned. He knew it. What he didn't know was how to escape the compelling grip of the mystery or the soul-deep need to know the fate of Erik the Learned.

". . . the whole table?" Serena asked.

He replayed the last few moments in his mind and answered her question. "I'll just need enough to spread out the pages."

"One whole table coming up."

While she cleared the table, he fought the temptation to just sit down on the floor and go through the manuscript pages right that instant. But he had felt the reluctance in her fingers when she handed over the portfolio. Having him rip into it like a kid opening a candy bar wouldn't make her any happier about sharing the pages. He had waited years. He could wait a few more minutes.

Erik was still telling himself that when he put the portfolio on a drafting table that was only partially cleared. As he lifted the scarred leather flap, his breath came out in a low sound that was both triumph and awe.

Curiously Serena watched him. Like Warrick, he seemed to recognize the pages. Unlike Warrick, he wasn't angered by them.

Erik was enthralled.

Silence stretched until it vibrated like a plucked harp string.

"Well?" she demanded.

"Well what?"

When he spoke, he didn't so much as glance away from the pages he had spread across the part of the table he had given her time to clear. He wouldn't have looked up for an explosion. Four leaves from the Book of the Learned lay before him, gloriously intact. No letters had been scraped away to make room for inappropriate—if beautiful—miniatures. No courtiers and castles of fifteenth-century French style had been drawn over a page of simple calligraphy: simple, but precious, for in those words lay fragments of the story of Erik the Learned.

He read quickly, silently, ravenously, translating the words in his mind.

I long for sons to marry the daughters of Simon and Dominic, and I yearn for daughters to marry the sons of my lord and friends. I pray for a wife like Amber or Meg or Ariane, women brave enough to love and strong enough to teach their fierce lords compassion.

It should be enough that my blood lives on in my sister Amber's children, blood joined by that of Duncan, her dark and beloved warrior. Their children will share marriage and estates and babes with those of Simon and Dominic. They will hold and protect this land as their fathers did.

Yet it is not enough.

I want more than my nieces and nephews, my godsons and goddaughters, and my friends' sons fostered in my home. Would to God that I had sons to foster in their homes, daughters to cast melting eyes at foster sons. That is the way lasting alliances are built. That is the way history begins.

No history will begin with me.

I do not know whether to damn the sorceress Serena or damn my Learned self for being unable to escape her. She is woven into my very soul. Would to God I could rip her out and be free to live as other men live, even Learned ones.

Enchantment makes fools of all men.

Especially Erik the Learned.

"Are they forged?" Serena asked when she couldn't take the silence any longer.

His head snapped up. He was still hearing echoes of a name in his mind, the sorceress's name he had known before he could have known it: *Serena.* "What makes you ask that?"

She thought of her grandmother's warning note, but all she said was, "Isn't that why people have things appraised? To find out if they're real?"

Erik smiled thinly. "Most people just want to know what they're worth."

Serena waited.

"I'll have to run some tests," he said.

And he would, for his own pleasure rather than for any personal doubt. The pages were real. He was as certain of it as if he had created them himself.

Then, like ice crystallizing across an autumn pond, freezing everything, came the certainty that he had done just that.

Thirty

"What type of tests?" Serena asked quickly.

Erik wrenched his attention back to the here and now, but still he saw the past so close, so real, like a colored shadow cast by an uncanny light. Or perhaps it was the opposite; the past was real and the present but a colored shadow of the past's vibrant life.

"Nothing destructive." Erik touched the edge of a page as though it was alive, breathing, whispering to his soul. "Script comparisons, text comparisons, technique comparisons, ultraviolet, visual examination of the vellum, that sort of thing. If there's still doubt, I'll take the pages to a lab that can do paint analysis as delicately as a butterfly makes love."

She frowned.

"This lab is very clever about not hurting the original," he reassured her, stroking one page again.

It was the care and the intense restraint of his fingertips touching the vellum that convinced Serena more than any words Erik said. He was a man touching something he cherished. No, loved.

Jealousy snaked through her, startling her. She told herself it was simply her reluctance to share the pages. She didn't quite believe it. But she did believe it would be wonderful to be touched like that, with caring and gentleness and the kind of longing that made breath back up in her throat.

Then she looked at the page that so fascinated Erik. She hadn't sent him a copy of this page, but she had sent one to Warrick. The heavily gilded, deeply complex design covered the full page. It would have shimmered even under thin moonlight. In daylight it was dazzling. By candlelight, it would be beauty and mystery woven together until the page breathed and trembled with life.

"That's my favorite," Serena said softly.

Erik jerked as though he had forgotten he wasn't alone. "The initials?"

She smiled crookedly. "You saw them very quickly."

"Practice," he said, knowing it was only partially true.

"It took me a long time to see the initials," she admitted. "The *E* and the *S* are so heavily intertwined that they're impossible to separate without destroying the pattern. The complexity is both beautiful and intimidating."

"Intimidating?"

"To a weaver, yes. Especially to a child who had seen nothing like it before, except in her dreams."

Slowly he focused on her. "I don't understand."

Her chin lifted in a gesture that was both self-conscious and defiant. "Did I ask you to?"

He hesitated. The shadows under her eyes left by a nearly sleepless night gave them a haunting darkness. "I want to."

"You won't believe me."

"Try me."

Serena looked at Erik's touch resting so carefully on her heritage, her dreams. She closed her eyes and said quickly, "I don't remember the first time I dreamed about that design. Mother was still alive, I know that much. She smiled when I tried to draw it. I couldn't write my own name, yet I was trying to create something so intricate that I couldn't even comprehend it." Serena shrugged and opened her eyes. Erik was watching her. His eyes were as wild and clear as a falcon's. "Anyway, I kept trying until I finally got it right."

"How long did it take you?"

"I finished it the night my grandmother was murdered. The dream I had of it that night was unbearably vivid."

"You dreamed of her death?" he asked sharply.

"No. Crazy laughter, the initials winding around each other like vines, a scream of inhuman pain . . ." She rubbed her arms and looked at the glowing, gold-drenched page. "I woke up sweating. I began drawing. I didn't stop until I had it all."

"How long did it take?"

"I don't know." She smiled raggedly. "Too long, according to Mr. Picky. Sometime into the second night, he started dropping choice morsels on the drafting table to lure me away."

"No crunchy bits?" Erik asked.

She made a sound that could have been a laugh or a throttled cry. "No. Just the juicy ones."

"Sounds irresistible," he said ironically.

"It's the thought that counts." Her voice was as dry as his, but her hands kept trying to rub goose bumps from her arms. "Anyway, I finished the drawing."

He thought over what she was saying and wondered about what she hadn't said.

"The design you dreamed," he said finally, stroking lightly down the margin of the illuminated page where initials were woven together in staggering complexity and beauty. "It was like this?"

"No. It *was* that. Big difference."

"It's not unusual for childhood memories to be very vivid and long-lasting."

She nodded, hesitated, then gave a mental shrug. Maybe he would be able to explain what she never had been able to understand. "I couldn't have seen the page before I dreamed it."

His eyebrows shot up. "Why?"

"G'mom never gave the pages to my mother, never visited mother after she ran away, never spoke to her after she changed her name to Charters. And I never saw G'mom until my own mother was dead."

"Yet you dreamed this page while you were still living with your mother?"

Serena gave him a slanting look. "I told you that you wouldn't believe it." She shifted her shoulders uncomfortably. "Not surprising. I don't want to believe it either. It's . . . eerie." She blew out a breath. "Anyway, it doesn't matter."

Erik wanted to agree with her. He couldn't.

"It might," he said.

"What?"

"It might matter."

Her chin tilted up. "Why?"

"Provenance," he said succinctly. "It's part of any appraisal. You're the only one alive who might have seen these pages in your grandmother's hands."

"Morton Hingham did. Her lawyer."

"Are you certain?"

She hesitated. Her grandmother could have used the safe-deposit box and never told Hingham what was inside. It would have been like her. "No," she said tightly. "So what?"

"To determine provenance, I need to trace the owners of these pages as far back as possible."

"I told you. They were passed down to the firstborn girl of each generation."

"No, you didn't tell me. But it will make my job easier. Who was your grandmother's mother?"

"I don't know."

"Try again."

"I told you. I don't know."

"All right. Who was your grandfather?"

"I don't know."

"Great-grandmother on your mother's side?"

"No."

"Great-grandfather?"

"No."

"Aunts, uncles, anything?"

"No. I'm the last of the female line. Of any line, for all I know."

Erik looked at her fiery hair and violet eyes and was certain she had stood in front of him once before like this, saying almost the same thing: *I am the last of the Silverfells line.*

The pager against his belt vibrated. He reached for it automatically, glanced in the window, and saw Niall's number. His very, very private number, the one even Dana hesitated to use.

"Excuse me," Erik said, reaching behind his waist. "It's urgent or he would have waited for me to call in."

"He?"

"S. K. Niall, one of my bosses."

Erik activated the scrambler, punched the automatic dial button, and waited.

Niall hit the answer button like a starving trout after a fly. "You've got a bogey."

"Down the street?"

"Name of William Wallace, aka Bad Billy. Former Navy. He was bounced out of Drug Enforcement Administration for 'excessive force' about ten years ago. Now he's a more or less licensed private investigator who is rumored to sell his unlicensed talents to the highest bidder. He started out with simple stuff, beating the crap out of deadbeats and stalkers, that sort of thing. Then he got into high-paying work. No proof, but I'm betting he's planted more than his share of trees on both sides of the border."

"Sounds like a real winner."

"Oh, he's cute all right. He usually works with Ed Heller, who's no better than he has to be. We're flying Lapstrake down to Leucadia right now as your backup."

"Divert to Palm Springs."

"Your place?"

"Yes. Don't take on the alarm system. I had some changes made."

"Bugger," Niall muttered. "Last time you nearly fried me."

"Joella still laughs about her handiwork. Next time, call ahead."

"No worries, boyo. When will you be there?"

"We'll leave in a few minutes."

Serena's left eyebrow went up. Erik had been looking right at her when he said "we."

"Stay there," Niall said. "Lapstrake can rent a car and follow you back."

"No. That would tip off the hound."

"What are you planning to do in Palm Springs?"

"Sketch bighorns."

It didn't take Niall long to understand. "Ahhh. All those lovely cliffs. A man could break his neck."

"Unless he was feeling friendly and conversational. Then all he would have to worry about is blisters from hiking in city shoes."

"All right," Niall said after a moment. "But I want the pager switched to GPS. If anything goes sideways, we'll find you from the coordinates."

"Global Positioning System, just like a crashed plane," Erik said dryly. "You really think he's that eager?"

"I don't know what to think until I know who hired him and why."

"Assuming he was hired," Erik said. "Big assumption."

Niall grunted. "Get going. Factoid and his minions are still investigating. If he turns up anything worse, I'll see you in Palm Springs myself."

"Right." Erik punched the END button and put the unit back on his belt.

"Sounds like you have a problem," Serena said.

"Not me. We."

"I don't see any problem."

"That's because you haven't noticed the clown down the street."

"Excuse me?"

"The guy who's sitting in a car admiring the back of his

eyelids while he waits for you to put these pages within his reach."

Serena's mouth firmed. "I have a bad feeling you aren't joking."

"I have a bad feeling you're right."

"I'll rent a new safe-deposit box."

"It would be awful crowded—you, me, my inspection gear, and the pages."

She almost smiled. "I get the point." Then she cursed under her breath. She really didn't want to turn loose those pages, but . . . "Okay, you can take them with you."

"With *us*."

"I have a weaving to finish up."

"You can't finish it if you're dead."

Serena's eyes stared at him in rich shades of twilight. "What are you saying?"

"You believe your grandmother was murdered, right?"

"Yes."

"Why?"

Again she hesitated. Again she saw no real option except to trust the familiar stranger known as Erik North. She opened the drawer of her design table, flipped through a folder containing her grandmother's few papers, and held out the note Lisbeth had written before she died.

Then Serena watched the change come over Erik as he read. He looked up from the paper and pinned her with bleak bird-of-prey eyes. He was furious and didn't care who knew it.

"Shit, lady. You really believe in living dangerously. You should have told me about this first thing."

"What I believe in is handling problems myself."

"So did your grandmother," he shot back, "and look where it got her. Burned alive."

Thirty-one

Still seething over Serena's lack of trust, Erik organized her departure with a few curt orders. Her grandmother had been looking for the missing pages when she was killed. Serena was looking for the missing pages and was now being followed.

It was the kind of simple addition that made his gut clench.

He didn't try to hide that he was loading the big leather portfolio into his own car. In fact, he did everything except light flares to catch the tail's attention.

Not that Erik expected the tail to take his word for it. If he was a pro, he would wait for a while to be sure the house was empty; then he would go through it like a stiff wind, searching for the pages. Or the tail could decide to follow Serena. Then he would simply start driving as soon as they did.

Erik was betting that the man would stay in Leucadia long enough to ransack the house. Probably he had a backup on the job or he had put trackers on their cars so he could catch up later.

It was what Erik had done in the past when he was trailing one of his sister's boyfriends, the one who had stolen the best of Erik's illuminated pages and gone to ground with them. The batteries on the little radio trackers had lasted for several days.

Erik had lasted as long as it took to get the job done.

Making sure the tail had a chance to see every motion, Erik put Serena's small overnight bag in the back of his SUV. Even with the backseats folded flat, there was very little room left for the bag. "Little Betty" was already installed in the vehicle, along with enough yarn to put a fringe around Africa. Then there was Mr. Picky's car carrier to add to the pile. Or underneath the pile, to be precise. Serena said the cat preferred not to watch the world whizzing by. It made him crazy. Then it made him sick.

"I knew it would all fit," Serena said, glancing into the interior.

"You sure you don't want Big Betty?" he asked sardonically.

"I'm sure I do. I'm also sure I won't get her."

She climbed in the passenger side, closed the door, and fastened her seat belt as though she always took off for unknown amounts of time with equally unknown men.

Hell, Erik thought irritably. Maybe she did.

He started to say something surly on the subject. Then he noticed the fine trembling of her fingers as she smoothed back the golden-red fire of her hair. No matter how cool she looked on the outside, on the inside she was flat scared.

It should have made him feel better. It didn't. Having raised his younger sisters, he knew too much about intelligent, independent, just-plain-stubborn women who wanted to do it all themselves. Serena was frightened now, but it would pass. When it did, he would have his hands full.

The thought of having his hands full of Serena Charters sent heat stabbing through his body in time to his quickened heartbeat. The longer he was close to her, the more he wanted to know her. Deeply. Biblically. Repeatedly. He could handle the hormone storm, but the flashes of medieval dream-memory were keeping him off-balance, wary, sniffing the wind like a staghound testing for danger.

He had always believed in a casual way that there were more things on earth than Western rationalism could explain. It only made sense; no single culture could have all the answers for all the ages.

In the same casual way he had always believed that inexplicable things happened to other people, not to him. He was a former college baseball pitcher, a medieval scholar, an illuminator, a hiker, a rock climber, and ninety-five percent a perfectly normal guy.

But having other people's memories wasn't normal, he admitted, climbing into his car and slamming the door. That last five percent could be a real bitch.

"I told you those were lemons, not oranges, on the tree in the backyard," Serena said.

"What are you talking about?"

"You. Sucking on a lemon."

"I'm not."

"You look it."

He gave her two rows of teeth in a carnivorous smile. "Better?"

"Go back to lemons."

When the engine started up, Mr. Picky began an unhappy yowling.

"It's all right, baby," she said soothingly.

She wiggled until she could put her hand between the two seats and poke a finger into his cage. Feline cries of distress turned into purrs.

Erik looked over his shoulder briefly, then looked again, harder. The big cat was sucking on her finger like a kitten. He had a dreamy expression of cat ecstasy on his broad face.

"Some pacifier," Erik said as he wheeled into the street.

"Beats listening to him once he gets wound up. He'll fall asleep soon and I'll get my finger back. Is that the car?"

"Beige Nissan?"

"Yes."

"That's the one. Don't stare at him."

"I was just trying to catch the license plate."

"I already have it."

The Nissan waited perhaps thirty seconds before it did a U-turn and followed.

Silently Erik cursed.

"He's following us," she said.

"I saw."

The Nissan stayed with them until they got on the northbound ramp to I-5. Then their tail turned away.

"Why did he turn around?" she asked.

"Maybe he needs gas."

But Erik doubted it. The tail probably had just wanted to be sure they didn't drop the portfolio off anywhere before they got on the freeway. Now he would go back and search.

Erik hit the accelerator. The vehicle surged forward like a predator after prey. He reached seventy-five miles per hour very quickly. He had bought the Mercedes not only for its agility off-road but for its speed on southern California's freeways.

Serena waited for Erik to keep talking.

He didn't.

"What are you going to do with the license number?" she asked finally.

"I already did it."

"Has anyone ever told you that you could piss off Pollyanna?"

"My sisters. Frequently. What do you think your grandmother meant about forgery?"

Serena's spine stiffened. He wouldn't answer her questions but had the brass to demand her answers. So she gave him the first one that popped onto her tongue. "Go to hell."

"I don't think that's what your grandmother meant."

"She would have if she'd met you."

Erik took a better grip on the steering wheel and his temper. "This isn't a game."

"So you say. But it sure has rules."

"What rules?"

"You ask. I answer. I ask. You don't answer."

"Shit."

"Yeah. Shit."

He glanced aside at her. She didn't notice. She was watching the side mirror.

"Did he follow us?" she asked.

"Not yet."

She let out a relieved breath. "If he's not on the freeway now, we've lost him." She caught Erik's thin smile from the corner of her eye. "Not that easy?"

"He saw me load the pages."

"That could have been a ruse."

His smile widened without becoming a bit warmer. Her grandmother might have screwed up at the end, but she raised a very bottom-line kind of grandkid. "Yeah, it could have. He's probably searching your house right now just to make sure."

"What? Call the police!"

"And tell them what? We're on I-5 headed north and we think someone is burgling your house?"

"Yes!"

"Even if the cops believed us, he'll be gone by the time they get there. The guy isn't new to the game."

"How do you know? Did you recognize him?"

"I sent his plate number to someone I know. A lot of information came back."

"Did he murder my grandmother?" Serena asked starkly.

"That wasn't part of the info."

"What was?"

He started to evade the question. Then he thought better of it. Knowing about Bad Billy might make her more cooperative.

"William Wallace, aka Bad Billy, is a PI up front, but out the back door he's muscle for hire."

"A bodyguard?"

Erik thought of Niall, who had spent some time being a bullet catcher all over the world. "Bad Billy isn't the legitimate kind of bodyguard. He's a cold piece of business. Depending on the price, he'll break your arm or your neck. A real junkyard dog."

"And you think he's after the pages?"

"You have a better reason to explain why he's following you?"

"How did he find out about the pages? I didn't tell anyone but you and the House of Warrick."

"Don't look at me. If I wanted your arm or your neck, I'd have it."

Serena didn't argue that. She couldn't. It was the only reason she was with him right now. She could trust him not to kill her.

At least, not before the Book of the Learned was found.

Even if her emotions cringed at the thought of Erik as a murderer, her intelligence told her flatly that she had to follow her grandmother's advice: Don't trust any man.

"Warrick didn't even think the pages were real," Serena pointed out, "so why would the House of Warrick hire a thug to watch me?"

Thirty-two

"I didn't say the House of Warrick hired anyone," Erik said carefully.

Except Rarities, of course, and he hadn't said one damned word about it. He would keep his mouth shut on that subject until Serena trusted him in more ways than with her elegant neck.

The longer he knew her, the more certain he was that the shit would hit the stratosphere when she found out he was, technically speaking, Warrick's representative.

"But no one else knew about the pages," Serena protested. "Who else could it have been?"

"Whoever gave you the pages knew."

"Hingham."

"Who?" Erik asked, even though he already knew.

"Morton Hingham, my grandmother's lawyer."

"Big office?"

"Small. Just a secretary-receptionist."

"Who meets friends for lunch and talks about families, husbands, boyfriends, babies, and work."

"A client's business is confidential."

"Yeah, it sure is supposed to be."

Serena thought of the blue-haired, lace-collared gentlewoman who was Hingham's secretary and shook her head. "I'm not buying it."

"You don't have to. There are other possibilities." The mail room of a big auction house, for instance. Though he knew already how she had sent the copies, he wasn't supposed to know. Besides, it never hurt to ask. Sometimes the answer changed in revealing ways. "How did you get the pages to Warrick?"

"Delivery service."

"To his home in Palm Desert?"

"No. To the House of Warrick in Manhattan."

"Where the mail room sorts all packages, security opens them, and then passes them—open, mind you—all the way to whoever is supposed to get them. Then that person asks other people for an opinion, and they talk to other people in the business, and in about two hours max the news of some fine sheets of Insular Celtic manuscript goes coast to coast and continent to continent."

"Surely the House of Warrick has more fabulous items come in every day."

"Possibly, but not through the mail room."

She compressed her lips. "But illuminated manuscripts are such a scholarly, narrow field. I can't imagine them attracting that kind of wide interest."

Erik shot her a fast look of disbelief before he gave his full attention back to the multilane, high-speed shouldering match known as Interstate 5.

"Money attracts wide interest," he said succinctly. "The equivalent of a medieval shopping list on a ragged piece of vellum can go at auction for thousands of dollars. A single illuminated leaf can go for tens of thousands. The *Hours of Saint-Lô* sold for 3.6 million dollars and change, and that was years ago. A lavish fifteenth-century French manuscript sold for more than five million about the same time as the *Hours*."

"Five million dollars . . ." Serena let her breath out. "For a book nobody has ever heard of."

"That's the whole point. Scarcity drives price. So does fashion. Right now, all things Celtic are in fashion, and therefore in unusual demand."

"But all I have is four leaves, not a whole book."

He thought of his own collection, where there were a few leaves of the Book of the Learned, plus copies of every page he had been able to trace through the marketplace. Then he thought of her grandmother's tantalizing warning: *If you decide to go after your heritage . . .*

The note implied that the whole book was intact except for whatever pages had been lost through the centuries. Even if only half was left, the idea of such a book was literally breathtaking. He wondered if Warrick knew. Then he thought about the shrewd old man and decided he probably knew. If he didn't, he would soon. One way or another, Warrick found out everything that went on in the illuminated manuscript trade.

Gently Serena eased her fingertip from Picky's sandpaper tongue. He kept on sleeping. "What would the whole Book of the Learned be worth?" she asked, wiping her finger idly on her jeans.

"More than the *Hours of Saint-Lô*. A hell of a lot more." His voice was neutral. "If they prove to be real, those pages you have are among the rarest of the rare. Illuminated pages, much less whole manuscripts, from the first half of twelfth-century Britain are very unusual. In Britain, unlike what became known as France, the twelfth century was a time of political and social consolidation rather than surplus wealth, and surplus wealth is what drives the creation of art."

"So my pages are unusual even for their own time?"

"As far as we know, yes. Especially in the choice of an illuminating style that was several centuries old at that time. But tomorrow someone could go into Great-granny's old linen chest and pull out something that would put everything we have to shame. If it's real." Erik's voice was sardonic. "Great-granny's old linen chest has a way of coughing up some clever boy's new forgeries."

Serena wanted to ask about the validity of her own pages again. She didn't. There wasn't any point. Erik didn't know anything more about them now than he had after he looked at them for the first time.

"So you think that lots of people might know about my pages," she said.

"Word of something new, Insular Celtic, and of that quality would go through the collecting world like a tornado through a trailer park. I'll bet everybody who is anybody is pulling strings and passing bribes to get a look at your pages."

She frowned. "Not much help there. Anybody could have sicced that junkyard dog on us."

"Yeah."

"So how do we find out who did?"

"When the right time comes, I'll ask him myself."

She started to laugh, then realized he wasn't joking. "That's ridiculous. It could be dangerous."

"So is driving fender-to-fender at eighty miles an hour. Just part of living in the twenty-first century."

He switched lanes while the speedometer spiked to the other side of ninety. He held the pedal down even after he had passed the gravel truck that was spewing seventy-five-mile-an-hour stones from both uncovered trailers.

He checked the mirrors. No one in the pack of cars behind him sped up suddenly to keep him in sight. So far, so good. In another mile or so, he would slow down to the speed limit and see if anything back there *didn't* want to pass him.

"I can't ask you to deal with a man who is known to be violent," Serena said.

"You didn't. I volunteered."

"But I can't afford to hire—"

"Forget it," he cut in. "I would pay to spend time—a lot of it—with those pages. This way we both get something we want."

She glanced in the side mirror. There were a few beige cars on the road. None of them were close enough to read the license plate. But then, Erik was driving like his tires were on fire. At this speed, it was hard to read anything smaller than a billboard.

"What about your boss?" she asked after a time.

Erik blinked, wondering where her agile, all-too-clever mind had led her. He lifted his foot and slowed to the speed limit. It felt like he was crawling. "What about my boss?" he asked cautiously.

"Won't he be upset that you're spending time on a project that has nothing to do with work?"

"I'm a consultant. My time is pretty much my own." All true, as far as it went. It just didn't go far enough to cover the connection between the House of Warrick, Rarities Unlimited, and Erik North. Not that it mattered; there was no conflict between what Rarities wanted and what Serena needed. But he didn't expect her to see it that way until she trusted him. "Besides, my other boss is interested in manuscripts."

"He is?"

"She is. Dana Gaynor."

Serena watched a black Ferrari doing about Mach 1 down the slow lane to get around them, but she didn't really see the sports car. She was trying to figure out the connections. "What kind of business do your bosses have? Auction house? Gallery? Museum?"

"No. They own the controlling interest in Rarities Unlimited."

"What's that?"

"Never heard of it?"

She shook her head, then paused. "Wait. Didn't I read something about Rarities a few months back? Someone had looted a site in the Yucatán, smuggled some gold artifacts to the United States, and someone from Rarities Unlimited found them and sent them back to Mexico."

"Close enough."

Actually it had been Shane Tannahill, gold collector extraordinaire, who had brought Rarities in on that one. People were always offering to sell him hot gold. They assumed that anyone who owned a casino was corrupt and wouldn't give a damn about provenance. Shane was careful to reinforce that impression. He wanted people to look at him and assume the worst.

In some cases it was true.

"Is that what Rarities does?" Serena asked. "Police the artifact trade?"

"The people at Rarities Unlimited buy, sell, protect, and appraise art and artifacts. If you want to sell something, but your insurance company doesn't want you to haul it from dealer to dealer and the best dealers don't want to come to you, we have a clean room at Rarities. You bring your goods, we appraise everything if you want, and we send out invitations. Everyone involved knows there won't be any robbery or rip-off under the roof of Rarities Unlimited."

"Bet Rarities charges a hefty fee," she said.

"Of course. It's not called Charities Unlimited. The owners, Niall and Dana, make a damn good living. They earn it, too. Twenty-four/seven, fifty-two weeks a year."

Serena shrugged, not impressed. Long hours were the price of self-employment. "So if I wanted to sell my pages, I could use Rarities as a go-between?"

Adrenaline kicked through Erik at the possibility that the pages might be for sale. Maybe Warrick wouldn't want all of them, especially if he believed they were frauds. Or maybe he was just trying to drive the price down. It was shark-eat-shark in the art trade.

"Yes. Do you want to sell?"

"No," she said instantly. "But you say that Rarities isn't an auction house?"

He loosened his grip on the steering wheel. It was just as well the pages weren't for sale. If they had been, he would have been obligated to negotiate for Warrick to purchase them. Any man who condemned those pages as forgeries on first glance didn't deserve to have them. Unless, of course, the canny Warrick knew something no one else did.

Thinking about that possibility put a lemon-sucking look back on Erik's face.

"Selling is just one service Rarities offers," he said. "Same for protection. If you have a valuable shipment, we'll courier it. If you have something to sell, we'll buy it from you or find someone who wants to. Rarities has an extensive client 'wish list.' If we find a match, we buy the item for our client."

"Buy, sell, appraise, protect." Serena ticked off each word on her fingers. "Reputation must be an important business asset for you."

"It is for anyone—appraiser, gallery owner, dealer, whatever. If you have a reputation for being dishonest, your client list reflects that. So do your sales. If you have a reputation for being incompetent, the goods you're offered reflect that."

"I can't believe the art and artifact business is made up entirely of scholars and saints," she said bluntly.

"It isn't. Getting the best price possible is part of the game. Lying or stealing to get your price isn't." Erik's tawny eyes flicked to the mirrors. Except for the slate-green baby pickup that had appeared a few minutes ago, everybody was speeding around the sedately moving Mercedes. A guy doing the speed limit was passed by anything on wheels, including seventy-year-old grannies driving thirty-year-old beaters. "Making each object look as good as possible is allowed," he continued. "Secret restoration isn't. Taking the last three sales as adequate provenance for an object is allowed. Ignoring dubious provenance isn't."

"Who enforces the rules?"

"The people in the business, mostly. If the error is bad enough, various law enforcement types take care of it. Why? You thinking about breaking some rules?"

"No. I just want to know what they are and if they apply to everybody in the game."

He smiled rather grimly. "I'll bet you never believed in Santa Claus, either."

"Did you?"

"Sure."

"And then you compared the opening of the average suburban chimney to the width of the average fat man's ass and made up your own mind."

He gave a crack of laughter. "How did you know?"

"You strike me as a bottom-line kind of man."

He thought of the twelfth-century pages that haunted him, the image of a sorceress with red-gold hair and violet eyes, and the pain of a man he had never met, never could have met, a man who had lived nearly a thousand years before.

Yet Erik North had his medieval namesake's precise handwriting, even down to the way he lifted quill from vellum with a slight upward flourish to the right. He was beginning to suspect that he had the other Erik's dreams, too, the colored shadow of a dead man's memories and emotions.

He shoved the uncomfortable thought aside. He would stick with the ninety-five percent of himself that was boringly normal.

He would have felt better about the decision if he hadn't sensed laughter ringing down through the centuries, hadn't seen Erik the Learned with his head thrown back and his tawny, bird-of-prey eyes alight with amusement at sharing the folly of another Erik as arrogant and selectively blind as himself.

Thirty-three

"The house is clean," Wallace said into his cell phone. "Security a first-grader could get through. No alarm system. No wonder she locked everything in her van."

"So she has it with her."

"I followed them to the freeway. Ed picked them up on the tracker a few minutes later. Still on the freeway. They didn't have time to stop off at a safe-deposit box."

"Stay with them."

"You still want both of us on it?"

"Yes."

"I could use some more men."

"You're being paid well enough right now for four men. Hire someone if you like, but don't bill me."

"But—"

Wallace was talking to himself. The client had already hung up. Nor could Wallace call back. He had tried tracing the number the first time the client hired him two years ago. He hadn't succeeded then. He hadn't succeeded at any time since.

But the money came in on time, and for some jobs it came from overseas, untraceable even for the IRS.

He didn't know if his client was male, female, or walked on all fours; voice distorters had come a long way since the first ones. These days it took a pro to tell when one was being used. Wallace was a pro. So he stayed with the odds and thought of his client as a man. If it had been a divorce case, he would have gone with a woman.

Wallace stuck a lump of chewing tobacco into his cheek and drove toward the freeway. He and his partner were getting triple time plus expenses. If the mysterious client wanted them to baby-sit at those rates, they would baby-sit. When it got down to the real job, the rates would go up. That was when he would earn every dime of whatever fee he negotiated.

He was looking forward to it. Something about blood had always given him a hard-on like nothing else—even sex. He didn't know why. He didn't care. The rush was worth all the boredom that came in between.

Thirty-four

Niall could have watched the transaction from one of the plush "viewing rooms" on the ground floor, which featured a one-way window into each clean room for those who didn't trust anything except their own eyes. He preferred watching from his office. The view was much better. There were two walls of flat-screen color monitors that gave him a look at everything on Rarities Unlimited's grounds except Dana's private quarters. So far, she had refused to allow any fiber-optic cameras into her small home, saying that if he couldn't protect her without spying on her, then she would bloody well just live dangerously.

At the moment, she was quite safe. She was with Risa Sheridan in the clean room, explaining to a client why the gold necklace his wife had picked up at Quartzite, Arizona's huge annual outdoor flea market was not only quite valuable but was probably part of a museum collection that had been stolen three years ago.

Niall dialed up the audio and settled in to listen. And watch. Risa, like Dana, was always worth watching. It was like seeing two wolves in drag stroll through a field of lambs, picking out the next meal.

". . . technique is old, yes," the unhappy client said, "but today's jewelers often imitate ancient techniques, don't they?"

"They're called replicas," Risa drawled. "Some of them are quite well done. If they're sold as ancient goods, then we call them forgeries. This isn't one of them."

"How can you be so sure?"

Dana knew Risa well enough to understand the meaning of the casual flick of her hand through her short black hair. Risa was getting tired of telling the stubborn man with the Hollywood haircut what he had already suspected: his wife's flea market coup wasn't legally theirs, so it wasn't going to make them rich.

"McCoy," Dana murmured into the nearly invisible lapel mike she always wore into a clean room for just these awkward moments.

"Coming up," Niall answered. He swiveled, hit an intercom button, and said, "Factoid. Now."

"Yo," came the puffing answer.

"You sound like you just ran upstairs."

McCoy made a guilty sound. "I was just, uh, checking around the departments."

"How's Gretchen?"

"Hot, man. *Hot.*"

"Tie it in a knot. Dana's in the number two clean room. She needs you."

"I'm there."

Niall watched Dana touch her left ear lightly and knew that McCoy had gotten through on her ear bug. He heard her request the Buyer Beware database, reference stolen gold jewelry, around fourth-century B.C., Asia Minor or more probably Greece, quite possibly the site known as Patikapaion. While she spelled out the last for McCoy, Niall switched his attention back to Risa.

She was closing in for the kill.

". . . the silk cord holding the gold beads is almost certainly more recent than my tentative date of fourth century B.C.," Risa's low voice continued. "The terminals on the necklace, what you call the fastenings, are a later addition. Though some attempt was made to match gold alloys, it wasn't entirely successful. If you doubt me, we'll test the fastenings and the beads, and tell you where the gold for each likely originated. It won't be the same place."

The man gave her a look that suggested he wasn't interested in testing anything.

"The beads," she said, "aren't modern but are, except for the fourth from the left, all of the same age and origin. If you'll look at the screen to your left again, I'll show you how I reached this conclusion. Under magnification"—she zoomed in on the piece with the computer-cum-camera that was part of the clean room's services—"you can see the wear pattern quite clearly, especially on the alternating decorated beads. The filigree is almost smooth. These beads are made of a soft, nearly pure gold and have rubbed against each other for a long, long time."

He grunted.

"Whoever added that one bead was probably the same person who added the fastenings," she continued. "The gold alloy looks quite similar. Again, there are tests to determine if the gold came from the same mine as the rest of the beads. We don't have a way to determine the age of gold, as I explained earlier. At this point, I'm confident that you have valid beads, except for one, and terminals—fastenings—of frankly dubious quality."

The man said something unpleasant under his breath. "For as much as you're charging for the appraisal, I'd expected something more, uh . . ."

"Sympathetic?" she supplied in a smoky drawl.

He shrugged and tucked his tie into his charcoal wool suit coat with the automatic gesture of a man who has spent a lot of time dressed for success. "Yeah, I guess so."

"Rarities sets the fees," Risa said. "I'm merely an outside

consultant. I have no financial interest whatsoever in anything but the truth."

"Yeah, well, you get a fucking gold star in your file for this one, and I get hosed."

"That's the nature of flea markets." Risa's smile told him that she no more believed the flea market story than he did. "People get hosed regularly in those places. I'm sorry you were one of them."

Neither one of them believed that, either.

"Ah, there we are," Dana said, pointing to another of the flat screens that circled the room. "This is Rarities Unlimited's own compilation of all stolen art and artifacts, both private and public."

The picture changed dizzyingly as it cycled through a series of necklaces made up only of gold beads. Each photo was numbered in the lower right-hand corner. Risa watched closely.

"Seventeen," she said.

"Zoom in," Dana said softly. "Split screen to show Mr. Morrison's necklace as well."

As McCoy manipulated the electronics, a picture of a string of golden beads filled half the screen. When Morrison's necklace was added to the other side, it was nearly a mirror image.

Even in the security room, Niall's untrained eye could see that the beads in the necklace in the clean room and the necklace in the database matched. Well, almost matched. One bead was a clinker.

"Startling similarity, wouldn't you say?" Dana asked mildly.

"That necklace doesn't have fastenings," Morrison pointed out.

"And it's missing a bead," Risa said. "Remove the later additions from your necklace and you have identity, not similarity."

"Data," Dana said into her mike.

Factoid talked into her ear.

"The necklace on the left used to be in the Hermitage," Dana said, listening as she talked. "When they were updating their catalogues recently, they discovered it was missing."

"Are you suggesting I stole it?" Morrison asked angrily.

"No. I am suggesting that you are in possession of a piece of stolen art whose rightful owner is one of Russia's foremost national museums." Dana's voice was an even alto that could be soothing or acid, whichever she thought would get the job done. Right now she was going for soothing. "If you would like Rarities to broker the return of the necklace, we will waive our appraisal fee. You will owe us nothing. In return, you will undoubtedly get a letter of appreciation from several international art organizations. A gold star, as you put it."

"No thanks." He reached for the necklace. "I'll try my luck somewhere else."

Risa smiled cynically. She had expected his reaction. Once you got beyond the ivory towers of universities, the art market was just that: a market.

"Your privilege," Dana said. "Naturally, it is our obligation to report to the proper authorities the presence of what we believe to be a stolen cultural treasure in the United States."

"Wait just a fucking minute!" he snarled. "You promised me confidentiality. I paid a fucking fortune to get you to—"

Niall didn't wait to hear any more. He was out of his office and opening the door to the clean room in twenty seconds.

". . . unless we discovered that the goods were listed as stolen, yes," Dana was saying when Niall opened the door. She wasn't surprised at his sudden appearance. Niall's rule of thumb was "Three fucks and you're out." Morrison had used up his quota, and a few more before Niall walked in. Dana had no objection to the language itself, but it was a good indicator of a frayed temper. "The policy of Rarities Unlimited was spelled out quite clearly in the contract you signed before we agreed to appraise your piece. If you need to refresh your memory, we'll give you another copy on your way out."

"But it's just a fucking necklace!"

"You're confusing this with the golden bells and jade rings the ancient Chinese used," Risa said blandly. "As an aid to sexual intercourse, they were quite valued."

"What are you talking about?" Morrison yelped.

"Jewelry used to enhance a man's erectile function," Dana said in an acid tone. "Fucking jewelry, as you described it."

Niall bit the inside of his cheeks so that he wouldn't laugh out loud. "Do we have a problem here, Ms. Gaynor?" he asked.

"I don't believe so. Mr. Morrison was just leaving with his necklace."

"I'll stop payment on my check!"

Dana shrugged. "Whatever you wish. We have lawyers on retainer. They might as well do something to earn their money." She looked at Niall. "Did the Louis XIV cabinet arrive?"

"We're uncrating it in the number four clean room right now."

"Excellent." She turned to Risa. "As always, a pleasure. I'd appreciate having your written appraisal as soon as possible. Whenever you want to review the tapes and select individual frames to include as photos in your report, let—"

"Tapes? Photos?" Morrison asked loudly. "What the hell are—"

"It's in the contract you signed," Niall cut in. "No images taken by Rarities will be used for publication without your written permission. The appraisal isn't for publication. It's for our files and yours. It will be a four-color beauty worthy of framing."

Morrison looked at the necklace like it was a snake. He held a losing hand and knew it. He might possibly sell the necklace before bureaucratic wheels turned him into roadkill, but he doubted it. Time to cut his losses and find another game.

"Fuck it," he said. "Keep the necklace. You want the name of the guy that sold it to me?"

"We're always interested in provenance," Dana said, her voice creamy again.

"Yeah, I'll just bet you are. Any chance of a finder's fee for me on this one?"

"We'll do our best to secure one. My office is free at the moment. Would you care for coffee or something stronger?"

With a muttered curse, Morrison followed Dana out of the clean room. His voice floated back, telling about a high-stakes poker game where cash, gems, and fancy jewelry were all part of the pot. The words *flea market* and *wife* weren't part of the conversation.

Risa watched Morrison stalk out of sight, enjoying every bit of it. Dana was one of the few people on earth Risa really respected. Niall was another.

Niall saw her X-rated lips turn up in a small smile. "What?" he said. "You've seen Dana in action before."

"Always a pleasure, but that's not why I'm smiling."

"Oh?"

"I thought I recognized Morrison. He's a regular at the Golden Fleece's version of your clean rooms."

Niall thought of Shane Tannahill's very private, very secure rooms on the top floor of the Golden Fleece. The rooms were rented out to people who didn't want to gamble in the noisy fishbowl of the casino's public rooms. "High roller?"

"Yes. Shane even plays poker with him occasionally."

"Morrison sure wasn't wearing his poker face today."

"He didn't know Dana was playing."

Niall's smile flashed wolfishly. "Live and learn."

Thirty-five

Serena stood in a guest room on the second floor of Erik North's bemusing castle. The view of the street was partially blocked by a blazing riot of bougainvillea, but she could see enough. Too much, actually.

"He's still out there," she said unhappily.

Erik didn't need to look over her shoulder to know what she was talking about. The green baby pickup had indeed followed them off the freeway, up the sand-scoured four-lane highway to the edge of the city, through the illogical maze of residential streets in old Palm Springs, and right up to the gate of his home.

"You want a different room?" he asked.

"One without a view of the street?"

"Yeah."

"If you wouldn't mind . . ."

He grabbed her bag off the bed. "Follow me."

She walked behind him, trying not to admire the flexed strength of his bare forearm holding her bag, his easy stride, and the fit of his faded jeans. Something about him made her palms tingle, and that made her feel like rubbing something—or biting it. It wasn't a feeling she liked or knew how to handle, because she had never had it before she met Erik.

When Picky began to wind around her feet, more than a little edgy and demanding in his new surroundings, she was glad of the excuse to pick him up. He allowed her seventeen seconds of adoration, then leaped out of her arms to continue exploring the house.

"How about this one?" Erik asked.

She looked at the open, sunny room with its baronial furnishings, high ceiling, and brass ceiling fan. The bedspread on the huge, raised bed was a machine-made tapestry that had once been jewel-toned but had faded over the years to a quiet kind of radiance. The rug was an old kilim with its hallmark slit-weave technique, which resulted in designs shaped like diamonds or triangles and diagonal stair steps marching across the center. The rug's yellow, red, green, and blue-black colors were also faded, yet still vibrant.

"Perfect," she said simply.

"How do you know? You haven't even looked out the windows."

Guiltily her head snapped up from studying the beautiful old handwoven rug. "I'm sure the view will be—" Her words stopped when she looked out the windows that took up most of the west wall. "Oh, the mountains! That's Dry Falls, isn't it?"

He smiled. "Especially this winter. We've hardly had enough rain to make a drool line down the stone cliff."

After a few moments Serena looked away from the view of her favorite mountains. The subtle signs of habitation that she had missed on her first survey of the room now came out clearly: sketches tacked on a big bulletin board near the closet door, several electronic charging cradles plugged in near the dresser, a portable computer humming quietly to itself on a bedside table that was also a desk, and a book detailing medieval designs open on a second bedside table.

"This is your room," she realized. "I can't take it."

"Don't worry, I had the housekeeper come in for a fast lick this morning after I left. Everything's clean, including the sheets."

"That's not what I meant. I can't move you out of your own room."

"You aren't. I am."

"But—"

"It will save me sneaking through your bedroom while you're asleep—"

"Sneaking—" she began hotly.

"—to check on our tail," Erik continued, ignoring her interruption. "The guest room has the best view of the street in the whole house. Besides, my bedroom is big enough to set up your loom. Little Betty would be a real squeeze in the other room."

She took a breath to argue, but the thought of having some stranger peering through her bedroom window made her skin crawl. "Let's go back to Plan A."

"The one where you stay at a motel?"

"Yes."

"Even with adjoining rooms, we'll be a lot more crowded there than we are here."

"Adjoining rooms. *We*. What are you talking about?"

"Watching your back while you watch mine. We're sticking together, Serena. Two have a better chance playing this game than one, and the best chance of all is to stay here. I have a good security system, a high wall, and an attack cuckoo."

She started to argue and found herself laughing instead. "Attack cuckoo. My God. We'd be better off whacking the guy over his head with my loom."

Erik grinned. "Good idea. Like I said, we'll have a better chance if we stay together."

She didn't look convinced.

He put his hands on his hips. "Look. If I was going to hurt you or jump on you, I'd have done it already. Can you say the same for the guy out there?"

"No."

"Then what's the problem here?"

The problem was that Serena was beginning to want to jump on Erik, but she wasn't about to say that out loud. She didn't even like thinking it. Yet there it was, as plain as the tingling in her palms and the heat growing in the pit of her stomach.

"No problem," she said through her teeth. "Let's get the loom tightened before the threads go completely wonky. I'll settle down once I have something to do with my hands."

He had a suggestion or two about that, but kept his mouth shut. Until her loom was set up, she could still change her mind and bolt, taking the pages with her. He didn't want that. He was dying to really examine them.

When he heard his own thought, he winced. *Dying to* wasn't a happy description at the moment, especially with some thug parked on the street just outside the gate.

Factoid, where the hell are those police reports on Ellis Weaver's murder?

Thirty-six

As soon as Serena began weaving, Erik took his computer to the guest room, plugged it in again, and started hunting for new additions. Even though McCoy hadn't called, he might have left something in the file.

He had.

"Thank you, O gods of geekdom," Erik muttered.

He called up the Book of the Learned file, turned the audio down to zilch—Factoid's running commentary tended to be loud and often obscene—and started reading about the night Ellis Weaver died.

The police work was about what he would expect of county cops whose major duties consisted of rousting prostitutes, scraping up human roadkill, and handcuffing mouthy drunks. Even if the cop work had been of the highest order, by the time the county fire truck emptied its tank and hosed down the smoking ruins of the cabin, there wasn't much evidence left to collect.

What they had found was gruesome. Enough remained of Serena's grandmother to prove in living color that a human being had burned to death. It was all there in the video file, the spine arched backward in death, the odd shreds of flesh or clothing that had escaped complete annihilation, the feeling of terrible screams echoing from the charred, open jaw.

Erik took a few deep breaths and let them out. He had seen autopsy reports and crime-scene photos before, but the grisly ones still turned his stomach. He forced himself to focus on the pages of written reports detailing evidence collected at the crime scene.

There wasn't much real evidence. Tire tracks leading in and out on the dirt road and footprints around the cabin . . . yeah, there were lots and lots of them. Every county cop with a set of wheels and an hour to kill had driven up the road to offer his professional opinion on what had happened. The fire crew had left tracks and puddles all over the place. The arson investigation team had been more delicate, but only after they finished cussing out everyone who had messed up the scene in the first place.

The closest thing to a neighbor was Jolly Barnes, a hermit who lived a half mile down the road. He hadn't heard or seen anything, because he had spent the night the way he always did—stinking drunk. Ellis Weaver didn't have any friends to question. There wasn't a lover, husband, ex-husband, or Peeping Tom. There was nothing worth stealing inside the cabin. No TV, no computer, no fancy electronics of any kind because there was no electricity. Ellis Weaver's idea of cash on hand had been a dish of small change and a few crumpled dollar bills. The truck she drove was older than most high school graduates.

The cops had tried. The investigator assigned to the case had made the rounds of all the grungy bars, sun-hammered trailer parks, hobo campgrounds, and biker hangouts. A handful of people had heard about the death. No one looked guilty. No one gave a damn. No one had any idea why anyone would want to fry some old lady who lived alone. She hadn't bothered anyone. They hadn't bothered her. End of interview.

There had been no blind phone calls to the sheriff's office hinting at a possible motive or suspect. No drunken bragging at any of the bars. No pissed-off girlfriend turning in an abusive boyfriend who just happened to like burning grannies. No informant pointing the way for an investigator to follow. No guilt-wracked amphetamine freak walking in to confess. Dead end.

After several weeks, fresher crimes claimed the attention of the overworked sheriff's department. Ellis Weaver's file remained open, but the conclusion wasn't likely to change: Death by homemade napalm bombs of one old lady at the hands of person or persons unknown. There hadn't been a crime like it before in the county. There hadn't been one like it since.

Erik looked out the window where the little pickup gleamed beneath a trail of moonlight and wondered if the man carried a box of soap flakes and a spare can of gas in the trunk.

Thirty-seven

Niall pushed back from his desk and stretched hard enough to make his tendons pop. A quick scan of all the screens showed that Rarities Unlimited was buttoned up for the night, except for the International Division. The people there went twenty-four hours a day. But that was his second in command's problem; Ruben Valenzuela was in charge of overnight security.

After another glance at the screens, Niall lifted his worn leather jacket off the back of his chair. If he hurried, he might get to Dana's kitchen before she added too much pepper oil to the stir-fry. She was always trying to get even for the nuclear curries he prepared.

The phone rang. It was his private line. Not his most private one, but not a line that many people had a number for.

"Yeah?" Niall said.

"Tannahill here. Sheridan isn't answering her unit."

"You want me to cry now or later?"

"I want you to tell me where she is."

"Flea-marketing."

There was a faint click from Shane's end of the line. Experience told Niall that the other man was walking his pen over his hand, and the click came from solid gold pen meeting solid gold Celtic ring. Niall wished he could watch the process. No matter how many times Niall tried the pen-walking trick, the damned thing kept leaping to the floor.

"Upscale fleas, I trust," Shane said.

"Museums."

Shane grunted. "Any news on a nice nearly solid gold illuminated manuscript page for my casino?"

"What kind of news are you looking for?"

"Price."

The laconic answer made Niall grin. He had only played poker with Shane once. It had been a learning experience. One of the things he had learned was how Shane had survived after he told his overbearing daddy to take his billions and shove them where the sun don't shine.

"The only one I know about isn't for sale," Niall said.

"Sooner or later, everything is for sale."

"Not this. Not today."

"When it is, call me."

"Norman Warrick gets the first call. If he doesn't want the pages or can't afford them, we'll let you know."

"What does the old buzzard want with that page among all the others? Besides, he likes fifteenth-century French stuff."

Silently Niall noted that Shane obviously had heard in fair detail about the manuscript pages that Serena Charters had. "I didn't ask. He didn't offer."

"You're acting as his go-between?"

"Not me. Erik North."

"What else can you tell me?"

"I'm hungry and Dana is cooking without my supervision."

There was silence at the other end, then the *click* that said

Shane had quit playing with the pen and had flipped it onto his palm.

"You're not the only one who knows about the pages," Shane said.

Niall's eyes narrowed. "Besides you, is there anyone in particular you want to talk about?"

"Not yet. But if Serena Charters was hoping to keep her pages quiet, she shouldn't have sent them through the House of Warrick's mail room."

"What else do you hear?"

"The pages are forgeries. The pages are Nazi loot. The pages are a local history of local political alliances. The pages are from a twelfth-century alchemy text and contain the secret to eternal life."

"Oh, Christ Jesus. We'll be ass-deep in geriatric millionaires."

"Young billionaires, too."

"Don't tell me you believe that crap."

"I believe that initial page is a fantastic example of Insular Celtic gold illumination. I believe that all the pages came from something that Erik North refers to as the Book of the Learned. I believe that Ellis Weaver's murder had something to do with—"

"You got into our files," Niall cut in angrily.

"—those pages," Shane continued without a pause. "I *know* I want that illuminated carpet page with the intertwined initials for the Golden Fleece's collection."

"How did you get in our files." It was a demand, not a question.

"McCoy is very good, but he isn't God."

"And you are?"

"No, but my daddy dearest wrote the software. He knows where all the trapdoors are hidden and how to open them. He made sure I learned even when I wanted to be out playing hockey in his very own private stadium."

"I'm switching software."

"To what?"

Niall snarled some words under his breath. There was nothing even half as good on the software market and both men knew it.

"I'll make you a deal," Shane said. "I'll tell McCoy how I got in your computer system if you'll guarantee that I'm first in line for those pages."

"I'd love to. I won't. It's called integrity, a concept you have at least a nodding acquaintance with. My name is on the contract with the House of Warrick and Rarities Unlimited."

"You think old man Warrick's a pillar of honesty?"

"I think he's a pillar of shit. What does that have to do with it?"

"Let me know if you change your mind."

"I won't."

"Warrick would sell you out in a nanosecond."

"Tell me something I don't know."

"You're a good man, S. K. Niall. Too damn good for this world."

Niall snickered. "Right, mate. I'm a regular fairy godmother blowing sparkling stuff out my arse."

Shane laughed once, roughly, then said, "There's something ugly oozing around those pages. Watch your back."

Before Niall could ask what he meant, Shane hung up. Niall looked at the phone, thought about dialing up Shane again, and decided against it. If the gambler had anything concrete, he would share it.

All the same, Niall didn't dismiss what Shane had said. Both men came from a long line of people who respected hunches, luck, and things that go bump in the night. Niall also respected Shane Tannahill for other reasons, one of which was that Shane had what every successful gambler had: a way of understanding people, cards, and circumstances that went beyond the rational surface of probability and odds.

Hunches, luck, and things that go bump in the night.

There's something ugly oozing around those pages.

As Niall stared out at the sea of lights and the overarching darkness that was Los Angeles, he decided to tackle Dana again on the subject of security cameras in her home. This time he would be a gentleman and a scholar about it. He would give her a choice.

She could live with cameras or she could live with him.

Thirty-eight

Serena didn't know what time it was when she realized that a phone was ringing at her bedside. She was so tired from throwing the shuttle, switching heddles and bobbins, and beating down the weft that she ached from her feet to the top of her head. She had only meant to lie down for a minute and stretch out the kinks. She had fallen asleep lying across the bed, with her scarf covering her eyes.

And now her stomach was growling.

So was the phone.

Sighing, stretching, shaking out the fatigue, she got up, settled the scarf around her neck, and reached for the phone. The instant her fingers plucked the unit from the charging cradle, she realized she wasn't at home.

"Er, North residence," she said.

"Where's Erik?" asked a brusque male voice.

"Who's calling, please?" Serena said in her most pleasant receptionist-dragon voice. Not for nothing had she paid her way through the early years of weaving as an office temp.

"S. K. Niall."

"Oh. His boss."

"One of them. Are you Serena Charters?"

"Yes."

"Where's Erik?" Niall asked again.

"I don't know. I was weaving and when I weave, the world goes away. I'm sure he's around here somewhere."

"Try his tower."

"Tower?"

At the other end of the line, Niall sighed. Obviously Erik had been correct: Serena needed a keeper. "His studio. On the top floor. Where are you now?"

"His bedroom." When Serena heard her own words, she winced and added hastily, "The guest room looks out on the street and the guy out there was looking in so Erik gave me his room."

Niall digested that. "Right. Go to the hall, turn right, go through the living room, take the hallway off the kitchen that looks like it leads to a pantry, open the door, climb the stairs, and bang on Erik's head until he puts down the damned quill or bitty little paintbrush and pays attention to you."

"What about if I just yell from here for him to pick up the phone?"

"He'll ignore you the same way he did the phone. When he's working, he's impossible."

"I resemble that remark."

"I wasn't going to point it out, but since you did, it's only polite that I agree."

Serena snickered and decided she might like Erik's boss. "Okay, I'm walking out the door and turning right . . ."

She got lost once, but only because Niall hadn't counted the coat closet as a door on the way to the kitchen. Soon she was climbing a lovely old spiral staircase up to the broad turret room that had looked so odd from the street. The door at the top of the stairs was open. Just inside the threshold, Mr. Picky was asleep on Erik's discarded jacket. The room itself was radiant with full-spectrum lights.

Erik didn't even notice her. He was working over a steeply

slanted table, having found that sleep just wasn't possible for him. His mind was too crammed with speculations, images, memories that he couldn't possibly have, fears that were all too rational, and a hunger for Serena that was like nothing he had ever known in his life.

His eyes blazed with reflected light like yellow gems. In his right hand was a small penknife. In his left was a long, creamy feather.

He didn't so much as glance at her.

"S. K. Niall wants you," she said.

Erik grunted, dipped quill into ink, and went back to writing.

"He's ignoring me," she said into the phone.

"Bugger. Try again."

"Erik, S. K. Niall is on the phone for you."

"Callhimback," Erik muttered.

"I think he mumbled something about calling you back," Serena said.

"Is he writing or illuminating?"

"He has a feather in his left hand, does that help?"

"Not if he's at the top of the page. How far down is he?"

Serena took a few steps and glanced over Erik's shoulder. "From what I can see, he's close to the bottom."

"Is he wearing a shirt?"

She blinked. "Er, yes. Why?"

"Put the phone in his pocket."

She hesitated, shrugged, and put the hand unit in the pocket on the left side of Erik's chest. She told herself that her fingers didn't tingle where they had slid over his shirt and come into contact with the vital heat of his body. Then she rubbed her hand over her scarf and told herself to think about something else.

He kept working as though she didn't exist.

"Erik?" Niall's voice rose from the unit held in Erik's pocket. "Yo, Erik. This is half of your paycheck calling you. Erik? Can you hear me? ERIK!"

Serena stared at the work that so held Erik's attention. After a few moments she drew in her breath and made a muted sound of appreciation. With every practiced motion of the quill, he replicated a way of writing that was ancient, difficult, and quite beautiful. Most of the letters looked familiar. Only a few of the words were. The rest were in a language that had died out long, long before Erik North had been born.

The sheet itself was nearly full of writing but for two rectangles in the midst of text. Each rectangle had a penciled design that was as intricate as it was ancient, based on a view of man and the universe that existed only in old Celtic manuscripts. Once the designs were filled in with paint and gold, they would be breathtaking.

Then she realized that Erik wasn't creating text, he was copying it from what looked like a very modern photograph pinned to the right-hand side of the drafting table. Except for the clarity of the copy—the original apparently had faded to almost invisibility—she couldn't see any difference between the two pieces of calligraphy.

Erik reached the end of the page about the time his caller reached the end of his patience. He laid the quill aside, dusted the vellum with sand, and grabbed the phone.

"Keep your shirt on," Erik said to Niall. "You know if I stop in the middle of the page it always shows, especially with the calligrapher whose work I'm copying right now."

"Is Serena still there?" Niall asked.

Erik looked up as though surprised to find her nearby. She was staring at his replicas as though she had never seen anything like them before. Probably she hadn't. Replicas as exact as his—down to the technique of tanning the vellum, mixing the ink, making his own colors from recipes a thousand years old—such works were as rare as the originals. More rare, actually. There were only a few people working in the world today who had the patience to do illumination and calligraphy exactly as it had been done in the Middle Ages. He was one of them.

The best one.

"Yeah, she's still here. Why?" Erik said.

"Serena doesn't know anything about what I'm going to tell you. If you want to keep it that way, pull your head out of your inkwell."

"It's out."

Niall's grunt said he wasn't sure. "Tannahill knows about her pages."

"Am I supposed to be surprised?" Erik asked, yawning. "He knows anything he puts his mind to knowing. Once I saw that gold carpet page, I figured he'd be sniffing around real soon. It's better than the one hanging in his gold gallery, and he never liked second place."

Serena listened with only part of her attention. She was staring at various works in progress that Erik had pinned to several drafting boards around the room. The writing was complete on each one. The illuminations were in varying states of completion. Unlike a weaving, where all colors were added as needed, illumination was accomplished in stages, one color at a time.

"Shane is doing more than sniffing around," Niall said. "He has his ear to the ground."

"Sounds uncomfortable."

"Listen, boyo. Shane is hearing things about those pages. Ugly things. Watch your back. Get that gun out of hiding."

"I—"

"Hate guns," Niall cut in impatiently. "I know, Fuzzy boy. I've heard it all before. And if you start wearing that nine-millimeter, you'll live to whine about it again. You still have someone parked out front?"

"Yeah. We're back to Bad Billy. The baby pickup took off a few hours ago."

"Probably didn't go farther than the nearest cheap motel."

"That's what I thought." Erik smiled thinly. "The good news is that in Palm Springs, even the cheap motels aren't cheap. He'll have to go all the way to Cat City for cheap. If a flare goes up, the cops might beat him back here."

"Don't count on it."

"I'm not counting on anything, most of all on a chunk of metal that can screw up fatally."

"Every gun jams sooner or later."

"If you don't use 'em, they don't jam."

"Sod it," Niall snarled. "You aren't stupid so don't act it. The smartest mouth in the world doesn't have the stopping force of the dumbest gun in the world. Wear that pistol or I'll tear up your contract right now."

"Shane really put the wind up your ass."

From the corner of his eye, Erik saw Serena walk closer to one of the drafting boards. The page on that one was almost finished. Only the gold foil itself remained to be added. A small "book" of extremely fine gold foil strips lay open in the narrow tray at the bottom of the table. The least stirring in the air lifted the corner of a foil strip, setting it to shimmering with light and hidden life.

Erik raked his fingers through hair that was two months away from its last cut and spiky from similar careless combing. "All right. Fine. I'll sleep with the damned thing."

"You do that. If I see you without it before I say all clear, the next thing you'll hear is the sound of your contract being turned into fucking confetti. Got that, Fuzzy boy?"

"Yeahyeahyeah." Then Erik cursed and said, "I got it."

He was talking to himself. Niall had already punched out.

Serena didn't notice. She had discovered a series of before and after photographs. The before ones were ratty, chewed, dirty, with their ink all but illegible and their colors faded to whispers. Only the elemental gleam of gold was untouched by time. The after pages were as luminous as gems, radiant with the color and beauty created by Erik North's patience and skill.

He was a forger.

A very good one.

And she had walked right into his trap.

Thirty-nine

Erik looked at the page on his drafting board waiting to be illuminated. Then he looked at Serena and frowned. She was pale, tight, and watching him with either contempt or anger flattening the line of her mouth. Maybe it was both.

He supposed he could sit here trying to guess what was on her mind, but his younger sisters had taught him that a man has about as much chance of figuring out how he stepped in the shit with a female as he has of getting himself pregnant. He could try ignoring her mood, but his sisters had cured him of that approach, too.

Unfortunately, they hadn't ever managed to teach him finesse. "What did I do wrong this time?"

Wordlessly Serena gestured in the direction of the before and after shots. The ends of her soft scarf fluttered as though trying to chase her fingers.

He followed the graceful arc of her hand. "So the place is messy. So what? I wasn't expecting a white glove inspection."

She gave him a *blow me* glare.

"C'mon, Serena. Spit it out. From the look of your mouth, it can't taste good."

"You're a forger."

The rush of pure, hot anger that went through Erik at the

contempt in her voice shocked him. It was shock that allowed him to keep his temper. Barely.

"Takes one to know one," he said through clenched teeth.

"I've never passed off any of my weavings as old pieces."

"But I'll bet you know the techniques of early weavers."

"Of course. I learned to weave on a back-strap loom just like—"

He talked over her. "And I'll bet you know which plants produced which dyes in the old days and the difference between wool and goat yarn and—"

"Every weaver who is any good knows—"

"—what tapestries differ from which wall hangings and the techniques weavers in various cultures used at different times in their history."

She put her fists on her hips and looked down at him—the handsome, arrogant son of a bitch sitting so at ease in the midst of all his forgeries. "Yes," she said tightly, "I know quite a bit about the history and tradition of various textiles in cultures from Stone Age string weaving to modern silk art kimonos. So what?"

"So if Rarities wanted an estimate on the worth or probable authenticity of a weaving, you could give them one based on your own learning and experience."

"What's your point?"

"It takes one to know one." His voice was soft, cutting. "If you want to know how a piece of ironwork was made, you go to a man who hammers iron for a living and ask him. If you want to know whether the technique of a weaving is in line with the date being claimed for it, you ask a textile specialist. If you want an estimate on anything, you go to someone who knows how that thing was made, when it was made, and from what it was made."

"There's a difference between an expert and a forger!"

His smile was as slicing as his tone. "I know. I just didn't think *you* did. I'm an expert on illuminated manuscripts, particularly Insular Celtic. I polished my expertise by doing what the old scribes and monks did—I made manuscripts by hand. In the process of teaching myself, I learned how to make a replica. Then I learned I had a gift for it. I love doing it. I'm not bad at it." He smiled thinly. "Screw modesty. I'm goddamn good. And I always, *always*, include an anachronism in my work so that anyone who examines it closely will know it's modern."

She wanted to believe him. She wanted it so much she was afraid to let herself. Without realizing it, she clenched her hands tightly on her scarf, sinking her nails into her palms. She felt the discomfort only at a distance, and only for a moment. The scarf seemed to thicken under her fingers, blunting the edges of her nails.

"Now," he added softly, "you tell me why I should trust a struggling artist whose grandmother's violent murder was never solved, an artist who as a result of that murder inherited some illuminated pages worth—"

"Are you accusing me of—" she cut in furiously.

"Be quiet," he snarled. "It's my turn to do the accusing and yours to do the listening. Why shouldn't I believe you killed your grandmother? Why should I believe that you didn't know your pages were forged? Why should I trust you at all after you turned down a million bucks for those same suspect pages? What's your game, Serena Charters? What do you really want?"

"To smack you until your ears ring."

He almost smiled. "What's your second choice?"

"Yell at you."

"You've already done that. Next?"

She scrubbed her hands over her face as though trying to wake up. He had no more reason to trust her than she had to trust him. They both knew it.

She had no way of proving she hadn't killed her grandmother.

He had no way of proving he hadn't sold his forgeries as the real thing.

"What a mess," she said bitterly. "If you don't trust me,

why did you bring me here? I might sneak in and murder you in your sleep."

This time he did smile. "Be kind of interesting to have you try."

Her head snapped up. She saw the light of amusement and something else in his golden eyes. Something hotter. "You don't really believe I killed my grandmother, do you?"

"No."

"Why?" she asked starkly.

"It's called trust. You should try it."

"I never learned how. G'mom . . ." Serena shrugged and fingered her scarf unhappily. "She never trusted anybody. I thought that was how it was for everyone. Arm's length, wary, never expect anything but bad news, never give anything you don't have to because there's never enough to go around."

Erik wondered how his sisters would have looked at the world if they had been orphaned at six instead of in their teens, and if their guardian had been flinty rather than full of hugs, paranoid rather than busier than a one-armed drummer. Erik hadn't been a perfect stand-in parent by any means, but his sisters hadn't seen the world as an enemy just waiting for an opportunity to eat them alive. In fact, there were times when he was afraid he had raised his sisters to be too open, too confident.

"You've already trusted me at least a little," he said finally. "Has it hurt you?"

"G'mom warned me particularly about forgery. You have all the qualifications for being a forger."

"Except one. I'm not."

Her lower lip moved as she bit into it from the inside.

"Would you trust Rarities Unlimited to tell you the truth?" he asked.

She tilted her head to the side, considering. "I think so, yes. Their reputation is all they really have, isn't it?"

"It's all anyone has."

She had the grace to look embarrassed. "I'm sorry. I don't mean to insult you. I'm just . . ."

"Cautious."

She nodded.

"To the point of paranoia," he added.

"No. If I was paranoid, I never would have come here with you no matter how fast you seduced my cat."

His lips curved and he looked at the animal in question, who was still asleep on his jacket. "It was mutual. The best seductions always are."

She was more than cautious enough to let that comment sizzle right on by her without comment.

For a few moments longer Erik watched the sleek pile of black fur on his jacket, but Serena didn't say anything. He wondered if telling her all of it now would send her running. Then he thought of the pages and homemade napalm and Bad Billy waiting out in the street.

Hell.

"Sit down, Serena," he said, standing and offering her the drafting chair. It wasn't particularly comfortable, but it was the only thing to sit on besides the floor.

She started to ask why she should sit, remembered his comments about trust and paranoia, and sat rather gingerly on the odd chair. At a long-legged five feet seven inches, she was used to having her feet reach the floor in any chair she used. Not this one. She had to hang her heels over one of the rungs and perch like a kid on Daddy's chair.

"I'm working for Rarities on these pages," Erik said.

"I had that figured out."

"Rarities is working for a client."

"I wondered about that. Who?"

"The House of Warrick."

Serena went still. "What do they want?"

"What did Warrick tell you when you saw him?" Erik asked.

"He looked at the pages, turned the color of tomato

sauce, and started trying to buy them. I didn't want to sell. He didn't want to believe me."

"How much did he offer?"

"I didn't hang around for his final offer."

"Why?"

"I was on my way out the door."

"You were in too big a hurry to find out what the pages were worth?"

"I didn't like his attitude."

"In what way?"

She wanted to tell Erik it was none of his business. Then she reminded herself that pushing people away was a reflex that she really should outgrow. Otherwise she might find herself alone like her grandmother, alone in a burning house. A sitting duck, and then a dead one.

"Norman Warrick acted like I was dog shit," she said tightly. "He wanted to know why I had waited a year to approach him. He called me a 'clever young girl' who wanted to take up where her 'purported' relatives left off."

Erik frowned. "Any idea what he meant by that?"

"Not a clue. Nothing nice, that's for sure. Personally, I think he's senile. I took the pages and left while he was still throwing offers at me. He was a really interesting shade of purple by then. I admit it; I hope he blew some circuits. You would have thought I was trying to rob him. Is that how it works in this business? You yell at each other until someone gives up?"

"Only if you know each other real well."

"I don't know him. I don't want to. I won't take that abuse from anyone."

There was anger in her eyes, but there was also distress. She hadn't liked the confrontation, hadn't liked being treated like excrement. Some people would have just shrugged it off. She hadn't been able to. It had hurt and embarrassed and then enraged her.

Erik shoved his hands into his pockets. It was either that or tuck stray strands of hair behind her ears, and then trace the curve of those same ears, and then give those soft lips a try.

Abruptly he turned and looked at the wall of before and after photos. Nothing that happened seemed to make his job any easier. Everything conspired to make it harder. Getting her full trust was looking close to impossible.

So the hell with half measures and subtlety. He didn't have the patience for all the sneaking around and pretending and half-truths and evasions and outright lies. That was why he worked for the Fuzzy side of Rarities. The demands of undercover work irritated him. He was too direct. His first and last impulse was to put all the shit on the table, deal with it, and get on with his life.

Abruptly Erik turned back to Serena. "My job for Rarities is twofold. First, I'm supposed to give Rarities my professional opinion of your pages. Second, I'm supposed to attempt to buy them from you on behalf of the House of Warrick."

Then he waited for what he had put on the table to hit the fan.

Forty

Serena's eyes widened and her mouth flattened into a narrow line. "I'm not selling them."

Erik measured the go-to-hell tilt of her chin. "Can you afford not to?"

"I've bumped along just fine so far without a lot of money."

"And you did it all yourself."

"Yes." She didn't bother to keep the satisfaction from her voice.

"What if Warrick offered a million dollars?"

"He already did."

Erik whistled softly through his teeth. Steep—for a forgery. "You turned him down?"

"Yes."

"Why?"

"Because he wasn't making sense. He said he wanted 'the rest of it' for that price. There isn't any 'rest of it.' The pages you saw are all that G'mom left me, and maybe all she had left, period. I don't know. I don't even know how to begin to find out." Serena picked up the ends of her scarf and rubbed its soothing texture over her temples. She was getting the kind of headache that made drugs look good. "Anyway, no amount of money would have tempted me, no matter how many or how few pages I find or don't find. I can't explain it, but I won't sell even one of the pages. I simply can't. They belong to me in a way I can't describe. It would be like selling myself."

"I know."

"Do you?" she asked wearily, rubbing her cheek against the soft scarf. But her tone of voice said that she doubted he understood at all.

"I feel exactly the same irrational attachment to the Book of the Learned," he said. "But I know I'll never have the money to outbid Warrick, so I have to endure the exquisite torture of watching something that is part of me sold on the open market. All I can do is ask—beg—you to let me make a replica of the pages before they go out of my life forever."

Serena lowered her hands and looked at Erik, really looked at him, for the first time since she had seen his work and decided he was a forger. His eyes were direct, clear, tawny, the color of single-malt scotch. His hair was the same shade of gold. His lashes and eyebrows were bronze, as was the shadow of beard that lay beneath his high cheekbones and stubborn chin. His mouth was bracketed by what could have been impatience or anger or both reinforcing the other, energy visibly seething around him.

She had seen him like this before, long, long ago.

And now, as then, it was his eyes that held her. The elemental fire in them, the intelligence, the power. Even when begging for a favor, he was in no way weakened. Like Mr. Picky begging for dinner, Erik was as much demanding as asking, even though neither cat nor man would ever see it that way.

"You're smiling," Erik said.

"You remind me of my dre—" She switched words at the last moment. "—my cat."

He glanced at the mound of black fur. "How so?"

"You don't want to know."

"Sure I do."

"You're both arrogant."

Erik blinked. "Arrogant? I'm begging here, lady."

Her smile widened. "You really believe it, don't you?"

"Yeah."

Her palms itched to run over his body as if he was indeed hers to pet and play with. The joys of born-again virginity paled whenever she was around him. He made her wonder what it would be like, if it would finally be unique with him, finally be satisfying all the way to her soul. She closed her eyes for an instant and let out a sigh that kept breaking. The uncanny material of her scarf lifted as though stirred by her breath.

"You're like a cat or a bird of prey," she said. "Arrogance is so ingrained in you, so normal, that you don't think of it as arrogance. You just loom over me and 'beg' for something that you could easily take by force."

"I won't."

"I know," she said simply. "That's why I'm giving it to you."

He looked at her mouth as she spoke. The cat in him wanted to settle in for some serious licking.

"Do you have a camera here?" she asked.

He nodded without looking away from her mouth.

"Take as many pictures of the pages as you like," she said.

"Okay."

She tilted her head, surprised by his lack of interest. "Erik?"

"He stepped out for a bit. I'm his evil twin brother. The one who thinks like a cat."

She blinked.

He bent down to her. "A cat with some serious licking in mind."

Her lips parted on a startled breath. "What?"

"This."

The tip of his tongue traced the outline of her lips and the sleek inner surfaces, tantalizing her until her hands came up and held his teasing mouth still.

At first he thought she was refusing the kiss. Then the tip of her tongue touched his, overlapped, curled. In a silence broken only by their quickening breaths, they tasted each other and found it both new and hauntingly familiar, wholly unexpected and somehow as inevitable as a river racing down to the sea.

They couldn't taste enough, couldn't share enough, couldn't get close enough. Suddenly his hands shifted and his arms tightened as he pulled her off the stool into the kind of hug that went from mouth to ankles.

She barely noticed the change of position. She was too consumed by tasting him more completely, sinking her fingers into the flexed muscles of his back, and feeling the hard thrust of his arousal against her belly. When she shifted her hips against him, he made a thick sound and lifted her so close that even her toes couldn't touch the ground. Slowly, slowly, he answered the motion of her hips with the hard promise of his erection.

The ragged, hungry sound she made took the world away. He barely kept himself from pulling her jeans off and taking her just the way they were, straight up and deep. Fighting himself, wanting to keep kissing her yet knowing that both of them were about to go under for the third time, he lifted his head just enough for his lips to shape words. "Last chance to say no."

She shook her head as though coming out of water. "What?"

He saw the hungry, dazed violet of her eyes, the flushed pink of her lips, and the wet gleam of a mouth that now tasted like both of them, like forest and mist and something hot, not quite sweet, incredible. His head dipped and he bit her lower lip with fierce restraint, and sucked on it the same way. "We want each other. Badly. Are we going to do something about it?"

Reality hit. Serena shuddered from a combination of surprise and the passion that had come from nowhere, sandbagging her.

"Oh. My. God." She let out an explosive breath. "I'm sorry. That's—it's not like me. I don't know what happened."

"Is that a no?"

She bit the inside of her lower lip. Her body was humming, flushed with a kind of heat she hadn't ever felt, certainly not after something as simple as a kiss.

"It better be."

"Why?"

"Does it matter?" she asked, embarrassed.

"Yes."

"I'm not on the pill and I don't carry condoms in my jeans," she said starkly. "Get the picture?"

"Yeah. But if you were and you did?" he asked.

Unconsciously she licked her lips, thinking about what it would be like if she had a condom or three in her pocket. "We'd be horizontal. Or vertical. Or any which way. That kiss was like nothing I've ever known and everything I ever wanted."

Breath hissed through Erik's teeth. "Damn, I've never had a woman get me so hot so fast. I could lose it just listening to you."

"No condoms in your jeans?"

He shook his head.

She sighed. "What a hell of a thing to have in common." Then she smiled crookedly. "But I remember enough from my dating days so that we can be safe and you won't have to take yourself in hand to get a good night's sleep."

He gave a crack of laughter. "If you were any other woman, I might settle for that."

"But you're not going to."

He shook his head.

"Why? I wouldn't mind." She looked at him and smiled. "In fact, I'd enjoy playing with you."

He let out another hissing breath. "You're killing me here. I don't trust myself not to seduce you the instant you put your hands in my pants. That's a first."

"Don't worry. I won't lose . . ." Her voice trailed off as she realized that she *had* lost control, and after just a simple kiss. If he had kept going, she would have been with him every bit of the way, and damn the consequences. She let out a seething breath that was very like his had been. "Okay. You're right. We can't trust ourselves." She gave him a puzzled look. "I want you to know this isn't me."

He smiled despite the jagged need digging into him, making him ache with every heartbeat, urging him to take what she offered, right here, right now, before she changed her mind. "Sure it's you."

"I don't know how to break this to you without increasing your already ample supply of masculine arrogance, but no man has ever turned me on with a kiss. Interested me, maybe, really intrigued me once or twice, but no bells, whistles, and rockets."

His smile became a very male grin. "Rockets, huh?"

"You're going to be impossible about this, aren't you?"

"Nope." He grabbed the loose ends of her scarf, brushed his lips over them, and tugged her closer. "I'm going to be so damned easy you won't know what hit you. C'mon."

"Erik?"

"Condoms in my bedroom. We should just make it."

They got as far as the bedroom door before their good intentions collided with the hunger that had blazed up in them so unexpectedly. She stumbled against him and then clung with a fierce kind of strength.

"Erik, can—?"

"Yes," he cut in.

"But you don't know what I'm going to ask."

"I don't care as long as you let me—"

He didn't finish. He couldn't. Her mouth was buried in his, her arms were around his neck, and her legs were wrapped around his waist. He laughed even as his kiss met and matched hers, hard and deep, the way they both wanted it to be. His hands went to her hips and he pulled her even closer while his fingers flexed, testing her resilient flesh. She made an incoherent sound and tried to get closer still, all the way close, inside his skin.

With a feeling of triumph unlike anything he had ever known, Erik carried Serena wrapped around him to the bed. He lowered her onto the coverlet parallel with the headboard, but still she didn't let go of him. Barely able to stand, head spinning with the violent beat of his own blood, he fumbled with one hand in the nightstand drawer and with the other freed his penis. Her blind, eager hands hindered as much as they helped, but even through the condom her fingers felt too good for him to complain.

In a few quick motions he stripped off her jeans and underwear. He didn't bother with his own—the two of them were too far gone to care about anything but completion. Standing by the side of the bed between her thighs, he had just enough control remaining to test her readiness with hungry, questing fingers. The pulsing heat of her response burned both of them. With a groan, he pulled her legs back around his hips. She lifted to him, both yielding to his need and demanding that he fill her.

Her eyelashes flickered as he took her with a long, powerful thrust of his hips. Heavy lidded, she watched the blaze of his narrowed eyes, the tautness of his face, and felt the clenched strength of his hips beneath her heels. She tried to smile, tried to say his name, tried just to breathe, but it was impossible. Her body wasn't hers anymore. It belonged to something unknown, unbelievable, urgent.

Acting instinctively, she drew off her scarf, flipped it around his neck, and pulled him even closer. The kiss he gave her was like being poured into fire. Abruptly she convulsed with an ecstasy that was as overwhelming and unexpected as passion itself had been.

He felt the first contraction hit her and gave up trying for any kind of self-control. He simply hammered into her and came with a force that left him spent and shaking, braced on his hands above her. Breathing hard, he fought to keep from pushing into her all over again and then again, harder, deeper, sending her over the edge once more, falling after her into a world of pure fire.

Dimly he realized he was moving, had been moving even as he thought, moving slow and deep, hard and long, and she was answering in the same sensuous rhythms, lifting against him, tugging at him with the velvet clenching of her need, sweet and sleek and twisting, then shivering and wild, unraveling, clinging, pulsing. And so was he, after her, with her, flung headlong into red oblivion, as though it had been a thousand years rather than a handful of seconds since they had drunk from the well of their shared sensuality.

Finally, with a hoarse sound that was her name, he collapsed onto the bed and drew her over himself like a blanket. She settled fluidly against him, utterly spent, shivering with the aftershocks of the pleasure that still speared through her at unexpected moments. He grabbed the corner of the bedspread in one hand and rolled completely over, wrapping them in warmth.

They were still wrapped together when they awoke deep in moonlight, steeped in each other. He peeled off the last of their clothes, leaving only the scarf whose texture enhanced his pleasure and hers. With a murmured word he wrapped her close beneath him. Nuzzling his rough cheek, shivering with pleasure when the scarf teased her breasts, she savored the feel of him as she shifted to make room between her legs. He kissed her shoulder softly. They didn't speak because there was nothing to say that could help them understand or even describe the peace, the ease, and the baffling rightness of being together.

Then she sought him even as he sought her. Aching, needing, they sank into each other, taking and being taken in turn. This time they were slow. This time they cherished.

This time the colored shadows overlapped, flowed together, and healed the hunger of a thousand years.

Forty-one

When Erik's mental alarm clock went off, Serena was sleeping as soundly as he wanted to be. With a silent groan, he sat up far enough to look at his laptop. Though the screen had dimmed, it hadn't gone dark, which meant there was a message waiting for him from Rarities. It was an important message, but not a Priority One, or the computer would have hooted at him until he shut the damn thing up.

Without turning on a light to alert whoever had the overnight shift out on the street, Erik smoothed the end of the scarf that clung to his cheek, kissed the cloth gently, and tucked it against her neck. Quietly he closed the computer, unplugged it, and carried it to the third bedroom. There was a night-light glowing between the twin beds there. It was the cheerful legacy of the last visit from his nephew, who was going through one of childhood's afraid-of-the-dark stages.

As soon as he woke up the computer, a hot link appeared on his screen. He activated it and found himself hooked up to the file Research had left for him. He scanned the provenance of his own sheets from the Book of the Learned, plus the sheets he had examined from various sources in the past. A click of the mouse presented the information schematically, according to the year most recently traded and working backward. Two of the sheets had been traced as far into the past as 1939. Most were edging back to the forties. Too damned many of them went back to fringe dealers who had gone bankrupt and sold their stock to other dealers by the storage container in the sixties.

Three of the sheets—the same ones that he had spent years trying to get permission to examine—were owned by a New Age spiritual-cum-financial adviser in Sedona, Arizona. Six years ago, when Erik had contacted the head monk, guru, soul adviser, channel, or whatever the flavor of the moment was, and asked about provenance for the pages, the man had maintained with a straight face that they had come to him direct from the Prime Nexus, so queries as to where and when he had purchased the sacred objects were pointless; they were a miracle, not something manufactured by man to be bought or sold.

Though Erik had tried every year, the head guru hadn't swerved in his story.

Erik clicked on the MORE link, which gave him the leaves' history in expanded form. A few moments later he discovered that he wouldn't be talking to the Great Blowhard any time soon. He had killed himself almost a year ago by setting fire to the inner sanctuary while he was in it. After the fire was put out, the place was a mess; the sacred golden objects were puddles and the miraculous pages were ash. Without the guru and the founding miracle of the manuscript sheets—sheets that Erik was certain had come from the Book of the Learned rather than the Prime Nexus—the sect had scattered in search of the next shortcut to wisdom, serenity, and eternal life.

Something nagged at Erik's stomach. Something cold. He told himself that people died all the time, too many of them died by fire, and a lot of them had once owned something valuable.

He kept telling himself, and he kept coming back to a conclusion that made ice congeal in his gut.

Frowning, he focused on the screen and scrolled down. Sheet number six, which was another one he had never been allowed to examine, had come full circle. A young enthusiast called Regina Jones had bought the palimpsest more than fifty years ago. Since then, it had been passed around, sold and resold, and sold again. Because the miniatures superimposed over the text were uninspired, it was the kind of item that was constantly "edited out" as someone's collection grew in stature and discrimination. Often such sheets went back to the original auction house to be resold. At present, Ms. Jones owned the sheet again, probably out of sentiment.

"Hallelujah," he breathed. "Now, Ms. Jones, do you still have your Medieval Mélange shop in Chicago, or have you moved to a warmer place?"

He clicked on the MORE link. Ms. Regina Jones had indeed moved to a warmer place sixteen years ago: Florida. Last year she had died there in her shop. Arson investigators said it was an insurance burning gone wrong. The commercial building where her store was located was losing money, someone torched the place for the insurance, and Ms. Jones had the extreme misfortune to be taking a late-night inventory in her shop at the time.

Erik realized his teeth were locked and his shoulders were knotted with tension. He didn't have to wonder why. There was a very ugly pattern and he couldn't ignore it any longer: owning leaves from the Book of the Learned had become bad luck, especially in the last year. Three people were dead by fire: Ellis Weaver, the Great Blowhard, and Ms. Jones.

It could be just a coincidence.

And snakes could read Shakespeare.

He clicked on the OPTIONS button and rearranged the data according to names most often mentioned. Not surprising, House of Warrick, Sotheby's, and Christie's were bunched at the top. What was surprising was that one D. J. Rubin was mentioned almost as often. Not until the last ten years did other dealers get mentioned frequently enough to merit another look. The Internet was really making inroads into traditional auction practices.

He made a list of three names and bounced it back to Rarities with a request to set up interviews. Then he clicked back on D. J. Rubin's link and read quickly. D. J. Rubin was a bargain-basement dealer who bought out other dealers' stock for cash. Not much cash, but the dealers who sold were bankrupt and welcomed the chance to unload what they could. D. J. Rubin hadn't bought anybody out for a long, long time. He had died in 1938 of a heart attack. His stock had been scavenged by other dealers, including the House of Warrick, which in those days hadn't been in a position to pick and choose its clients. In fact, the House of Warrick, like many family businesses, had nearly gone under in the Great Depression. But Norman Warrick had pulled the company through with his skill and his unerring eye for the genuine among all the garage-sale junk.

Erik smiled bleakly. That explained Warrick's aversion to frauds; his entire reputation rested on his ability to find the genuine. That meant there was going to be a real professional pissing contest over the validity of Serena's leaves from the Book of the Learned.

The more Erik saw of them, the more certain he was that they were genuine.

Maybe the old man was getting senile after all. If so, the House of Warrick might be in trouble. Garrison and Cleary would have to ease the old man out before he tarnished the Warricks' business reputation with a series of stupid decisions.

But right now Warrick was the least of Erik's problems. Working quickly yet overlooking nothing, he reviewed the data again, rearranged it again, and then again, using different criteria each time. Nothing he saw changed his mind.

Shane Tannahill had been right. Something ugly was oozing around pages from the Book of the Learned.

For a moment Erik sat very still, playing various scenarios in his mind with the speed of a Defense Department computer. No matter which way he approached the interlocking problem of himself, Serena, an unknown murderer or murderers, and the Book of the Learned, he came to the same conclusion.

He wasn't letting Serena out of his sight.

Period.

He picked up his communications unit and called up Lapstrake's roving number. It was answered on the first ring.

"What's up, Erik?"

"Me, checking on the tail. Is it Bad Billy?"

"Yeah. They switched off about an hour ago. It's hell only having two guys. Eight hours on, eight off, eight on and on and on until it's over. Bet they get real tired of pissing into relief tubes."

"Ah, the glamorous life of a P.I."

Down on the street, Lapstrake snorted, stretched, and walked a few feet in one of the generic step-vans that Rarities often used for stakeouts. This particular van advertised itself as a rental job, reliable and priced right. Lapstrake looked out the back peephole. "No lights are on. Are you crawling around in the dark?"

"For a few minutes. Then you'll see lots of lights."

"Chinese fire drill time?" Lapstrake asked sardonically.

"Not quite. I'm taking Serena to watch the sunrise on top of a ridge."

Lapstrake groaned. "Lucky us. How close you want me to work?"

"You don't need to go hiking. Just let me know if I have more than one bogey. If I do, take them out quietly, but be sure Bad Billy stays with me."

"Quietly, huh? How much time do I have?"

"Half an hour if you're lucky. Twenty minutes if you're not. Call me if you run into problems."

"Call you what?" Lapstrake retorted, and disconnected. He had a lot to do and not much time to do it in.

Back in the darkened house, Erik hit the number seven

button on his unit with his thumb. Instantly Niall's second-most-private number went out into the ether.

"This better be good, boyo" was Niall's surly greeting.

"Somebody is burning people who have leaves from the Book of the Learned."

Niall said something beneath his breath. Erik didn't recognize the language and didn't ask for a translation.

"Short form," Niall demanded.

"I just gave it to you."

"Give me more."

"Three people connected to the Book of the Learned have all died in the last year. Serena's grandmother in southern California, a Sedona guru in northern Arizona, and Ms. Regina Jones of Florida. All three were burnings. One was called a random act of violence, one was called a suicide, and one was called an insurance arson."

"Bugger," Niall said viciously. "Anything else?"

"None of the leaves have a provenance older than 1939. Or if one does, we haven't found it yet. It's real slow searching the pre-sixties stuff because most of it is only on microfilm."

Niall grunted. "That's Dana's problem. I want you and Serena at Rarities headquarters. Our plane will be waiting at the Palm Springs airport in two hours."

"It will wait, all right. Serena and I are going on a little hike before we bail."

Back in L.A., Niall stared at the phone as though it had licked him. "Say *what?*"

"We're going hiking."

"Like bloody hell you are! I'm giving you a direct order to—"

"Dana's my boss," Erik cut in. "She gave me my head on this one."

"Boyo, I'll *hand* you your head if you fuck this up."

"Fine."

That was all Erik said. He didn't think his boss wanted to hear that if he fucked up, he would probably be out of Niall's reach. As in dead. Not that Erik was particularly worried about that possibility. Once he left civilization behind, he had the oldest and best ally of all: the land.

"I'm waking Dana up," Niall said flatly.

"Let her sleep. Whatever she says won't make any difference. I'm going to have a chat with Bad Billy, and I'm going to do it where he knows he has to listen. Serena's coming with me. Until this is over, she'll never be out of my sight. It's not negotiable."

"Are you ready to tear up your contract over this?" Niall asked.

"Consider it fucking confetti. You can bring in someone else, but don't hold your breath expecting Serena's cooperation. She trusts me like an old friend. A very old one."

It was just *how* old that didn't bear thinking about.

"There's more to this than the manuscript, isn't there?" Niall said finally.

"Yes. I just wish I knew what."

"Find out, boyo. The plane will be waiting when you get back from your sunrise jaunt. And leave your communications unit on GPS so we'll know where to find the body."

"Does that mean I'm not fired?"

"As long as you don't die before I can kill you myself."

Niall broke the connection before Erik could.

With a disgusted word, Erik looked at his watch. He had a little time before he began the wild-goose chase. Enough time to scan Serena's sheets into the computer and forward them to Rarities.

While he was at it, he would take a closer look at the gather marks. There was something about them that tantalized him. There was a pattern he had sensed without realizing it, a pattern that went beyond the natural development of an artist's style through all the years it took him to complete the Book of the Learned. At least that was the way Erik remembered it.

As for which Erik was remembering, he really didn't want to know.

Forty-two

Serena couldn't ignore the watery noises any longer. She blinked groggily, trying to figure out where she was. When she remembered, she sat up in a rush.

Mr. Picky flexed his claws, hanging on to the blanket and the warm body beneath.

"Erik?" she called out, wincing and coaxing the cat to retract his claws. "Where are you?"

"Well, praise the Lord," Erik answered from the adjoining bathroom. "She's alive after all." He came to the doorway and looked over at her with eyes that gleamed like gold coins. "I was beginning to wonder if I'd killed you the fourth time. Or was it the fifth?"

He was freshly showered and shaved, wearing jeans, flannel shirt, and a lightweight jacket. Looking at him made her heart turn over with memories and new need.

"Want to try again?" she asked before she thought better of it.

"Hell, yes."

She waited. He didn't do anything more than look at her like a man who was remembering just how good she tasted.

"Unfortunately," he said, "you're going to need your strength for something else."

"What about you? What do you need?"

"You know damn well what I need, but for now I'll settle for my hiking boots."

"Hiking boots," she muttered beneath her breath, realizing for the first time that he was wearing socks but no shoes. "Of all the things to need before the sun comes up. I suppose the macho dawn raider is going to Braille his way over a mountain instead of sleeping in like any sane person would after a night like we— Let go of me, Picky!"

"What? I can't hear you," Erik said, but the hidden laughter in his voice suggested he could. "Better get up, honey. The sun won't stay down forever."

"I'll get up as soon as I get this wretched black hair ball off my stomach."

This time Erik didn't bother to swallow his laughter. Obviously Serena wasn't a morning person. She looked as grumpy as Picky at being disturbed. Not that Erik would have minded crawling into bed with her. In fact, if she stayed there about ten more seconds, he might do just that.

Serena shoved cat and covers aside and surged out of bed before Erik's evil twin brother could take over again. She stalked toward him, too sleepy to be embarrassed about being naked but for the scarf that slid over her skin.

Erik took a hissing breath through his teeth. Hair a wildfire around her arms and shoulders, skin like pale cream satin, breasts tipped with pure pink, and another fire burning between her thighs.

"Damn, but you're beautiful," he said hoarsely.

She gave him a look of stark disbelief and grabbed her nightgown off the back of the desk chair. The "gown" was a man's size XXL brushed-silk shirt in a rich shade of teal blue. As a sultry sexual tease, her shirt was a nonstarter. But for comfort and softness against her skin, it beat any expensive lingerie she had ever owned.

He almost groaned at the sight of her wrapped in loose yet clingy folds of silk, her hair a waterfall of fire over her breasts, a fey scarf peeking out from beneath her hair.

With both hands she swiped her hair away from her face. Her braid had come loose during the night, which meant that her hair looked like it had been combed by a hurricane.

Hurricane Erik, to be precise.

"If I'd known you were a dawn raider," she said distinctly, staring up at him, "I'd have gone to bed earlier."

"We'll try that tonight."

"Going to sleep earlier?" she muttered.

"No. Going to bed earlier."

She smiled despite the morning grouchies. Now that she was awake enough to know the difference, she felt really good. A little stiff here and there, but humming with energy and at peace with the world. Even her scarf seemed especially soft and springy.

"You look smug," he said.

"I feel smug." She stretched.

Erik looked away and told himself all the reasons why he couldn't take her back to bed. Or on the floor. Or anywhere. The relentless, reckless surge of his own body surprised him. After last night, all through the night, he should have been as hard to raise as the dead.

No such luck.

"Where's the portfolio?" he asked roughly.

"Bottom drawer of the big dresser, where Picky can't get to it and sharpen his already lethal claws."

Erik looked as horrified as he felt. "He wouldn't."

"You never had a cat, did you?"

"He would."

"If he thought of it, yes. As the supposedly smarter of our dynamic duo, it's up to me to see that Picky doesn't get an opportunity to do things he shouldn't do."

Erik looked at the yarns scattered around, and smiled as

he remembered how unexpectedly soft a pile of yarn had felt under his naked back. "What about your weaving stuff? Doesn't Picky go after it?"

"We had some issues about it at first," Serena said dryly.

"I'll bet. Who won?"

"We both did. Picky decided he'd rather stay away from my yarns and looms, and be allowed in the house than be a full-time outside cat." She yawned, grabbed her hair in both hands, twisted it into a loose knot at the nape of her neck, wrapped the scarf around everything, and tied it at the top of her head. She was beginning to take the material's flexibility and usefulness for granted, as though it was simply another part of her body. "Are you through studying the sheets? Is that why you need the portfolio?"

"I haven't begun to study them. Your illuminated pages are in the climate-controlled safe along with some other things," he said. One of which *wasn't* the gun. Not anymore. The bloody thing was in a holster at the small of his back, right next to the Rarities communications unit. "I'm going to use the empty portfolio as bait."

The cool anticipation in his eyes took away the last of Serena's sleepy fog. "Bait?"

"Get dressed, honey. We're going for a hike."

What he didn't say was that she was part of the bait. At least he was afraid she was. That was why he wasn't going to leave her in his home by herself, no matter how fancy his security system was. A system was only as good as the speed and quality of the response it got when it sounded the alarm. Without him, the security system was simply a very expensive way to startle unwanted visitors.

Not that he didn't trust Lapstrake to keep Serena safe.

All right, maybe he didn't. Not entirely. Reading those files had made him realize that Serena's grandmother hadn't been paranoid. She had just known more than he did about what was at stake.

"A hike?" Serena repeated. "You're kidding." Then she took another look at his eyes. "You're not kidding."

"Right the second time."

Despite the presence of Lapstrake parked down the street, watching the watcher, Erik didn't want Serena out of his sight. Even if it had been Niall himself on duty out on the street, Erik wouldn't have left Serena behind. It wasn't that he distrusted Niall. He didn't. Hell, he would leave his sisters to be guarded by Niall—or Lapstrake, if it came to that.

But not Serena.

It wasn't rational. It wasn't normal. And it wasn't something Erik could fight in himself. It simply *was*. He had a grim certainty that something final would happen if he and Serena were divided again.

Nothing had been rational since he had seen Serena's eyes, the violet eyes of the sorceress in pages a thousand years old come to life. He didn't need Niall to tell him that he was being unreasonable. He knew it, accepted it, and it changed nothing. He wasn't going to be separated from her.

End of argument.

"What if I don't want to go for a hike?" Serena asked, turning away.

"I'll sympathize every third step."

"Be still my beating heart." She flipped open her suitcase, looked at him with unreadable violet eyes, and said, "While I shower and get dressed, take Picky out to a nice sandy spot in your yard. It's the only type of cat box he recognizes."

"What if he runs off?"

"He never has, and he travels with me when I have to go to L.A. or San Francisco. He knows just what a highway rest stop is for."

"Gotcha."

Erik grabbed the sleepy black fur ball, tucked it under his arm, and headed for the backyard. Picky made a sound that could have been questioning or threatening. Erik chose to believe the former.

"Son, I'm taking you to a sandpile you won't believe. Best you'll have until you go to that Great Cat Box in the sky."

Forty-three

NEAR PALM SPRINGS
SATURDAY DAWN

"Erik, wait! I've got a rock in my shoe."

Pausing, he looked back at Serena as he had every few steps since they had started up the steep, dry trail that led away from the equally steep, equally dry dirt road that had dead-ended at the trailhead. The air was crisp, scented with chaparral, and so clear that everything had a knife edge, even the dawn. The first tiny curve of the sun was above the eastern horizon just enough so that long fingers of red and dark gold light speared across the desert. Down on the flats streetlights still glittered and café signs flashed in cold neon rainbows, coaxing sleepy people in for a cup of coffee and a handful of sugared grease.

Below Erik and Serena, perhaps two hundred yards down the mountain, a man-shaped shadow followed them, pausing when they paused, moving when they moved. Unlike them, he didn't use flashlights to find his way. That told Erik the man was using some kind of night-vision glasses, which was why Erik was tempted to spear him with an occasional blast of "random" flashlight. Through amplifying glasses, even a distant flashlight could be blinding.

But he didn't give in to temptation because he didn't want to discourage their tail. "Bad Billy" was more used to city surveillance than country chases. He didn't instinctively take advantage of natural cover, the night shadows or the pools of strengthening light, or the terrain itself. Not that he was stupid. He wasn't. He hung back in open places where his dark figure might be spotted against the lighter landscape, and he closed in whenever he thought he could get away with it.

Erik was certain that the portfolio itself hadn't been out of Bad Billy's sight for more than a minute at a time. That would change just as soon as they got over the ridge. That was when Wallace would start to get nervous and rush things. That was when even a very cautious man made mistakes.

Somehow, he didn't think Bad Billy was overly cautious.

Erik went to Serena and gripped her high up on her left arm. "Brace yourself on me and get rid of the rock in your shoe."

As soon as he was close enough, she began to speak in a very soft voice—he had already told her not to whisper, because whispers carried much farther than a low, murmuring sound.

"Is he still following us?" Serena asked, fiddling with her shoe like she was fishing out a rock.

"Yeah."

"Hell. How much farther do we have to walk?"

"I thought you liked to hike."

"Not when some stranger's eyes are boring into my back."

Erik didn't argue. His neck itched something fierce. "In another quarter mile there's a good place for an ambush."

She stiffened. "You said you were going to be careful!"

"Keep your voice down," he murmured. "Laying an ambush is a very careful business."

"But—"

"Let's go," he cut in impatiently. "He'll have to take off the glasses soon, no matter how much he dials them down. Then it will be our turn. And I don't want it to be too light."

He led off at a brisk pace. She followed no more than two steps behind. The portfolio poked out of his rucksack like a quarter panel of plywood. When she had pointed out that it would be invisible in the darkness, so how would their shadow know they had it, Erik had said three words to her: *night-vision lenses.*

Serena was sorry she had asked. After that, with every step she took, she had wondered if the man was staring at her close-up and damned personal while she struggled along the trail in her cutoff jeans, sweatshirt, and running shoes. And scarf, of course. It was the only thing that had kept her from freezing. At first she had been so cold she was sure their shadow could count her goose bumps with his high-tech glasses. But after a mile on the steep trail, she had warmed up. Soon she would be hot. Wherever full sunlight touched, the temperature went up about ten degrees.

For the last half mile they had been out in the open, scrambling up the steep shoulder of a ridge. She was thinking about pulling off her sweatshirt and tying it around her hips. Maybe then her skin wouldn't crawl every time she thought about the goggle-eyed stranger staring at her butt.

Instead, she moved her scarf until the ends of it trailed down her back. Not much as concealment went, but it made her feel better anyway. Right now, she would take all the feel-good she could get. She liked to hike, but she usually stuck to a trail. Apparently Erik didn't, or else he was following the kind of trail only a mountain goat could love.

As she scrambled upward toward the last nearly vertical pitch, pebbles turned like marbles under her feet. She skidded, grabbed a shrub that smelled like cedar, and caught her balance. At least the greenery at this altitude didn't have thorns. The first time she had tripped, she had nearly gone facefirst into some cactus.

He looked back when he heard a low curse. "Need a hand?"

"I've got two, thanks."

He smiled, but for the benefit of Bad Billy—who was hanging back farther and farther, either as a precaution against the growing light or because his feet hurt—Erik said clearly, "We'll make better time on the other side of the ridge. The cave is only a mile from there. And stop worrying, honey. The pages will be safe there until we find out what's going on."

"They better be." There wasn't any cave and she knew it.

"Trust me."

"I can't believe you said that."

Erik laughed.

After a moment, so did she. Despite the early hour and the man following them, the beauty of the dawn kept sneaking up on her. The air was crisp yet silky. The scents were subtle yet heady—heat stored overnight in the biggest rocks, midnight cold in the shadows, plants that were both brittle and resinous, clean dust that was finer than powdered sugar, a feeling of space and time everlasting. Ahead, black-velvet mountains condensed out of the night in endless geometries. Sunlight was a living thing: shifting, changing, making the delicate tracks of a lizard leap out in sharp relief against the dust. The wind was alive, too, rising with the sun, breathing over the land in a long, remembering sigh.

"Beautiful, isn't it?" Erik murmured.

She nodded and stroked the scarf that snuggled so comfortingly against the pulse in her neck. "Sunrise in the desert makes me think of a tapestry that weaves together light and time and life. And death. Death is always there, just beyond life, defining it." She willed herself not to look at the man following them. "G'mom loved sunrise. She would weave through the night just to see the first light of dawn falling on her loom. She called it God's illumination, more precious than gold."

"So she was a 'dawn raider'?"

Serena didn't have to turn to see Erik's smile. She could

hear it in his voice. "More like a night raider. My grandmother loved the darkness, loved the silence."

"You don't."

She yawned. "Once in a while it's great. But I love all the thousands of colors sunlight brings. I love the burning heat of the sun in summer and the patience of hidden seeds waiting for the rains to come. I love the birdsongs and the flight of a butterfly and a horizon that's a hundred miles away in all directions."

"You love the desert, period." His fingertip traced her smile, touched her scarf, slid it aside to feel the pulse of her life quicken at his caress. He wanted to do more, much more, but it wasn't the time or the place. "Let's go. The sooner I have a talk with that clown down the hill, the quicker we can start looking for the rest of the Book of the Learned."

The rising sun slanted across his face, turning his eyes to golden crystal, so vivid that they stopped her breath. "The rest of it?" she said huskily. "Are you talking about the pages G'mom lost?"

"And, I hope, the pages she didn't."

"What do you mean?"

"I've been thinking about that note she left you." He had been thinking about the pages, too, and he kept coming back to a single conclusion that he couldn't prove and couldn't ignore. He lowered his voice still more, leaning down until his lips were brushing Serena's ear. "She was trying to tell you that she'd lost some pages, but that she still had most of the book."

Serena took a deep breath. The air smelled of dawn and desert and man. "What makes you say that?"

"Early this morning—"

"Correction," she cut in dryly, "late last night. *This* is early morning."

He smiled. "Whatever. I got the bright idea of checking gather marks and marginalia on the duplicates I have, and on your pages. I think Erik used the red dots in the seal on every fourth page as a counter. If I'm right, your grand-mother gave you pages from the front, middle, and end of the book. At least I'm guessing it was the end."

"How many pages?"

"Close to six hundred originally."

Her head jerked up so quickly she almost knocked against his chin. "But where's the rest? Why didn't she give it to me?"

"Maybe she wasn't sure it would get to you."

"Morton Hingham wouldn't have—damn, she really was paranoid, wasn't she?"

"From the way she died, she had reason to be."

Serena flinched. She didn't like thinking about her grand-mother's death by fire. "Then the rest of it is lost."

"No. Not if you do what your grandmother told you to do: Think like her. Think hard, Serena. Think fast. *Think as though your life depended on it.*"

Without waiting for her to say anything, Erik turned and began striding up the final seventy yards to the top of the ridge. Hands on her hips, Serena stared at him. His ease with the steep, rough land both pleased and irritated her.

"Big guy, you don't want to know what my grandmother would think of me climbing around a mountain with a ma-cho man at dawn," she muttered. As for last night . . . well, her grandmother had had a child, so maybe she had known all about the compelling heat and an ecstasy that was like the phoenix, death and resurrection in one.

But that was something Serena wasn't going to think about. Not with some high-tech Peeping Tom following them. She shifted the canteen that was poking a hole in her hip and set off up the slope. By the time she got to the top, she was breathing deeply and pulling herself along on every bit of shrubbery she could trust. They hadn't hiked up to the tree line yet, but some of the shrubs were taller than a bas-ketball player.

"Watch the top," Erik called back softly. "It's covered with loose rocks. Go to the right."

The last twenty feet of the scramble was a nearly vertical

cliff. She saw where Erik had wedged his boots into cracks or pockets, taking a diagonal route to the top instead of the easier-looking, more natural route up the center. She took a deep breath and followed him, angling off to the right as he had. She didn't have the skill or upper body strength to pull herself up using only her fingers or clenched fists, but she was agile enough to find other ways to climb than brute strength.

As she pulled herself up and over, she saw why he hadn't gone straight up. At the center of the cliff, just back from the lip and invisible from below, there was a hump of rubble that featured rocks of every size from grapes to cantaloupes. If she had tried to climb out at that spot, she would have grabbed loose stones and probably tumbled right back down the rocks.

"Nice going," Erik said approvingly as she slid down the other side and into his arms. Reluctantly he released her, but he let his hands caress her every bit of the way. "See that pile of boulders down there?"

Serena told herself that she was breathless after the scramble up the slope. It was true as far as it went; it just didn't include having her heart turn over when she felt the lingering touch of his hands.

"Boulders," she said, forcing herself to concentrate on something other than the smell of heat and man. She licked her dry lips and told herself that she didn't want to taste him. Not at all. She knew what sweaty skin tasted like. Salt. Big deal. So why was her mouth watering? "Those big rocks about twenty yards away," she asked, "the ones that look like they were assembled by a drunken giant?"

"Yes." His nostrils flared as he drank her scent. He wanted to drink more, and he wanted it with a force that shocked him. "There's a hollow with enough room to hide in there."

She looked doubtfully at the boulders. "For a rabbit, maybe."

"I hid there during a thunderstorm once. The opening is on the far side. Watch for snakes."

"What are you going to do?"

"Wait for Bad Billy to reach that last ten feet."

"And then?"

"I'll think of something." Erik's eyes narrowed. "Have you ever used a gun?"

"Does a rabbit gun count?"

"Did you hit anything?"

She raised one eyebrow. "I rarely missed. G'mom made a really tasty rabbit stew. It was a break from pinto beans and jalapeño peppers."

"Okay." He reached behind his back, under his lightweight jacket, and drew the nine-millimeter gun from its holster. "Safety's on," he said, pointing. "The first shot requires a double pull. After that a single pull gets it done."

She accepted the gun, taking care to keep the muzzle pointed away from both of them. That alone reassured him. He watched while she took the safety off and put it back on a few times, getting used to the feel of the mechanism. Then he clipped his communications unit on the belt he had loaned her—after he had cut a row of new holes for her much smaller waist.

"I've already put in Niall's private number," Erik said. "If something goes wrong, hit TALK, take off the safety on the gun, and *stay hidden.* If Bad Billy is dumb enough to come looking for you, shoot him and keep on shooting until he gives up or you run out of bullets. Don't be girly or coy about it, either. You'll be fighting for your life against a murderer."

Her eyes widened, then narrowed as she realized what he hadn't said: if someone came after her, it would be over Erik's dead body. "Keep the gun," she said starkly.

"I've got a much better weapon."

"What?"

"The land."

Her eyelids flickered. She wanted to ask a hundred questions and make a thousand objections, but none of them would change Erik's mind or their circumstances, and she knew it.

"Don't look so worried," he said, smiling. "I plan to keep the upper hand all the way with Bad Billy. But if I don't . . ." His mouth flattened. No matter what, he would see that she wasn't hurt. "Niall will tell you what to do."

Before she could say anything, both of them heard the rattle of rocks from the other side of the ridge. Wallace was on the move up toward them. From the sliding, grating sounds he made, he wasn't having an easy time of it.

Erik jerked his chin toward the boulders.

Serena's mouth tightened into an unhappy line, but she didn't argue. There was no time and she knew it. She headed for the boulders, found the opening, and tossed a handful of pebbles into the gloom beyond. No snake rattled a warning. She went in headfirst and began mentally revising Erik's plans.

For openers, she wasn't going to sit and suck her thumb while he risked his life.

Forty-four

Risa Sheridan stared at the ringing phone like it was a rat. Outside her modest hotel room, L.A. was up and moving, but not very fast. Saturday morning wasn't a big hustle-bustle time in the city. Most folks were still sleeping off Friday night.

Resentfully she looked at the clock. Nobody should be calling her before 7 A.M. on a Saturday morning, which meant that somebody in another time zone had forgotten about the three-hour difference between East and West coasts, or someone didn't care, or was awake in the same time zone and thought she should be awake, too.

She was betting on the latter.

"Yes, Mr. Tannahill," she said to the dark, empty room as she reached for the phone. "Whatever you say, Mr. Tannahill. And have I mentioned lately what a dear, sweet, kind, relentlessly demanding bastard you are?"

She picked up the phone. "I didn't ask for a wake-up call."

Shane ignored her. "You didn't mention that the International Antiquarian Book Exposition was in L.A. this weekend, either."

"Mr. Tannahill. What a surprise."

In Las Vegas, high above the twenty-four-hour hustle of the Golden Fleece, Shane smiled thinly at the complete lack of inflection in his curator's voice. The gold pen in his left hand began turning over lazily, walking across the back of his fingers like an acrobat doing slow flips.

"Have you been to the exposition yet?" he asked.

"No."

He waited.

So did she.

"Go," he said.

"Everything that you might be interested in was shown to one or all of the major museums before the festival opened," Risa said. "Unless you're telling me to sift the dregs, I can't think of a reason to go there."

"I can."

"I await enlightenment."

Shane wished he could see Risa's lush mouth form the biting words. He had never touched her, because he didn't fool around with employees. That didn't mean he was blind. He was just too smart to get tangled up with a female tiger like Risa Sheridan. Yanking her chain, however, was always entertaining.

"Because I told you to," he said.

"Brilliant."

"And because the Huntington Library, which would be a logical choice for what I'm talking about, is rumored to be having financial difficulties."

"It's a library. Of course it's short of money."

"It's a scholarly kind of library. No sex appeal, which means no big exhibits to bring in cash. The grounds are huge. Takes an army to keep it up. Very expensive, so the administration probably has been cutting corners, saving on basic maintenance, selling off some of the stuff in the basement, that sort of thing."

Risa saw where the explanation was going. "So they're not acquiring right now."

"It's nice to work with a smart woman."

"Try hiring your casino girls by their IQ rather than their bra size."

"Same problem the Huntington has—no sex appeal."

"Some men have gotten past the tits-and-snicker stage."

"Not enough of them to fill my casinos."

Risa gave up the losing end of that argument. "Are you after anything in particular at the antiquarian garage sale, or do you just want me to look around?"

"Look all you want, but listen even harder. If anyone wants to talk about the Book of the Learned, I'll be happy to make them rich."

She straightened as the last of the I-need-coffee haze disappeared from her mind. "Is it here?"

"That's your job. Find out. And Risa?"

"Yes?"

"At the first hint of danger, get out."

"Danger?" She frowned. She had had her share of obsessed collectors screaming and threatening her. She had met dubious dealers in back alleys at night. Unpleasant, but part of the business, especially for an aggressive, ambitious curator like her. Shane knew that as well as she did. In fact, he positively encouraged it. "What have you heard?" she asked sharply.

"Nothing. That's why I'm nervous. It makes me think that whoever has the Book of the Learned is keeping folks quiet the old-fashioned way."

"What's that?"

"Killing them."

Forty-five

Wallace, aka Bad Billy, eyed the last twenty feet between himself and the top of the ridge. He was cursing steadily, monotonously, and very quietly. Although he always went to work with an overnight kit in hand, nobody had bothered to tell him that the slack-wristed Palm Springs scholar whose house he was watching was actually a fucking mountain goat. If the woman hadn't slowed Erik North, Wallace knew he would have been lost after the first mile.

Not that it had been a picnic so far. If he hadn't been in shape, he would have been on his hands and knees, panting. Just as soon as he could, he was going to get a pair of really expensive hiking boots and put them on the client's bill.

But for now he was stuck trying to climb a cliff wearing old running shoes. It could have been worse, he supposed. He could have been in a tux and leather shoes like the last job.

He looked at the cliff one more time, listened carefully, and heard nothing. His orders hadn't said anything about beating the crap out of North, but they hadn't said anything about *not* doing it, either. North wouldn't be so hard to keep track of if he had a busted ankle. Or neck.

Wallace took the cliff where the route looked easiest—straight up the middle. By the time he realized his mistake, it was too late. He had run out of places to put his hands, much less his feet. He would have to climb down and try a different route. Swearing under his breath, he felt around with his toe for the foothold he had just abandoned. His shoe grated over rock and slid off.

"I'd offer a hand, but we haven't been introduced," said a voice from over his head and to the right.

The P.I. was too shrewd to lose his balance by looking up suddenly, especially when the voice was between him and the rising sun. He looked up slowly. Very slowly. He saw a man crouching on his heels, silhouetted at the edge of the cliff, and very much at ease with heights and tricky footing. For all the tension he showed, the guy might have been standing on a pitcher's mound.

But it wasn't until Wallace focused on Erik's eyes, pale against the shadows of his face, that he knew he had made a big mistake. The guy might make his living by drawing pictures in books, but he wasn't anybody's Tinkerbell. The only good news was that North's hands were empty. All Wallace had to do was support himself on one foot and one hand while reaching across his chest and into his shoulder harness for his pistol.

Yeah. Right. He would just have to wait until he climbed down for that little pleasure.

"You want a name?" Wallace asked.

"I have one. What about you?"

"David Farmer."

Erik looked at the man who was clinging to the rocks with both hands and one foot. Wallace wasn't sweating much or panting, which spoke well for his physical condition. He hadn't even paused before lying, which spoke well for his wits if not for his morals.

Not looking away from his quarry, Erik selected a baseball-size rock from the rubble at the top of the cliff and wrapped his hand around the cold stone. "All right, David Farmer. What are you doing out here?"

"Walking. Then I got lost. You know the way out?"

"There are several ways, but unless you start telling me the truth, you won't need any of them."

"Great," Wallace said sarcastically. "First I get lost and then I get found by a paranoid survivalist."

"Life's a bitch, ain't it?" Erik's smile was even less comforting than his eyes. "Want to start all over again?"

"Look, I'm sorry you don't believe me. I'll just climb back down and—"

"You make one move," Erik cut in calmly, "and I'm going to start dropping rocks on you. By the time Search and Rescue finds you—if they ever find you—they'll assume you're just one more dumb tourist who thought Mother Nature was a sweet old lady and cougars really would rather eat carrots than kids. You with me so far?"

"Yeah."

"Third chance. Who are you?"

Wallace thought about sticking with David Farmer. Then he thought about how he had underestimated Erik North so far. But no longer. There was no doubt that the man above him was cold enough to stone him off the cliff.

And smart enough to get away with it.

"William Wallace," he hissed through his teeth, trying to force a smile.

"Why are you walking around in the wilderness at dawn?"

"You tell me," he retorted. He had been wondering about just that thing for the last two miles. Surely there were better places to hide the portfolio.

Thoughtfully, Erik balanced the rock at his own eye level on his flattened palm, as though testing the missile's weight and balance. Some internal equilibrium shifted. The rock started to fall, heading straight for Bad Billy's face.

"All right! All right! I'll talk," Wallace said quickly, cringing against the cliff.

Erik caught the rock with a movement that was so fast it made Wallace blink. Then Erik went back to balancing the rock on his palm.

"I'm watching the leather case," Wallace said.

"Why?"

"I'm being paid."

"Who hired you?" Erik asked.

"I don't know."

"Wrong answer."

The stone rolled off Erik's hand and over the edge of the cliff. It missed Wallace, but not by much. Both men listened while the rock bounced, grated, bounced again, then rolled off down the steep slope at the bottom of the cliff. The stone rolled for a long time, caroming off anything bigger than itself with unhappy crunching sounds.

"How far do you think you'll roll?" Erik asked, picking up another rock. This time there was nothing casual about the way he handled it. He looked like the baseball pitcher he once had been.

Wallace began to get nervous. "I told you the truth. I don't know who hired me."

The next rock smacked into his shoulder. It could just as easily have been his nose. Both men knew it. Only one of them sweated over it.

"I don't know!" Wallace said, his voice rising.

Rocks rained down one after another, thrown so swiftly that he couldn't have ducked even if he had been on the flats. A cut opened up high on his cheek. The back of his head throbbed. He tried to crawl into the cracks on the cliff, but there wasn't nearly enough room.

He had been pummeled before, but never while clinging to a cliff. It terrified him almost as much as the certainty that Erik North was playing with him like a cat idly toying with a mouse before he moved in for the kill.

"Please," Wallace said hoarsely. "You gotta believe me. I don't know!"

"I don't believe you."

More rocks rained down. Wallace slipped and barely caught himself.

"Stop!" His voice broke. His breath sawed. "I'm telling you, I don't know! I tried, but he's too slick. I've worked for him on and off for ten years, and I don't know his name!" He took another broken breath and hunched his shoulders against more punishment. "The bastard's real good, whoever he is. Or she. Could be a woman, I suppose. I just don't fucking know!"

Erik wished he didn't believe Wallace. But he did. The man was shaking.

"How do you get paid?" Erik asked.

"Now it's cash sent to an overseas bank. At first, it was small, nonsequential bills mailed to my P.O. box."

"From what city?" Erik knew that the detective would have been curious enough to check the mailing envelope.

"L.A. twice, New York twice, Miami, Denver, Dallas, Seattle."

"The boy—or girl—gets around." Erik flipped the fist-size rock from palm to palm as though it was as light as a tennis ball. "Who do you think it is?"

"Not a clue," Wallace said in disgust, but his shaking was subsiding. "And I've tried to find out. Believe me."

Erik did. The possibilities for blackmail must have appealed to someone like Wallace, especially once he began doing the kind of illegal, high-ticket jobs that required payment through an overseas account. "How are you contacted?"

"By phone. The number is blocked. The call isn't traceable."

"Man or woman?"

"Could be a Pekingese. It's hard to tell with a high-end voice distorter." He wiped his sweaty, blood-streaked forehead against the back of his hand. "You mind if I climb down? My hand is getting tired."

"So is mine. Want to see who drops what first?"

Wallace gave up the idea of trying to pull his weapon under the pretense of climbing down the cliff.

"What kind of jobs do you usually do for your mystery client?" Erik asked.

"Background checks."

"Bullshit."

Wallace considered hanging tough and trying to make his first answer fly. Then he looked at Erik's eyes. There was more light now, a lot more, but it would take something hotter than sunlight to warm up those eyes. "Once or twice I leaned on some people."

"Who?"

"A bellman who was robbing rooms. A check artist who liked to use the names of the rich and anonymous."

"An old lady in Florida?" he asked casually. "Fire?"

Wallace didn't flinch.

"A guru in Sedona?" Erik asked, watching the other narrowly. "Fire again."

Wallace looked confused.

"An old woman in the Mojave Desert?" Erik continued. "Napalm, this time."

"What is this, some kind of state-by-state tour of pyros?"

More rocks rained down. Wallace's look of confusion went back to stark fear. "I don't know what you're talking about!" he shouted. "I've worked in a lot of states, okay? I'm not a torch! It's not the way I do things!"

Erik weighed the answers and the rock in his hand. Wallace undoubtedly knew more than he was telling, but he hadn't flinched or sweated at being questioned about three deaths by fire, so he wasn't going to be any help there. He could stone Wallace right off the cliff, but there was little point. All Erik really wanted was the name of whoever had hired Wallace. Wallace didn't have that name.

Something moved at the edge of Erik's peripheral vision: Serena's scarf, lifting on a breeze too light for him to sense. He turned his head just enough to see her clearly, but not enough to take his attention away from Wallace.

Serena was standing to his right. She walked forward until she could see the man on the cliff—and he could see the barrel of the gun pointing straight at him. Her knuckles were white around the gun. Her legs trembled, but the gun barrel didn't.

"Is he the one who murdered my grandmother?" Serena asked.

The quality of her voice made the hair stir on the back of Erik's neck. This was a woman who would fight for whatever she loved and let hell take the loser.

"I never did an old woman," Wallace said instantly.

"Good thing it wasn't her grand*father*," Erik said, not knowing if he believed the professional liar. "Right, Bad Billy?"

Wallace shut up.

Erik felt like dropping the rock he held and a few more for good measure. Men like Wallace gave him a pain real low down in his butt. They were barbarians swaggering through civilization, taking advantage of the rules while breaking them, giving nothing back to the world but a raised middle finger.

"Do you believe him?" Serena asked.

"Until I have a better reason not to, yeah. Nothing we found in his file suggests he likes to burn people. He prefers bullets or tire irons." Erik flipped the rock back and forth in his hands, thinking fast. "Okay, Bad Billy. You're going to climb down off that cliff and go back to your car. We're going to watch, but not from any of the places you'll expect us to be. If you're a good boy, your car will still work when you get there. If not, you'll have a hell of a long walk back home. Any questions?"

"Think you're real tough, don't you?" Wallace asked bitterly.

"I'm better than tough. I'm smart. Any time you don't believe it, I'll be happy to demonstrate. Again."

Wallace was just barely smart enough himself to bite back all the gutter talk he wanted to share. He ignored Serena, dismissing her as an amateur. If he wasn't stuck here on the cliff, he would have fed her the gun by now.

"Start climbing down," Erik said. "I don't have to tell you what will happen if you don't keep your hands in sight, do I?"

"Fuck you," Wallace said roughly.

"Not in this lifetime."

"Fucking pansy-assed—" Wallace slipped, scrambled, flailed, caught himself.

And came up with a gun in his hand.

The unfamiliar double-pull on the trigger made Serena's first shot go wide. The rock Erik fired at Wallace was right on target. It hit the man like a club, numbing his gun hand, sending the weapon flying. Serena's second shot was wild, because the instant Erik released the rock, his arm kept on swinging, knocking her gun aside. Wallace didn't see, because he was back to hugging the cliff. In his mind there was only one threat, and its name was Erik North.

"Let the land take care of it," Erik said to Serena without looking away from Wallace, who was rapidly losing his hold on the cliff. One good hand just wasn't enough. "Less questions that way."

She stared at Erik for a moment that sent ice down her spine. She had always sensed a warrior's cold pragmatism beneath his smile, but she had never really felt it. Until now.

Wallace slid like a sack of mud to the bottom of the cliff and started rolling down the ridge. After about twenty yards, a big rock stopped him. For a few moments he lay there, dazed. Then he pulled himself to his feet and looked up to the top of the cliff.

No one was there.

He turned and went painfully down the slope, wondering if his car would be where he had left it.

It was.

But it didn't work.

Forty-six

"What do you mean, you lost them!"

Wallace grimaced. Even the distorter couldn't conceal the anger in his mystery client's voice.

"You moron. How could you lose them? Where?"

"Up a fucking mountain, that's where. North led me on a runaround, dumped me off a cliff, and drained my gas tank. When I got to a place where my cell phone worked, I called my partner, then I called you."

"Find them. Fast."

"I plan on it. You care what shape he's in when I'm done?"

"No."

"What about her?" Wallace asked.

"Just get me those pages any way you can."

"You're not paying me enough for Murder One."

"I'll put a hundred thousand in an account in your name with the Bank of Aruba."

"Two hundred."

"One-fifty. Don't fuck up again, Wallace. Dead men don't spend money."

Forty-seven

No sooner had Erik and Serena walked in the front door of North Castle than his pager went off. He looked at the pager window. Dana.

From upstairs came the sound of the vacuum cleaner. Lila-Marie was hard at work keeping house.

"I forgot to ask how Mr. Picky feels about vacuums," he said.

"Loves 'em. Being vacuumed is a special treat."

He gave her a sideways look. She had been tight and pale for the hike back to his SUV. During most of the drive, she had been quiet, watching him as if she hadn't seen him before.

Then she had asked: *Do you do this sort of thing often?*

Not if I can help it.

Oddly, that had seemed to reassure her. She had sighed, leaned into the car seat, and said: *It's new to me.*

Didn't look like it. You did just fine, Serena. A real mama tiger.

Her smile had been brief, but real.

So had his.

"I'm serious," Serena said, listening to the vacuum upstairs. "It took Picky a while to get what he wanted through my dense brain, but he managed. He drools in ecstasy when I vacuum him."

"Maybe I should tell Factoid to try it with Gretchen."

Serena blinked. "Excuse me?"

"If you ask, I'll tell you, but you won't want to know."

She looked at the expectant curve of his mouth and decided not to take the lure. "Okay. I'll go check on Picky."

In disbelief, Erik watched the lithe flex and sway of Serena's hips as she climbed the stairs. If she had been one of his younger sisters, he would have been pestered until he told her more than she wanted to know. That would have been fun, kind of, but mostly it would have been irritating.

No doubt about it, Serena wasn't his little sister. Thank God. The things he wanted to do with her didn't come under the category of brotherly, except maybe in ancient Egypt.

Smiling, he keyed Dana's number into the cellular.

"What's up, boss?" he asked.

"I was going to ask you the same thing."

"Like I told Niall as soon as I got off the mountain, I'm still studying the pages when I'm not leading Bad Billy on a wilderness hike."

"Hmm. Niall didn't say anything except that you would be late coming here. Did Wallace enjoy the outing?"

"Doubt it."

"Did he survive intact?"

"More or less. No marks on him that couldn't be accounted for by a careless hiker taking a header down a small cliff."

"Excellent." Dana all but purred. "Did you learn anything?"

"He doesn't know who hired him."

"Do you believe that?"

"For now," Erik said. "It fits the pattern. He's the type who would blackmail someone if he thought it was worth the trouble. Since whoever hired him knows he's a leg-breaker, a black-bag specialist, and quite probably a killer, he's paid accordingly. I have to assume that anyone who can afford him would be worth shaking down."

"Did Wallace try to intimidate you?"

"Yeah. He didn't know the difference between tough and smart."

"You're both."

"Nope. I'm smart but I'm tapioca. Just ask Niall."

Niall's voice came from somewhere close to Dana. "Balls."

"You've assured me that Fuzzies don't have them," Erik said, smiling because Niall couldn't see it.

When Niall answered, his voice was much clearer. Obviously he had grabbed the phone from Dana. "You wearing a gun?" he demanded.

"Only because you made it a deal-breaker."

"It still is, boyo."

"I can't hear you over the vacuum cleaner," Erik said loudly.

Dana must have reclaimed the phone from Niall, because it was her voice that said, "Don't even think about it. If Niall says you carry, you damn well carry."

Erik shrugged. "You're the boss."

"Do keep it in mind while you attend the International Antiquarian Book Exposition in L.A."

"Say again?"

"You heard me. If anyone asks, Rarities has a client who wants an opinion of a fourteenth-century Book of the Hours."

"What kind of opinion?"

"Is it worth the money Pinsky is asking."

"No. Morgan Pinsky always asks too much. See? I just saved you mileage to L.A."

"You know you're dying to go through all those boxes of loose leaves to see if there's a nugget in with the dross," Dana said. "If Pinsky is within bargaining distance of a bearable price, and the manuscript is as represented, buy it."

"Define bearable."

"Under one million. His asking price is two and change."

Erik whistled. "Pinsky has delusions of grandeur."

"Perhaps. And perhaps he has a beautifully illuminated Book of the Hours with the name of a French duke in the front and the coat of arms of a royal bastard throughout."

"What about the Huntington Library?"

"They told him it didn't meet the needs of their collection. I've told the hotel to expect you and a guest. Several, actually. Niall insists that you not be left alone."

"Don't forget the twenty-pound cat."

"What?"

"Maybe twenty-one by now. Picky has a serious canned salmon habit and where Serena goes, he goes."

"If the hotel can handle toddlers, it can handle a cat."

"Is Pinsky expecting me?"

"Of course not. The fair runs through tomorrow. Expect to stay."

"I have several dealers I have to talk to about missing leaves from the Book of the Learned," Erik began, trying to control his impatience. "Can't the Pinsky stuff wait?"

"I assume you're talking about Albert Lars, Reginald Smythe, and Janet Strawbinger, all of whom have owned sheets that originally came from the Book of the Learned, despite their present fifteenth-century French surface."

"Yes," he said impatiently. "I went over all this with—"

"Bert and Reggie will both be at the exposition," Dana cut in. "Bert, as always, is living beyond the allowance his parents give him. They're ninety and ticking along just fine. Probably good for another decade, so money is the way to Bert's heart. Reggie, as always, is living from sale to sale. Again, money will open his doors. The third dealer whose background you requested—"

"Strawbinger."

"Yes. Strawbinger. She's overseas. Germany. One of the old castles is cleaning out its basement. Her balance sheet is healthy enough that something other than money might be required to get her attention, unless she loses her head over the contents of the castle and is strapped until she sells some of it."

Erik shrugged. "She was the least interesting to me of the three." He thought quickly, balancing various demands. "All right. I've already digitized Serena's pages and loaded them on my computer and in the Rarities archive. We'll bring the real pages in, leave them in one of Rarities's vaults, do the Exposition dance, and then she and I are loose."

"Except for a few operatives tagging along, fine. What do you have in mind?"

"Finding the rest of the Book of the Learned."

Silence.

"It's the only way I'll be able to put a price on the pages Serena has, which is the only way I can fill your client's request," Erik added smoothly.

Dana laughed. "That's what I like about smart men—they're almost always worth the trouble they cause." Ralph Kung's voice in the background demanded her attention. Cleary Warrick Montclair was tired of being on hold. "Damnation, that woman never gives up," Dana said. "Switch her to my second phone."

Niall grabbed the first phone and talked fast to Erik. "Watch your back. Wallace isn't called Bad Billy just because all the other monikers were taken."

"Is he really good for murder?" Erik asked.

"In court or out?"

"Out."

"He's rumored to be, and now you've pissed him off. Don't be the Fuzzy dickhead who makes those rumors a reality."

Forty-eight

The long, monotonous thunder of huge jet planes sliding down out of the sky to land at Los Angeles International Airport didn't penetrate the hotel's faux-marble lobby. In the bar adjoining the lobby, patrons with wire-rim glasses, wilted shirts, tweed or corduroy coats, and bad hair were the order of the day. There were more martinis crossing the bar than microbrews or wine. From the look on the cocktail server's face, the antiquarian book folks tipped the way they dressed—badly.

Erik glanced away from the bar lobby to the easel that supported a placard welcoming everyone to the International Antiquarian Book Exposition and instructing them to please sign in on the lower mezzanine level. He stifled a sigh that was part wistful, part impatient. The wistfulness came from the unquenchable hope that somewhere, somehow, amid all the first-edition Hardy Boys and Betty Boop posters, there would be an undiscovered page from the Book of the Learned. His impatience came from the same source: so much crap, so little gold.

But then, the same could be said of everything. Hotel lobbies, for example.

According to Lapstrake, the good news was that Wallace's partner had indeed arrived at North Castle but had gotten there too late to catch Erik and Serena. No one had followed them to L.A. Erik thought they might have picked up a shadow at the Retreat—the small, very fine hotel Rarities always used for clients—but he couldn't be sure. He was, however, certain that no one had followed them to this hotel.

Yet.

And he was going to stand around the lobby for a while just to see if that changed.

"You rushed me out the back door of our quiet, luxurious hotel in Beverly Hills for this?" Serena asked, looking around the loud, echoing lobby of the airport hotel. The clients at the Beverly Hills Retreat had all been expensively, if sometimes casually, dressed. Not the people at this hotel. She hadn't seen such a wretched collection of clothes since her thrift shop days. "Some of the suit coats those men have on are old enough to qualify for museum status." She looked at the fifteen-by-fifteen-foot lavender silk-flower arrangement, complete with real dust and spiderwebs. "As for the hotel decor, forget it. I'm sure trying to."

"Yeah. I told you that you'd envy Picky before this was over."

"You were right. From a hotel that feeds their feline guests lobster tidbits and puts them up on satin pillows in a room the size of Rhode Island, to . . ." She looked at the spider busy rolling up a fly for a midnight snack. "This."

"You'd never guess that there are millions of dollars in rare and old books downstairs, would you?"

"Not from looking at the fairgoers," she said, glancing toward the lobby bar.

"Most of them are exhibitors, not spectators."

"They put all their money in their stock rather than in their wardrobe?"

"Somewhat. But mostly it's the professorial thing. Bad clothes, bad teeth, great mind."

"Don't forget the bad hair."

Grinning, he combed his fingers through his needs-a-haircut mop. "Are you talking about me?"

"Not even on your worst day," Serena said absently, studying a man—no, it was a woman—whose hair was three inches of henna and one inch of white right next to the pink scalp. "You have gorgeous hair. I'd kill for it."

"I'd rather have yours falling like fire all over my bare skin."

The words and the sensual heat in his tawny eyes drew her, made her breath stop. "Don't talk like that," she said quickly.

"Why not?"

"It's distracting."

His glance traveled over her like hands, remembering. "Yeah, it sure is." He made himself look away, scanning the lobby for someone who was glancing at them too often or who looked like the file photo of Ed Heller that Factoid had sent as a .jpeg.

A woman with the body of a Playmate and the grace of a ballerina came gliding up to Erik. Serena gave the woman a good look. Though not beautiful in the Hollywood sense of the word, she was somehow compelling. Her hair was a sleek slice of midnight. Her eyes were wide-set and delft blue. Her mouth made you think of burgundy wine and sex. Her voice was humid, steamy, southern.

"If Shane had told me you were going to be here, I wouldn't have kicked as hard about coming," she said.

"Risa! Where did you come from? It's been forever since I've seen you." Erik bent down to give Risa a hug and a kiss.

Serena told herself that she wasn't jealous. Then she told herself again. She was going for a third time when he released the stunning woman and grinned down at her with obvious pleasure as he made introductions. Serena and Risa shook hands while they gave each other the kind of once-over only another woman could.

Risa wondered where Erik had found the aloof, brooding redhead with the witchy bedroom eyes and the kind of lithe, elegant body that Risa had wanted all of her life. Not to mention a textile jacket that was so extraordinary she had a hard time keeping her hands off it. Odd that such a striking woman would wear such a dull scarf as an accessory, but there was no accounting for individual style.

"Don't tell me your boss has you combing through the dustbins, too," Erik said, pulling Risa's attention away from Serena. "What did you do to piss him off this time?"

"I'm breathing." Risa turned back to Serena. "Where did you get that fabulous jacket?"

"I made it."

At first Risa thought it was a joke. Then she realized it wasn't. "Well, there goes that dream."

"What dream?" Erik asked.

"The one where I buy a jacket like that and attract the lover of the century."

"Hey, I offered," Erik said.

She rolled her eyes. "Only *after* you were sure I was over my crush on you, and then you only did it to salvage my pride when my boyfriend dumped me for a rich girl who could pay for his Ph.D."

"He was a loser, a pretty boy with no morals."

"I'm sure you're right, darlin'," Risa said slowly, letting the natural smokiness of her voice increase with the drawl. "It comes with being a big bad older brother." She winked at Serena. "But I'm friends with Erik's sisters, which means I can get even. He has no secrets from me."

"Really?" Serena grinned, liking Risa better with everything she heard. "Can I buy you a glass or three of wine?"

"You can do the girly bonding thing over my secrets later," Erik cut in. "Have you been down to the floor?" he asked Risa.

The shrug she gave made light move over the tailored

coarse silk jacket she wore. Serena had thought the jacket was black, but the glints of light in it were an intense, almost fiery blue, rather like her eyes.

"I've been there," Risa said. She put her slender, manicured hands in the pockets of her tailored black slacks. "The usual stuff."

"What is Shane after?"

"You'll have to ask him."

"Damn," Erik muttered. "I was afraid of that. He's heard about that carpet page of gold foil and touches of color, hasn't he?"

Risa simply raised her sleek eyebrows.

"Well, I'd rather he got it than some other people I could think of," Erik said, but he wasn't happy at having more competition. Tannahill was an enigma. Trustworthy up to a point—that point being when Tannahill wanted to acquire something. Then it was a new game, with new rules. As in no rules.

"So you'd rather Shane buy the golden goody than Norman Warrick?" Risa asked.

"So Shane *is* after that page."

Risa smiled like a cat. She was every bit as competitive as her boss was. "You know him better than I do."

"Nobody knows Shane."

"Odd. He said the same thing about you. I agreed with him, and I know you better than anyone except perhaps Niall." Risa's smile became deeper as she turned to Serena and handed her a business card. "Don't let Erik talk you out of having drinks with me. I think we might find we've got a lot in common."

"Smart women in a world run by men?" Erik said, a pained expression on his face. It was his sisters' favorite gripe.

Risa blew him a kiss from ripe, sultry lips. "You guessed it."

Serena watched the other woman stride away. She covered the ground quickly, but somehow it looked easy, luxuriant, as though she had all the time in the world to be lazy.

"I can't believe you turned her down," Serena said.

"I don't rob cradles."

"She's not that much younger."

"Not now. She was then."

"So what happened to now?"

Erik looked at Serena. "What do you mean?"

"Why aren't you two lovers?" she asked bluntly.

"We like each other too well to ruin a good friendship with what we both knew would be short-term sex."

"How do you know it would be short-term?"

"Ever look at a pair of shoes and know without trying them on that no matter how great they look, they're going to pinch?"

"Sure. It's called experience."

"That's how we knew."

Serena's dark-red lashes lowered over her eyes for a moment. "Okay."

"What does that mean?"

"Just that. Okay. It makes sense. Only teenagers have to go over a cliff to find out it hurts when you land."

Erik opened his mouth, closed it, and gave her a slow smile. He would never understand a woman's mind, but that didn't prevent him from enjoying the quick ones. "I like you, Serena Charters."

"I'm learning to like you, Erik North."

"An acquired taste, is that it?"

She licked her lips, remembering just how he tasted.

"You're killing me," he said. He bent and kissed her quick and hard and deep. Then he said in a low voice, "I like Risa, but I don't trust her in this. She's an ambitious, intelligent woman with a lot to prove. She has made some acquisitions for Shane that were frankly borderline as to methods and/or provenance. She wants those pages because her boss doesn't promote losers."

"Are you sure you like her?"

"Yes, a whole lot. That doesn't make me blind." He kissed Serena hard again and buried his face against the fey scarf in the curve of her neck. He was baffled by the need he felt to reassure himself that she was here with him, within reach, as though if he turned away for an instant she would be gone for a thousand years. "Now let's go see if we can find another leaf or two of the Book of the Learned."

Serena wanted to tell Erik to wait, her head was spinning and she really wanted to keep on kissing him. Then she heard her own thoughts, shook her head briskly, and strode after him to the escalator. As she followed him down, she smiled and said silently, *G'mom, some of them just might be worth the trouble. He doesn't crowd me even when he's so close the only thing I can breathe is him.*

That was a first.

In fact, she had thought it was impossible. But the proof was right in front of her, riding down the escalator, looking around the lower mezzanine with the eyes of a hungry bird of prey. The supple leather suit coat he wore with casual slacks and scuffed-enough-to-be-comfortable loafers fitted him like a dark-chocolate shadow. She decided that he had a perfect build, strong without being muscle-bound, and big enough to make her feel as deliciously feminine as Risa's mouth.

Then Serena remembered what he had said about Risa: *Don't trust her in this.* Erik lived in a world where trust was a commodity that could be rationed. She lived in a world where she had learned to trust no one. Not really. Not all the way.

Yet she wanted to trust him all the way, even though she knew that was foolish. She couldn't help it. She trusted him not to kill her. She trusted him as a lover. Now she was sliding toward trusting him not to hurt her in ways that weren't physical but were very real nonetheless.

She didn't need her grandmother's advice to know that trusting Erik like that was stupid. He had come to her because of the mystery surrounding the Book of the Learned. He would leave when the mystery was solved. End of story. End of affair.

At best, she would be hurt. At worst, she would end up like her grandmother. Murdered.

But unlike her grandmother, Serena wouldn't know why she had died.

Forty-nine

Erik stepped off the escalator, waited for Serena, and led her to the registration table that waited near the hallway just beyond the rest rooms. He could have dropped a Rarities business card on the rumpled woman behind the table and been given two VIP passes. But he would rather pay ten bucks apiece for visitor passes and site maps and not have some PR person hovering over him, telling him how important this or that exhibit was, and how this book exposition was the ultimate destination for discriminating collectors from all over the world.

If he didn't know that already, he wouldn't have come in the first place. Or, to be precise, Dana wouldn't have sent him.

Because no matter how much professionals bitched about all the junk that could be found at affairs like this, there was always something spectacular, too. Something that a museum couldn't or wouldn't afford. Something that was labeled one thing and was actually another. Something that just filled a gap in a private collection or sent a collector off on a whole new tangent. That was why everyone came: the hunt. They never knew what they might find.

And the exhibitors came because they never knew what they might sell.

"The manuscripts are down this way," Erik said, looking at the site map.

Reginald Smythe's booth was down the center aisle, just where a novice would be expected to start looking. The good news was that Erik had never dealt professionally with Smythe, so he wouldn't be recognized as a knowledgeable buyer. The bad news was that the indirect approach took longer.

But it left him with a fallback position.

"Play along with me," Erik said quietly. "You wanted to come here and you're my fiancée. Don't mention anything about anything unless I do it first. Okay?"

"I guess."

"I don't want to be guessing."

"Okay. I'm arm candy and you're the big man."

Erik was still laughing when she followed him into a long hall with doors opening off it on one side. As she stepped through after him, she discovered that all the doors led to the same place—a huge ballroom. The room had been partitioned into subrooms that held booths of various sizes and differing contents for sale.

Staring around, trying not to trip because she was looking everywhere but where she was headed, she walked beside him down a narrow corridor between booths. Though the exhibit floor was far from crowded with customers, a hum of conversation hovered just below the threshold of hearing, punctuated by sudden words and phrases.

". . . biggest choir book I ever saw. Size of a card table and illuminated with . . ."

". . . not since the Lindisfarne Gospels has there been a . . ."

". . . sure it was commissioned by Charlemagne, but I can't prove it. That's why the price is so . . ."

"You sell anything yet?"

". . . illustrated page from *La Divina Commedia*. Look at the fine . . ."

". . . believe this leaf came from a Carolingian Bible. All the internal evidence points to a ninth-century . . ."

Serena wondered if her eyes were spinning like pinwheels. She wanted to look at everything, but Erik had his hand wrapped around her upper arm and was all but frogmarching her down the rows of fascinating manuscripts. Every so often she dug in her heels for a better look, but he didn't let her linger nearly long enough.

". . . see, signed right there, Bartolomeo Sanvito. I assure you, this is as fine a fifteenth-century book as you will . . ."

"Hey, you sell anything yet?"

Serena turned, but couldn't see the questioner who was going down a parallel aisle saluting various exhibitors with the same question.

". . . the quality of this historiated initial. Sumptuous! The epitome of sixteenth-century . . ."

". . . exquisite lapis blue in the Madonna's robe, but it's the gold foil that gives this . . ."

"No, it's late East Anglian style. Look at those faces. They could have been copied from the Luttrell Psalter."

"You sell anything yet?"

Erik felt Serena's unwillingness to be dragged any farther and almost smiled. He managed to bully her as far as Reggie Smythe's booth before her patience ran out. Not that he blamed her. Anyone who made textiles as medieval-feeling as she did would be fascinated by the designs and illuminations of medieval books, particularly in the British style, which owed a lot to the designs and symbols of Celtic ancestors.

Pretending reluctance, muttering, he stopped trying to pull her farther down the aisle. She planted her feet and looked past the shoulder of a worn tweed jacket to the page under discussion. He glanced at the page the gently crazed exhibitor was trying to sell to a customer who also wore an exhibitor's badge. More exhibitors swapped goods at these events than sold them outright to walk-ins.

"I'd be willing to talk about a trade for your fourteenth-century leaf from a French Epistle Lectionary," said the exhibitor. A smudged badge with the words REGGIE SMYTHE on it had been fastened crookedly to the man's suit coat.

"I'll bet you would be," said the customer, unimpressed. "But if you throw in that damaged leaf from Chartier's 'Le livre des quatre dames' we might have something to talk about."

"Damaged!" Smythe stepped back as though he had been struck. His shaggy salt-and-pepper hair fairly bristled with disdain. "Only a cretin would consider the normal, beautiful marks made by the passage of time and use on vellum as *damage.*"

The other man shrugged. "If you haven't moved either of these by closing time on Sunday, look me up. I'm over by the exit sign on aisle G."

Smythe smiled grimly and turned to Erik and Serena, ignoring the other man who, despite his words, was still hanging around and looking at the leaf. "Lovely, isn't it? Would you like to examine it more closely?"

"You sell anything yet?" came faintly from another aisle.

"No, thanks," Erik said before Serena could speak. Then he thought, what the hell, nothing ventured nothing gained. Niall would faint at the almost direct approach, but Niall wasn't here. "My aunt is an antiques nut. You have any early twelfth-century pages written in the Insular Celtic style? Secular, not ecclesiastical." He spoke slowly, with the air of a man who has carefully memorized what he is supposed to look for.

"Secular? No."

"How about any, uh, palimps—palimpsests?" Artfully he stumbled over the unusual word.

"Partial or entire?" Smythe asked, smiling genially.

"Either one is fine, I guess. She didn't say."

"Secular?"

"Doesn't matter."

"Age?"

"Hell, I don't care," Erik said easily, "but she's excited

about fifteenth-century illumination." He shrugged. "I guess it's nice enough, if you go for that sort of thing."

Fifteenth-century illumination was the style he had found on all but one of the overwritten pages he had tracked down from the Book of the Learned.

"*Nice.*" Smythe winced. "Um, yes. Fifteenth-century illumination is considered by many to be the peak of the illuminator's art." He cleared his throat and ducked beneath the counter. He emerged with a cardboard carton. Inside, like pictures in colorful cardboard frames, there was a batch of vellum leaves of various ages, quality, and condition. "These," he said, selecting quickly, "are what you're looking for."

Erik took the box, hefted it, and decided that it was time for his fallback position: screw subtlety. He ignored Smythe's recommendations and began flipping through the framed leaves with a speed that said either he knew exactly what he was looking for or he didn't care about what he was seeing. He left it to Smythe to decide which.

Serena waited until Erik was nearly through the stack before she gave up being polite and leaned in over his shoulder to see for herself the flashing bits of gold and color and calligraphy. When he felt her interest—and her warm breath on his neck—he commented on the pieces almost as quickly as he could flip through them. He had concluded he wouldn't find anything important in this booth by playing dumb. Reggie was a bottom feeder.

"School exercise," Erik said curtly about one crudely written page. "He had a long way to go for a passing grade."

"Thirteenth century, not fifteenth."

"Wonder who mixed his colors? Looks like he used urine instead of vinegar, and he'd been drinking too much milk."

The leaf whipped by before Serena could do much more than register a rather sickly, faded green.

"Lampblack ink, not oak gall and iron. Wrong for the purported time and place. Matches the drawing, though. Inept."

Smythe glanced at the leaf in question and didn't argue. He

had taken it in trade along with several quite nice fourteenth-century leaves. Win some, lose some.

"Idiot. He used gold paint before the other colors instead of after. Must have thought he was working with gold foil. Bet his teacher whacked his knuckles but good over that one."

Two leaves whipped by, leaving the last one.

"Could have used a better lunellum," Erik said, dismissing the last leaf.

"A what?" Serena asked, leaning in even more.

He took a breath that tasted of sweet woman. Above the scarf her neck looked as smooth as cream. It had felt just as rich on his tongue.

"A lunellum is the curved knife they used to scrape the hide clean," he said absently, breathing deeply again, savoring her nearness, wondering if the scarf would mind being bitten. Gently, of course. The odd thought made him smile. "This vellum looks like it was chewed up and spit out."

The exhibitor flinched but didn't disagree. It was a truly ragged example of the art.

"The good news is that the illuminator was obviously still learning his trade, so a piece of good vellum wasn't wasted on an incompetent artist," Erik said.

He wondered if he was going to have to question Reggie outright about the sheet he had listed for sale on the Internet. Or maybe the sheet had already been sold.

Damn.

"So far these aren't palimpsests so much as erased and written-over school exercises," Erik said bluntly. "Do you have anything better or are you wasting my time?"

Without a word Smythe went to another box. This one was slimmer and the pages were stored flat within their cardboard frames. Smythe opened the box carefully.

Serena's breath went out in a rush that stirred the hair near Erik's ear and made his heart kick over in double time.

"Gorgeous," she said. "Not my favorite style, but gorgeous

all the same." She looked at the sticker in the corner of the frame: $1,100.

Erik didn't say a word. He simply speared the exhibitor with a glance. "What's wrong with it?"

"What do you mean?" Smythe asked.

"Get real. This looks like the work of the Spanish Forger. If it is, you wouldn't be hiding it in a box."

The exhibitor cleared his throat and gave up hoping that this customer didn't know a whole lot about illuminated manuscripts. "I thought it was, too, until I put it up against some originals. If one can call a forgery an original, that is."

"Do you have any other pages like it?" Erik asked. "I like to have more than one to choose from."

"No, not with me."

"In your shop?"

Reggie tugged uselessly at his crooked name badge. "Actually, I don't have any like this. I've sold one or two through the years." To be precise, he had sold this page before, but he didn't think it was necessary to be precise. No point in confusing the client.

Erik could have told him when and where the sheet had been sold before, but what he wanted to know was the oldest source. The *first* person to put the sheet on the market. That was the person he wanted to talk to. "Where did you get anything like this sheet in the beginning?"

"At the time, I was buying from a lot of estate sales, the kind that don't have a real inventory because the goods aren't worth the effort."

"Can you remember the first time you saw a page like this?"

Reggie looked at Erik. "Young man, I've been in the business for thirty-five years. It's hardly likely that I would remember a page as insignificant as this, is it?"

"Only if you got burned."

"If I did, I didn't know it at the time." Pointedly, he went back to the page at hand. "I'm guessing this is a pastiche drawn from the Spanish Forger's work. An angel from one page. A castle from another. A dragon from a third. A Madonna from a fourth. Excellent artwork, but not, I'm afraid, authentic. Quite a beautiful capital *F*, though, don't you agree? Great depth and balance despite the, er, eclectic nature of the composition."

"A forged pastiche of authentic forgeries," Serena said under her breath. "I'm getting another headache."

"What about the text beneath?" Erik asked.

"Secular. From what I can tell, it's probably twelfth-century. That's why I brought it out. This box is for, er, special buyers with particular needs."

Erik wondered if "special" was another word for stupid. Or "dishonest." But it wasn't his problem. Finding out if this leaf had been cut from the Book of the Learned was. "Did you put it under a lamp?"

Smythe didn't ask what kind of lamp. UV was the only one that made sense in this context. "Yes. There was a faint trace of an initial beneath. Another *F*, perhaps—or a *B*."

Or an E *and an* S *combined.*

But Erik didn't say it aloud. "Text?"

"No. This was probably cut from a practice sheet or from the extra sheets at the front or back of a manuscript."

"Forgers do it all the time," Erik agreed. "That way the vellum, at least, is the right age."

"But if vellum was so valuable, why did the original owners waste it on blank pages?" Serena asked.

"Remember how pages came in those days, one full hide at a time?"

She nodded.

"The hide could be folded to make any number of smaller and smaller pages in multiples of two, four, or eight. Today printers still make pages in multiples, called gathers or quires, which means you end up with blank pages if the text doesn't come out even."

She nodded again.

"It happened more often in the past. A lot of times there simply wasn't enough text to fill all the pages of a gather," Erik said. "Or sometimes books were gathered but not finished. And sometimes the presence of blank pages at the front and back of a manuscript was a statement of the importance of the book itself. An early example of conspicuous consumption."

An old image came to Serena, twisting like a darkly glittering current through her memory. "You mean like a book cover of hammered gold set with rubies and sapphires and pearls and either rock crystal or badly cut diamonds? With designs that are—"

Erik went still for an instant, then said across her words, "Yeah, just like the one we saw at the Huntington." Before she could object that they hadn't even been to the Huntington, he turned to Smythe. "Two hundred."

"Eight," Smythe said automatically.

"Try again. This isn't worth shit to a collector." Erik stroked the side of Serena's cheek and slid his fingers beneath the silky scarf, silently asking her to play along. "I'm only buying it because my fiancée thinks it's pretty and I forgot her birthday last week."

Serena bit the inside of her lip so she wouldn't laugh out loud. Slowly she rubbed her cheek against his palm and batted her eyelashes at him like a good little fiancée. "You're so sweet. But you don't have to buy me anything. I meant it when I said I wasn't mad."

"For you, darling, it's a pleasure." Erik dropped his hand and began flipping through the few leaves in the box. Nothing stirred his interest.

"Five hundred," Smythe said quickly, sensing a sale slipping away.

"Two-fifty."

"Would you like it wrapped?"

Erik nodded curtly, paid for the leaf in cash, and grabbed Serena's arm. He pulled her a few steps away where no one could overhear them and demanded, "Where did you see a book cover with jewels and hammered gold?"

Serena thought the clarity and intensity of Erik's eyes would be really attractive if they weren't aimed at her in something close to anger and accusation. But they were.

"I—just an old memory, that's all. Probably from school." But neither of them believed it.

"Was it a Baroque style, or full of fleurs-de-lis, or plain or fancy or—"

"It was more Celtic than anything else," she said. "Bold yet intricate. Like the initials *E* and *S* on my pages, but *not* the initials if you know what I mean."

"Could you draw it?"

"I could try. Why?"

"How old is your memory? As old as the memory of the intertwined initials?"

She quickly saw his point. "You think I saw this cover at the same time."

"I think if I put all that work into a manuscript, I or one of my descendants might just decorate the hell out of it as a way to prove its importance."

Serena closed her eyes and tried to recall the memory more clearly. The harder she tried, the more vague the memory became. She made a sound of frustration rather like an angry cat. "I'm sorry. I can't help any more than that. I just can't see it."

He wanted to push her but sensed it wouldn't do any good. "Let's look at some more leaves. Maybe it will jog your memory."

"And if it doesn't?"

"We'll search the databases at Rarities."

"What if—"

"What if we die tomorrow?" he cut in impatiently, then wished he had bitten his tongue instead.

"You're so comforting."

"Yeah," he said, disgusted. "A regular snuggly bear." He

gave her a fast, fierce kiss. "Come on. There's a lot of crap to look at and not much time."

"Before we die?" she shot back sardonically.

He didn't answer. He had just seen someone who looked like the file photo of Ed Heller.

Fifty

Heller was pretty sure Erik North had made him. Wallace had warned him that Erik was tricky, but Heller hadn't believed it. Chrissake, the guy was a friggin' scholar. Even worse, a nancy-boy artist. Wallace must have been half-asleep to get caught on that cliff.

But Heller had to admit that Erik had real quick eyes.

The good news was that all Heller had to do was make a log of who Erik and Serena met at the fair, interview anyone they talked to without making any fuss, and tuck the targets in bed at the Retreat. Same thing tomorrow. No sweat. The dude with the bad hair—Smythe, Reginald, called Reggie, white male, Caucasian, about fifty years old, Boston residence, divorced—had been more than happy to talk about anything, including what he had just sold to the young man who knew a lot more about manuscripts than he had let on at first.

It had been all Heller could do to shut Smythe up before he started talking about his pet turtle and the sows at the dry cleaner who should go back on welfare instead of breaking the buttons off his shirts.

This kind of investigating was a lot easier than kneeling in rosebushes or cactus to take a close-up picture of the little woman with somebody other than her old man banging away between her thighs. Some operatives really got off on watching sex. Heller didn't, unless the little woman was built or the guy was really hung. Then it was kind of fun to watch them bounce.

"You sell anything yet?"

The familiar words yanked Heller back to his present job. He looked down the aisle with a frown. Someone ought to put an elbow in that jerk's throat. He must have asked that question a million times in the last fifteen minutes.

Heller's stomach growled. He pulled a granola bar out of his jacket pocket and opened it. As soon as he bit into the stuff, he remembered why he preferred peanuts straight up rather than crushed with honey and whatever else his wife was selling as health food that week.

Maybe Erik would get hungry soon. The café across the lobby from the bar hadn't been very full at all and the french fries had smelled good enough to eat.

Heller almost sighed. Someday he wouldn't have to haul around whole grain and fake chocolate, and lust after french fries. Someday he would be on the same gravy train as Wallace. He would be getting steak and pussy whenever he wanted. If he got a couple thousand for breaking an arm here and there, then whacking some dude should be worth ten thousand, easy. Hell, twenty. He would be shitting in high cotton, as his dead granny used to say.

The next time Wallace offered to cut him in on the good stuff, he was going to say yes.

Fifty-one

Risa Sheridan smiled at the young dealer who was trying to impress her with his knowledge of illuminated manuscripts and sex. It was No Sale all the way, but he didn't know it yet. She still had a few more questions to ask. She had better get some useful answers, too. Shane Tannahill wanted that gilded carpet page, which various people at the fair had already assured her was a contradiction in terms: carpet referred to painting and gilded was just a golden highlight. She simply had smiled and kept on asking.

If Shane wanted a gilded carpet page, she would get him a page where there was a lot more gold than colored paint and the design incised in the gold went from border to border. Her biggest problem was that she knew she wasn't the only one doing the looking for him. Shane believed in the shark model of employee advancement: throw them all in the same pool and see which shark swims the longest.

She planned on being the last shark. What she didn't know was how many other sharks Shane had thrown into the pool with her. All she knew for certain was that she wasn't the only one he had sent after the page. There were a lot of sharks he could call on for help. Unfortunately, competitively speaking, she wasn't the meanest shark in the pond; there were things she wouldn't do to win. Not many, but enough so that she could look herself in the mirror long enough to put on makeup.

Not everyone Shane hired was so fastidious, which meant she had to be the quickest and the smartest.

"So, you've heard of some Insular Celtic pages," she said, "but you don't have any to show me?"

"Nothing that's new to the market, but this is, like, a fine example of the time and period you want."

She looked at the leaf with an interest she didn't have to pretend. Her trained eye saw echoes of Celtic jewelry in every stroke of the illuminator's drawing. The style of the designs alone allowed her to place the leaf within a half-century and a few hundred miles of its time and place of origin. But telling the earnest scholar across the glass case from her that he had missed placing the leaf by a century and a country wasn't the way to get information from him. So she widened her eyes, licked the lips that seemed to fascinate men—for no reason that she had ever understood—and gave the young man an up-from-under-long-eyelashes look that was guaranteed to make him think with his dick.

"Is this like the pages you heard about?" she asked.

He wished it was. He really did. Almost as much as he wished he knew this lush-mouthed woman well enough to break some old civil laws about sex with her.

"Uh, no. They were painted. This is, like, drawn." He pointed to the initial, which indeed had been rendered in red ink rather than paint. "But this kind of drawing is the hallmark of Insular Celtic style and, like, technique."

"Then the other pages, the ones you heard about, wouldn't be as valuable?" she asked, telling herself that she wouldn't, really would *not*, start using, like, that word instead of, like, anything else.

Sighing, he memorized the pouting curve of her lower lip.

"Actually, they're, like, more valuable, because they're more rare. If they're, like, real."

"Real? As in authentic?"

"Yes. It's always, like, a question when utterly new material comes on the market. Especially . . ." His voice faded as he belatedly remembered that he was supposed to be selling manuscripts today, not lecturing to graduate art historians about the duties and pitfalls of becoming a curator to private collections. He smoothed a hand over hair that was already becoming distressingly thin. Like his mother's brother, he was going to be bald by thirty-five. "New material always, like, raises new questions."

"So Warrick is trashing the pages?" she said, reading between the lines.

He hesitated, then shrugged. Obviously, he wouldn't be the first to bring up the House of Warrick's discreet and damning warning about the pages. "Among others."

"Really? Who else has seen them?"

"No one. But if Norman Warrick says the pages should be, like, approached with great care, well, no one is going to stand up and say otherwise. Whoever owns those pages will have, like, a hard time selling them."

She smiled. Shane would be glad to hear it, because it would bring the price down and scare off other buyers. But she wouldn't tell him yet. She would let him sweat.

Not that a man as rich as Shane ever cared about money. Or anything else, for that matter.

"Thanks for your time," Risa said. "You've taught me a lot. I'll look at Insular Celtic pages with, like, a whole new appreciation now."

"If you have any more, like, questions, I'd be, like, happy to . . ."

She waved without looking back.

He stared longingly after her. It wasn't until she merged with the crowd around the multimillion-dollar Book of Hours that the young scholar realized that he had been, very gently, taken in by the woman with the lush, brain-numbing mouth.

Anyone who already knew about Warrick's distaste for the newly discovered pages didn't need, like, help picking out a really nice example of early-twelfth-century British illumination in the archaic Insular Celtic style.

Fifty-two

"People are still jammed around the book," Serena said as she watched the discreet shoving match that resulted from people trying to get closer to the fair's multimillion-dollar attraction.

Erik didn't look up. He appeared to be concentrating on a selection of leaves from an Italian lady's Book of Hours, but his attention was on two men in suits who sat with their chairs against the wall. Their bodies were turned toward each other and they leaned close together, as though to shut out the rest of the room. The men must have believed the low rumble of background noise in the ballroom would cover their conversation. In most cases, it would have. But Erik had exceptional hearing and the man who was doing the selling had the kind of voice that carried.

". . . to pay a million. She doesn't know what she has. There hasn't been anything of this quality since the Book of Kells."

"Are you certain she doesn't know?"

"If she did, she would have a multimillion-dollar price tag on it, wouldn't she? It's a repeat of that fine Italian Gospel last year. One inheritance. One dumb heir. One good buy for us."

"Yes, but—"

"Look," he cut in, "anyone who doesn't appreciate what they own doesn't deserve to own it. If she takes a few thousand dollars for a multimillion-dollar piece of art, well, that's the price she pays for being a cultural moron."

"As long as it's legal."

"No problem. They haven't managed to pass laws against being stupid yet."

Neither of the men mentioned ethics, because neither of them was interested.

"So you think you can get the manuscript for a few thousand?"

"Maybe. I might have to go as high as a hundred thousand, because she's being coy and saying she doesn't have the whole thing but word is that she does. She's just milking the price. You front the cash and I'll take twenty percent of the resale."

"Fifteen. And that's half again what a finder's fee would be."

"Yeah, but without me you—"

"Fifteen," the money man cut in impatiently.

"Okay. Fifteen. But I'll need the money fast. Word is already out about the leaves she sent to Warrick."

"Yeah. And the word I've heard is that they're fake."

"Fake, schmake. My source says they're solid gold."

"Who's your source?"

"Same as always."

"Yeah? Who's that?"

"A little bird."

Erik was still looking at an illustration of a fifteenth-century artist's idea of what the Epiphany looked like when one of the two men strode past in a hurry. It was the man whose voice carried so well, the one who talked to little birds.

"Sell anything yet?" the man asked over Erik's shoulder.

"No," said the proprietor, a young woman named Marianne who was watching Erik from the corner of her eye. "You?"

"Hell, no. Nobody buys at affairs like this. We're just a free floor show."

When the man cut over to another aisle and began querying every other proprietor about sales, Erik looked up. "Who was that?" he asked Marianne.

"V. L. Stevenson. He has a booth down by the front, but he's never in it."

"Probably why he hasn't sold anything," Serena said.

Marianne's eyes said she would just as soon Erik had been alone, but her voice was polite. "You're probably right. Most proprietors will share duties with nearby booths, but . . ." She shrugged and didn't say the obvious—with a wanderer like V. L. Stevenson, sharing was a fool's game. She leaned closer to the page Erik was studying and pointed at a picture with a blush-pink fingernail. "The interesting part of this manuscript, in addition to its use of gold foil, is the fact that it is one of the earliest known examples in which the Pepysian model book was used for the decoration."

"What's that?" Serena asked.

"Medieval clip art," Erik said. "It was a book of sketches of birds and such that illuminators and miniaturists copied from when they were decorating manuscripts."

"No such thing as copyright back then."

"No need. Copying was a requirement if there was to be any spread of literacy or religion at all. Before page numbers, the illuminated capitals and miniatures served as a way to remember which page a particular sermon began on, so the decorations got copied, too."

"Before mechanical printing, it was an honor and a duty to make your manuscripts available to less fortunate religious orders," Marianne said. "Rich monasteries would loan out their books to be copied by poorer monasteries who couldn't afford to commission such expensive works from scratch."

Serena looked at the leaf. It was colorful enough, but to her eye badly composed. The birds looked like they had been haphazardly glued in place to keep from falling off the page.

"Then the printing press came along," Erik said, turning

to another leaf. This one was less colorful. Red initial capitals only on important sections. "That ended the need for hand copying. By modern times, people were sneering at copies as inferior, but before that originality wasn't prized. Quite the opposite. It was suspect."

"Makes sense," Serena said. "Most of the first books were religious, and in religion, originality is another name for heresy."

Erik grinned and ran his fingertips over her long red braid. "Quick, aren't you?"

"Quick enough to rap your knuckles if you go after my scrunchie," she said, referring to the twist of elastic and cloth that secured the end of her braid. She was discovering that he loved unraveling her hair. "You mess my braid up, you put it back together."

"I'll look forward to it." Smiling, he turned to Marianne. "This manuscript is interesting but it doesn't quite meet my needs. Do you have any palimpsests, particularly any from the fifteenth century? Miniatures and capital letters are preferred."

"Sorry. Our specialty is entire manuscripts. Have you tried Reggie Smythe?"

"Yes."

She frowned and looked around the room as though for inspiration. "Oh, of course! Albert Lars. Down at the end of aisle J. He has a huge collection of illuminated singulars and oddities." She wrote quickly on a business card. "If you can't catch him in his booth, try this number. He does a lot of after-hours showings."

"Thanks, I will," Erik said warmly.

He meant it. He didn't want to make Ed Heller's work any easier than he had to, and he had begun to think no one would recommend good old Bert to him, thus giving him an excuse to pursue the other dealer who had a known connection in the past to some pages from the Book of the Learned. Maybe Heller would miss the connection. Maybe not. It was worth a try.

Erik pocketed the card and began working his way slowly toward aisle J, talking with proprietors and staff all along the way, hoping Heller's hand would go numb from taking notes on whom they had talked to and what had been said. By the time they got to aisle J, Serena's eyes were looking a bit glazed.

"Okay. I think I have it now," she said. "They're called miniatures because they were originally done in red paint, which was called *minium*."

"Right. Thus, *miniaturist*—one who paints in red. Then the other colors came along. The name didn't change but the meaning did."

"Got it. Miniatures are independent of the text rather than part of it like capital letters. In fact, miniatures might not have anything to do with the text at all."

"Right."

"The plural of codex is codices."

"Yes."

"I think I already knew that. Just like index, whose plural used to be indices but now is indexes. Think the same thing will happen to codex?"

"Only if people start using it as a synonym for 'book.' "

"I don't see that happening. Most people aren't even sure what *synonym* means."

He laughed.

She kept talking. It was how she organized disorganized facts in her mind. Picky was used to it. He ignored her. Erik was more fun. He seemed to enjoy her.

"Chrysography is writing with gold ink," she said, sorting through the jumble of new terms in her mind. "Glair is the binding medium. Actual powdered metallic gold gives gold ink its color. There was something else . . ." She frowned. "Oh, yes. Glair is made from egg whites. Yuck. Who do you suppose first figured out that it was that sticky?"

"The mother of the first kid who dropped an egg and glued his pet mouse to the floor with it."

Serena snickered. "*Hexateuch* and *incunable* are real

words. The former means the first six books of the Old Testament. The latter means any book printed before 1501. Primer is another name for the Book of Hours, taken from the Hour of Prime, which was the first hour in the daily cycle of devotion. Since most people learned to read—if they learned to read at all—from the Book of Hours, today we call early teaching books primers."

"All that and beautiful, too. Awesome."

"Ha ha," she said without emphasis. "Insular Celtic means something different to everyone."

Erik laughed. "Only if you're talking about time periods. That's why I usually add 'early twelfth century' to the description. It's a shorthand way of saying a Romanesque period manuscript in Insular Celtic style."

"So Erik the Learned was an anachronism?"

"Maybe. And maybe the complex yet exuberant Celtic style spoke to his soul more than the classical Romanesque style. Whatever, it was a choice he made, not a necessity. He wasn't an ignorant man. He knew what was happening over on the Continent. Perhaps he even fought in one of the Crusades. Certainly he had friends or allies who had fought the Saracen."

"How do you know?"

"The Book of the Learned names one of Erik's allies as Dominic le Sabre, called the Sword. He was a Norman knight who received his fiefdom in England as a reward for outstanding service in the Crusades."

"Generous of the king."

"Up to a point. The king of England was one shrewd bastard. He gave his 'Sword'—the nickname described a hell of a fighter and a leader of men—land and marriage in the borderlands, where the Saxons were still reluctant to bow to the English king. In one swoop the king got rid of a brilliant Norman warrior-leader, put a powerful ally in place on the enemy lines, and smacked the uppity Saxons right in the face."

Serena thought of the elegant, lovingly made pages her

grandmother had left to her. "Somehow it doesn't seem possible that such beautiful, intricate art came from a time of political backstabbing. Front-stabbing, too. Did I mention outright war?"

Erik glanced up in time to catch her swift frown. "Monasteries with high walls and secular castles with palisades and moats existed for a reason. If it wasn't war, it was bandits or ambitious neighbors. In those days, the force of arms brought more peace than the confessional. The Borderlands, the Disputed Lands, the Scottish Marches, the Lowlands . . . by whatever name, the north of England and the south of Scotland have seen more than their share of bloodshed." He shrugged. "Blood was probably the first ink."

"Cheerful thought."

"Realistic."

Serena didn't argue. She had seen the way he casually looked around the crowd every few minutes. The way he was doing now. "Find it?" she asked tightly.

"What?"

"Whatever you're looking for."

He caught a glimpse of Heller's broad face and short, pale hair. "Yeah. I found it."

"Who is it?"

"No one you want to know."

Idly Erik thought about letting Heller follow him to some quiet place where they wouldn't be interrupted by well-meaning bystanders. Then he discarded the idea. Heller wouldn't know anything more about the mysterious employer than Wallace had. Less, probably. Wallace called the shots in that partnership.

"Looks like Bert isn't here," Serena said.

Erik stopped watching Heller out of the corner of his eye and looked at Bert's empty booth.

"If you're looking for Mr. Lars's private showing," said a slim young man in the next booth, "it's across the hall in the Silver Room. Don't worry about being late. He's not a stickler for formality."

"Thanks," Erik said.

"What are we going to do now?" Serena asked under her breath.

"Go to Bert's party."

"We weren't invited."

He gave her a sideways glance. "Buyers are always invited to Bert's parties."

"Then why is it in a private room?"

"You'll see."

Fifty-three

Erik gave one of his Rarities Unlimited business cards to the rumpled gatekeeper at the door of the Silver Room. Thirty seconds later, Bert appeared in the doorway, smiling like a crocodile. He was a tall, thin man with wispy blond hair, a raw silk shirt and jeans, a scholar's stoop, and the sensibilities of an ex–porn producer. He greeted Erik like an old friend or a person with something to sell—warm handshake and a manly punch in the shoulder.

Bert had been a Hollywood producer in another life. At least, that's what he told people who cared enough to ask. It was the truth, after a fashion. He had indeed produced movies. Some of them even had dialogue.

Much to his wealthy family's relief, he had turned to a more reputable means of expressing himself: he began collecting medieval artifacts. He had quickly moved from arms and armor to more portable items. Jewelry of various kinds and value, with a particular Celtic specialty, had been his passion for a few years. Then he had settled upon illuminated pages. Not entire manuscripts, just pages. As he had said more than once, you can only look at one page at a time anyway.

"Hey, boy, where ya been keeping yourself?" Bert asked.

"Long time no see. Come in, come in. If I'd known you were in town, I'd have sent an invitation by courier." Without waiting for a response, he gave Serena the thorough twice-over look of a man who knew all the uses of power, ambition, and the casting couch. "Is this your Tush du Jour?"

Serena managed a thin smile. Men like Bert were the reason she had spent the last four years as a born-again virgin. The only difference between him and some of the men who had cured her of the opposite sex was the calculation in his pale blue eyes.

Erik started to introduce her, but she cut him off.

"Don't bother," she said easily. "Tushes and horses' butts don't need to exchange names."

Bert's smile changed into rough laughter. "Watch it, boy. Those smart ones will be collecting alimony before you see forty."

"The smart ones don't get married," she said with a glittering smile. "Use 'em and lose 'em."

"Wish I'd met you before you grew teeth," Bert said, and his smile looked genuine.

"She was born with them," Erik said. "Trust me."

"Never figured you for the dominatrix type."

"Neither did I," Erik said. "Life is full of surprises. The best of them carry black velvet whips."

Serena gave him a sideways look that promised retribution. His smile said that he was looking forward to it and had a few ideas of his own.

"Man, you're twisted. I like that," Bert said, drawing them farther into the room. "The goodies are along the far wall. You and Trixie want a drink?"

Erik almost choked as he made the connection between dominatrix and Trixie. He heard something close to a snicker from Serena's direction before she coughed.

"Thanks," he said, swallowing hard against laughter. "We're fine for now."

"Great. Let me know what you need. It's yours." With that, Bert went back to working the small crowd in the room.

"Bert's one of a kind," Erik said blandly.

"Thank you, God," Serena retorted. "How long do you think it took him to perfect his act?"

"Sometimes I think it isn't an act."

"You're scaring me."

"Don't worry, Trixie. I'll take care of you."

"Blow me," she said succinctly.

"That, too."

Before she could say anything, he took her arm and headed for the far wall. He didn't know all the players, but he could often tell their home geography at a glance. People from the East Coast wore leather shoes with slacks and open-necked shirts. The local males wore jeans, running shoes, three-hundred-dollar shirts, and two-thousand-dollar sport jackets. Two of the women—local, no doubt—were dressed like sex trophies. The other two women looked like overworked faculty wives at an upscale college. None of the trophies were interested in the pages. The women in dark dresses, sensible pumps, and pearls were very interested in what lay beneath the glass cases.

So was Erik. Followed by Serena, he did a quick circuit of the offerings. Occasionally he pulled out his hand-sized communications unit, entered notes, or queried the databases at Rarities.

The pages in the Silver Room were a revelation to Serena, who thought of illuminated manuscripts as proper, even prissy, manuscripts dealing with man's spiritual aspirations. But like everything else human, illuminated manuscripts came in more than one flavor. Bert collected the flavors that most shocked the twenty-first century's still fundamentally Puritan view of bodily functions, including but not restricted to sex.

Serena bent down and looked into a case with horrified fascination. The creatures in the margins were grotesque, their genitals exaggerated, and their actions graphically perverse.

"I'm afraid to ask, but—" she began.

"What are they doing?" Erik cut in, smiling.

"No! I already know way too much about that. I was just wondering what the text was like."

"It's a fragment of the Gospel according to Mark."

"You're kidding."

"Nope."

"Then why . . . ?"

"The decoration?"

"Decoration," she said neutrally. "Now there's a word I wouldn't have thought of to describe demon proctology."

He laughed and looked back down at the page in question. "Maybe he's just taking his buddy's temperature."

"Maybe my name is Trixie."

Shaking his head, he gave up teasing her. "When these manuscripts were created, hell was very real. It was the home of all sin, all that was grotesque, all that was forbidden to man by God, and all of it was described in detail within the Bible itself. Unfortunately, many of the people associated with the manuscripts, from scribes to secular owners and more than a few priests, simply weren't literate. They got their inoculation against hell from the marginalia and decorations, with grotesques meant to scare man back to the path of righteousness by showing what would happen to you in hell."

Serena looked around the room at the people staring into the cases. "They don't look worried."

"They aren't. Different culture entirely. They're buying historical curiosities or adding to private or scholarly collections centered around perversity as seen through the ages."

Serena bent over another case and tried to see its contents in a seminary library. She was still trying when Bert came back.

"See anything you like?" he asked her.

Erik answered, "Not yet. We were hoping you had come across another of those fifteenth-century miniatures of the type you sold to the House of Warrick when you first started out in business. Palimpsest, remember? Gorgeous miniature on top and twelfth-century writing underneath."

Bert's smile hardened. "I don't do stuff like that anymore."

"Too bad. That's all I'm interested in these days. Who did you buy it from? Maybe they have some more or know where I can find some. I'll be glad to guarantee you a finder's fee."

"You lost me."

"I'm talking about the miniature that you sold to the House of Warrick fifteen years ago," Erik said with an easy smile. "That kind of palimpsest is my new passion. I'm prepared to pay very well to support it. Why shouldn't you get some of the benefit?"

"It was a long time ago. I don't remember who sold it to me."

Erik didn't believe him. "Why don't you think about it some more? Give it a chance. It seems like the memory of your first big sale would stick with you. Could you check your records?"

"Sorry. I only keep five years' worth of records or I'd be buried in paper."

Erik looked at Bert's pale eyes and wondered why he was lying. "Too bad. You could make a lot of money on this. If you remember anything, call me."

Bert hesitated. "How much?"

"Depends on how good the lead is. Five thousand, minimum."

A flicker of surprise showed on Bert's face. "I'll think about it."

"You do that. While you're at it, think about ten thousand, tax free."

Bert looked like he was doing his thinking right now. "You got it on you?"

"What do you think?"

"How long will it take you to get it?"

"A few hours," Erik said.

"You know where my house is?"

"I can find it."

"Be there at nine tonight. Small bills only. Nonsequential."

"I can be there sooner than nine."

Bert smiled. It wasn't nice to see. "Forget it. I need the time."

"For what? A brain scan?"

Bert's laugh wasn't any nicer than his smile had been. "Anything that's worth ten to you might be worth more to other people. So bring some extra cash, pal. I just love auctions. Gives me a big hard-on every time."

Fifty-four

Despite the cozy honey tones of the Retreat's large suite, Niall's blue eyes didn't look welcoming. Neither did the gun he checked with a few quick, efficient motions. Satisfied that it was good to go, he shoved the gun into his shoulder holster.

"Look," Erik said for the fifth time, "you don't have to go with—"

"Are you deaf?" Niall interrupted impatiently. "I'm bloody well not. I heard you loud and clear. Now you hear this, Fuzzy boy. Anytime you're carrying thirty thousand in cash, you get company. Especially with a slimy item like Bert. That man's biography would gag a skunk."

Serena looked from one man to the other. Whether by accident or design, both were wearing a dark shirt, dark pants, and a dark jacket. Both had on the kind of shoes that could handle sidewalks or rough country with equal ease. Erik wore a black baseball cap over his bright hair. Niall didn't need a hat; his hair was already the color of midnight.

"Show me yours," Niall said in a curt voice, holding out his hand.

Erik's mouth flattened but he reached behind his back, drew his gun, reversed it, and handed it to Niall butt-first. The older man checked it out, grunted approval, and handed it back.

"Clean and loaded," Niall said. "You're wasted on the Fuzzy side."

Erik checked the safety, holstered the gun, and didn't say a word.

"I feel left out," Serena said sardonically, her empty hands on her hips. "No black cat clothes, no weapon, just blue jeans, running shoes, and a red sweater."

"Then stay here," Erik said, "the way I told you to."

"I don't take orders from you."

"No shit."

"Can she use a gun?" Niall asked Erik, heading off a continuation of the argument that his arrival had interrupted.

"I would have shot Wallace if Sir Galahad here hadn't knocked my hand aside," she said.

"But you wouldn't have liked shooting him," Erik said savagely.

"Are you saying you would have?" she challenged.

He didn't answer. He couldn't without undermining his position, and he knew it. But that didn't make him any less angry. No matter how she fought it, he knew that she would spend more time regretting violence than he would. That didn't mean she wouldn't get the job done; it just meant that she shouldn't have to be the one to do it.

Niall looked at Serena with new approval. "Good on you. And don't worry about the red sweater. In low light, red is the first color to look black."

"I was being ironic about feeling left out," Serena said to Niall. "Are you familiar with the term *irony*?"

"Never heard of it," Niall retorted. "I work with a delicate little flower who wouldn't know irony if it bit her on her perfect ass."

Erik turned toward the door. "Don't start arguing with Serena. It's not worth the time you'll waste."

"And I suppose you're a mountain of sweet reason?" Serena said bitingly.

"I thought you'd never notice."

The door shut behind Erik. Hard.

Serena told herself that she wasn't being stubborn, he was being overprotective. Either way, it shouldn't hurt the way it did. The fact that it hurt enough to make her eyes sting made her madder than ever.

"Don't worry," Niall said calmly. "He'll get over it. It takes a man a while to get used to a strong woman."

"No need for him to bend his stiff neck," she said, yanking open the door. "As soon as Mr. Warrick gets the message that my pages aren't for sale, Erik can go back to screwing numbingly sweet young things that wouldn't say shit if their mouth was full of it."

"Doubt it," Niall said, following her out the door. "Once a man bites into something with zest, he's ruined for cotton candy."

He was talking to himself. Serena had caught up with Erik and was matching him stride for stride.

Fifty-five

The silence inside Erik's silver SUV was thick enough to slice
and serve on crackers. He ignored it just as he ignored Serena.

*She had always been like that—independent, determined,
carrying life's savage demands like a banner into battle.*

The thought was Erik's, yet not quite his. Just as the image
of Serena mounted on a battle stallion was both Serena now
and a different Serena—smaller, delicate without being fragile, thinner mouth bracketed by pain, *fleeing, always fleeing,
because the mist retreats and he is there, always there beyond
the mist, waiting for vengeance.*

*The man I loved beyond death, wronged beyond death, Erik
the Learned sorcerer, who would kill me and the child of his
loins.*

*She was looking at him, straight into his soul stretched
across time, eyes violet with agony and regret, and a hope that
would not die.*

Help us!

Do not repeat our mistakes!

Cat's paws of ice pricked over Erik's skin. The vision had
been so clear, so real, he could still see the woman's fear and
smell the spicy sachet lifting from her beautifully woven
robe.

Quickly he glanced at Serena. She was staring at him, her eyes dilated, her mouth pale. He wondered what she had seen. Then he was afraid he knew.

Abruptly he stopped fighting what he couldn't understand and couldn't control. All he could control was his own response. He let go of the steering wheel with one hand long enough to brush the back of his fingers over her cheek.

"Don't worry," he said roughly. "If there's a way, we'll find it."

As though they had always been lovers, she turned her head and brushed a kiss across his palm, comforting him as he had comforted her.

If there's a way . . .

From the backseat, Niall watched both of them. He didn't know what had happened, but he knew something had. For an instant there had been a presence in the car that crackled like hidden lightning, the smell of spice and time, despair and hope. . . .

Things that go bump in the night.

With a silent curse, he checked his shoulder holster. The heavy gun butt was still there, still cool despite the warmth of his body slowly seeping through the leather. The solid reality of the weapon reassured him on the same primitive level that had recognized something distinctly unordinary arcing between Erik and Serena.

Then Niall thought of Dana's motto, she of the breathtaking intelligence and equally breathtaking pragmatism: If you can't beat it, don't fight it.

"We won't stop throwing money at Bert until he tells us what he knows," Niall said.

"Whose money?" Serena asked. "I can't even afford to keep Picky in cat food."

"Our money. If Bert can lead us to the rest of the Book of the Learned, Dana will consider the money well spent."

"Why? It still won't be for sale," Serena said.

"The art," Erik said simply. "Not the owner, not the client. The art is all that matters, all that will endure."

She let out a long, fragmented breath. Everything was happening too quickly, moving at light speed when she was more comfortable with the patient, timeless weaving of thread upon thread. "I wish my grandmother had left me more information."

"She thought she left you enough," Niall said. "Use it. Something like the Book of the Learned belongs to human history, no matter who keeps it from century to century."

"How do I think like a dead woman?" Serena asked.

A primeval oak forest, the sound of hunting horns, the thunder of horses' hooves digging up clots of darkly fragrant earth, a peregrine's wild cry . . .

"How am I thinking like a dead man?" Erik asked tightly.

When Serena looked at him, her eyes were violet with more than the flickering light of L.A.'s night. She saw two Eriks, one a few inches shorter and every bit as strong, hair and beard cut to wear beneath a battle helm, quick, confident to the point of arrogance, as fierce as the peregrine that rode his leather-clad arm. His eyes, Erik's eyes, staring at her, demanding . . . *something.*

She gave him an almost frightened glance and didn't say anything more. She felt as she had the night her grandmother died, when time had been the unbound leaves of a book and she had turned them to find a design a thousand years old.

Out in the rain-slicked night, a siren wailed up and down like the voice of darkness.

Erik turned onto a side street, parked, and turned off the lights. Nobody drove by. Nobody turned off and parked behind them. "Lapstrake must have decoyed him."

"Hope Dana enjoyed the ride," Niall said dryly. "It really cheesed her to let him drive her new toy."

"At least she had the good taste to buy a silver Mercedes SUV," Erik said.

Niall shook his head. "She's a holy terror in that thing. Eats sports cars for lunch. They have to slow down for bumps and rain gutters. She flat flies over 'em."

Erik started the engine, flipped on the lights, and got back on the urban highway. A few miles later he turned onto one of the numberless small side streets that were thrown over the outlying areas of Hollywood like a badly woven net. Cars had been parked haphazardly along the streets, narrowing the passage to one lane through many blocks. It was illegal, but it happened all the time in old neighborhoods where houses were divided into rental apartments and there wasn't enough parking for one car per bungalow, much less two or three.

The clapboard bungalows were crowded together like beach houses, except there wasn't a beach for miles. All that existed in the way of nature was a dry ravine overgrown with brush, feral grapevines and ivy, windblown trash, and the dry weeds of seasons past. In a few weeks new grass awakened by last week's rain would poke through the mat of dead foliage and debris, but now there was only a feeling of abandonment.

Bert's house certainly wasn't what people expected to find in the hills overlooking a chunk of L.A. His bungalow was small, old, surrounded by narrow, winding streets lined with aging eucalyptus trees whose brittle branches broke off in every high wind. There were lights on in the front of his house, just enough to show off the weeds in the disreputable front yard.

"Don't park close," Niall said.

"Don't tell me what I already know," Erik retorted.

He didn't even slow down while Niall looked the place over. He drove two blocks farther before he squeezed into a space between two cars that looked like they cost more than the houses they were parked in front of. But this was Hollywood, where looks were deceptive. For all their shabby modesty, the bungalows were within easy commuting distance of hundreds of thousands of jobs, which meant that the land cost five times what the houses were worth. If the view had been good, the bungalows would have long since given way to expansive and very expensive houses, but the only view was of a brush-choked hillside and the neighbor's needs-a-coat-of-paint house.

"Looks like party time," Niall said as he got out of the car.

"For some people, it's always party time," Erik said, locking the SUV with a single motion of his thumb on the fat key.

Cars were parked everywhere but on roofs. The young and the hip mingled with the older and the jaded in bungalows so small that a party of ten was a crush. A couple walked by in the center of the street, sharing a cigarette; neither of them looked old enough to be out after curfew. The smell of marijuana hung in the air behind them like incense.

Serena dodged between a polished Porsche and a dusty Lexus. If there was a sidewalk, she hadn't set foot on it yet. Despite the recent rain, the weeds were dry enough to leave foxtails clinging to her socks and jeans. Once the heavy smell of pot dissipated, the air was fragrant with the herbal scents of eucalyptus and dried weeds.

There was a car parked in the side yard that passed for a garage at Bert's house.

"There's an alley behind," Erik said.

He started forward, only to be hauled back by Niall's hard hand wrapped around his arm. "Security goes first, boyo. Fuzzies bring up the rear and take care of the clients."

Erik started to argue with Niall but knew it would be useless. He locked his jaw, took Serena's arm, and followed the older man so close they could touch him.

"Wait here," Niall said in a low voice.

Serena began to object, but the sudden pressure of Erik's fingers on her arm silenced her.

Fifty-six

Niall went to the car, touched the hood, and felt only chilly metal. The vehicle had been parked long enough for the engine to become stone-cold. There were other cars parked out front in the street, but they looked like the party two houses down—young and expensive.

He did a quick circuit of the bungalow. The backyard opened onto an alley that was either unpaved or had been buried in dirt and neglect. There weren't any cars in the alley, but there was another party going on a few houses up on the other side. A low fence gave a casual air of privacy to Bert's yard. French doors led from what was probably a back bedroom to what once had been a garden. Except for a light over the kitchen sink, the rear of the house was dark.

Quietly Niall went back to the front yard. "So far, so good," he said softly to Erik. "Let's see if he's home. You first, this time. Serena, stay with me."

As he spoke, Niall grabbed Serena's arm. His fingers wrapped around the trailing end of the scarf. He lifted his hand, rubbed it, and gave the scarf a narrow look. The bloody thing felt like a steel brush, yet she was stroking it with her fingertips like it was velvet.

Erik stepped up onto the small front porch and hit the

doorbell. Instead of chimes or a buzzer, the cries of a woman revving toward climax announced that visitors had arrived.

"Must be the soundtrack from his last movie," Erik said blandly.

"Hope she got an Oscar," Serena muttered.

Bert opened the door. He was wearing jeans and the kind of colorful, woven silk sweater that had been popular two decades ago. From the look of the cuffs, he had worn the sweater at least that long. The paunch that his suit had disguised was on proud display, straining the colorful yarn. A tumbler full of what smelled like room temperature gin was clenched in his hand. He took a big swallow that should have burned like gasoline all the way down, but apparently he was used to it. He didn't even clear his throat.

"Who's that?" he asked, looking at Niall.

"My money man," Erik said.

"Hope you brought lots of cash, pal."

Niall looked bored.

"Yeah, well, come on in," Bert said. "You got here first. Drink, anyone?"

"No thanks," Erik said for all of them.

"Suit yourself." Bert glanced at his glass, swished the oily liquid around with a jerk of his arm, drank, and headed to the kitchen for more. He had a few jiggers to go before he reached the desired state of numbness. "Sit down if you want," he called back over his shoulder as he went into the kitchen. "The other bidder should be here any—"

Breaking glass, Bert's terrified scream, and the reek of gasoline all exploded out of the kitchen at once. Erik started for Bert at a run, only to be hauled up hard by Niall and thrown toward Serena.

"Get her out of here!" Niall snarled. "Don't go out the front, he'll be waiting!"

Before the words left his mouth, another burst of burning gasoline hit the floor and exploded into fire, but this bomb came through the side window and into the living room, setting fire to everything between them and the front door.

More missiles rained down and exploded, vomiting flames everywhere. The fuel wasn't gasoline. Not exactly. It was napalm, sticking to everything it touched, and burning, burning, *burning*.

The kitchen was a sheet of fire. Bert's screams rose above even the violence of flame.

"Hallway!" Erik yelled.

Serena was already running toward the soothing darkness and into the mess that was Bert's bedroom. She spotted the French doors and raced to them. They were locked. After giving the handle a yank, she reached for a chair to smash the glass. Erik beat her to it, grabbed the heavy wooden chair, and swung it hard. Glass and wood burst outward.

Bert's screams ended beneath the explosive violence of another firebomb.

Gun drawn, Niall leaped through the smashed doorway and swept the backyard. There was nothing but shadows that changed as flames leaped and another bomb exploded.

"Alley!" Niall growled to Serena.

"But, Erik—"

Niall jerked Serena through the opening and shoved her toward the alley before he turned back to look for his friend.

Erik was already running back into the bedroom, his face a mask of soot and rage. Niall didn't need to ask about Bert. The stench of more than jellied gasoline was rising into the night.

"Out," Niall said tersely.

The two men caught up with Serena as she scrambled over the sagging fence and dropped into the alley. The instant Erik landed in the narrow lane, Niall grabbed Erik's jacket and yanked it off his body. His shirt came next. Then his cap. The clothing fell to the ground and smoldered sullenly.

"Any on your pants?" Niall demanded in a low voice.

"Not that I know of," Erik said, rubbing his shoulder where his shirt had almost burned through.

"You'd know. Napalm is bad cess. Any ID in your shirt or

jacket?" As he spoke, Niall stripped off his own jacket and gave it to Erik.

"No. Serena, are you—"

"She's fine. She had the sense to put that barbwire scarf over her hair." Niall kicked the burning clothes aside. "You first. Serena in the middle. *Move.*"

Erik headed down the alley toward his car, shoving his arms through the jacket sleeves as he went. As soon as his left hand was free he pulled his gun from the holster at the small of his back and flipped off the safety. He moved through the alley quickly but not carelessly. He watched every shadow.

There were no lights in the alley. None were needed. The raging orange flames provided more than enough illumination. Some of the neighbors in back and on either side of the burning house had abandoned TVs or parties and raced for garden hoses. They were already sending streams of cold, chlorinated water over cedar shake roofs and crispy lawns and wooden slat fences.

Some of the party folks weren't that smart. They trotted closer to the fire, gawking and hooting as though it was just part of the evening's entertainment.

Niall and Erik searched the faces of the milling people. There was no one who looked furtive or familiar. No one just standing apart with a grin of sexual ecstasy on his face.

A soft, terrifying *whump* came from the burning house. Fire blossomed and spat flaming seeds in all directions. A woman screamed as eucalyptus trees burst into flames.

"Get out!" Niall shouted at the people standing back down the alley, much too close to the fire. They were staring, shocked, at the inferno their neighbor's house had become. "Run!" he yelled.

Some people listened. Others stayed, only to run when there was a second explosion. For a few of them, it was too late. Flaming debris rained down on them, sticking to their clothes and flesh. They stumbled away into the darkness, screaming.

Erik hoped someone would help them. He couldn't, not without putting Serena at risk. That he wouldn't do.

Shouts came from all up and down the street, but no one really noticed the three people in the alley. Holding his gun down along his left leg so he wouldn't panic the partygoers, Erik cut between two houses to the street. His vehicle was only thirty feet away. Right-handed, he pulled the key from his jeans and released the locks.

"Get in and shut the door fast," he said to Serena without looking at her. He was looking everywhere else, searching for the pale glint of a gun or the flashing arc of a bottle of burning napalm dropping down out of the night.

As soon as she was inside the car, Niall emerged from the shadows between the houses. He held his gun down along his right leg and mingled with the curious people who were running out of every house on the block and staring toward the faint glow two blocks down. If anyone noticed his shoulder harness against his dark shirt, or the dark gun against his black pants, no one reacted.

Erik stood near the driver's door, watching shadows and people. He wasn't worried about being conspicuous; the houses up and down the block were gushing people. Most of them carried drinks or exotic cigarettes in their hands. Some of them noshed on canapés and chips while they peered down the street.

"In," Niall said tersely when he reached Erik's car.

Erik flipped on the safety, holstered his gun, and slid behind the wheel.

Niall took a last look around before he got quickly into the backseat. He didn't holster his gun. "Go. No lights. Open the windows. Serena, get down on the floor."

"But—" she began.

"*Do it*," Niall snarled. "I need a clear field of fire."

She slid off the seat and crammed as much of herself into the footwell as she could while Erik started the car and opened all the windows so Niall could shoot out if he had to.

"Are you going to call it in?" Erik asked Niall.

"I already did, so don't dawdle, boyo. The fire department around here is close by. Not that it will do Bert any good. He's toast."

Moving slowly despite the adrenaline storm lighting up his blood, Erik drove away from the burning bungalow, pulled out onto the narrow road, and headed out as though he had nothing more urgent on his mind than finding the next party. Only a few of the people seemed to understand what all the excitement was about down at the end of the next block.

Erik wanted to get out before everyone caught on.

"Lights coming on," he said.

"Can I sit up now?" Serena asked.

Niall grunted.

She took that as an assent and clambered back into the seat.

Erik flipped on the headlights.

A few blocks later, the sound of a siren punched through the night, coming closer with every second. At least two other sirens lifted and cried from other directions, closing in fast.

Erik looked ahead, swore, glanced right and left, and said tightly, "Hang on."

He spun the wheel hard to the left, diving headfirst between two parked cars. The front wheels bumped up over the curb and dug in eagerly, eating lawn until the rear wheels were out of the narrow traffic lane. He killed the lights and waited.

Siren screaming, a paramedic truck rocketed down the only open space, which was the center of the street between parked cars. Before Erik could back out, more lights and sirens warned of approaching emergency vehicles. He gauged the distance, added up the time it would take him to back out and straighten up, and decided that he would stay out of the way of whatever was turning onto the narrow residential road.

A few seconds later, a brush truck bristling with fire axes

and brush cutters lumbered by, lights spinning in blinding array. On its heels was a ladder truck that came within inches of trashing parked cars on both sides of the road.

Erik's eyes met Niall's in the rearview mirror. Neither man said anything, but both of them kept looking around for anyone who might be racing away from rather than toward the source of all the excitement. Other than doors opening up and down the street to see what the fuss was all about, there weren't any people outside. Any vehicle that might have been trying to get out this way would have been stopped by the oncoming fire trucks.

Back toward Bert's bungalow, flames climbed up eucalyptus trees in a graceful, devouring fountain. From where Serena sat, she couldn't tell how many other houses were involved.

"Hope those boys are good at their work," Erik said, his voice rough with adrenaline. "It's been a dry winter." But he was looking at the vehicle's navigation computer rather than the fire. Grids flashed as he tried alternate routes out.

"Yeah," Niall said. "That rain we got wasn't enough to wet down the underbrush and wood shingles. Get going, boyo. They'll be putting up roadblocks."

"No shit."

A final glance at the computer confirmed that there were a lot of tiny lanes and the occasional barely passable alley ahead. None of them led where Erik wanted to go unless he got through one of two possible intersections before the cops closed them down.

He backed out and drove like he had a light bar and sirens until he got to the first intersection.

Too late.

A sheriff's patrol car was already laying out flares. Erik could wait like a good citizen for permission to cross, or he could try another route.

He turned and went back two blocks and over one until he reached a narrow lane that was more a fire access road joining two old subdivisions than it was a road for civilian vehicles. Just to discourage the public, railroad ties had been thrown over both ends of the lane.

Erik pulled the gear lever into low range and bounced over the railroad ties. When he was back on the street, he switched back to all-wheel drive and raced for the second intersection. He got there just as a patrol car did.

The SUV slid through the intersection before the cop got out of his car.

"One down. One more to go," Erik said, glancing at the nav computer.

Other sirens called in the night, but they weren't close enough yet for him to worry about.

A block away, a police car's flashing lights approached the next intersection from the opposite side. Without hesitating, Erik floored the gas pedal. The big engine gave a happy roar. The Mercedes shot forward like a rocket off a launch pad. They were through the intersection and into a driveway, lights out, before the patrol car reached them. The lady cop gave Erik a hard look as she drove by, but there were more urgent things for her to do than yell at a macho driver.

The cop raced a half block to the intersection, squealed to a stop, jumped out, and began laying down flares to divert traffic from the fire.

Erik backed out and gunned away from the blockade, back to the anonymity of L.A.'s urban jungle.

Niall laughed. "Like I keep saying, you're wasted as a Fuzzy."

All Erik said was "If she got my license plate, you're paying the ticket."

Fifty-seven

Dana glanced up from her desk as Erik, Niall, and Serena came into her office. Her nose twitched and she grimaced. "Smells like someone had a gasoline spritzer."

"Napalm, actually," Niall said. "Not commercial grade—soap flakes, gasoline, and a flare for a fuse—but it got the job done just fine."

Dana shot to her feet. Her dark eyes went over Niall, searching for injuries.

"Check your Fuzzy," he said, hooking a thumb in Erik's direction. "He didn't get in out of the petrol rain fast enough."

"I thought that looked like Niall's jacket," she said, glancing at Erik. "Anything permanent besides clothing?"

"No. Just singed here and there."

She gave him a probing look, accepted his assessment, and turned back to her partner. "Shall I expect official inquiries?"

"Don't think so. Erik got us out before the official types got in place. They'll be too busy scratching their balls over the homemade bombs to worry about us."

"Excellent. I'd hate to call in any more favors." She looked at Erik. "Dead end?"

"Very dead," he said flatly. "Bert died before he could tell us where he first purchased one of the written-over pages of the Book of the Learned."

Dana's eyes narrowed. She sat down again. Her hands began playing an imaginary flute. After twenty seconds her fingers abruptly stilled. "Let's reassess what we have, what we don't have, and where we might get it. Quickly."

"Before it starts raining gasoline?" Erik asked sardonically.

"Precisely." She picked up a telephone and punched in a number. "Michael, how are you? You know the guests in room nine?" She waited. Then her eyebrows rose. "Yes, the ones with the starving feline. Has anyone requested a room close to theirs?" Her eyes narrowed. "Who? Are they in yet? Good. When she arrives, put her at the opposite end of the building and start painting all the rooms around nine. No, I don't care what color. Just make it look good."

Dana hung up before she started swearing in German.

Niall winced. "What is it?"

"Cleary Warrick Montclair is moving into the Retreat for an indefinite stay. Son and lover—excuse me, security adviser—are with her."

"How did they know we would be at the Retreat?" Erik asked her.

"The connection between the Retreat and Rarities Unlimited isn't a secret." Dana sighed and swore. "Bloody hell. I guess I should have returned more of Cleary's calls. That female would try the patience of a stone. She should see someone about her attachment to her father. It's more suitable to a girl of five than a woman over fifty."

"Haven't you told her I won't sell my pages?" Serena asked.

"Many times."

"Then why is she coming here?"

"She doesn't believe me. She wants to talk to you herself. I told her it was out of the question. She didn't believe that, either."

Serena's chin came up and her eyes narrowed. "She will. I never want to deal with her or her father again."

"Norman Warrick often has that effect on people," Dana said dryly. "That's why Garrison is the front man for the public. After he scattered wild oats in the army, he majored in charm at Harvard. Oh, that reminds me, Serena. Garrison called earlier, asking me to pass a message along to you, as he couldn't reach you. He would like to take you out to lunch tomorrow. He feels that there is a misunderstanding between the two of you."

"I don't care if he's as charming as sin. My pages aren't for sale."

"Is he?" Erik asked.

"What?" Serena said, looking at him. Wearing Niall's dark jacket open across a naked, furry chest, with soot streaking his cheek and his blond hair spiky from wind and impatient fingers, Erik looked distinctly uncivilized.

"Is Garrison as charming as sin?" he asked.

"Oh." Serena shrugged. "He's very polished. So is Paul Carson in his own way. Handsome, too. It doesn't make up for Warrick. Nothing makes up for that kind of rudeness."

"But Garrison would like to try," Erik said.

"I'm not interested."

"Good," Erik said. "I'll see that he gets the message."

"I'm quite capable of telling him myself."

"That's okay." He pulled her close and kissed her hard. "I don't mind giving him the good word."

"What word?"

"Good-bye."

Amusement and irritation flickered over Serena's face. Amusement won. Erik had the smug look of Picky after a successful hunt. "You remind me of my cat."

"I'm not going to ask."

"You sure?"

He laughed and kissed her again. "I'm sure."

Niall gave Dana a sidelong look and a knowing smile. She

winked. Then she picked up the phone and punched in Factoid's red alert, answer-or-die number.

He picked up on the fifth ring, sounding breathless. "What!"

"Where are you?"

"Uhh . . ."

"Never mind. Can you be in the computer command center in half an hour?"

"Shit."

"I'll take that as yes."

"Shit. I—she—we—chocolate syrup—*shit.*"

"Half an hour." Dana hung up and looked at Niall, eyebrows raised. "I do believe that's the first time I've ever heard the boy dither."

"What did he say?" Niall asked.

"Something about chocolate syrup and shit."

Niall choked, then started laughing. So did Erik.

"What?" Dana asked them.

Both men shook their head and kept on laughing.

She gave them a disgusted glance, stood, and stalked toward the door. "Come with me, Serena. We'll leave the baboons to howl while I bring you up to date on what we have on the Book of the Learned. Gentlemen, when you have recovered what minor wit you were born with, we'll be in clean room number three."

Fifty-eight

Coffee steamed gently in front of Serena and Erik. Dana and Niall were drinking tea that was strong enough to melt glass. Niall's had milk in it. Dana's was straight. Screens around the room featured a digital image of each of the seventeen known pages of the Book of the Learned. Other screens were blank, waiting for a command.

Factoid's face talked down from a central screen and his surly voice came out of a speaker. He was in the computer command center of Rarities. Other than a sticky hairdo and a streak of chocolate on his chin, he looked normal—for Factoid.

"Okay," he snarled. "One through seventeen. Earliest known provenance. Starting at screen one and working up: 1963 . . . 1959 . . . 1944."

"Who first owned the page on screen three?" Erik asked quickly.

"Derrick James Rubin."

"Go on. But give me names as well as dates."

Factoid said something everyone ignored as irrelevant.

Even worse, uninspired. Then he started over. "One—1963, Christie's, bought from private individual now deceased, dead end; 1959, Sotheby's, brokered for private individual, page was a birthday present from father, now deceased, dead end; 1944, Rubin estate, no catalogue, dead end; 1956, Sotheby's, they're still looking for origin on microfilm; 1958, Christie's, checking microfilms; 1944, Rubin estate, no catalogue, dead end; 1948, brokered by Warrick's, they're checking for origin; 1962, Mirabeau Auctions via private individual, now deceased, said to have been in family for generations, dead end."

Erik sat motionless while the irritated computer tech ran through the screens. Erik let the names and dates roll through his mind while he searched for a pattern. By the time Serena's pages were up for discussion, all that was certain was that searching microfilm files was a hell of a lot slower than searching computerized databases.

"The last eight screens belong to Serena Charters, inherited from grandmother, now deceased, dead end. Claimed to have been in family for generations."

Everyone stared at the screens in silence.

"Except for screen eight," Erik said, "Serena's are the only sheets that aren't palimpsests."

"Say what?" Niall asked.

"Written over. Show him, Factoid."

Muttering came from the speakers, but the rest of the screens split to show the sheet under normal light and under UV. The writing beneath was ghostly yet unmistakable in the UV panel.

"Give me everything you have on screen eight," Erik said.

"Looking . . ." Factoid said. "According to family legend, the Blackthorns bought it from one of the poor Scots immigrants who were shoved out during the Highland Clearances and Improvements." He yawned. "That could take it all the way back to the Battle of Culloden, or 1746 for the historically impaired among us. Since the Blackthorns are descended from a Scots soldier in the British army—who spelled thorn with an *e*—they've been in the U.S. since before it was the U.S. So has the page."

"Show us the other side."

"It's blank."

"I know. Show it. You get better resolution here than I do at home."

Factoid muttered and said, "Screen nineteen."

"There. In the corner. See the gather mark?"

"Yeah. So what?"

"Put the gather marks from Serena's pages up with it."

Factoid shut up, zoomed in, cut, pasted, and had gather marks up for comparison.

"Good," Erik said. "I thought so. This page was cut from the gather on screen three."

"So?" Dana asked.

Erik shrugged. "So it looks like whoever had the book cut out a fancy illuminated page from the front of the book and sold it. Probably for food or to pay a debt."

"Does that mean that Rubin's pages go back to the Blackthorn family?" Serena asked.

"No. All of Rubin's pages are palimpsests. This one hasn't been erased."

"Where does that leave us?" Dana asked.

"With the good probability that the Book of the Learned came to America in the eighteenth century, was passed down through the generations, and the occasional leaf was snipped out when the going got really tough."

Serena closed her eyes and saw her grandmother's note. *We've lost some pages through the centuries, but damned few. Until my generation.*

She didn't realize she had spoken aloud until she opened her eyes and saw Dana and Niall staring at her.

"Don't stop," Dana said.

A wave of sadness mixed with exhaustion swept through Serena. The adrenaline that had kept her going after the fire was ebbing fast, leaving her stranded and flat. "It was my grandmother's note to me, part of her will."

"Tell them the rest of it," Erik said.

"Haven't you already?" Serena asked wearily. "They employ you. I don't. You're theirs."

"Wrong. I'm my own man."

"He's got that right," Niall said curtly. "If he was mine, he'd take orders better."

"If he was mine," Dana said, "he'd live in L.A. and work for us full-time. But he lives in Palm Springs and chases mountain goats."

"Sheep," Erik said.

"Whatever."

Serena looked at Erik with shadowed violet eyes, wanting to believe, wanting to trust.

Afraid to.

Trust no man with your heritage. Your life depends on it.

If she didn't follow her grandmother's advice, would she be wise or just as foolish as all the firstborn of her generation?

Don't repeat our mistakes!

Serena groaned. Now she was getting advice from her imagination. Soon she would be as wild-eyed as her grandmother. "It doesn't matter," she said. "G'mom was paranoid. After tonight, I know why."

Dana and Niall looked at each other.

"Please," Serena said bitterly, "I may look soft and slow, but I'm not. It's damn clear that whoever Bert's mystery bidder was murdered my grandmother when she tried to track down the missing pages. This same person murdered Bert before he could tell us the original source of a page. Then this person did their best to murder me. Someone really doesn't want the Book of the Learned to be whole again."

"What worries me," Erik said roughly, "is that this person is ready, willing, and damned able to murder. That's been proved at least four times in the last year."

Niall said sharply, "What?"

Erik ticked off the murders on his fingers. "A woman in Florida. A New Age monk. Serena's grandmother. Bert. They have two things in common. Each died by fire. Each was the last known link in a chain leading to pages taken from the Book of the Learned."

"But I don't know anything about the missing pages," Serena said quickly.

"Not yet," Erik agreed. "But after four murders, do you really think this person—or persons—will take the chance that you might?"

Fifty-nine

Dana's calm voice cut through the silence that followed Erik's words. "Tell us what you do know, Serena. Maybe we can help, if only by offering more, and more difficult, targets."

Serena put her elbows on the table, saw the scratches on her arms from the wild scramble over a dead man's fence, and grimaced. Absently she rearranged the scarf that had protected her hair from a fiery rain. In a gesture that had become a habit, she stroked the textile with her fingertips and felt as though she was being stroked in turn. The cloth soothed her. Perhaps it was simply the tangible connection to the past, the textured assurance that something outlived even a murderer's brutality.

"Grandmother was the firstborn female—as far as I know, the *only* child of either sex—in her generation," Serena said slowly. "She had custody of the Book of the Learned. Somehow she lost it. Or, at the very least, parts of it. Erik thinks she had most of the manuscript and left it for me." Serena sighed wearily. "If she did, she left it in such a way that I can't figure out how to find it."

Silently Dana's fingers played an intricate Renaissance piece on the modern steel of the clean room table. "Do you think that any of the murder victims knew where the whole book was?"

"No," Serena said.

"Erik?" Dana asked.

He thought about it, tested various patterns, and shook his head. "No."

"All right. We'll table the location of the whole book for now," Dana said. "For some reason, the murderer—I tend to believe there is one, for the simple reason that anything conspiratorial that two or more people know is on the six o'clock news within a week." She glanced at Niall.

Niall hesitated, then nodded. "I'll go with that. For now."

Erik nodded.

"I'm a weaver, not an investigator" was all Serena said.

Dana turned to Erik. "You mentioned four murders in the last year. Who was first?"

"Ellis Weaver."

Serena cleared her throat. It probably didn't matter, but it might. She couldn't take the chance. With a mental apology to her dead grandmother, she said, "The name I knew her by was Lisbeth Serena Charters."

All three people stared at her.

The speaker that carried Factoid's voice said, "*Fuck. Minute.*"

"When she decided to make a new life for herself, she chose the name Ellis—which is a run together form of *L. S.*—and the last name Weaver because that's what she did," Serena said.

"What about the name Charters?" Erik asked. "Was it hers by law or by choice?"

"The one time I pinned her down, she said it was her grandmother's maiden name."

"What was your grandmother's third name?" Erik asked coolly.

Serena looked blank.

"The name before she chose Charters," he explained.

His eyes were as distant as his voice. He was furious. Just

when he thought he had won her trust, she proved that she had barely trusted him at all. She would have sex with him, trust him not to kill her while she slept in his bed, hell, in his arms, but the rest of it, the day in and day out ordinary kind of trust that builds true intimacy . . . no, so sorry, the lady just wasn't buying into that.

Serena's chin came up. She met his anger with level eyes. "I don't know."

"Don't know or won't say?" he shot back.

"I. Don't. Know."

He didn't say anything. He didn't have to. His disbelief was as plain as his narrowed, glittering amber eyes. "Factoid?"

". . . minute."

"While he searches databases," Dana said, "let's pursue the possibilities of four murders in one year."

Erik's glance cut sideways to Dana.

Her dark eyebrows rose. He looked positively baleful. How like a man. It was fine for him to keep secrets, but not for his lover. "I've never seen you in non-Fuzzy mode. Impressively male. Full testosterone rush. No wonder Niall wants you back."

With an effort, Erik throttled his temper. He closed his eyes, thought of all the times his sisters had driven him to the wall, and reminded himself that this, too, shall pass. When his eyes opened, they were still cold but they were no longer furious.

"Where do you want to start?" he asked Dana.

"Ellis Weaver's death note suggests several things," Dana said blandly.

Serena looked startled. "How did you know about—oh, of course. Erik."

"Yes. Erik." Dana looked at him. "I guess you didn't mention it to her, hmmm?"

"I didn't know you wanted me to keep Serena posted on every little thing I told you," he said. His voice was as tight as the line of his mouth.

Dana's left hand waved gracefully. "It is the nature of

businesses and families to have secrets. I'm sure Serena didn't take your keeping business secrets any more personally than you took her keeping her family secrets."

Niall strangled a laugh into a cough and studied his hands as though they had just grown fur.

Erik looked at the other man. "Such sweet reason. How have you avoided strangling her?"

"Clean living and constant prayer," Niall said dryly.

Dana ignored them and glanced at Serena. "Did your grandmother ever say anything about when the leaves first went missing?"

"No."

"You sound quite certain."

"I am. Until her death note, she never mentioned the Book of the Learned to me. Not by name. She talked about my heritage, and how my mother had forfeited the right to so much as look at it."

"By running away?" Dana asked.

"No. By taking the name Charters. Grandmother was afraid that it might lead back to her."

"Even though she used the name Weaver?" Erik asked.

"Yes."

"What was she afraid of?" Niall asked.

"She never said. She just spent her life hiding."

"And one of the things she was hiding was the Book of the Learned," Niall said. "The name Charters must be tied to it somehow."

"I'll bet the book descended through the grandmother whose maiden name was Charters," Erik said.

"Interesting," Niall said, "but not particularly useful except as a measure of Ellis Weaver's paranoia."

"Fear," Serena corrected softly, rubbing her palm against her scarf. "When she was discovered, she was murdered."

Niall grunted. "All right. So what gave her away?"

"Probably the questions she asked when she decided to go after the missing pages of the Book of the Learned," Erik said. "It's the only thing that fits the pattern of the murders."

"It does?" Dana asked. "How?"

"Think about it. She must have known where the missing pages went. Or she hired someone who found them."

"Wallace?" Niall asked.

"He has my vote so far," Erik agreed. "Put Shel on it. Check Morton Hingham's records. She would have hired an investigator through him, the same way she kept her truck registered in his name and her taxes paid on her property in her assumed name."

Dana reached for one of the portable phones that were scattered throughout Rarities. Very quickly she was talking to Shel.

"Why do you think it's Wallace?" Serena asked.

"He's still alive," Erik said bluntly. "He has the background to make homemade fuel bombs and lure law-enforcement types down blind alleys when they investigate a murder. And three out of four of those murders were written off as random or suicide."

"What about Bert?" she asked with a shudder.

"I'll bet it's written off to a meth lab or a drug war," Erik said. "Or simply kept open and never solved, because the cops don't connect it to the other murders."

"Aren't we going to tell the police?"

"No hurry," Niall said. "You and Erik are the only obvious targets left, and you'll be well covered."

"Erik?" Serena said unhappily. "Why would he be a target?"

"Same reason Bert was," Niall said easily. "Bert knew something. Whoever chucked those bombs can't be certain that Bert didn't tell us before he cooked."

Serena flinched. Erik put his hand over hers and gave Niall a hard look. Erik might be pissed off at Serena, but he was damned if he would let Niall upset her.

Niall smiled widely. *Gotcha, boyo. Or rather, she has you.*

"But Wallace said he was working for someone else," Serena objected. Then she said quickly, "Forget it. I'm not thinking very well. Of course he would say that, even though he was clinging to the cliff and Erik was firing rocks at him."

Dana smiled like a cat. "You didn't mention that part, dear boy."

Erik ignored her.

"Like I said, you're wasted as a Fuzzy," Niall said.

Erik ignored that, too. "At least now we know how to draw him out into the open without putting Serena at risk."

Serena blinked. "We do?"

Niall nodded and said to Erik, "Good. Because that was my next suggestion and I knew you wouldn't go for it when I asked her."

"What was?" Serena demanded. "What are you talking about?"

"Bait," Niall said succinctly. "Erik just volunteered."

Sixty

"Only if there's no other way," Dana cut in quickly. "You know how I feel about putting nonsecurity types in the line of fire."

"We don't have enough time to put Fuzzy boy through a brushup course," Niall said, his voice impatient.

"I'm not suggesting that," Dana said with deadly clarity. "I am simply saying that we will try all other avenues first." She looked from Niall to Serena. "The most obvious course is to find the Book of the Learned and use *it* as bait. From what Erik told me, your grandmother believed she had left enough clues that if you followed her instructions, 'the Book of the Learned will follow.' "

"I've tried," Serena said, rubbing her aching scalp. "I simply don't get the point she was trying to make. Or points."

"Was your grandmother always paranoid?" Niall asked.

"Cautious," Serena corrected. "Yes. As long as I can remember."

"And longer," Erik said. "She refused to speak to your mother after your mother ran off and changed her name to Charters."

Slowly Serena nodded.

"That suggests to me that the name Charters was closer to her than she admitted to you," Erik continued. "Her own maiden name, perhaps. That would be the only reason she would get so angry when her daughter used it, putting it into the public records where anybody who was persistent enough could find it."

"Factoid?" Dana said sharply. "Did you hear that?"

Silence, then "How long ago did she last use the name Charters?" came out of the speakers.

Three people looked at Serena.

"No more recently than forty-five years ago, certainly," Serena said. "She would have been about thirty-five years old, give or take."

"Give or take what?" Factoid said sharply.

"I . . . five years?"

"I'm asking you," Factoid muttered.

"I don't know. She was approximately eighty when she died. At least, I think she was. Maybe it was just something I assumed."

"What was her birth date?" Factoid asked.

"I don't know. We didn't celebrate it. We barely celebrated mine. In fact . . ." Serena frowned. "I remember arguing about it. Awful. A real screamer on both sides. I wanted my birthday on its real day. She tried to get me to change my birthday and last name just after I came to her, but I wouldn't. It was the only thing I had of my own mother. I refused to let it go."

"Which state was your grandmother married in?" Factoid asked.

"She never said."

Factoid said something that sounded like *fuck*.

"That's two," Niall said.

Silence.

Erik said, "Serena is thirty-four. Her mother ran off when she was seventeen. Assuming she got pregnant pretty quick, she was eighteen when she had Serena. Serena was thirty-three when her grandmother died. Assume Ellis—Lisbeth—was eighty when she died. That makes her, at most, twenty-nine when she switched identities. She could have been as young as nineteen. Look for marriage licenses featuring a maiden name of Charters in that time span."

"A joke, right?" the speaker snarled.

"No."

"Well, *suck*, man! That puts me lip-deep in microfilm again! None of the states have computerized *dick* from the old days."

"Pull in every researcher we have except the ones working with April Joy on the Singapore project," Dana said instantly. "If that's not enough, hire more."

Factoid flipped the switch off and yelled obscenities until he ran out of breath. Then he flipped the switch on again and said, "Working."

"While he tears his retro lime-green hair out," Niall said, "let's explore another route to the truth."

"Such as?" Dana asked.

"Such as when did Ellis-Lisbeth start after the missing leaves?" Niall looked at Serena.

"I don't know," she said. "Her note didn't say anything about it, but if I had to bet, I'd guess it was a few months before she was murdered."

"I agree," Erik said. "That's how the murderer found her after all those years. She had to come out of hiding to reclaim the pages."

Niall grunted. "Does that get us anywhere new?"

"Not me," Erik said. "Dana?"

She shook her head. Her fingers were doing the flute thing again.

"Serena?"

"No."

Silence.

"Did you ever see the Book of the Learned?" Dana asked Serena finally.

"Yes, I think I did. Or did I dream it?" She frowned, wondering how she could sort out dream and memory. Or if it was even possible.

"When?" Dana asked.

"I . . . sometimes I can almost . . ." Slowly Serena pulled the stretchy band off her thick braid, shook it out, put her face in her hands, and rubbed her aching head. Hair the color of fire tumbled down and piled like burning coals on the steel table.

"What do you remember?" Erik asked softly.

"The initials intertwined. Grandmother's hair a tarnished silver with a halo of lantern light. Something whispering like dry hands rubbing. Gold gleaming and running and sliding and flashing when she turned pages in a thick, old book. A book whose cover was an etched gold plate studded with gems. A book whose marker was a piece of uncanny cloth woven by a sorceress long dead. It looked just like the scarf . . ." Serena tilted her head up and saw Erik watching her with eyes like hammered gold. "A dream. That's all. Just a dream."

"The cloth isn't a dream," Erik said.

"What cloth?" Dana asked.

Sighing, Serena reached beneath her hair. The cloth, as it often did, had somehow wound itself securely around her neck. Not tightly. Just not so loose that it got in the way. "I couldn't bear to leave the scarf behind once I'd touched it," she said, unwinding the old cloth from around her neck, "so I'm telling myself it looks better for being worn."

Erik glanced at the cloth and smiled at the complex play of color, texture, and design. The fabric was radiant, almost incandescent, as though it brimmed with life. "If it looked any better, it would glow in the dark." He held out his hand. "May I?"

She draped the textile over his hand, but didn't completely let go of it herself. "You're right. It looks richer now than it did before I wore it."

"Maybe it's like vellum. Maybe it needs to be touched to retain its highest gloss." He stroked the fabric with his fingertips, then rubbed it against his cheek. If he noticed that Serena hadn't let go of the scarf, he didn't say anything.

"Incredible texture. Soft but not filmy, solid but not harsh, velvety but with no direction to the nap."

And it had never felt better than last night, wrapped around both of them like a vibrant colored shadow, caressing their naked skin. But there was no need to talk about that. Like the lovemaking itself, it was private.

He spread the cloth over his palm and admired the ripple of light across the unusual surface. "Like holding a rainbow."

Dana and Niall looked at each other. Neither of them saw anything particularly spectacular in the piece of fabric Erik was admiring. It was interesting, but hardly deserved the reverence in his words and expression.

Niall leaned closer, started to pick up the fabric, and promptly dropped it. "Don't know what you're raving about, boyo. Feels like scratchy English tweed to me. About as flashy, too."

At first Erik thought the other man was kidding. Then he realized that Niall was quite serious. Erik held the cloth out to Dana. After a slight, reluctant tug, Serena let go.

"What about you?" Erik asked Dana.

She picked up an edge of the fabric, ran it between her fingers, and said, "I'm with Niall. Factoid?"

"From here it looks like a piece of burlap."

Serena looked at Dana and Niall, then at Erik. "I don't get it."

" '. . . the cloth a guardian stronger than armor and a lure to just one man. Uncanny cloth woven by the sorceress Serena of Silverfells,' " Erik quoted softly.

"Is that from the Book of the Learned?" Serena asked.

"The book, Erik the Learned's memory, a dream." Erik's mouth twisted into a wry line. "I'm not sure it matters. Nearly a thousand years ago this was woven by Serena of Silverfells." He laid the cloth over Serena's hands but didn't let go of it himself. "Now it belongs to another Serena, also a weaver. And so does the Book of the Learned. All she has to do is remember."

Unease rippled over her like a cool breath. He was so certain, his eyes so clear, as deep as time, waiting . . .

Her fingers clenched in the fey cloth. "I can't remember what I never knew!"

"You will."

Her chin tilted. "You lost me on that last one."

"Then you'll just have to trust me, won't you?"

She bit the inside of her lip, then realized that they both were holding the ancient, extraordinary cloth, their fingers touching, overlapping, locking together. Slowly she let out a long breath that was almost a sigh of surrender. "I don't have much choice, do I?"

"You always have a choice," Erik said roughly. "That's what scares the hell out of me. If you choose wrong, you die."

Sixty-one

Cleary Warrick Montclair paced one of the Retreat's spacious suites and looked at her watch.

"Shit," she hissed between her teeth.

"What?" Garrison asked.

"It's too late to talk to them tonight."

Her son sighed. "Then relax, Cleary," he said patiently. He had learned at a young age that she preferred to be called that name rather than the more generic "mother," especially when she was stressed and impatient. Lately, that had been one hundred percent of the time.

"How can I relax when Daddy is so upset?" Abruptly she realized she was almost shouting. She took a slow breath. "Where's Paul?"

"Through the connecting door, like always," Garrison muttered, but not loud enough that his mother could hear. If she wanted to pretend she was the virgin Sister Cleary, it was no skin off his butt. At least Paul took some of the hysterical edges off Cleary. Garrison supposed that was a good enough reason to tolerate the older man, even though Paul often acted like he was in charge. Yet Garrison admired Paul as much as he resented his unswerving business sense. Personalities never made Paul lose his temper. "Want me to get him?"

"Yes."

Garrison made a show of going out the hall door, walking down forty feet to the left, and knocking on the door of the room next to Cleary's. The door opened quickly. Paul looked surprisingly fit and youthful in sweatshirt and jeans.

"Is something wrong?" he asked Garrison.

"Cleary is upset. She wants you."

Impatience flitted across Paul's face. Then he went back into his room, picked up his key card, and stepped into the hall.

Cleary was waiting by the door. She opened it before Paul could knock. "You've got to do something! Daddy can't take much more of this waiting and the negotiations with the other houses have stalled and we're going to lose everything unless we get going but they're not back in their rooms and our man in the lobby hasn't seen them and—"

As soon as Paul stepped into the suite, the hall door shut abruptly in Garrison's face. He looked from the blank door to his empty highball glass and decided that another drink was just what the doctor ordered. In his own room. There weren't any women in the lobby bar that were worth the effort to screw.

As far as he was concerned, the only good news of the day was that his dear sweet granddaddy had refused to leave Palm Desert. For that, Garrison was very grateful; if he had been forced to put up with Warrick on top of flying out from Manhattan to be at his mother's beck and call, he would have undoubtedly killed someone.

As he stalked down the hall, Garrison wondered how much Serena Charters was going to cost the House of Warrick before she got what she wanted.

Or better yet, what she deserved.

Sixty-two

The Retreat's ventilation system was so efficient that only a trace of fresh-paint smell made it into the two-bedroom suite Erik and Serena shared. They didn't get a chance to enjoy the privacy. No sooner did they walk over the threshold into the room than Lapstrake stepped out from behind the door and shut it.

"Hello, Ian," Erik said. "Have you met Serena?"

"No." Lapstrake smiled down at the tousled redhead who had the kind of sultry eyes that set a man to dreaming. "Hi, Serena. I'm Ian."

"Good-bye," Erik said to Lapstrake, opening the door before Serena could say anything. "Niall wants to talk to you."

"You sure?" Lapstrake asked, looking over his shoulder at Serena.

"Yeah." With an ungentle nudge, Erik got Lapstrake out the door, shut it, and threw the dead bolt.

She raked hair back from her face. "That was remarkably rude."

"He's too handsome by half."

"Is he?" She yawned. "I didn't notice."

"Yeah? What color were his eyes?"

"Hmmm. Let's see. I've got a fifty-fifty chance on this one. Light?"

"Dark." Erik looked at her oddly. "You really didn't notice, did you?"

"One handsome blond is all I can handle at a time."

"Ian is dark-haired."

"Gosh, you know him so well. Maybe I'm the one who should be jealous."

Erik laughed out loud in surprise. Then he tugged her into his arms and simply held her. "You're good for me," he said softly. "After tonight, I wasn't sure I'd be really laughing anytime soon."

Her arms tightened and her heart turned over as she remembered him running back toward Bert's kitchen while fire rained down all around.

"You could have been killed," she said huskily, kissing his warm, bare skin beneath Niall's jacket. "Are you sure you're all right?"

His breath hesitated, thickened. He pulled her closer and buried his face against her neck. The soft scarf caressed his lips before he nosed it aside to taste the tantalizing skin beneath. "Getting better every second."

She pulled away and looked at him. "I meant the fire. Are you burned anywhere?"

"Yeah. It's terrible. Wanna see?"

She laughed at his rakish expression. Then she forgot to breathe as his mouth closed over hers. He tasted of hunger and time, darkness and need. Despite the unanswered questions between them, everything female in her responded. Whatever happened in the future, at the moment it was enough that they both were together now, both alive.

"Serena?"

"Yes," she whispered. "Oh, yes."

It was the last coherent word either one of them said for a long time as they rediscovered how well they fit together, how deep, how right. The fire they found together was the fire of the phoenix, healing rather than murderous, generous rather than deadly.

When she finally lay more asleep than awake, smiling, her lips against the slow beat of his pulse, he gently eased his wrist free of the clinging scarf. Slowly, trying not to wake her, he slipped from her and went to the heavily draped window. His laptop computer on the bedside table gave enough light for him to avoid furniture.

One of Serena's pages took up the whole screen. The background of gold foil on the page shimmered. The colors applied to the complexly intertwined initials shone like intricate gems.

None of the beautiful light was enough to soften the curve of his lips as he stood naked by the bedroom window and nudged the drape aside just enough to allow him a one-eyed view of the world.

"That's not a very nice smile," she said lazily from the bed. Under the sheet she was as naked as he was, except for the scarf, which had ended up wound around one of her wrists. And his, too, now that she thought about it.

He let the curtain fall back the bare half inch he had opened it. Turning, he came back to the bed. The hard line of his mouth shifted into a true smile as he caught the red-gold shimmer of Serena's hair against the pale wood of the headboard. He lifted the covers, inhaled the heady scent of Serena and intimacy, and slid in beside her.

"It just started to rain," he said quietly. "Heller is going to be cold, damp, and pissed off sleeping outside in his baby pickup. I, on the other hand, am going to be warm, comfortable, and very satisfied in here with you."

She wasn't nearly as amused as he was. The idea of being followed just wasn't something she could smile over, even a smile as nasty as his had been. "Where do you suppose Wallace is?"

"Nursing a headache." And, if God was kind, some broken bones in his hand.

But Erik didn't say anything aloud about his hope. Despite Serena's willingness to use his gun when they were threatened, she had a softer heart than he did. It must have been her mother's contribution to the genetic mix. From everything he had found out, it sure hadn't been her grandmother's.

He cuddled Serena against him, savoring the feel of her body while it fitted to him as easily as though they had always been lovers. "You have any more flashes about designs or gold covers set with gems or anything else about the Book of the Learned?" he asked.

She put her arms around him, enjoying the strength and resilience of his shoulders. Then she sighed. Flashes were a good description of what those memories were like . . . sudden lightning against the dark backdrop of forgotten years.

"It was so long ago." Hearing her own words, she almost smiled. "In kid terms, anyway. For me, the years between one and five are a lifetime lived by someone else, someone I don't really know. Five to ten isn't much better. Ten to fifteen is a blur, sixteen to twenty is somewhat better, and I'm prepared to discuss intelligently the years between twenty-one and today."

"When did you move out of the cabin?"

"On my eighteenth birthday. G'mom encouraged me. She said I never would amount to anything if I hung around the cabin waiting for her to die."

He whistled silently. "Not your average loving granny."

"She was a realist who didn't have much patience with people who couldn't pull up their socks and get on with life. She might have been short on hugs, but she didn't abuse me. Never so much as raised her voice. She did her duty. Always."

He kissed the subdued fire of Serena's hair as he said, "And it was always a duty, never a pleasure."

"Her only pleasure was in weaving and . . ." Serena's voice died as a ghostly lightning flickered against the lost years of childhood.

"And?" Erik asked quietly.

"Reading, I think."

"Did she have a lot of books?"

"No. None."

"Yet you remember her reading?"

"Yes."

Erik waited. He knew memory could be elusive and yet as solid as the San Jacinto Mountains rising out of the desert. When Serena didn't say anything more, he nuzzled her hair and said quietly, "Can you describe the memory?"

She let out a long, sighing breath. "I woke up and saw her face lit by lantern light. She was looking down at the table and smiling. That's why I thought I was dreaming. She never smiled in daylight, except sometimes when she was weaving. But she wasn't weaving. She was just sitting. That was odd, too. Her hands were never still. Weaving, sewing, drawing water from the well, tanning rabbit skins for a downscale trading post in Palm Springs that sold junk to tourists . . . she was always busy at some task or another, even at night."

He made a low sound of surprise. With every word Serena portrayed a lifestyle that could have existed one hundred years before, or two hundred, or a thousand; lifetimes when night was relieved only by fire.

"What was she looking at when she smiled?" he asked. "What was on the table in front of her?"

"Something beautiful. Something that was like a ripple of light whenever she . . ." Serena's voice died.

"Turned a page?" he suggested.

She closed her eyes. It didn't help. Memories of clots of fire exploding and Bert screaming poured through her like molten glass. "I don't know. I can't see it." She drew a steadying breath. "But that must be it. Or am I simply manufacturing something to fill a gap in memory and none of it is true?"

"You didn't manufacture that design of intertwined initials. Or the cover you sketched for Dana just before I told her you'd had enough and dragged you out from under her velvet-sheathed steel claws."

"Did I thank you for that?"

He grinned and kissed the corner of her mouth, licked lightly, remembering. "Oh yeah."

Her smile came and went swiftly. "How much of my memory do you think is real?"

"My name is North, not Proust."

"Where's a philosopher when you need one?" she retorted.

"Drinking hemlock tea."

She smiled in spite of the restlessness that swept through her like an autumn wind. She could almost see the memory/dream/image of her grandmother in lantern light, smiling.

Almost. But not enough to look through her grandmother's eyes and see what had made her smile.

If there was anything to see.

Damn!

"Let it go," Erik said.

"What?"

"Whatever is making you tighten up and frown. Let it go and enjoy the last of the wine Dana sent as an apology."

"Eat, drink, and be merry, for tomorrow you'll—" Serena stopped abruptly.

Erik's hand closed over hers. "You'll be fine."

"That's not how the saying goes."

"It is now."

He lifted her hand to his lips. Under the cover of a kiss, he slid his tongue between her fingers. The noise of rain bursting against the window covered her gasp, but the sudden speeding of her heartbeat was quite apparent at her wrist. Delicately he probed the telltale pulse with the tip of his tongue.

"Are you trying to distract me?" she asked.

"Yeah."

"You're succeeding very well."

"Want to see what else I'm good at?"

Desire swept through her, softening her in a scented rush. "I can't wait."

His fingers stroked, probed, found her ready, and his own breath broke on a surge of hunger. "You don't have to wait."

In one long motion he locked himself inside her.

Beside the bed, the intertwined initials shimmered and burned as though they were alive.

Sixty-three

Screens around the clean room showed each of the seventeen sheets taken from the Book of the Learned. At the bottom of each screen was the earliest known provenance of the pictured page. At the moment, no one was paying any attention to the displays.

Paul Carson and Cleary Warrick Montclair were isolated behind a one-way mirror with Niall. Both men were watching Cleary closely. She had the fractured eyes and vibrating body of a woman running too close to the edge of her control.

Beyond the one-way mirror, Garrison Montclair sat on one side of the clean room's steel conference table. Serena and Erik sat opposite Garrison. Dana sat at the head of the table. Various refreshments lay ignored in the center.

"Thank you for agreeing to this meeting, Serena," Dana said, her voice as creamy as her eyes were cold. She was furious at having been forced into the confrontation. But the choice had been clear: if she wanted the House of Warrick's cooperation tracing the illuminated pages, she would have to keep Cleary informed of everything that occurred in the search, no matter how minor the detail. "Ms. Warrick Montclair is intensely worried about her father."

Erik, who was facing the one-way mirror, didn't bother to hide his sardonic expression. If Dana's arm-twisting could be called agreement, Serena had agreed. To be precise, she had literally thrown her hands in the air and said, *Fine. I'll talk to Garrison. And then I'm leaving!*

"Garrison, I believe you are acting as spokesman?" Dana said, looking at him with no favor at all.

Erik made a disgusted sound. Talk about an understatement. Paul had all but carried Cleary screaming into the spy room. Cleary had wanted to convince Serena face-to-face of the importance of selling the pages—and the Book of the Learned itself—to the House of Warrick. Dana had vetoed that idea. Serena had repeated that refusal to Paul Carson in a word of one syllable.

Garrison smiled engagingly. He looked quite fresh in his slate-colored flannel slacks and open-necked, long-sleeved white shirt. If his eyes showed the effects of too little sleep and one too many martinis, he wasn't worried about it. Anyone with Cleary for a mother was bound to look frayed from time to time.

"I second Dana's thanks," Garrison said, giving Serena a look of frank understanding and sympathy. "I also apologize for my mother. She's an excellent businesswoman, but when it comes to family she loses all perspective."

Serena's expression wasn't encouraging. It said more clearly than words that she was heartily sick of hearing about Cleary's problems. "I'm here," Serena said. "If you thought I would be smiling about it, you don't know me."

Garrison sighed. "I'm sorry, Serena."

"So am I," she said evenly.

He smiled.

She didn't.

"I believe you had a proposition to put before Ms. Charters," Dana said. The look in Dana's eyes said she wasn't going to be throwing rose petals at Garrison no matter what the outcome of the meeting.

"So much for the amenities, is that it?" Garrison asked ruefully.

"Exactly." Dana waited.

"All right." He took a sip of the coffee he had been ignoring. As he put down the cup, he looked directly at Serena. "The House of Warrick is prepared to pay you one million dollars for the four leaves of manuscript you have in your possession and your written agreement to cede to the House of Warrick all interest in whatever manuscript those pages once were part of."

Serena didn't even pause. "No."

"Ms. Charters . . . Serena," Garrison said, rubbing his forehead wearily, "may I ask why?"

"Would you sell the heart out of your body for a million dollars?" Serena retorted.

He looked startled. "Er, no, of course not."

She touched the uncanny scarf she wore around her throat. Against her forest-green blouse, the scarf was a gold-shot green. Last night, against a black shirt, the scarf had looked like gleaming midnight. In any light, it gave her skin the iridescence of pearl.

"In some way I can't explain," she said finally, "those pages are as much a part of me as your heart is a part of you."

"Forgive me," Garrison said, frowning, "but I find it difficult to believe that a woman of limited means would turn down a million dollars for four manuscript leaves that wouldn't sell for a thousand dollars each on the open market."

"Which brings up an interesting point," Erik said, pinning Garrison with predatory eyes. "Why is the House of Warrick willing to spend a million for pages that Norman Warrick is saying are fraudulent? Are you afraid that someone else might disagree and undermine faith in the old man's abilities? Someone like me? Because I can't wait to go one-on-one with your grandfather on the subject of the worth of Serena's pages. They are as true as they are beautiful."

"No one from the House of Warrick has officially announced an opinion on those pages one way or another."

"Interesting," Erik said neutrally. "Yet everyone who is anyone in the illuminated manuscript business knows that Norman Warrick thinks Serena's pages are frauds."

Garrison made an impatient gesture. "I can't be responsible for gossip. As for being worried about my grandfather's reputation—bullshit. He has been wrong in the past—though rarely—and the House of Warrick hasn't crumbled. The reason we're offering a million is emotional rather than professional. My mother has her panties in a twist for fear that Grandfather is going to blow a valve over the pages, which would throw a real spanner into our negotiations with a coalition of auction houses. This is a crucial time for the House of Warrick. Her solution is to buy the pages and save her father's life and the family business. If that sounds unreasonable to you, take it up with Cleary. I am sick of the subject." He switched his gaze to Serena. "Please, I beg you, think about it. My grandfather insulted you, but don't you think that killing him is more than the insult deserved?"

Erik came to his feet in a rush. All that kept him from going over the table after the younger man was Serena's hand on his wrist.

"If I was keeping the pages out of pique," she said distinctly, "you would be right. I'm not. The pages are mine. They will remain mine. This discussion is over."

"One million, one hundred thousand" was Garrison's only response.

"No."

"A million and a quar—"

"No," Serena cut in savagely. "Not for any price. Don't you understand? *No part of the Book of the Learned is for sale.*"

"Darling, everything is—"

"I believe that concludes the meeting," Dana said over

Garrison's cultured voice. "You have presented your offer and your reasons for urgency. Ms. Charters has unmistakably declined."

A door slammed in the hallway outside. The clean-room door opened just far enough to show Cleary's furious face before Niall put his big hand on the door and shoved it shut. She started to claw at his hand, then began sobbing hysterically.

"Get her out of here," Niall said to Paul.

"Of course. Sorry. This has been very . . . difficult."

Cleary leaned against Paul and cried with hoarse, racking sounds.

Niall grunted and released his hold on the door. As he had expected, it opened very quickly and Dana stepped out. She made a point of closing the door behind her and blockading the doorknob with her own body.

"We'll send Mr. Warrick the final bill," she said distinctly.

"You're quitting?" Paul asked, startled.

"We signed a contract to attempt to buy Serena's pages. We've attempted. No sale."

"No!" Cleary said harshly, pushing away from Paul. "I won't have that little bitch telling lies about Father losing his grip as an appraiser. He's sharper than ever. When you find out where those pages really came from, you'll see. She'll rue the day she came to Daddy with a handful of lies and turned our lives upside down!"

"Cleary, look at me," Paul said. With a steady pressure of his palm he turned her face toward his. "Are you sure you want this? The more you push it, the more strain it will be on you and your father. If you step back and let things die down, Ms. Charters and her pages will probably be forgotten in a few months."

"Never," Cleary vowed. "I'm going to ruin her and her goddamned pages if it's the last thing I do. Don't you understand? All the House of Warrick has is its reputation, and Daddy *is* that reputation!"

Paul looked at her reddened eyes, felt the tension vibrating in her body, and knew he wasn't going to win this round. Cleary wasn't going to be rational, much less reasonable, about her father and the House of Warrick. "Okay, we'll do it your way. It doesn't matter one way or another. Life is a game and nobody gets out alive, not even Norman Warrick." He tucked Cleary against his chest and looked over her head at Dana. "Finish it. The House of Warrick is good for it."

"Finish it?" Dana asked. "By that I assume you mean trace the provenance of the pages?"

"Yeah. And keep us informed, of course. Cleary will insist."

"Hourly?" Niall asked in a hard voice.

"If not more often," Paul said with a twist to his mouth that was harder than a smile.

"Does this mean that the House of Warrick will redouble its efforts to go through its own files?" Dana asked. "Unless Serena can piece together enough childhood memories to find the whole Book of the Learned, we're at the point where all other avenues of investigation are closed. Sotheby's and Christie's have put themselves out as much as they are willing to. That leaves Warrick's files."

Paul nodded curtly. "I'll see to it myself."

Dana released the doorknob and stepped aside just in time to keep from being run over by Garrison.

"Is Mother—Cleary—all right?" he asked Paul.

"She'll be fine as soon as all this is settled."

"What's to settle? It's over."

"Not quite," Paul said coolly. "Cleary wants Rarities Unlimited's research into Serena's pages to continue."

"But that's crazy! No matter what we find out, it won't—"

"It will ease Cleary's mind," Paul interrupted. "Surely that's worth a few thousand dollars?"

Garrison looked beseechingly at the ceiling. Then he shrugged. "Yeah. Sure. Whatever. Fuck."

Dana's eyebrows rose. "The amended contract will be ready in a few hours. I'll send it over to the Retreat for signatures."

She was talking to Garrison's back.

"Send the revised contract to Palm Desert," Paul said. "That's where Cleary will be. She wants to get back to her father."

With that, Paul urged Cleary down the hall. Halfway to the outer door, she tipped her face up and said something.

Paul stopped, looked over his shoulder, and called to Dana down the hall, "Hourly updates, unless a new course of investigation offers itself. Then you will notify us immediately. Agreed?"

Dana would just as soon have eaten raw snake, but she was a businesswoman and the House of Warrick was a very good client. "Agreed."

Sixty-four

The remains of Chinese takeout lay scattered across the clean room's steel table. Chopsticks stuck rakishly out of empty white cartons. Napkins smeared with hot mustard and hotter pepper oil were stuffed into other cartons. Green tea lay cold in the bottom of mugs, forgotten. Bottles of Tsingtao beer waited in a tub of half-melted ice, unopened.

Serena's chin was propped on her hand. Her glazed eyes looked at the wall of screens without really seeing any of the bold calligraphy or glorious illumination. She and Erik—with Niall, and even Dana from time to time—had spent most of the day trying to discover anything new from the data on the sheets.

Whenever Research had new information to add, it appeared on the appropriate screen. It had been several hours since anything new appeared. The House of Warrick had traced another sheet through aging microfilm to the Rubin estate.

Dead end.

Erik also looked at the screens without seeing them, but

that was because he was chasing the tantalizing pattern that kept whispering to him. There was more to be discovered about the previous owners. He was certain of it. The pattern was there, nearly within reach . . .

He almost closed his eyes and became completely still, as though the pattern was a wary roadrunner he was teaching to eat from his hand.

Niall looked at him. When Serena would have spoken, a gesture from Niall cut her off. He leaned close to her and said quietly, "Leave him be. This is why Dana fought me to keep him in Research. He has a scary knack for finding patterns where others see just a jumble of information. He and Shane Tannahill are enough to make you believe in things that go bump in the night. But Shane turned Dana down flat. That's when she stole Erik from me."

Serena looked at Erik and remembered another man who had been good at finding patterns, a man who rode with a peregrine on his arm and a staghound pacing beside his horse. *He would have come to her like that, proud and free, but she had needed him too much to leave the fate of Silverfells to a proud man's choice. So she had woven a lure that only one man would come to. And he had come.*

Enthralled.

She had hoped he, the man who saw all patterns, would see the perfection of the one they wove together; because if he had not been the man he was, he would have shunned the offered lure.

In the end, he had seen only his own humiliation. He, the pattern master, fooled by an uncanny weaver. He, the pattern master, had become the lover of the last sorceress of Silverfells, a clan forbidden to the Learned. He, the pattern master, had been mastered by her.

Then hatred had eaten love.

Then mist had descended, dividing them.

Serena saw the words so clearly, the capitals picked out in gold and silver, the smaller letters as black as the truth they revealed. She saw them—but had never seen the page where they were written.

Yet the words were there, shimmering in her mind.

Cool air prickled over Serena's skin. It wasn't quite fear. It was a heightened awareness, an acceptance that there was more to life than could be seen, touched, tasted, heard, smelled. There was time itself. Time endlessly described by poets and philosophers, time nailed to walls or chained around wrists by the powerful, time cut into pieces by mathematicians and scientists until each segment was named, numbered, defined by the beating heart of an atom . . .

And never understood.

Silently she realized that time would never be understood, for no one even understood the child who lived before the adult, sharing one body through all the changes of life.

Erik straightened abruptly. "Is Factoid still there?"

". . . minute," came the muttered response from the speaker.

"Now," Niall said curtly.

"*Suck.*" There was a rustle and slam as though something had hit the wall. "I'm here!"

"Do you have the computer breakdown I requested?" Erik asked.

"Which one?" Factoid retorted.

"Stylistic hallmarks of the Spanish Forger set against the stylistic hallmarks of the pages I— "

"Yeah, yeah," Factoid cut in. "Close, but no cigar. Definitely a forgery of a forger. The guy's real good, though."

Erik nodded. "When was the change? In the forties?"

"Suck, man, if you already knew, why did you put me through the burning hoops?"

"I was guessing. Now I'm not."

Serena started to ask what he wasn't guessing about, but Niall shook his head.

"Using the second forger's style," Erik continued, "search the databases for matches on whole or partial manuscripts."

"Oh, sure," Factoid said sarcastically. "Have it in two shakes of a stripper's tit. *Fuck.* You think I'm some kind of magician?"

"I'm not listening," Niall said to no one in particular.

"Yes," Erik said.

Factoid cracked his knuckles spectacularly, cut the speaker, and got to work.

"What was that all about?" Niall asked Erik mildly.

"Not yet. If it's a false trail, I don't want to mire anyone else's speculations in it."

"And if it isn't a false trail?"

"Life will get very interesting."

"You know about the old Chinese curse, don't you?" Niall asked.

"Which one?"

"May you live in interesting times."

Sixty-five

"We're not getting anywhere," Erik said, pushing away from the steel table. "We need new information."

Niall sucked up the last cold noodle from a soggy carton before he spoke. "At last count, Dana had fifteen researchers combing data."

"Not that kind of information."

"Then what?"

Erik looked at Serena. Her eyes were dark, haunted, almost bruised. He didn't need any particular pattern skills to guess that she was seeing fire rain down out of darkness and knowing all too clearly what her grandmother must have seen and felt and tasted in her last instants of life.

"We're looking in the wrong place," he said. "We need to follow Ellis-Lisbeth's directions."

"Glad to, boyo," Niall said. "What in bleeding hell were they?"

"To think like her. To remember Serena's childhood."

"Oh, well, piece of cake." Niall's deep, ironic voice mocked every word he spoke. "What's holding us back?"

Serena's eyes focused on Erik. "I've tried. But all this"—
she waved her hand to take in the room with its high-tech
screens, cameras, communications equipment—"distracts
me. It just feels *wrong*."

"I know. How can we help?"

"Hypnosis?" suggested Niall.

"Won't work," she said. "I tried it once to see if it would
explain my dreams of mist and forest and a loom I'd never
seen filled with patterns that haunted me, people speaking a
language that was old before Chaucer." She shrugged. "I
found out I don't hypnotize worth a damn."

"Not surprising," Erik said.

"Why?" she asked.

"Hypnosis requires suggestibility and trust," Erik said
matter-of-factly. "You're about as suggestible as a stone wall.
As for trust, well, we've already been around that track once
or twice, haven't we?"

She smiled thinly. "Bet you don't hypnotize worth a
damn, either."

"Bet you're right," Niall said before Erik could. "It's one of
the things I liked best about him. He drove Dr. Cooper nuts."

"If you really want to help me remember," she said to
Erik, "let me go back to G'mom's house. Even though I know
nothing is there, I can't shake the feeling it will help me remember something."

"Forget it," Niall cut in. "You're not leaving headquarters
until we catch the murderer—or murderers."

Serena kept looking at Erik.

"The desert sounds like a great idea," he said. "I've had
about as many walls and computer screens as I can take. I always keep camping gear in the SUV. How does that sound?"

"Like a bloody stupid idea!" Niall snarled.

She ignored him and smiled at Erik. "I haven't slept out
since I was a girl."

"There's no feeling quite like it." He smiled at her in return, the lines around eyes and mouth almost sad.

"Do you have a lantern?" she asked suddenly. "The old-fashioned kind that runs on kerosene or white gas and is pressurized with a little hand pump and has silk mantles that burn with a clear light that is almost as good as sunlight."

"Is that the type of lantern your grandmother used?"

"No," Niall said. "Repeat, NO."

"Yes," Serena said over him. "Can you find one? The sound and sight and smell of it burning against the darkness is my most vivid childhood memory."

"And smell triggers more memory than any of the other senses," Erik said. "Good idea. Very good. I have one of the old lanterns at home. I've always loved the light. Sketches done by lantern light have a special quality." He held out his hand.

She took it, lacing her fingers deeply with his.

"I'm getting Dana," Niall said harshly. "You fucking well better be here when we get back."

Erik glanced at Niall. "Don't dawdle. It's a long drive."

"Anybody following us?" Serena asked.

"Not that I've picked up," Erik said, glancing automatically at all the SUV's mirrors.

Except Lapstrake, of course, and Erik hadn't exactly spotted him in the surprisingly heavy evening traffic leaving L.A. He simply knew that Lapstrake was out there somewhere, leading Heller on a merry chase in Dana's SUV, with one of the security women riding shotgun in a red wig.

Niall hadn't liked letting Erik and Serena leave headquarters without guards. He had argued about security with Dana until the walls vibrated; then he had stalked off to orchestrate the inevitable.

Despite their burning impatience to be away from the carpet of lights and humanity that was L.A., it was almost two hours before Niall declared that he had done all he could. When Erik and Serena had driven away from Rarities Unlimited, they were alone.

As far as Erik could tell they were still alone.

"We don't have to do this," he said to Serena. "Niall is

right about the risk. If Lapstrake didn't decoy Heller success-fully, we could end up with a lot of company out in the desert."

"Are you worried?"

"If I thought I could do this without you, I would."

"You're worried."

"Fucking A," he said sardonically.

"But only about me, not about yourself."

Erik didn't bother to argue that. "If I get hurt, it's my own fault. If you get hurt, it's my fault."

"That's crap."

"That's the way I feel about it."

"I can't be responsible for your irrational emotions."

"Bloody hell," he said through clenched teeth, hearing echoes of his own arguments years ago. "Are you sure you don't know my sisters?"

Serena smiled and touched his cheek. The masculine tex-ture of heat and beard stubble made her smile soften. "I'd like to. Are they as smart and stubborn as you?"

He blew out a breath, then said starkly, "I don't want to lose you again."

Again.

"And that's as emotional and irrational as anything I've said tonight," Erik muttered.

"But much more sensible," she said.

His only answer was in the hard set of his shoulders.

She hesitated, then let out a long sigh. "Erik, I feel it, too. I didn't want to. I'm not even comfortable thinking about it." She touched the scarf that nestled around her throat as though protecting her vulnerable pulse. "Yet it . . . *is*. I knew you before I met you. You knew me. I see another man in you sometimes, like a colored shadow thrown by unearthly light." She hesitated. "Do you see another woman in me?"

"Yes. Sometimes. I'm not real cool with it, either. I'm too much a creature of the twenty-first century to be comfort-able with anything you can't reproduce in a lab under speci-fied circumstances."

Serena made a muffled sound and then laughed out loud. "Put that way, our worries sound ridiculous. The most important things haven't been reproduced in any lab—creativity and imagination, laughter and grief, time and memory, hate and love and yearning. Everything that makes us human."

He ran the back of his fingers over her cheek and down to the ancient cloth against her neck, warm with her warmth, vital with her life. "How did I ever lose you in the first place?"

"I'm guessing we were as stubborn and proud then as . . ." Her voice died, but they both knew what she had been about to say . . . *as we are now*.

"Yeah," he said. "That would explain it."

It wasn't a comforting insight.

They drove in silence to his home to pick up a lantern that they hoped would be rich with memories of her childhood.

Sixty-six

It would have been more symmetrical to incinerate the old man while he slept, but that would attract too much attention. At least there wasn't any need for caution or stories about being stranded by a broken radiator hose. The old man was dead drunk. Dead easy.

Breathing through clenched teeth, a shadow in black clothing stood over the pile of blankets that passed for a bed. The stench rising from the mound was enough to make eyes water; cleanliness hadn't made the hermit's short list of virtues.

"Old man, how can you stand the smell?"

Black-gloved hands reached out. A quick, jerking twist of bristling chin against thin shoulder, a dry snap, and the transformation was complete.

Dead drunk to dead.

Satisfied that no one would become curious about any strange vehicle parked in the dusty yard, the attacker went to the car, drove it around in back, and threw a drab tarp over it. Night glasses were put in place and adjusted for the surprising light of the stars. Only then did the intruder walk into the darkness.

The deadly shadow moved quickly over the rough land. It wouldn't do to be late. It was going to be a busy night at the cabin where Lisbeth Charters had lived in solitude and died under a hail of fire.

Sixty-seven

The helicopter shot a spear of white light over the empty land. Caught in harsh illumination, Joshua trees seemed frozen in horrified surrender, their spiky arms stretched high. The spear of light swept on, quartering the area around the burned-out cabin, looking for fresh tire tracks or vehicles.

Niall didn't expect to find anything, but he was a careful man. It had saved his life more than once.

"Looks clean," he said finally into the microphone in his helmet. "Take us down."

The chopper dropped out of the night like an elevator with a death wish. At the last instant, the pilot adjusted the controls. Butterfly-tender, the chopper's metal runners kissed the ground.

"You're going to misjudge someday," Niall said into his microphone. "It better not be on company time."

Larry's grin was a slash of white against the glowing amber of the console lights. Fifty feet up the road, the ruins of a dead woman's home rose out of the little hollow. "What do you think, Ian?"

The sound of the rotors dropped to a tolerable roar as Lapstrake unhooked the safety harness and reached for his helmet. Before he pulled it off, he said, "I think you're almost as good a pilot as you think you are. It's the 'almost' that's giving me gray hair."

Larry laughed while he watched both men switch from helmets to very discreet, portable, battery-driven communications gear.

"You read me?" Niall asked. The hair-fine microphone at the corner of his mouth picked up his words.

"Four by four," Lapstrake answered.

"Let's go. The way Erik drives, he might not be more than an hour or so behind us. We have to choose our positions and be in them by the time his headlights clear that little rise."

Carrying backpacks, both men dropped to the ground and shrugged their gear into place.

Though the landing had been light, the helicopter wasn't. The landing skids had dug into the dirt road's rain-softened surface. Beneath that top inch or two, the baked earth of the desert lay hard and untouched.

Lapstrake looked at the chewed-up road. "What if Erik spots the marks left by the chopper?"

"Then he'll know what he already suspects," Niall said coldly. "No way in hell I was going to let him go without backup, no matter how much the two of them bleated about having to get away from the crowd in order for Serena to remember."

He glanced around. Even without the benefit of the night-vision glasses that he had slung around his neck, he could see that there wasn't as much cover as he had expected. The trees—if you could call them that—were more like spiky, many-armed scarecrows than real trees. Only Factoid could have hidden behind one of them.

"Rocks?" Lapstrake asked, pointing toward the closest of the random stacks of boulders that poked up out of the rolling desert.

Niall grunted. It was a little obvious, but it wasn't like Erik was going to come hunting. It was more a matter of giving him a feeling of space. Freedom. "Yeah, the rocks. Let's get rid of the light show."

He looked toward Larry and made a gesture with his hand that suggested rotors winding up.

Larry took the hint. The rotors spun more quickly as the engine revved. Dust, grit, and small pebbles made life a misery for everything within reach of the rotor wash. The chopper vibrated like an eager hound and leaped up into the night. The white shaft of the powerful landing light swept over the two men as the helicopter swung to a new heading.

Side by side, eyes closed against the whirlwind, ears throbbing from the unleashed roar of the metal beast, the two men waited for the air to calm and their night vision to return.

They didn't see the shadow separate from nearby boulders. They didn't hear anything come up behind them. Without warning something grabbed their hair and slammed their heads together with a vicious cracking sound only the attacker was conscious long enough to hear.

A different kind of night fell on Niall and Lapstrake, the kind of night a man would be lucky to survive.

Working quickly, the shadow dragged the slack-bodied men behind the boulders. The slow, dark welling of blood from each man's skull announced that they were still alive. The attacker considered that fact, then shrugged. If there were questions to ask the men later, they probably would still be alive. If there weren't any questions, they could die in a few hours just as well as now. A smart person kept as many options open as possible.

The attacker was very smart.

Lifting from the silence beyond the hollow came the sound of a distant vehicle. Soon it would be close to the hermit's turnoff. Then would come the turnoff to the informal target-shooting range. Then would come the ruts that led to the destroyed cabin.

The shadow worked with redoubled urgency. Backpacks were jerked off and flung beyond reach into the boulders.

Quick fingers ripped duct tape off a roll and wrapped it around wrists and ankles with swift motions.

Within two minutes Niall and Lapstrake had their hands bound behind their back and their ankles strapped together. A few turns of tape across each man's mouth and around their head ensured that if they came to before they died, they wouldn't be able to tell anyone about it.

With a smooth efficiency that told its own story, black-gloved hands frisked the fallen men. First Niall's weapons, then Lapstrake's, were stowed behind the attacker's waist-band. Pocketknives were discovered and hurled into the darkness well beyond reach of even a conscious, unbound man.

Satisfied that the two men were fully helpless, the attacker slipped away and merged with the darkness once more, waiting for the final participants to arrive.

Sixty-eight

Lantern and camping gear stowed in back of the SUV, Erik and Serena turned off the highway onto the asphalt county road that connected the nearly uninhabited Mojave Desert with the bright lights and crowded ambitions of urban southern California.

No lights turned off behind them.

He hadn't spotted any lights following him from the freeway to his home. No little pickup truck or pale Nissan sedan had been parked in front of North Castle, waiting for him to return. Nor had anyone been nearby, watching with binoculars.

Or if there had been someone, he or she hadn't gotten into place quick enough to pick up the SUV when it left North Castle. No one had followed them from Palm Springs to the lonely county road leading east into the Mojave Desert.

Along with cars and concrete, they had left behind the lid of clouds that had settled over L.A. and was trying to engulf Palm Springs. Even without clouds, there wasn't as much light as usual. There was no moon to separate the night into slices of silver and shards of black. Beyond the reach of the headlights, a bowl of stars glittered brilliantly overhead, almost bright enough to cast radiant, ghostly shadows.

Erik kept on checking the mirrors all the way up the asphalt road to the dirt road that led to shacks inhabited by a determined, far-flung handful of desert hermits. Lisbeth had once been one of them. The most resolute one. Her cabin was the farthest away and the best hidden.

Serena woke up when he turned off the county road onto the dirt road that twisted up and over several miles and many rumples in the desert floor, branching off to cabins or dead ends where the locals came to play with their guns. In the bright glare of headlights, the dirt showed signs that another vehicle—or vehicles—had been on the road since yesterday's rain, but no matter how often Erik checked, he didn't see any moving lights anywhere in the landscape ahead of or behind him. The graded dirt road stayed empty.

Unless someone was driving without lights.

As an experiment he killed the headlights and went with parking lights alone. Then he went with nothing at all. It was slower, but safe enough as long as you were sure you were the only one driving in stealth mode. The graded road didn't have any potholes or rocky outcrops to snare the unwary. The ruts leading to the burned cabin were a different matter. They would require care and good light, especially after a rain.

He turned the headlights back on. If he was going to hit one of the big-eared local deer or a roving coyote, he wanted to see it coming.

"Well?" she asked, watching him check the mirrors.

"So far so good. Lapstrake must have decoyed Heller back in L.A. No one picked us up leaving my place in Palm Springs. No one is in our rearview mirror. Or in our windshield, for that matter."

"Then why do you look like you're attending a funeral?"

In the muted glow of the dashboard lights, Erik's smile

wasn't much more cheerful than his expression had been. "Guess I'm just naturally a happy sort."

"I think you're cranky for lack of sleep. You should have let me drive part of the way and slept."

"I don't need much more than five or six hours a night."

"Yeah? Any other vices I should know about?"

His smile softened into a real one. "Vice, huh? How much sleep do you need?"

Serena put the window down partway. Clean, crisp desert air poured over her in a reviving stream. "I'm a steady seven hours or more kind of person." She inhaled deeply, letting the dry, pungent air seep into her, past her conscious mind, all the way down to the deep places where memories slept. "G'mom wasn't a big sleeper. The older she got, the less she slept."

"That's pretty common after sixty or so. I don't think Granddad slept more than two or three hours a night." While Erik spoke, his glance kept shifting from mirrors to road. The farther up the graded road they came, the more turnoffs they passed, the less tire tracks there were. "Any guess about how many people live out along this road?"

"There are five houses, counting G'mom's. Hers is the most remote. The turnoff we just passed leads to Jolly Barnes's house—shack would be more accurate."

"Jolly?"

"Yeah. You know, tall guys are Shorty and skinny guys are Hefty and—"

"Sourpusses are called Jolly," Erik finished. "Gotcha. I take it Jolly isn't?"

"He might be a regular wiggling puppy for all I know. I never got close enough to him to find out. Between the dreadful hand-rolled cigarettes he always smokes and the fact that no liquid ever saw the inside of his cabin or the outside of his body unless it came in a box of wine and then right out of him, Jolly is enough to wilt cactus at ten feet."

Erik laughed despite the uneasiness prowling through him. He told himself the bug-crawling feeling on his neck and forearms came from just the darkness, just the multiple tire tracks on a rarely used road, just the approaching site of a murdered woman . . . anything but the man's voice that was like his and not like his, an utterly familiar stranger speaking in the silence of his own mind, warning him that flesh was frail and death was final and arrogant pattern masters could make mistakes just like anyone else.

Silently he wondered if he should have let Niall come along.

The voice in his mind had nothing to say on that subject.

Thanks, buddy, he thought sarcastically. *Be sure to let me know if I can ever help you out.*

Then he realized he was talking to the five percent of himself that he usually did his best to ignore. Not good. Next thing he knew, he would be seeing someone else in the mirror and speaking a kind of English that had been out of fashion for centuries. That was when the guys with the nets and really long-sleeved shirts would come for him.

"That turnoff goes to a ravine," Serena said, pointing toward the right. "People use the place to turn bottles into little pieces of glass."

"How far off the road?"

"Less than a mile."

Erik turned the wheel and bumped down to the local target shooting place. Nothing was there but shattered glass glittering in the headlights and the darker gleam of spent brass casings. He turned around and drove back out to the road.

"See those ruts at the edge of the headlights on the left?" Serena said a few minutes later.

He made a noise that said he was listening.

"Those lead to Grandmother's cabin," she said.

"Where does the rest of the road go?" he asked, stopping at the ruts rather than turning off.

In the headlights, vehicle tracks were clear on the surface of the unraveling road. The tracks led away from the ruts that ended in a burned cabin.

"There's a wash about a hundred feet up the road. It's im-

passable except on foot. Some people park and hike farther
into the desert from there. Most people just turn around and
go back to wherever they came from."

Erik drove up the little spur just to be certain that no one
was staked out there, waiting. The ragged turnaround/parking
area was empty. No one had parked there over the weekend
and not come back. There were no fresh human tracks, nothing but desert and a four-foot drop into a damp-bottomed
wash.

Without a word, he turned around just as previous vehicles had since the rain and headed back the same way he had
come.

"You're thinking like Grandmother, aren't you?" Serena
asked as he drove back to the ruts leading to what was left of
her grandmother's house and her own childhood.

"What?" he asked, scanning the ruts before he turned
onto them.

"Paranoid."

He didn't argue her point. He should have felt better after
he proved to himself that they were alone. There was no one
parked where they shouldn't be. Even more reassuring, the
tracks he was leaving now were the first ones to mark the ruts.

He wasn't reassured.

And the bugs didn't stop crawling on his neck and forearms.

He took a better grip on the wheel and settled in for some
bumps and surprises. If he had been able to come up with a
better way to open Serena's memory, he would have. He
hadn't.

So be it.

"How about you?" he asked. "Are you thinking like her?"

"I've never understood my grandmother, which was why
her advice to think like she did when she was my age seems
useless. I have a hard time even imagining her in her thirties,
much less thinking as she would have thought then."

"A woman alone, raising a child on a raw little homestead
in the desert, all the conveniences of the early nineteenth

century." Erik shook his head. "No, I don't see you doing that. But you had points of similarity with her."

"Both women?" Serena suggested dryly.

"Both weavers. Both bound to the Book of the Learned in ways that are . . ." He hesitated. ". . . uncanny."

For a time there was only the crunch and growl of tires over uneven, rocky road to disturb the silence. Then she sighed.

"What's the point in denying it?" she asked. "The instant I saw those pages, something in me shook off a long sleep and said, 'These are mine.' It was the same for the scarf, except even more intense." Her fingers caressed the ancient weaving. "Even as I say it, it sounds nuts, but . . ." She shrugged. "It doesn't change anything. You can label it any way you want. I don't care anymore. It's real. That's all that matters to me."

"I know how you feel."

She gave him a look he couldn't read in the shadowy interior of the vehicle.

"I first saw a piece of the Book of the Learned when I was nine," he said. "It grabbed me like nothing has before or since. Except you. No," he said before she could speak. "I don't have to like it. You don't have to like it. But it's damned real. I've chased that book my whole life. I dream of it, of writing its pages, of flying stormy skies like a peregrine and coursing the forest like a staghound. I dream of a woman with the violet eyes of a sorceress and hair like fire, watching me with anger and love and fear and desperation in her eyes. I suspect I watched her in the same way."

There was a taut silence, a sigh, two words: "You did."

Though her words were soft, he heard them. Something twisted deep in him, something like anger and love and fear and desperation.

"I don't like the feeling of living someone else's life," Serena said tightly.

"Neither do I."

"Would you cut yourself off from the Book of the Learned because of that?" *From me?* she asked silently.

"I'm not sure I have the choice." His voice was as grim as the set of his mouth.

"Let me out."

His head whipped toward her. "What?"

"Let me out here," she said evenly. "Turn around and go home. I promise you, if I ever find the Book of the Learned or any more of its pages, I'll give you as much access to them as you need. If I don't have children, the book will be yours to pass on to your children. Agreed?"

"Serena, what in—"

"Stop the car," she said urgently across his words, reaching for the door handle.

He slammed on the automatic locks and the brakes at the same time. "What the hell is wrong with you?"

"Nothing. It's you, not me."

He looked at her narrowly and felt the twisting inside himself again, colored shadows rippling, time overlapping, rage and love and desperation.

"*You came to me once, drawn by a pattern you refused to see. I paid for being the lure. You paid for being lured. Our child—*" Her voice broke. She shook her head. "Never mind," Serena said bleakly. "It was a long time ago. But what is the past and all its pain for, if not to learn? So go back to what you understand, Erik North. Let me go where I must."

"I'm not letting you go anywhere without me until I know what the hell is going on!"

"Is that your choice, freely made?"

"What are—"

"*Is it?*"

Silence filled the car. Then he understood: she would never again take choice from him. The twisting ache in his gut eased. "Yes. My choice, freely made."

She lifted her fingers from the door handle.

In a silence that seethed with uncanny shadows, they drove the last quarter mile to another Serena's cabin.

Sixty-nine

"The loom was there," Serena said quietly.

Night was kind to the ruined cabin. The soot marks didn't show on the high stone walls. The charred ends of roof beams didn't look like black, rotting teeth. The shadows in the corners seemed to be part of the natural darkness rather than swirls of windblown debris and ashes.

She held the gently hissing lantern up so that the north corner of the cabin was illuminated. The jagged fingers of glass that still stuck up from window frames flashed briefly in the light. She moved the lantern again, remembering.

"Someone took the potbellied stove after she was murdered. I hope it works better for them than it did for us. Every time the wind blew from the northeast, smoke backed up into the cabin. That's why G'mom liked to use the hearth, even though it didn't warm the corners of the room quite as well."

"Which part of the room did you sleep in?" Erik asked.

In the lantern light, he was all glowing bronze and stark black shadows, except for his eyes. They were pure gleaming gold.

"The west corner. We shared a bed at first. When I got too

big for that, she made up a pallet for me at the foot of the bed, closer to the hearth, but not next to it. G'mom was always very worried about fire. Ironic."

Serena turned slowly, taking the lantern with her. The feel of the cooling night, the warmth of the lantern close up, the subtle flicker of the light fed by pressurized gas, the distinctive smell of petroleum and hot glass, all were familiar to her. She could feel echoes of memories whispering . . .

She held her breath as memories rose, only to turn and slide back into darkness. But they left part of themselves behind. Part of her childhood.

He watched her, light and darkness combined, her eyes a flash of violet at midnight, her hair as wild as fire itself, light in one hand and time in the other; and he had never wanted her more.

With an effort he forced himself to look away. He stared at the hearth, which was opposite the loom. The floor there was stone. In fact, it was stone everywhere. He sat on his heels and watched light quiver over the floor's rocky mosaic with each breath Serena took.

Beneath the soot and ruin, there was a pattern to the floor. Lisbeth Serena Charters had taken a lot of care choosing and placing stones. Like the walls, the floor was a composition of selected colored rocks rather than an aimless mixture of whatever stones were handy.

"What is it?" Serena asked.

"The floor. I'm surprised she didn't lay wood." He stood up. "Much easier than stone."

"That kind of wood cost money. Besides, even if she could have afforded wood, she didn't want it. She was really, really careful about fire. All right. She was paranoid." Serena shrugged. "The loom was as far away from the little hearth as it could be and still be inside the walls. The baking oven was outside, and everything she could make of stone was made of stone. One of the worst scoldings I ever got in my life was when I started playing with burning twigs from the hearth as though they were Fourth of July sparklers. She doused them—and me—with a bucket of water and yelled at me for being thoughtless: '*Don't you know how easily old threads and papers burn*?' "

"Threads?"

"Her weaving materials. She called everything thread, not yarn."

He looked around the small living space. If there had ever been shelves on the walls, they were gone. Not even holes were left. "Did she have a lot of papers?"

"Just my old school stuff. She used it to start fires."

"Family photos?"

"None that she showed me."

"And no books."

"Not that I remember. Unless you count my schoolbooks and the old telephone books in the outhouse."

"I thought you didn't have a telephone."

She smiled slightly. "We didn't. She got them from somewhere. Cheaper than toilet paper."

He blinked, then laughed. "Amazing woman, your grandmother. So you both slept in this one room, ate here, worked here, everything. This room was your grandmother's life."

"Pretty much. I walked to the bus stop for school, unless she was going into town to sell weavings or rabbit pelts or buy beans or flour."

He nodded, but he was thinking about something else. Patterns. The pattern of a frightened woman who had one thing she valued so much she had spent her life hiding herself—and it.

"It's here," he said simply.

"What?"

"The Book of the Learned must be hidden here. It's the only thing that fits her pattern."

"Then it's lost," Serena said. "We're standing in its ashes."

"She feared fire because she was worried about protecting the Book of the Learned. She would have prepared for it."

Serena looked through the burned-out doorway. "She

cooked outside. Maybe she hid it somewhere out there, away from any fire."

Erik glanced beyond the lantern light to the wide, dark sweep of desert. He thought of the woman who had had enough strength and determination to build her house with her own hands from native stone, and to live in what she had built for almost a half-century. Such a woman would have been able to walk out over the land and go anywhere she pleased, taking the Book of the Learned with her.

And hiding it.

"If she prepared well enough," he said, "the book isn't lost. But it's a hell of a long way from being found."

Saying nothing, Serena studied the cabin through half-closed eyes, trying to remember it exactly as it once was. She went and stood where her pallet had been. Nothing was left but her memories. And stone.

G'mom had chosen her building material well.

"Take the lantern," Serena said absently.

Erik stepped to her side and lifted the lantern's wire grip from her hand.

"Now go where the loom was," she said. "No. More to the right. More. She didn't like having fire too close to her work. Yes. Right there."

Ignoring the ashes and dirt, Serena sat where she had once slept. Eyes almost closed, she remembered where the loom had been, how it had looked by lantern light when she awakened and her grandmother was weaving, weaving, graceful as flame, enduring as the land itself. She had lacked tenderness, but she had always been there when Serena awakened in the night.

Always.

Wrapped and warmed by covers her grandmother wove, Serena had been quiet as the night, lying half awake, eyes almost closed. She had loved to watch through the rainbow haze of her own lowered eyelashes while her grandmother worked. Usually she fell asleep that way.

But sometimes, especially in the first year after her

mother died, sleep didn't come or came only raggedly, and the child awoke. She soon learned to be quiet, not to disturb the woman who was now her only security.

Sometimes such stillness was rewarded by a special dream, a dream of wondrous beauty, of hammered gold and colorful gems molten with reflected light, time and the lantern pulsing softly while glorious pages turned, rich with feeling and memory . . .

"You're awake, girl. Don't try to fool me. I know."

Silence and a child's unnaturally still body.

"You ever speak of this, to anybody, and I'll drive out of here and leave you alone. You'll be as dead to me as your mother."

A stifled whimper, no more. Then silence.

"You forget this. You forget all of it!"

Silence.

Then later, much later, the grating of stone over stone in the darkness.

And in the morning, a dream no one talked about.

Ever.

Serena let out a ragged breath. She was surprised to feel tears running hot over her cheeks, dropping cold onto her hands. That, too, was like childhood.

"I saw the Book of the Learned," she said, looking up.

Erik's eyes were a gold as rich as the cover of the book had been, but they were alive, watching her with all the warmth her childhood had lacked.

"Yes," he said. "You told me."

"I mean, I really saw it."

"Yes. You described what you were seeing of your childhood as it came back to you." And she had said it in a child's voice that tore at his heart.

She saw that he believed her and sighed. "You were right. The Book of the Learned is here."

He nodded, more concerned about her than anything, even the book. "Are you okay?"

Her smile wavered, but it was real. "Yes. Sometimes remembering is painful, that's all."

"Painful." He almost smiled. "Oh, yes. It's all of that. May I move the lantern now?"

"What? Oh. Yes. Sorry. I wasn't thinking."

"Remembering is a kind of thinking. A very special kind." He took several steps toward the north corner of the cabin. "Was the loom right up against the wall?"

"No. It was a reverse-weave loom, so G'mom had to leave space to check the design."

He gave her a blank look.

"The back of the weaving was toward the weaver," Serena explained, "so to see the design, she had to walk around to the other side, which faced the wall. She hung a mirror on the wall to check it through the warp threads, but the best way was to check it face-to-face."

"Why did she weave that way?"

"Do you really want a lecture on the reasons for—"

"No," he cut in hastily. "I'll take your word for it. So the loom was about three or four feet out from the wall?"

"Closer to three feet. The braces on the loom stuck out about two feet on both sides of the frame. She wouldn't have needed much more room than that. She kept the loom out of the way as much as possible. The cabin is small and G'mom wasn't a big woman, for all her self-sufficiency. She was maybe five feet three and really lean, as if life and the desert had sweated out all her softness."

"So the braces kept the loom frame about two feet from the wall. Could she step over the braces?"

"Easily."

He sat on his heels and stared at the floor that would have been behind the loom before it burned. After a few moments he brushed aside small piles of charred wood and ashes. In the side light, a stone bobbin looked like a palm-sized, reclining ghost. Absently he picked up the bobbin and rolled it on his left palm while he moved the lantern around with his right. There were other ashes, other bobbins. He dropped the one he had and with the side of his hand swept everything away from the wall, to the place where the heavy loom would have stood.

"How wide was the whole loom?" he asked.

"Six feet, at most, including the frame. There were rollers at the top and bottom to take up woven fabric and let out more warp threads for weaving."

Though he nodded, she doubted if he was really listening. She got up and walked over to him. Standing out of his light, she watched his eyes probe the wall and floor as though he could see through them. She had an odd certainty that he was using a lot more than ordinary vision to study the stones.

Pattern master.

She ignored the unwanted murmur in her own mind. "What are you looking for?"

"An opening," he said without looking up.

"Into stone?"

"The wall isn't thick enough, even at the bottom, to protect the book from damage by fire. It has to be the floor."

She dropped down on her knees and began sweeping burned debris off the stone with both hands. Bobbins rattled and grated, rolling in eccentric circles on the rough stone floor with an unhappy noise that made her bite her lip.

Like bones disturbed in a crypt.

"Go away," she muttered.

Erik looked up in surprise.

"Not you," she explained. "The other Serena."

"Oh. Her. Tell her to take the other Erik with her."

Her head snapped up. "You, too?" Then, quickly, "Of course. Damn. Is he as handsome as you?"

"Is she as beautiful?"

"I'm not beautiful."

"I'm not handsome."

She opened her mouth, sighed, and swept strands of hair away from her face. "All in who's doing the looking, is that it?"

"Yeah, that's it." He ran the back of his fingers down her cheek, leaving a trail of soot. "Beautiful."

She rolled her eyes. And then she smiled almost shyly.

He tugged at her scarf, savoring the special feel of the cloth. Without warning he planted a lingering kiss on the neck he had revealed, and then went back to staring at the stone floor as if he had never stopped.

Ashes and dirt had darkened any scrape marks that might have been left by use, but nothing could erase the faint outline where stone had worn against stone each time the hole was opened or closed. There was a reddish stone set off-center in the faint rectangle. It was part of the pattern that was woven through the floor itself.

And it looked loose.

"Gotcha," he said softly. "Take the lantern again."

She grabbed the wire and moved back a little to give him more room.

Delicately he probed around the edges of the reddish stone, which was the size of his fist. It wobbled very slightly. He pressed harder on that spot. The rock tilted up and came loose. He picked it up and set it aside.

The top of a steel eyebolt that was more than an inch wide at the eye gleamed slightly against the greater darkness in the small opening. He knelt and gripped the ring.

"She would have had a tool for leverage, probably a fire poker, but I think I can . . ." His shoulders bunched as he heaved upward on the heavy ring.

"Let me help."

"No room." He grunted, shifted his weight, and pulled again.

With the grating reluctance of something that hasn't been shifted in a long time, the lid of stone pulled free.

Both of them stared down into the opening. It was as long as his forearm and almost as wide, too deep to see the bottom. He reached for the lantern just as she shifted it and stared in.

Empty.

Disappointment speared through her. Then she saw that the darkness wasn't even.

There was something at the bottom of the hole.

She lowered the lantern until both of them could see the bundle of black cloth.

"Go ahead," he said, reaching for the lantern. "It's yours. Get it."

She set the lantern down. "There's room for both."

Together, breathless with hope, adrenaline roaring in their ears, they reached into the hole with one hand apiece and eased the surprisingly heavy bag into the light. Reverently they set it on the stone floor.

After a moment Serena picked apart the bow on the rawhide tie and unlaced the handwoven sack. As the cloth fell to the floor, she drew in a sharp breath, pleasure and disbelief together.

Covered in beaten gold, incised with two intertwined initials, studded with polished gemstones, the Book of the Learned shimmered like a dream in the lantern light.

"Well, ain't that pretty."

Erik and Serena whirled to face the voice.

Wallace was standing in the doorway of the cabin. The blue steel of the gun in his bandaged hand gleamed as coldly as his smile.

He was still smiling when he shot Erik. "That's for the cliff, asshole."

Seventy

The impact of the bullet spun Erik around and dumped him on his back across the Book of the Learned while pain spread in blinding waves up from his right side. Serena threw herself over him, both protecting him and searching frantically for the wound.

"Gun," Erik muttered against her ear.

She lifted her head and stared at him. Glazed with pain, his eyes bored into hers, willing her to remember what he had told her once before. She shoved one hand beneath him and held her other over the wound on his side.

"Get away from him," Wallace said harshly.

Serena ignored him and continued groping frantically beneath Erik. The butt of the gun bumped coldly against her fingers.

"You silly bitch! Get away or I'll shoot right through you!" Wallace yelled.

A shot caromed off the stones. Grit peppered Serena's face. "Don't be stupid!" she yelled without looking up. "If you shoot through either one of us you'll ruin the book and all you'll have to show for your time is two bodies and a handful of shit!"

Wallace had expected anything but the rough edge of Serena's tongue. Adrenaline hummed through him, giving him the erection that only violence could. If he killed her now, he would be stuck beating off. Fucking a corpse just wasn't as good as having a live one, willing or unwilling.

He took a long stride to the right and immediately felt better. He could see Erik's hands. They were slack, empty. His own bandaged right hand ached from the kick of the gun, but it had worked well enough to put a man down and keep him there.

"Okay, bitch. Show me your hands."

"Before or after I keep him from bleeding all over the book?" She had her fingers through the trigger guard, but finding the bloody little safety was—

"Show me your hands!"

Serena spun around, shooting as she turned, hearing Erik's advice ringing in her memory: *Don't be girly or coy. Just shoot and keep on shooting.*

Her first two bullets were wild, but so were Wallace's. His injured hand just wasn't as quick or accurate as it should have been. Ricochets slammed around unpredictably, chewing chips out of stone.

The rest of Serena's shots weren't wild. She didn't count how many times she hit Wallace. She just clenched her teeth and fired until the gun was empty and he was lying sprawled and motionless against a blood-spattered wall.

Distantly she realized that she was still pulling on the trigger and Erik was talking to her.

"It's over, Serena. Listen to me. You're all right. He's not going to get up again."

Numbly she lowered the gun.

Erik looked at her bleached skin and bleak eyes, and wished he could wipe the past few moments from her memory. But he couldn't. He knew he should tell her to get Wallace's gun, but he wasn't going to do that, either. He didn't want her to get any closer to the bloody mess than she already was.

Besides, it was a dead certainty that Wallace wasn't going to be doing any more shooting.

"Look at me, Serena. Not at him. At me."

She turned toward Erik, took a wrenching breath, then another. The sight of blood pulsing down his right arm shocked her back into control. She went to her knees beside him in a rush.

"You're bleeding too much," she said, dropping the gun.

"A little blood always looks like a lot."

She saw the ruined cloth and gore along his ribs. "If you tell me it's just a scratch, I'll shoot you myself."

"No worries," he said through his teeth. "It's not a scratch."

"I have to stop the bleeding."

"Pressure."

Without a thought to its venerable history, she began yanking the scarf off her neck.

"Stand up and get away from him."

For a shocked instant both Erik and Serena thought the voice was Wallace's. Then Erik looked past her at the black-dressed figure standing in the doorway, holding a gun on them.

Seventy-one

"Paul Carson," Erik said grimly.

The gun in Paul's hand was pointed at Serena. It didn't jerk or waver.

"I'd rather not shoot you," he said matter-of-factly, "but I haven't yet decided whether you're in on the scam with North and Wallace."

"Wait," she said. "You don't understand. There's no—"

"Move, Serena," Erik cut in. A pattern had just condensed in his mind. An ugly one.

"But—" she started to object.

"Do it."

Unwillingly she stood and backed away from Erik. Her steps brought her no closer to Paul. He smiled at her caution.

"Commendable, if a bit late," Paul said, but he was watching Erik with the eyes of a man who knew who his enemy was. "I see you're too clever to grab at straws."

"There's no scam," Serena said urgently. "I remembered where the Book of the Learned was and we got it, and then Wallace shot Erik and I—I shot Wallace."

Paul slanted a speculative glance at her. "Thank you. It saved me the trouble. You surprise me, Serena. You must have more of your grandmother in you than anyone thought. That was one tough old bitch. Like you, she wouldn't negotiate no matter what the price."

"So you killed her," Serena said.

He shrugged. "She was threatening the House of Warrick."

"The woman in Florida?" Erik asked. "The guru in Sedona? Bert?"

"Of course." He looked at Serena with pale eyes that felt nothing, saw everything. "Put your hands on top of your head and turn around, and walk backward to me. If you get between me and your boyfriend while you do it, you're both dead."

She believed him. He wasn't like Wallace, pumped up and flushed with adrenaline, wanting an audience. Paul was steady as a stone and every bit as hard.

"I thought fire was more your style," she said bitterly.

"Whatever keeps the cops guessing," Paul said. "You have three seconds, Serena. Two."

She turned around and awkwardly started walking backward.

"Keep you hands on top of your head," he ordered. "Keep backing up. More. Slowly, Serena. Stop. Good. Move just once and he dies."

Erik watched like a predator.

Paul didn't give any opening. He was cool and professional. Deadly.

"Where's your car?" Erik asked casually.

"In back of a dead man's shack."

Erik didn't have to ask who had died. There was only one house within easy walking range: Jolly's. "And Wallace's car? Where did he hide it?"

"In front of the old man's shack, right where I told him. Right where the police will find it when I notify them."

"Anonymously, of course," Erik said. "You don't want to disturb their fantasy that Wallace worked alone."

Paul didn't bother to answer the obvious. Holding the

gun on Erik, watching him, Paul reached out with his left hand to search beneath Serena's jacket for weapons. The first thing his groping fingers found was the scarf dangling loosely around her neck.

He screamed and shoved her away as though he had grabbed burning napalm.

Erik's left arm moved in a blur. One of Lisbeth's stone bobbins hurtled across the cabin and buried itself halfway in Paul's temple. His scream stopped as quickly as it had begun. He toppled backward over Wallace and went down hard. He stayed there.

The stench of gunfire, blood, and death clung to everything.

Erik forced himself to his feet. He thought he would pass out before he picked up Paul's gun, but he felt a lot better with it in his hand.

"Sit down before you fall down," Serena said, her voice strained.

"I'm—"

"You're shot, that's what you are," she cut in savagely, "so just shut up and sit down."

Erik compromised. He shut up.

She whipped the scarf off her neck, folded it into a thick pad, and held it over his ribs where blood was coming out much too fast. Breath hissed through Erik's teeth as pain tried to send him to his knees. The only thing that kept him upright was the knowledge that Serena wouldn't be able to get him into the car on her own.

To her surprise, blood discolored the hastily made bandage but didn't immediately soak through. Gritting her teeth, she pressed harder to slow the hot red flow. She didn't know how much pain Erik could take without fainting, but she was afraid she was going to find out. She watched him with anxious violet eyes.

Pale, trembling, smeared with ashes and blood—she was the most beautiful thing Erik had ever seen. He started to tell her when Niall spoke from the darkness beyond the ruined walls.

"If you shoot me, boyo, go for the heart. I've already got a pisser of a headache."

Erik's smile looked more like a feral snarl. "What took you so long?"

Niall stepped into the light of the lantern. He was as pale as Erik and almost as bloody; scalp wounds were worse for bleeding than anything but tongues.

"You look like hell," Erik said.

"You should see the other guy," Niall said.

He glanced at the gun in Erik's hand, recognized it as the one taken by the attacker—Paul or Wallace, from the look of it. Apparently Niall had been slotted to be the bad guy, complete with murder weapon in his dead hand. Sweet. Really sweet.

"Has that gun been fired tonight?" Niall asked as he went to check on Paul and Wallace.

"Not by me."

Niall grunted. "Good. It's mine."

He saw the oddly shaped stone sticking out of Paul's skull, checked for a pulse, didn't feel anything conclusive, and started frisking him. When he checked for a sleeve knife, he saw Paul's hand.

"Christ Jesus," he muttered. "What did you do to him, hold his hand against the lantern until he confessed?"

Erik and Serena exchanged puzzled looks and said nothing.

Niall collected all the weapons he found and put them across the room. When he was finished, he put his hands around his mouth and hollered, "Come on in, Ian. Dana's Fuzzy took care of it."

"I had a partner," Erik said, giving Serena a bittersweet smile. "I'm not sorry Wallace is dead, but I'm sorry you were the one holding the trigger down."

Niall gave Serena an approving look. It changed to surprise when he spotted the gleaming gold cover and pools of colored gems on the floor behind her. "I take it that's the prize."

"Yeah," Erik said.

"Sit down before you fall down, boyo."

"Take your own advice," Erik retorted. "I'm feeling better every second. It's not nearly as bad as I thought when the bullet hit. Serena has the bleeding under control."

Niall walked over and looked at the thick pad of cloth Serena was pressing against Erik's ribs. "Bet that stings like a bitch," he said neutrally.

"No bet," Erik said through his teeth, "but it's easing up quicker than I expected."

Niall reached out to the pad. "Here, let me have a—shit!" He snatched back his hand and shook his fingers as though they had been singed. "What's on that thing, acid? How can you stand it against the wound?"

"What are you talking about?" Erik said. "It feels cool and soothing."

Niall looked at his fingertips in the lantern light. They appeared normal. Felt normal except for a residual tingle. "Bloody hell."

Serena heard an echo of laughter in her head and sensed the satisfaction of a weaver whose uncanny skills had lasted into a time when such things were neither known nor thought possible.

"A lure and a weapon," Erik murmured, remembering. He touched the cloth with new appreciation. "Nifty painkiller, too."

Ian Lapstrake stepped—or staggered—into the light of the lantern. One side of his head was bleeding freely. So were several cuts on his fingers.

"What happened to you two?" Serena asked, looking from Niall to Lapstrake.

"We had a meeting of the minds," Lapstrake said roughly.

"Bastard came up behind us when we were still blind and

deaf from the helicopter taking off," Niall explained. "Rang us like bells. Then he taped us up and left us behind a pile of rocks."

"We'd still be there, if it wasn't for Niall's shoelaces," Lapstrake added, looking at his bloody fingers ruefully. "I was working behind my back, so it took me a little while to figure out where the razor strip began and ended." He glanced up, pinning Erik with dark eyes that weren't smiling at all. "Anything else need doing before we call 911?"

Erik understood the real question: *Anything you want to hide before the cops get here?* "I don't think we need any stage dressing. It was ambush and self-defense all the way. I'd like to keep Serena out of it, though."

"Which gun?" Lapstrake asked, looking around.

"Mine, behind us," Erik said. "Wipe it down and hand it to me, okay?"

"But—" she began.

"You'd be doing me a favor," Niall said quickly. "Dana is Satan in spiked heels when a client ends up doing our job."

"I'll hold on to this," Erik said as he eased her hand away from the cloth pressed against his ribs. "Go get the Book of the Learned. See if a Learned pattern master can tell us what all the killing was about."

"Maybe they believed that crap about the secret to eternal life," Niall offered.

"Wallace might have," Erik said. "Paul? No way. His kind doesn't believe in anything."

"What kind is that?" Niall asked.

"Psychopath."

Slowly Serena went to the ancient book that had cost so many lives. She wiped her hands on her jeans and frowned at the imperfect results. Then she saw that some of Erik's blood was already on the cover, darkening the luster of gold. She decided there was nothing she could do to the Book of the Learned that time and man hadn't already done many times over. With a final swipe of her hands over her jeans, she carefully opened the book.

She couldn't read the writing on the first loose vellum pages, but she could recognize that it wasn't the work of Erik the Learned. The calligraphy was less perfect, less patient, somehow more feminine. It wasn't simple text that met her eyes but what appeared to be a list of names linked to other lists.

Gradually she realized that she was looking at a genealogy. One word appeared again and again, and from it came the next generation to be listed.

She turned the page over. The list continued on the other side. The writing varied in style, individual despite the strict rules of calligraphy. The lines were small, almost cramped in an obvious attempt to use as little of the precious vellum as possible. But still there were pages.

The appearance of the list changed through time as the shape of the letters and the words themselves changed, becoming more recognizable. Fascinated, she watched the language evolve into more modern spelling, a more modern alphabet, Arabic numerals, cursive writing. Then she turned another page and saw a name leap up from it in endless combination.

Serena.

Each woman's maiden name changed into a married name or simply descended unchanged to the first female child of the next generation. The marriages, births, and deaths of each Serena's relatives weren't recorded unless there were no girls born and a collateral line was designated. But one thing didn't vary: only the firstborn female of any given generation carried Serena as some part of her name.

Ignoring the surnames, Serena whispered the first and middle names of her female ancestors, reading faster and faster until the names blurred into a kind of litany.

Cassandra Serena. Serena Elspeth. Kenna Serena. Serena Elen. Beatrice Serena. Elisabeth Serena. Mary Serena. Serena Margaret. Serena Victoria. Lisbeth Serena. Marilyn Serena. Serena Lyn.

Abruptly she realized that she had read her own name

aloud and that of her mother, her grandmother. For the first time she focused on the surnames, her mother's maiden name, her grandmother's married name.

Shocked, Serena made a sound that could have been disbelief or pain or both combined.

"Serena?"

She looked up and found Erik watching her with his vivid bird-of-prey eyes.

"What is it?" he asked.

She tried to speak, couldn't, and tried again. "Norman Warrick is my grandfather."

Seventy-two

The doorbell chime's melodious fifteenth-century harmonies blended oddly with the stark rise of desert mountains beyond the Warrick estate's high walls. Mentally bracing himself, Garrison Montclair opened the front door.

A single glance catalogued what waited for him: Dana, Niall, Erik, and Serena stood on the imposing front porch. Niall and Erik looked like they had tangled with a train—all bruises and bandages. Dana was a rapier sheathed in black, ready to slice. Serena's fiery hair was unbraided and tied at her nape with a black ribbon. Her eyes were uncomfortable to look into, the kind of violet that slid off into a midnight that wasn't in any hurry for dawn. She was carrying what appeared to be a large package wrapped in a shapeless black cloth bag.

"Thank you for coming here rather than insisting that we go to Los Angeles," Garrison said. "This has been a shock for everyone. While we're all eager to help clear up this mess in any way we can, Cleary really shouldn't be traveling until she feels better."

If she ever did. Watching her wail for her dead lover had been one of the most disturbing experiences of Garrison's life. Warrick's contempt for his daughter's condition hadn't helped.

"Come in," Garrison said, stepping back. "I don't know what we can tell you that we didn't tell the police, but . . ." He shrugged. "Frankly, I'm hoping you can tell us something."

Erik looked at the clean-shaven young son of wealth and said, "I'm sure you are."

"It's hard to believe you can know someone for ten years and not know he's crazy," Garrison said.

"That's why you think Carson did it?" Niall asked casually. "He was a nutcase?"

"It's the only explanation that makes sense to me."

"Perhaps your grandfather will have the insights that are supposed to come with age," Dana said smoothly. Her smile was like a knife sliding out of a sheath. "I take it he's home?"

"He's in the throne room." Garrison smiled sourly. "But if you call it that to his face, he'll throw you out. Follow me."

When Serena hesitated, Erik ran the back of his fingers softly down her cheek. "You don't have to come."

"He's my grandfather," she said in a low voice.

Erik started to say something, then simply touched her cheek again. Together they followed Garrison into the huge room. Serena gave the sumptuous rugs and wall hangings no more than a swift glance. Her fingers were locked around the Book of the Learned. It was the ancient manuscript's designs and colors that filled her mind, the genealogy that led through time to herself and a grandfather she had never known.

And wasn't sure she wanted to know.

Norman Warrick was sitting in the intricately carved ebony chair that gave "the throne room" its nickname. Against his dark clothes, his face was pale, almost translucent. So was his hair. But his eyes were the same clear, cold hazel Serena remembered. They watched her unblinkingly.

Not until Cleary moved did Serena see her. Instead of her

usual fluffed and curled hairstyle, Cleary had skinned her hair back into a bun that made her look every one of her fifty-odd years. The brown tailored pantsuit she wore added neither color to her face nor grace to her starkly thin body. The only thing truly alive in her was her eyes. They bored into Erik with naked hatred.

"What is this nonsense?" Warrick demanded in a surprisingly strong voice. "I'm looking for provenance as fast as I can and still run a business. Without Paul, it's going to be a lot slower. He was my right hand as well as my head of security, and the staff knew it."

Cleary flinched. Color flared on her cheekbones, then faded. "I handle the staff," she said dully.

"Bullshit. Paul kept things running. He was just smart enough to let you think you were doing it." Warrick turned away from his daughter and focused on Serena. "Well, I suppose you've come to your senses and decided to sell me those tarted-up pages. You should have done it when I first offered. The price now is a hundred thousand, and that includes all of it."

"All of what?" Serena asked carefully.

"Don't be as stupid as you look." Warrick turned impatiently to Dana. "If Rarities says those pages are good, you'll regret it."

"Not as much as you will," Erik said. "They're better than anything you got out of the Rubin estate."

For a moment Warrick went still, then he turned his whole body and stared at Erik. "I've bought and sold hundreds of estates in my lifetime," Warrick said. "Hell, thousands. Who's Rubin?"

Garrison's mouth thinned and his eyes closed. He glanced toward Cleary. She was still glaring at Erik as though he was reptilian rather than human.

"A man whose estate you bought in 1940," Erik said.

"Did I? Then there will be a record of the estate's contents somewhere."

"There was no inventory."

Warrick smiled. His teeth were unnaturally white. "Then you have a problem, don't you?"

"No," Dana said distinctly. "You do. The police are still looking for a motive in the Carson-Wallace case. When we tell them that your employee—your right-hand man, I believe you called him—started murdering people a year ago because they—"

"That's a lie!" Cleary shot to her feet and stood, swaying with a combination of sedatives and an emotion too violent to be chained. "Paul wouldn't kill anyone!"

"Really?" Dana turned and looked speculatively at Garrison. "Your grandfather is mean enough to murder a kitten, but not spry enough in the time period that concerns us. You, however, are."

"Ridiculous!" Cleary's voice climbed into an unpleasant screech. "Garrison would never—"

"That leaves you," Dana cut in smoothly, turning to Cleary. "Shall we start discussing dates and alibis?"

Cleary's mouth opened. Nothing came out but a high, thin sound.

"Sit down and shut up," Warrick snapped at his daughter. "God deliver me, why are all females so useless?"

"Try having a baby without one," Serena suggested.

He glared at her and his silence said that her comment was beneath an answer.

"What did you do to my grandmother that she spent her life hiding from you?" Serena asked.

"What is she blathering about?" Warrick asked Dana.

"Your first wife, Lisbeth Serena Warrick, maiden name Charters," Serena said. "She married you during World War Two. Then she left you in Manhattan, took her baby, and went alone across the continent. She started over in the desert not fifty miles from here. She changed her last name to Weaver, her first name to Ellis. She lived in stark poverty for the rest of her life in order to hide her real identity. Why? What did you do to her?"

Cleary put her head in her hands and started to cry quietly. Garrison went and put his hand on his mother's shoulder, but his eyes were on his grandfather.

"She was a tiresome, rude country girl," Warrick said, dismissing Lisbeth's life with a wave of his hand, "but she had a good eye for art. She stole some very valuable manuscripts from me. That's why she hid all her life. She knew what I would do if I found her."

"Burn her to death?" Dana suggested mildly.

Warrick shot her a cold glance. "Don't be ridiculous."

"She isn't," Serena said in a biting voice. "But you are." She stripped off the black cloth and let the Book of the Learned gleam in the room's genteel light. "You expect me to believe that my grandmother stole this from you."

In the sudden silence, Cleary's whispering sobs sounded like shouts.

Warrick leaned forward. "That's mine. Bring it here."

"It's my inheritance from my grandmother."

"Which she stole from me!" Warrick bellowed.

He pointed with a shaking finger toward the rich glow of gems and gold. "How else would a poor, unlettered hill girl get a piece of art like that?"

"From her mother," Erik said, "who got it from her mother, who got it from her mother, all the way back to the early twelfth century, when Erik, called Glendruid or the Learned, created the book and gave it to Alana Serena, the firstborn daughter of the last survivor of the Silverfells clan, Serena, called the sorceress."

"Fairy tales for children," Warrick said, but he never looked away from the Book of the Learned gleaming almost within reach. "Lisbeth's people were dirt farmers who came from dirt farmers who came from crofters who were so useless the Scots lairds cleared them from the land and replaced them with sheep. Are you asking anyone to believe that a manuscript worth millions was passed down through generation after generation of miserable poverty?"

Dana looked at Erik with new respect. "You were right. He must have been up all night with his lawyers."

"Or his killers," Niall said.

"What bullshit are you slinging now?" Warrick demanded. "You want lawyers? I have a building full of them in Manhattan and more in Chicago. You want to fight me over this?" His clear, burning eyes focused on Serena. "Take the hundred thousand as a reward, leave the book, and get out."

"Go to hell," she said through her teeth.

Warrick leaned back and looked at Dana. "Which side are you on?"

"The same one as always: the art's," Dana said crisply. "It stays with Serena, who got it from her grandmother, who ran from you to prevent you from butchering any more of the book in order to keep the House of Warrick afloat after the Depression and World War Two."

"So you admit she stole it," Garrison said swiftly. He didn't trust his grandfather to keep his temper much longer. Once he lost it, the situation would head for the toilet even faster than it was going now.

"The ownership of the manuscript is clear," Erik said. "It's written in a genealogy in front of the book. It is Serena's."

Garrison shrugged, unimpressed. "One of America's foremost duplicators of old manuscripts happens to be fucking the woman who's claiming the Book of the Learned on the basis of some line of descent conveniently written in the book itself. Pretty thin, when millions are at stake."

Niall put a cautionary hand on Erik as he stepped forward.

Garrison ignored both of them, focusing only on Dana. "I assume you can prove Grandfather actually was married to that woman, whatever her name was."

"Lisbeth Serena Charters," Dana said. "Yes. We have a copy of the marriage certificate."

"Good. That proves a marriage took place," Garrison said calmly. He turned to Serena. "Since they were married, the book is at least half Grandfather's in any case. Under the circumstances, he is being generous to give you a finder's fee. If you insist on fighting him, you'll spend more on lawyers than any part of the book is worth."

Erik clapped his hands mockingly. "Very good, Garrison. Harvard wasn't wasted on you. You can sell snake oil with the best of them. I can't wait to hear your explanation of your grandfather's forgeries of Renaissance illuminations over pages cut from the Book of the Learned and sold to people who trusted the House of Warrick's reputation."

"Prove it."

Erik's smile was as cold as his eyes. He turned to Warrick. "You almost got away with it. All those years, selling and re-selling what you *knew* were forgeries. Almost fifty pages chopped up into pieces you could sell into the market as real. How many forgeries in all, Warrick? Three hundred? Five hundred? And that was just from the Book of the Learned alone. I'm sure other manuscripts underwent 'improvement' by your hand. A lot of money, no matter how you add it up. Or did you do it just to prove how good you were and how stupid everyone else was? Greed and arrogance are the most common motives for forgery."

Cleary looked at her father with drenched, wounded eyes. He didn't even glance her way. He was riveted on the young man whose eyes were as metallic and as ancient as the cover of the Book of the Learned.

"Just in case someone saw through the fraud," Erik said, "you illuminated in the style of the Spanish Forger, a forger who worked before you were old enough to draw a straight line. Clever, but that goes without saying. You were always a clever, clever man. What a shock it must have been when Lisbeth got in touch with you and demanded that you return all the pages of the Book of the Learned that you had stolen. But she had to take a risk. She had to give you a point of contact. She chose a post-office box. You sent something there, she picked it up, and Paul Carson followed her to her home. She was murdered there that same night."

Warrick shoved to his feet and bent forward, braced on an

ebony cane. "Murder? What are you blathering about? Lisbeth ran away, that's all."

"Someone burned Lisbeth to death a year ago," Erik said distinctly. "Shortly after that, a man was murdered in Sedona and a woman was murdered in Florida, both by fire. A few days ago, Bert Lars was murdered by fire. The connection between all the murders is simple. Each person knew where the forgeries ultimately came from: the House of Warrick. Once those people were dead, the provenance was simply lost in time or assumed to have come from the estates of dead men who kept no inventories. Convenient and perfectly acceptable in all but the most exacting art market."

Garrison stared at his grandfather. "I always knew you were a cold son of a bitch, but . . . murder? Didn't know you had it in you."

"He didn't," Cleary said distinctly. "When Paul showed him Lisbeth's letter demanding the return of the pages, Father laughed. He said she could go to the cops for all of him, he would be dead before the lawyers sorted it out, and dead men don't give a damn. *But I did,*" she said fiercely. "I've spent my life working to make the House of Warrick the leading auction house in the world. I wasn't going to let some blackmailing old bitch ruin me!"

Warrick tilted his head and studied the woman who was connected to him by a brief sexual spasm that had occurred so long ago he couldn't remember it. "You? You killed Lisbeth?"

"Paul did." Cleary's chin lifted proudly. "For me. Paul loved me. But you wouldn't know about that kind of love, would you?"

"Neither would Paul," Warrick said, disgusted. "Stupid female. Paul loved his own comfort. If Garrison had been the only way into the House of Warrick's money, Paul would have fucked him rather than you. Probably had more fun of it, too."

Shrieking, Cleary shot out of her chair and launched herself at her father with murder in her eyes. Garrison grabbed her and held her as gently as possible until her screams subsided into a shattered kind of silence.

"Get her out of here before she drools on something valuable," Warrick said.

Garrison looked at his grandfather over his mother's bent head. "Shut up. Just. Shut. Up. Too bad you weren't on Paul's kill list. You can't die soon enough for me."

Stunned into silence, Warrick watched while Garrison picked up his mother and carried her away from the man who never should have had children at all.

"Are you happy now that you've turned my grandson against me?" Warrick asked Dana bitterly. "But if you expect to prosecute anyone, forget it. You have your pound of flesh. I have a university full of psychiatrists who will be happy to swear that Cleary isn't competent to stand trial."

Dana and Niall exchanged looks. Dana nodded slightly.

Niall spoke for the first time. "We're willing to let Paul Carson go to his grave as a murderer working with one hired hand, William Wallace. We even have a motive: he was protecting the House of Warrick's reputation during the delicate sales negotiations between you and—"

"How did you know about that!" Warrick interrupted. "No one but—"

"When more than one person knows," Niall cut in impatiently, "there's no such thing as a secret. A lot of what you were selling was your reputation. Linking you to a trade in forgeries—much less the creation of those forgeries—would have killed the sale and left Cleary a much less wealthy woman. As Paul expected to marry Cleary as soon as you died, he had several million dollars' worth of motive for murder."

Warrick sat slowly, then nodded. "Makes more sense than her mewing about love."

"In return for keeping your reputation intact," Dana said, "you will agree to open your files so we can trace the missing pages from the Book of the Learned. You can put whatever face you want on it, but I would suggest you say that you have reason to suspect the pages are forgeries and you're willing to buy them back for their most recent purchase price since the error was originally yours in identifying them as valid pages."

Warrick grunted. "I'll think about it."

"Not good enough," Dana said crisply. "You will agree now to help make the Book of the Learned whole or you won't. There will be no waffling."

Warrick's mouth thinned until it disappeared into the grim lines of his face. "Agreed." Then he pointed to Serena. "But if you think I'm going to do anything else to help that misbegotten bitch, you're mistaken. I will never acknowledge her as my granddaughter. Never!"

Serena smiled with all the savagery of the last sorceress of Silverfells. "I will hold you to that." Then she looked at Dana. "Get it in writing."

Without another glance at her grandfather, Serena turned and walked out, carrying the Book of the Learned in her hands.

Seventy-three

Serena sat at her loom, flanked by colorful yarns hanging from bobbins. Her unbound hair shifted and burned with each motion she made as she worked the heddles and threw the shuttle with tireless, timeless rhythms of her body. She worked as she had for the last two nights, in candlelight, with Erik reading aloud from the Book of the Learned.

The pattern that was growing under her deft hands was as old as the intertwined initials of E and S, and as new as the peace she felt each time she looked up and saw Erik watching her, smiling. She had been terrified that he would bleed to death before the paramedics came, but he had been right when he said that the wound wasn't as bad as it appeared. The medics had muttered about ribs like steel plate and how lucky he was. Healthy, too.

He had healed with a speed that made Niall mumble about weird cloth and things that go bump in the night.

"Go on," Serena said to Erik, her voice husky with memory.

"You sure you want the story to end?"

"I'm sure I want to know *how* it ends."

He laughed. It caused a small twinge along his ribs, but only a small one. Whatever had been woven into that old cloth was better than penicillin. His wound had healed the way corn grew in Kansas—while you watched. He still wore the scarf wrapped around his ribs beneath his shirt. Every time he took it off, he started to hurt.

He took the hint and left the uncanny cloth in place.

"You're going to torment me, aren't you?" Serena said with an exaggerated pout. "You can read it and I can't, so you're going to make me beg."

He looked at his beautiful fire-haired lover and felt an ache like time twisting through his gut. "Never."

He began to read aloud.

Today the mists parted for me.

She waited within them, hair like fire, eyes like amethyst. When she saw her cloak held tenderly in my hand, the cloak brought to me by the daughter I never knew I had, she smiled despite the tears burning silver on her cheeks.

I held out my hand, asking.

She came to me, answering.

The crystal bells of Silverfells sang around us.

When Erik stopped reading, the silence in the room quivered with candle flames and the whisper of leaves of time turning and returning. Gently he closed the Book of the Learned.

"I'm glad they got past their unhappiness," Serena said, putting aside her shuttle.

"More like pigheadedness," he said dryly.

"That, too." She sighed. "Think of it. She bore twins alone and raised them alone. She was last of an outlaw clan, protected only by uncanny mists that kept retreating farther inward each year when Erik the Learned went back to seek . . . What was it he sought, revenge?"

"I'm sure that's what he told himself. He had enough pride for a regiment of men."

"You don't think he wanted revenge?"

"I think," he said deliberately, sliding his arms around her, "that once he got his hands on his beautiful witch, revenge would have been the last thing on his mind. He spent those thirteen years of separation in living hell."

"What about her?" Serena objected. "She hardly had an easy time of it."

"At least she had children to love." He bent and tasted her neck with deliberate intent.

She tilted her head to give him access to more skin. "And a lover whose memory was like a knife in her heart every time his smile flashed on his son's face or his daughter's eyes burned gold while she wove."

"My point exactly." Teeth nipped lightly. "Pigheaded. You're not going to be like you're ancestor, are you?"

"Are you saying I might be pigheaded?"

"Yeah."

"So are you."

"Yeah. What are we going to do about it?"

Smiling, she looked over her shoulder at him. "Enjoy every bit of it while we look for the rest of the Book of the Learned."

"Good idea. Any time limit? Even with Warrick cooperating, Cleary on meds, and Garrison back to being charming, it could take years to track everything."

"No time limit." She lifted her head proudly and looked him in the eye. "How about you?"

He drew in a slow breath. It was scented with spice and cloves, alive with overlapping colored shadows and the trembling song of crystal bells.

Silently they looked at each other, accepting what neither could understand.

He had sun-bright hair cut so that it would fit beneath a war helmet. His cloak floated on a breeze, revealing the chain mail hauberk beneath. A peregrine falcon rode his left arm. At his feet lay a staghound the size of a pony. He was watching a woman weave on a loom that was taller than a man. Her unbound hair tumbled in a fiery torrent down her back to her knees. She was looking over her shoulder at him with eyes the color of woodland violets. Instead of castle walls, they were surrounded by a rain-drenched forest, as though nothing on earth existed but these two people caught in the mists of time.

"I want a thousand years," Erik said. "Minimum. We've earned at least that much."

Author's Note

To my knowledge, the Book of the Learned doesn't exist. But it could have. Stranger things happen all the time.

Don't believe me?

Let me tell you a story that is as strange as it is true . . .

For thirty-four years I have been well and truly married to the only man I ever loved. In addition to being husband, lover, friend, and father of my children, Evan is a hardheaded contrarian who will take either side of any argument that is offered. If one isn't offered, he'll offer it himself.

Ten years ago, we went to Britain for the first time. With Maxwell as a last name, it was inevitable that we would end up seeing Scotland. My maiden name, Charters, is also Scots, a corruption of the name Charteris. But we didn't go to Scotland for a personal, sentimental journey. We just wanted to see the islands that had had such an impact on Western civilization.

After several days in London, we piled into a rented car—where everything but the clutch, brake pedal, and gas pedal were reversed—and set off on our adventure down the wrong side of the road. By the time we reached the border, we were tired of superhighways and modern concrete. Once over the border, we got off on the first country lane we found. It wound along beside a windswept shallow bay, the Solway Firth. When I spotted some ruins rising out of the land, I was thrilled. A lot of buildings in England were quite old, but hardly ruined.

It took a while, but Evan was game. Heading for the ruins with nothing more in the way of directions than "There, I see it again! Turn left!" we found ourselves on smaller and smaller "roads" until we were driving on one lane with tall hedgerows crowding up on either side and no place to hide if we met oncoming traffic. When we finally got to what was left of the castle, we discovered it was part of the Scottish National Trust. And it was closed for the season.

I didn't think a few pictures would rupture international relations, so I started photographing the magnificent red ruins. Evan saw a plaque and walked off to see what it offered. A minute later he called and waved me over. When I got there, he simply pointed to the plaque. The wonderful sandstone ruins were all that remained of Castle Caerlaverock (Nest of the Meadowlark), which had been built in the twelfth century.

Caerlaverock had been the Maxwell clan stronghold.

We were stunned by the coincidence of time and place and us. Curious, we went to the nearby town and bought a pint for one of the locals at the pub. He told us that we should go to the Maxwell museum in Maxwellton (Maxwell Town).

We got there just before the museum closed. While Evan admired arms and armor, I did a fast circuit to see what I wanted to concentrate on. The first thing I saw was a map showing all the Scottish clans. I was surprised to discover that my own clan Charteris had claim to a fingernail of land hanging on to the vast lands of the clan Maxwell.

Nearby was an oil portrait of a fierce Maxwell. Beneath it was the clan history. I started reading. And then I started laughing out loud, laughing so hard I had to lean on the wall.

Evan came out of a library room to see what had come over his wife. All I could do was point to the history. He read and discovered what I already had: the Maxwell clan had

fought on the *wrong* side of every major battle after 1066 . . .
including the Spanish Armada! Three times various English
kings laid siege and after six months managed to tear down
the Maxwell castle walls, strip them of land and titles, and
force them to bend their stiff necks. And three times the
English kings were forced to give back the land and titles and
war hardware, because England needed a warrior clan to
fend off the Vikings, who made a habit of landing in the Solway Firth and raiding. The fourth time the Maxwells put an
English king to the trouble of a six-month siege, they eventually got their land and titles back, but not the right to build
a castle. The Vikings were contained; there was no more need
of the headstrong clan Maxwell.

The Maxwells were contrarians to a man.

That, at least, hasn't changed in a thousand years.

Evan didn't think it was quite as funny as I did. He
pointed out that my ancestors had been fighting and losing
right alongside the Maxwells, as their duly obedient vassals. I
gave him an *oh sure* look. To prove his point, he led me to the
library, where a curator was watching over several huge
leather volumes. They turned out to be Maxwell genealogies
compiled in the nineteenth century. Smiling oddly, Evan
motioned for me to read.

I began scanning through the volumes, moving backward
in time with each turned page. At first I mentioned given
names and short life spans to Evan. Then I fell silent. On
those yellowed pages I kept seeing one name over and over,
and what I saw was an explanation of something I had never
expected to understand: from the moment I first saw Evan in
California in 1963, I felt that I knew him in some impossible
way. He felt the same about me.

Now we knew why.

Maxwells and Charterses had been intermarrying for
nine hundred years.

I figure it took that long for two hardheaded clans to get it
right.

If you enjoyed *Moving Target*,

Then take a sneak peek at the

Following brief selection from

RUNNING SCARED

Electrifying suspense from Elizabeth Lowell

Now available in hardcover

from William Morrow

The silvery disc of a nearly full moon kept Virgil O'Conner awake. He liked it that way. At eighty-one, he had long since decided that watching shades of darkness twist across the Arizona night was better than being in their grip and screaming himself awake.

"I'm sorry I took it," he whispered to the night. "Sorry, sorry, sorry, sorry . . ."

The darkness didn't answer. It never had.

His heart faltered, skipped, and settled down. He let out a long breath that wasn't quite relief. He wanted to die, but not yet. Not until the dead forgave him for touching their sacred gold.

Neck rings of braided gold chains, as smooth and heavy and supple as he once had been.

Armbands as wide as his spread fingers. Hammered gold covered with symbols so eerie and beautiful they raised the hair on his scalp.

Cloak pins as big as his hand, pins carrying the likeness of an animal, yet frighteningly human.

A mask that was more than human.
Shapes of gods or demons or dreams long dead.
Twenty-seven pieces of gold. Beautiful gold.
Deadly gold.

A chill condensed on his skin. Automatically, he reached for his lap robe, but its soft warmth couldn't heat the freezing in the marrow of his bones.

He was a dead man screaming.

"No," he said hoarsely. "I didn't mean it! I never sold any of it, even when I needed money. I worked two jobs. Worked hard. I could have melted it all down or . . . or . . ."

His voice died into a whispery rasp. He knew the spirits that hounded him couldn't hear his words. He wasn't a channel. He couldn't reach his tormentors to explain his innocence.

Unless, just maybe, he held some of their gold in both hands. No gloves this time. Nothing to protect his flesh. Just his skin and potent gold.

The thought made him shudder. He had touched the gold once, long ago, with his naked fingers. He had never touched it that way again. He didn't even want to think about touching it. But he kept thinking about it just the same, reliving every black instant of the night years past when he had followed his dead great-uncle's instructions, borrowed a metal detector from a military store, and went digging.

The sacred oaks where neither Romans nor Angles dared to go. Nine hills. Six groves. Three man-rocks facing in. One spring. Three times three times three of gold.

He jerked his head sharply. He didn't want to remember. It made his heart twist as it had that night, pain lancing through every cell in his body, in his soul.

"Hold tight," he whispered to himself. "Just till tomorrow. Midnight. That's when they'll finally understand why I did it."

Or he would die.

He wasn't sure if he really cared which happened—life or death. He only cared that the gold stop killing him by inches.

"Hold tight. Tomorrow. Midnight."

Even though Risa Sheridan was only an occasional consultant to the international firm of Rarities Unlimited, she didn't resent flying from Las Vegas to Los Angeles for a few hours of work. She never knew what treasures a client might have brought to the company's headquarters so that Rarities could "Buy, Sell, Appraise, Protect." All she could be certain of was that whatever she would be inspecting was at least 400 years old—and usually much older—because ancient jewelry was her specialty.

Risa's feeling of anticipation flattened when she looked through the double glass doors that led to Rarities' offices: Shane Tannahill was already on the other side of the bulletproof glass. Despite the fact that she had left Las Vegas before he did, her boss had beaten her to Los Angeles.

Shane had one of his hands tucked into a pocket of his black slacks. The other hand anchored the soft leather jacket he had slung over one shoulder. A visitor's badge hung on a chain around his neck. Angular face impassive, jade green eyes narrowed, dark hair neatly trimmed, he lounged against the guard desk. Waiting for her.

He wasn't a patient man.

Bloody L. A. traffic, she said silently.

It wasn't her fault that a semi-truck hauling gasoline had turned over on Sepulveda, blocking the easiest exit from the airport and thoroughly screwing up the city's already over-burdened surface streets.

And making her late.

Her pulse might have kicked with more than irritation when she spotted Shane, but her steps didn't hesitate or quicken. Nor did she check that her short black hair was smoothly in place and her unstructured blue jacket was hanging straight. Other women might have licked their lips for that extra shine or sucked in their belly or stuck out their chest to look their best for Shane Tannahill.

Not Risa.

She had fought to get where she was. She loved her job as curator of gold objects for the Golden Fleece, Shane's Las Vegas entertainment complex. She wasn't going to lose everything she had worked for simply because of his handsome face and killer grin. Better that she rub her boss the wrong way than the right.

Shane's work ethic was simple and inflexible: no lying, no cheating, no stealing, and no sex. He didn't touch the female employees. End of subject. But if a woman didn't want to accept that, and he was interested in an affair, he would find her another job. Only then would a good time be had by all.

No matter how intelligent, appealing, rich, and maddening Shane might be, Risa wanted her job more than she wanted to do laps around the sex track with any man. Even one of the few who had ever really interested her.

It's the forbidden fruit thing, Risa told herself briskly. *No man is that sexy after you wake up with him. Or without him, for that matter.*

The guard released the automatic locks for Risa. The door swung open.

She gave the uniformed man a bright smile. "Good morning, Jersey. How's the thumb?"

Jersey, who was about seven feet of muscle and bone, blushed. "Who told you?"

"Mmmm" was all she said. She didn't want Shane to know how often she and S. K. Niall chatted. Shane was friendly with the two heads of Rarities, but that friendship didn't slop over into business. He wouldn't be pleased knowing that his curator talked several times a week with Niall ("rhymes with kneel, boyo. I'm not a bloody river"). At the moment, the Golden Fleece didn't have enough business with Rarities to justify such frequent communications. But Risa was lonely and Niall was safely involved with Dana Gaynor, the other head of Rarities.

"I can't believe I slammed my thumb in the desk drawer," Jersey muttered.

"Yeah, Dana really ought to wear a warning bell when she walks around," Risa sympathized, fighting a smile.

Shane didn't bother to fight it. He flashed the kind of grin that made men and women alike blink and draw closer, as though to a fire.

Jersey's blush deepened.

"You'll get used to Dana's walk," Risa said. She tossed her purse on a moving belt like those at an airport checkpoint and strolled through the metal detector's field without setting off a single buzz. "All the men do. Eventually."

"Uh, yes'm." But Jersey was shaking his head while he watched the screen that displayed the contents of Risa's purse. Nothing but the usual. The metal alarm didn't quiver. The nitrate alarm didn't go off. Neither did any of the other chemical alarms. Not that he expected anything like that to happen—not with a consultant. But he wasn't paid to make personal judgments. He was paid to put everyone who walked in those doors through the scanners, and that included Dana Gaynor and S. K. Niall.

Shane took Risa's purse as it popped out the other end of the scanner. He tossed it to her with a quickness that had caught more than one person off guard.

She snagged her purse with a deceptively lazy movement of her arm. He wasn't the only one with good reflexes. "Thanks." She turned to Jersey. "Anything else?"

"Just this." He handed her a staff pass dangling on a long neck chain. "New rules."

She put on the chain and the colorful bit of plastic that stated she was a consultant. "Since when?"

Shane answered before Jersey could. "Since someone threatened half of Rarities Unlimited."

"Dana was threatened?" Risa asked, startled.

"No. Niall."

"Whew," Risa said, blowing out a breath. Besides being a friend, Niall was half-owner and head of security for Rarities Unlimited. Dana owned the other half and ran the "Fuzzy" or Fine Arts side of the company. "Remarkably stupid of whoever made the threat." She gave her boss a speculative glance out of eyes that were a clear, dark blue. "When?"

"Three days ago." Shane started toward the elevator at the end of a wide, short hallway. "They're waiting in the Number Two clean room."

Without missing a beat Risa matched her boss's long-legged stride. If it strained the hem of her knee-length fitted skirt, too bad. No way a man was going to have her at a disadvantage. "What was the guy mad about?"

"He had a tray of Roman cameos he wanted appraised," Shane said. "Turned out most were pretty good forgeries. He didn't like it, so he started yelling and cursing. Niall showed up real fast and escorted the client out. The client didn't like that, either. Said he was going to send someone to teach Niall some manners."

"Dumb and dumber." She shook her head at the client's lack of insight. Not to mention simple smarts. "Niall isn't as big as Jersey, but he's a lot tougher."

The corner of Shane's mouth kicked up and his eyes gleamed with sardonic humor. "Meaner, too. And I'll bet on mean every time."

"No argument here." Risa's mouth turned down. She knew

better than most people just how far mean could go. Growing up cockroach poor taught you all about the difference between mean, tough, and merely big. You learned to size up men and situations fast—and accurately—or you paid in pain.

Shane slanted a speculative glance at his curator. She was very businesslike in her dark tailored skirt and loose, jewel-blue jacket, her hair a sleek black cap, her makeup understated, her curvy figure all but hidden, and the kind of mouth that could make a man forget all the reasons he shouldn't bite it. He almost hadn't hired Risa because of her body and those sin-with-me lips. Then he had measured the unflinching intelligence in her eyes and remembered the ambition that had fairly radiated from her resume.

Risa was everything he had wanted and more than he had bargained on getting when he asked Niall to help him find a trustworthy gold curator who would agree to live in Las Vegas.

Niall had sent Risa.

Knowing that he would probably regret it, Shane had hired her. Then he had kept as much distance as possible from his new curator.

Given the nature of her work, it wasn't enough space for comfort. Getting ready for his upcoming "Druid Gold" show had them stepping on each other's shadows for months. More than once he had thought about finding another curator so he could have sex with this one. But he needed Risa's expertise and her fierce intelligence more than he needed an affair, so they just kept circling each other like strange dogs that didn't know whether to bite or lick.

Most of the time Shane was thankful that Risa put up as many GO AWAY signs as he did. The rest of the time it irritated him that she was every bit as wary of him as he was of her. He couldn't help wondering why she kept backing up. Certainly not out of fear of losing the only good job around. In the past year a well-known private museum and two wealthy collectors had offered Risa employment. He knew because he had bettered their offers in order to keep her.

But his common sense told him that he should have let her go. She was the kind of trouble he really didn't need.

Risa tapped on the door of the Number Two clean room, so called because it was a safe, neutral territory where buyer could meet seller and not fear fraud or outright robbery. In this case Shane was the designated buyer. At least that was what Rarities' client hoped.

"Sorry I'm late," Risa said to Dana and Niall, who were going over some papers on the long metal table that ran down the center of the room. "A gas tanker truck flipped on Sepulveda."

"You two should be honored," Shane said.

"Why?" Dana asked, looking up.

"I'm her boss, and she didn't apologize to me."

Risa's eyes narrowed. She didn't say a word.

Niall cleared his throat. Shane and Risa had been at sixes and sevens from the first day they met, but lately the air was beginning to smoke whenever they were in the same room. With a mental sigh, he decided to start looking for a new opening for Risa; if she didn't quit pretty soon, Shane would fire her. On the plus side, Shane was noted for his generous severance packages. Maybe she was pushing for that.

"Why should she apologize to you?" Dana asked, stacking the papers with brisk motions. "Rarities is paying for her time at the moment, not you."

"Ouch," Shane said.

"One day you'll learn, boyo," Niall said, grinning. "The lady could teach cutting to a sword."

Shane cocked a dark brown eyebrow at Niall, who was kicked back in his chair as though he didn't have a worry in the world. "Voice of experience, I presume."

"Bloody right." His low-voiced growl was at odds with his amused blue-green eyes and clipped brown hair. He shifted his broad shoulders and reached for his shirt buttons. "Want to see my scars?"

"I don't think his heart could stand it," Dana said. "And Risa is far too young for such a manly display."

"Hey, y'all, I'm thirty-one," Risa drawled, letting her

Arkansas upbringing pour through her smoky voice. "That's old enough to know better than to let some male show me his, um, scars."

Dana's laugh made her look much younger than Risa suspected she was.

"Right," Niall said. "If you're not interested in a manly striptease, how about a look at some old gold jewelry?"

Without waiting for an answer, he pushed back and walked to a long, spun-aluminum case at the far end of the table. The box was about the size that a professional pool player might use to protect his favorite cue. There was a similar, smaller box on the opposite end of the table.

"Recorders on," Dana said to no one in particular.

"Running," answered a disembodied voice from a ceiling grille.

"Is that Factoid?" Shane asked, gesturing toward the grille.

"No," Niall said, "Our research guru is off today."

"With Gretchen?" Shane asked, smiling. Joe-Bob McCoy, aka Factoid, had a permanent lech for his boss, the Head of Research. Gretchen Miller was twice his age and half-again his weight. A real Valkyrie.

"At the moment she's working with Ian Lapstrake and Lawe Donovan," Dana said. "The Rutherby inheritance."

"Too bad," Shane said. "I've got a great menu for Factoid to try out on his next date with Gretchen, assuming he ever talks her into another one. Food guaranteed to make the woman of his dreams lust for him."

Niall snickered. "What is it—oysters twelve ways?"

Dana rolled her dark eyes. When it came to matters biological, men were such simple creatures.

"A bit more elaborate," Shane said. "First, a bunch of candles surrounded by agates."

"Why?" Niall asked.

"Guaranteed, time-tested aphrodisiac."

Dana snorted softly.

Shane kept talking. "Shrimp cocktail, celery soup, endive salad, halibut with paprika and juniper. Wine, of course.

Benedictine and chocolate for dessert. Then the night of your dreams awaits."

"For that, I'd even eat endive," Niall said.

Dana cut him a glance that said she would remember his words and use them against him. He hated endive.

Without realizing it, Risa let out a soft moan at the thought of Benedictine and chocolate. "You're killing me. All I get for lunch is carrots and celery."

"Why?" Shane asked, startled.

"The usual reason. I can't afford new clothes if I eat my way out of these."

"Are you hinting for another a raise after the one that I was forced to give you to—"

"Argue on your own time," Dana cut in. Then she said to Risa, "The client's request is that you do a 'cold' appraisal. Visual inspection only."

"Cold appraisal for hot goods?" Shane suggested.

Dana gave him a look that could have frozen fire. "The provenance on these goods is above reproach. The collector is merely reluctant to invest in a full appraisal if, after a quick look, the goods seem to be less than they were advertised to him."

Shane smiled and tugged on his forelock like a peasant standing before his lord.

Dana ignored him, though her lips twitched around what might have been an answering smile. She had a weakness for men who were smart, easy on the eyes, and hard on the opposition.

Niall opened the first aluminum box and lifted the lid. Inside, each within its own individually cut nest, pieces of gold jewelry gleamed.

Instantly, Risa forgot everything else in the room. She went to the open case and simply stared at the contents. After a long, silent minute, she began talking. "First impression. Celtic, of course. Styles and techniques range from La Tene to Mediterranean. Age could be anywhere from fifth century B.C. to fifth century A.D. If you need dates on individual pieces, it will take several days for detailed stylistic comparisons with artifacts in museums, published papers, auction catalogs, online collections, that sort of thing. Most of my references are in Las Vegas, because you said you only needed a fast look."

"If a more detailed appraisal is required, would you need the actual artifacts, or would the virtual ones do?" Dana asked.

With intent, narrowed eyes, Risa looked through the collection again. "Did you search for modern machining marks when you had these under the 'scope?"

"The client assured me there were none," Dana said. "We checked, of course. Nothing caught our expert's eye."

"Right." Risa let out a breath. "Then I'd start with the virtual and go to the real only if I ran into problems."

Dana nodded. "So noted."

"For now," Risa said, "of the nine real objects in this case, one shows obvious signs of recent repair—the gold alloys simply don't match. Two of the pieces have repairs that appear much older, but that's only a preliminary visual examination. Some of the rest certainly could use repair, but that's to be expected. In all probability, they're two thousand years old."

"You think they're genuine?" Dana asked. "Again, this is a non-binding, verbal opinion based solely on a limited visual examination."

Risa waited while the legal niceties were recorded before she said, "I haven't seen anything to put me off. Yet." Nor had she seen anything that made her heart kick with excitement at being in the presence of a truly fine artifact. A showstopper, as her boss would say.

That was what Shane needed to launch his new gallery on New Year's Eve. That was what she hadn't found yet—a centerpiece for his Druid Gold show. She couldn't help wondering how much more time he would give her. And who else he had looking.

Shane might have made his fortune gambling, but he never left anything to chance.

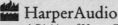